ST

D1423181

THE SERPENT MAGE

By the same author

BLOOD MUSIC
EON
THE INFINITY CONCERTO

THE SERPENT MAGE

Greg Bear

CENTURY

LONDON MELBOURNE AUCKLAND JOHANNESBURG

First published in Great Britain in 1988
(simultaneously in paperback and hardcover)
by Century Hutchinson Ltd
Brookmount House, 62-65 Chandos Place
London WC2N 4NW

Century Hutchinson South Africa (Pty) Ltd
PO Box 337, Bergvlei, 2012 South Africa

Century Hutchinson Australia Pty Ltd
PO Box 496, 16-22 Church Street,
Hawthorn, Victoria 3122, Australia

Century Hutchinson New Zealand Limited
PO Box 40-086, Glenfield, Auckland 10
New Zealand

British Library Cataloguing in Publication Data

Bear, Greg
  The serpent mage.
  I. Title
  813′.54(F)   PS3552.E157
  ISBN 0 7126 1672 1
  ISBN 0 7126 1677 2 Pbk

Printed and bound in Great Britain by
Anchor Brendon Ltd, Tiptree, Essex

This book, finally, is for Kristine
—unbeknownst to herself,
a kind of Beatrice

1951–1971

1

The pale, translucent forms bent over Michael Perrin once again. Had he been awake, he would have recognized three of them, but he was in a deep and dreamless sleep. Sleep was a habit he had reacquired since his return. It took him away, however briefly, from thoughts of what had happened in the Realm.

He is pretending to be normal, one form said without words to her sister, hovering nearby.

Let him rest. His time will come soon enough.

Does he feel it?

He must.

Has he told anybody yet?

Not his parents. Not his closest friends.

He has so few close friends . . .

Michael rolled over onto his back, pulling sheet and blankets aside to reveal his broad, well-muscled shoulders. One of the forms reached down to squeeze an arm with long fingers.

Stop that.

He keeps himself fit.

The fourth figure, shaped like a bird, said nothing. It stood by the door, lost in thought. The others retreated from the bed.

The fourth finally spoke. *No one in the Council knows of this.*

It was a surprise even to us, the tallest of the three said.

Michael's eyelids flickered, then opened. He caught a glimpse of white vapor spread like wings, but it could easily have been the fog of sleep. With a start, he held up his left wrist to look at his new watch. It was eight-thirty. He had slept in. There would barely be time for his exercises.

He descended the stairs in a beige sweatsuit, a gift from his parents on his last birthday. There had been no candles on his cake, at his request. He did not know how old he was.

His mother, Ruth, was reading the newspaper in the kitchen. "French toast in fifteen minutes," she warned, smiling at him. "Your father's in the shop."

Michael returned the smile and picked up a long oak stick from beside the kitchen pantry, carrying it through the door into the back yard.

The morning was grayed by a thin fog that would burn off in just a few hours. Near the upswung door of the converted garage, his father, John, was hand-sanding a maple table top on two paint-spattered sawhorses. He looked up at Michael and forearmed mock-sweat from his brow.

"My son, the jock," Ruth said from the back steps.

"I seem to remember him still carrying stacks of books around," John said. "Don't be too hard on him."

"Breakfast lingers for no man," she said. "Fifteen minutes."

John wiped the smooth pale surface with his fingers and applied himself to a rough spot. Michael stood in the middle of the yard and began exercising with the stick, running in place with it held out before him, hefting it back over his head and bending over to touch first one end, then the other to the grass on both sides. He had barely worked up a sweat when Ruth appeared in the doorway again.

"Time," she said.

She regarded her son delicately over a cup of coffee as he ate his French toast and strips of bacon. He was less enthusiastic about bacon—or any kind of meat—than he had been before . . .

But she did not bring up this observation. The subject of Michael's missing five years was virtually tabu around the house. John had asked once, and Michael had shown signs of volunteering. . . . And Ruth's reaction, a stiff kind of panic, voice high-pitched, had shut both of them up immediately. She had made it quite clear she did not want to talk about it.

Just as clearly, there were things she wanted to tell and could not. John had been through this before; Michael had not. The stalemate bothered him.

"Delicious," he said as he carried his plate to the sink. He kissed Ruth on the cheek and ran up the stairs to change into his work clothes.

Michael had not yet assumed the position of caretaker at the Waltiri house. The time was not right.

After two weeks of job hunting, he had been hired as a waiter in a Nicaraguan restaurant on Pico. For the past three months, he had taken the bus to work each weekday and Saturday morning.

At ten-thirty, Michael met the owners, Bert and Olive Cantor, at the front of the restaurant. Bert pulled out a thick ring of keys and opened the single wood-framed glass door. Olive smiled warmly at Michael, and Bert stared fixedly at nothing in particular until he was given a huge mugful of coffee. Shortly after the mug was empty, Bert began issuing polite orders in the form of requests, and the day officially started. Jesus, the Nicaraguan chef, who had arrived before six o'clock, entering through the rear, donned his apron and cap and instructed two Mexican assistants on final preparations for the day's specials. Juanita, the eldest waitress, a stout Colombian, bustled about making sure all the set-ups were properly done and the salad bar in order.

Bert and Olive treated him like a lost son or at least a well-regarded cousin. They treated all their employees as if they came from various branches of the family. Bert had called the restaurant his "United Nations retirement home" after hiring Michael. "We have a red-headed Irishman, or a lookalike anyway, and half a dozen different types of Latinos, and two crazy Jews in charge."

Michael served on the lunch and early dinner shifts, and he studied the people he served. The restaurant attracted a broad cross-section of Los Angelenos, from Nicaraguans hungry for a taste of home to students from UCLA. Lunchtime brought in white-collar types from miles around.

This morning, Bert's mug of coffee did not settle him firmly into the day. He seemed vaguely distraught, and Olive was unusually subdued. Finally, a half-hour before opening, Bert took Michael into the back storeroom behind the kitchen, among the huge cans of peppers and condiments and the packages of dried herbs, and pulled out two chairs from a small table where Olive usually sat to do the books.

Bert was sixty-five, almost bald, with the remaining white hair meticulously styled in a wispy swirl. He could be relied upon to always wear a blue blazer and brown pants with a golf shirt beneath the blazer, and on his right hand he sported a high school class ring with a jutting garnet.

He waved this hand in small circles as he sat and shook his head. "Now don't worry about whether you're in trouble or not. You're a good worker," he said, "and you wait tables like an old pro, and you're graceful and you could even work in a snazzy place."

"This *is* a snazzy place," Michael replied.

"Yes, yes." Bert looked dubious. "We're a family. You're part of the family. I'm saying this because you're going to work here as long as you want, and we all like you . . . but you don't belong." He stared intently at Michael. "And I don't mean because you should be in a university. Where are you coming from?"

"I was born here," Michael answered, knowing that was also not what Bert meant.

"So? Why did you come *here*, to this restaurant?"

"I don't know what you're geting at."

"The way you look at customers. Friendly, but. . . . Spooky. Distant. Like you're coming from someplace a hell of a long ways from here. They don't notice. I do. So does Juanita. She thinks you're a *brujo*, pardon my Spanish."

Michael had learned enough Spanish as a California boy to puzzle out the *brujo* was the masculine for *bruja*, witch. "That's silly," he said, staring off at the cans on their gray metal shelves.

"I agree with her. Maybe even, pardon me, a *dybbuk*. Juanita washes dishes, and I taste the food and maybe yell once a week, but that's both our opinions. Both ends of the rainbow think alike."

· "What does Olive think?" Michael asked softly. Olive reminded him of a slightly plumper Golda Waltiri.

"Olive would like to have half a dozen sons, and the Lord, bless him, did not agree. She adores you. She does not think ill of you even when she sees the way you 'learn' our customers, the way you *see* them."

"I'm sorry I'm upsetting you," Michael said.

"Not at all. People come back. People, who knows why, enjoy being paid attention to the way you do it. You're not in it for the advantage. But you still don't belong here."

The room was small, and Bert was wearing his look of intense concern, raised brows corrugating his high forehead. "Olive says you have a poet's air about you. She should know. She dated a lot of poets when she was young." He cast a quick, long-suffering look at the ceiling. "So why are you waiting tables?"

"I need to learn some things."

"What can you learn in a trendy little dive on Pico?"

"About people."

"People are everywhere."

"I'm not used to being . . . normal," Michael said. "I mean, being with people who are just . . . people. Good, plain people. I don't know much about them."

Bert pushed out his lips and nodded. "Juanita says that for somebody to become a *brujo,* something has to happen to them. Did something happen to you?" He raised his eyebrows, practically demanding candor. Michael felt oddly willing to comply.

"Yes," he said.

Having struck paydirt, Bert leaned back and seemed temporarily at a loss for what to ask next. "Are your folks okay?"

"They're fine," Michael said abstractedly.

"Do they know?"

"I haven't told them."

"Why not? They love you."

"Yes. I love them." The dread was fading. Michael did not know why, but he was going to open up to Bert Cantor. "I've tried telling them. It's almost come out once or twice. But Mom gets upset even before I begin. And then, it just stops, and that's it."

"How old are you?"

"I don't know," Michael said. "I could be seventeen, and I could be twenty-two."

"That's odd," Bert said.

"Yes," Michael agreed.

The story spun itself out from there, across several days, each day at eleven Bert drawing up the chairs and sitting across from Michael with his corrugated forehead, listening until the lunchtime crowd arrived and Michael began waiting tables.

On the fourth day, the story essentially told, Bert leaned

back in his chair and closed his eyes, nodding. "That," he said, "is a good story. Like Singer or Aleichem. A good story. This part about Jehovah being a Fairy, that's tough on me. But it's a good one. And I'm not asking to insult you—but, it's all true?"

Michael nodded.

"Everything's different from what the newspapers and history books say?"

"Lots of things are different from what they say, yes."

"I'm asking myself if I believe you. Maybe I do. Sometimes my opinions are funny that way. You're sure it's better here than going to college?"

He nodded again.

"Smart boy. My son James, from a previous marriage, he's gone to college, the professors there don't know *frijoles* about people. Books they know."

"I love books. I've been reading every day, going to the library after I read all the books my folks own. I need to know more about that, too."

"Nothing wrong with books," Bert agreed. "But at least you're trying to put things in perspective."

"I hope I do."

"Well," Bert said, with a long pause after. "What are you going to do about yourself?"

Michael shook his head.

"I feel for you, with a story like that," Bert said. Then he stood. "Time to wait tables."

The winter passed through Los Angeles more like an extended autumn, crossing imperceptibly into a wet and clean-aired spring such as the city had not seen in years, a sparkling, green-leafed, sun-in-water-drop spring.

The pearls appeared in Michael's palms six months after his return from the Realm, in the first weeks of that spring. They nestled at the end of his lifeline, insubstantial, glowing in the dark like two fireflies. In two days' time, they faded and disappeared.

The pearls confirmed what he had suspected for some weeks. Events were coming to fruition.

So ended the pretending, his time of normality and anonymity, the last time he could truly call his own.

*   *   *

Rain fell for several hours after dinner, pattering on the roof above Michael's room and chirruping down the gutters. Moonlit beads of moisture glittered on the leaves of the apricot and avocado trees in the rear yard. Rounded lines of clouds, their bottoms turned orange-brown by the city lights, moved without haste over the Hollywood hills.

Michael had come upstairs to read, but he put down his book—Evans-Wentz's *The Fairy-Faith in Celtic Countries*—and went to stand before the open window, feeling the moist air lap against his face.

The night birds were singing again, their trills sharp and liquid by turns. The trees seemed alive with song. He hadn't heard them singing this late in months; perhaps the rain had disturbed them.

Michael closed the window, returning to his bed and leaning back on the pillow. He slept naked, disliking the restriction of pajamas while he lay in bed, while his mind acted like an antenna, extending itself and receiving, whether he willed it or not . . .

Tomorrow, Michael would leave the home of his parents to live in the house of Arno and Golda Waltiri and assume control of the estate. He had planned the move since telling Bert and Olive he was quitting, but the time had never seemed exactly right.

Now it was right. Even discounting the pearls, unmistakable signs were presenting themselves stacked one upon the other. He was having unusual dreams.

He turned off the light. Downstairs, a Mozart piano piece —he didn't know which one—played on his father's stereo. He felt drowsy, and yet some portion of his mind was alert, even eager. Moonlight filled his room suddenly as the shadow of a cloud passed. Even with his eyes closed to slits, he could clearly make out the framed print of Bonestell's painting of Saturn seen from one of its closer moons.

For the merest instant, on the cusp between sleep and waking, he saw a figure crossing the print's moon landscape. The print was not in focus, but the figure was sharp and clear. A young—very young—Arno Waltiri, smiling and beckoning . . .

Michael twitched on the bed, eyes closed tightly now, and then relaxed, falling across continent, sky and sea.

He saw—in some sense became—

* * *

Mrs. William Hutchings Cunningham, widowed only a
year, addicted to long treks in the new forest beyond her Sus-
sex country home. She walked gingerly, her booted feet sink-
ing into the damp carpet of compacted leaves, moss and loam.
The early spring drizzle beaded in the fine hairs of her wool
coat and cascaded from ferns disturbed by her passage.

The dividing line between the new forest and the old was
not well marked, but she knew it and felt the familiar surge of
love and respect as she crossed over. The great oaks, their
trunks thick with startling green moss, tiered with moons of
fungus, rose high into the whiteness. Her booted feet sank into
the loam and moss and piles of leaves.

Mrs. Cunningham felt herself become a part of the deep
past whenever she crossed into the old forest. There was so
little of it left in England now; patches here and there, converted to housing projects with distressing regularity, watched
over by (she felt) corrupt or at the very least incompetent and
uncaring government ministries. She swung her goosehead-
handled stick up and poked the empty air with it, her face a
mask of intense concern.

Then the peace returned to her, and she found the broad flat
rock in the middle of the patch of old forest, near an ancient
overgrown pathway that arrowed through the trees without a
single curve or waver. The trees had adapted themselves to the
path, not the other way around, and yet they were centuries
old. So how old was the path?

"I love you," she said, with only the trees and the mist and
the rock as witness. Carefully maneuvering around a slick
patch of wet leaves and mud, she sat on the rock and let her
breath out in a whuff.

It was here and not by his grave, which was in a neatly
manicured cemetery miles and miles away, that she came to
hold communion with her late husband. "I love you, William," she repeated, face downturned but dark brown eyes
looking up. She closed her eyes and leaned her head back to
feel the mist's minute droplets land on her face.

"Do you remember," she said, "when we were just married, and there was that marvelous inn, the Green Man, and
the innkeeper wanted to see identification, wanted to know
how old we were?"

For some, such a process, day in and day out, would have

signified an unwholesome self-torture. But not for her. She could feel the distance growing between herself and the past, and she could feel the wound healing. This was how she kept a bandage on those wounds, protecting them with a bit of ritual against the abrasions of hard reality.

"Do you remember, too—" she began, then stopped abruptly, her eyes turning slowly to the path.

A tall dark figure, walking on the path miles beyond the trees, yet still visible, approached the rock on which she sat. It seemed she waited for hours, but it was only a minute or two, as the figure grew larger and more distinct, coming at last to the extent of the path that Mrs. Cunningham would have called real.

A tall, pale-skinned woman arrived at the rock and paused, drifting forward as if from ghostly momentum as she turned to look at Mrs. Cunningham. The tall woman had dark red hair and a thin ageless face with deep-set eyes. She was dressed in a gray robe that was really a translucent black. Mrs. Cunningham had not seen her like before.

She felt a feather-touch at the back of her thoughts, and the woman spoke. With each word, the uncertain image became more solid, as if speaking finished the act of becoming part of this reality.

"I am on the Earth of old, am I not?" the woman asked.

Mrs. Cunningham nodded. "I think so," she said, as brightly as she could manage, or dared.

"Do you grieve?"

"Yes." Mrs. Cunningham's expression turned quizzical, with a touch of pain.

"For a loved one?" the woman asked.

"For my husband," she replied, her throat very dry.

"Silly grief, then," the woman said. "You do not know the meaning of grief."

"Perhaps not," Mrs. Cunningham conceded, "but it feels to me as if I do."

"You should not sit on that rock much longer."

"Oh?"

The woman pointed back up the path. "More of my kind coming," she said.

"Oh." She stared at the path, head nodding slightly, eyes wide.

The tall woman's pale face glowed against the dark trees and misty sky. "I say that your grief is a silly grief, for he is not lost forever, as we are, and you have paid mortality for infinity, which we cannot."

"Oh," Mrs. Cunningham said again, as if engaged in conversation with a neighbor. The woman's eyes were extraordinary, silver-blue with hints of opalescent fire. Her red hair hung in thick strands down around her shoulders, and her black gown seemed alive with moving leaves in lighter shades of gray. A golden tassel hanging from her midriff had a snaky life of its own.

"We are back now," she said to Mrs. Cunningham. "Please do not cross the trod hereafter."

"I certainly won't," Mrs. Cunningham vowed.

The woman pointed a long-fingered hand at the rock. Mrs. Cunningham removed herself and backed away several yards, slipping once on the patch of leaves and mud. The woman drifted down the path, not walking on quite the same level, and was surrounded by trees away from Mrs. Cunningham's view.

She stood, her lips working in prayer, and then returned her attention to the direction from which the woman had come. "The Lord is my shepherd," she murmured. "The Lord is my shepherd. I shall not want—"

There were more, indeed. Three abreast and of all descriptions, from deepest shadows without feature to mere pale wisps like true spirits, some dripping water, some seeming to be made of water, some as green as the leaves in the canopy above, and following them, a number of beautiful and sinewy horses with shining silver coats . . . and all, despite their magnificence, with an air of weary refugee desperation.

Mrs. Cunningham, after a few minutes, decided discretion would be best, and retreated farther from the path—the trod —with her eyes full of tears for the beauty she had seen that day, and for the message of the woman with red hair in the living black gown.

Paying mortality for infinity . . .

Yes, she could understand that.

"William, oh *William*," she breathed, fairly running through the woods. "You wouldn't *believe* . . . what has . . . just happened . . . here . . ." She came to the boundary and crossed into new forest, and the sensation dulled but did not leave her entirely.

"But whom will I tell?" she asked. "They're back, all—or some—of the faerie folk, and who will believe me now?"

Michael opened his eyes slowly and stared at the dawn as it cast dim blue squares on the closed curtains.

Behind the vision of Mrs. Cunningham had been another and darker one. He had seen something long and sinuous swimming with ageless grace through murky night waters, watching him from a quarter of the way around the world. In that watching there was appraisal.

On the morning of his move, Ruth offered one last time to help him get settled in the Waltiri house. Michael politely refused. "All right, then," she said, dishing up one last home-cooked breakfast of fried eggs and toast—consciously leaving out the bacon. "Promise me you won't take things so seriously."

He regarded her solemnly.

"At least *try* to loosen up. Sometimes you are positively gloomy."

"Don't nag the fellow," John said, holding one thumb high to signal friendly banter and not domestic disagreement.

Michael grinned, and Ruth stared at him with wistfulness and then something like awe. He could almost read her thoughts. This was her son, with the strong features so like his father's and the hair so like her own—but there was something not at all comforting in his face, something lean and . . .

Fierce. *Where had he been for five years?*

Michael walked with suitcases in hand in the pale rich light of morning. Dew beaded the lawns of the old homes and dripped from the waxy green leaves of camellia and gardenia bushes. The sidewalks steamed in the sun, mottled olive and gray with moisture from last night's rain.

He passed a group of nine school girls, twelve or thirteen years old, dressed in uniforms of white blouses and green and black plaid skirts with black sweaters. They averted their faces as they passed but not their eyes, and Michael sensed one or two of them turning, walking backward, to continue staring at him.

The possibilities offered by his appearance seldom concerned him; he appreciated the attention of women but took little advantage. He still felt guilty about Eleuth, the Breed who had given her life for him, and thought often of Helena, whom he had treated as Eleuth had deserved to be treated.

For that and other reasons there was a deep uncertainty in him, a feeling that he had somehow twisted his foot at the starting line and entered the race crippled, that he had made bad mistakes that lessened his chances of staying ahead. He was certain about neither his morals nor his competence.

He set the bags down on the front porch of the Waltiri house. Using the keys given to him by the estate's attorneys, he opened the heavy mahogany door. The air within was dry and noncommittal. Plastic sheets had been draped over the furniture. Gritty gray dust lay over everything.

He took the bags into the hall and set them down at the foot of the stairs. "Hello," he said nervously. Waltiri's presence still seemed strong enough that a hale answer wouldn't have surprised him.

The upstairs guest bedroom was his first project. He searched for a storage closet, found it beneath the stairs and pulled out a vacuum cleaner—an old upright Hoover with a red cloth bag. He cleared the hardwood floors of dust upstairs and down and unrolled the old oriental carpets and the stair runners. Removing yellow-edged sheets from the linen closet, he made up the brass bed and folded the plastic covers into neat squares.

He then went from room to room, standing in each and acquainting himself with their new reality—devoid of Waltiri or Golda. The house was his responsibility now, his place to live for the time being, if not yet his home.

Michael had spent most of his life in one house. Getting accustomed to a different one, he realized, would take time. There would be new quirks to learn, new layouts to become used to. He would have to re-create the house in his head and cut new templates to determine his day-to-day paths.

In the kitchen, he plugged in the refrigerator, removed a box of baking soda from the interior and unchocked the double doors to let them swing shut. The pantry—a walk-in affair, shelved floor-to-ceiling and illuminated by a bare bulb hanging from a thick black cord—was full of canned and dry goods, all usable except for a bloated can of pineapples that rocked to his touch. He threw it out and made up a shopping list.

In the triple garage behind the house, a 1939 black Packard was parked next to a maze of metal shelves stacked high with file boxes. Michael walked around the beauty, fingering a moon of dust from its fender and observing the shine of the chrome. Enchanting, but not practical. Leaded premium gas (called ethyl in the Packard's heyday) was becoming difficult to find; besides, it would draw attention—something he wanted to avoid—and be incredibly expensive to maintain. He peered through the window and then opened the door and sat behind the wheel. The interior smelled new: leather and saddle-soap and that other, citrusy-metallic odor of a new car. The Packard might have been driven out of the showroom the day before.

Wedged between the seat and seat back on the right side was a folded piece of ivory paper. He pulled it loose and read the cover.

Première Performance

THE INFINITY CONCERTO
Opus 45
by Arno Waltiri

8:00 P.M. November 23rd
The Pandall Theater
8538 Sunset Boulevard

Within the fold was a listing of all the players in the Greater Los Angeles Symphonia Orchestra. There were no other notes or explanations. After staring at the program for several minutes, Michael replaced it on the seat and took a deep breath.

Parked outside by the east wall of the garage, in a short cinderblock-walled alley, was a late 1970's model Saab. Michael unlocked the door on the driver's side and sat in the gray velour bucket seat, resting his hands on the steering wheel.

This was much more practical.

He had ridden Sidhe horses, *aband* from point to point in the Realm, and touched a myriad of ghostly between-worlds, and yet he still felt pride and pleasure at sitting in a car, knowing it would be his to drive whenever and wherever he pleased. He was a child of his times. After a long search for the latch, he popped open the hood and peered at the unfamiliar engine. The battery cables had been unhooked. He reattached them to the posts.

Michael knew enough about fuel injection systems not to depress the gas pedal when starting the engine. The engine turned over with a throaty rumble on the first try. He smiled and twisted the wheel this way and that, then backed it carefully out of the alley, reversed it on the broad expanse of concrete before the garage and drove to the supermarket.

That evening, he inspected the living room fireplace and chimney and brought wood in from where it had been stacked beside the Packard. In a few minutes, a lusty blaze brightened the living room and shone within the black lacquer of the grand piano. Michael sat in Waltiri's armchair and sipped a glass of Golda's Ficklin sherry, his mind almost blank of thoughts.

He was not the same boy he had been when he entered Sidhedark through the house of David Clarkham. He doubted he was a boy at all.

The Crane Women had trained him well; he didn't doubt that. He had survived the worst Sidhedark had to offer— monstrous remnants of Tonn's early creation; the ignorant and frustrated cruelty of the Wickmaster Alyons; Tarax and Clarkham himself. But what had he been trained for? Merely to act as a bomb delivering destruction to the Isomage, as Clarkham had called himself? Or for some other purpose besides?

The flames danced with wicked cheer in the broad fireplace, and the embers glowed like holes opening onto a beautiful and deadly world of pure heat and light.

He drowsed, grateful that no new visions bothered him.

At midnight, the rewound grandfather clock in the foyer chimed and awoke him. The fire had died to fitful coals. He went up to his bedroom and sank into the cool, soft mattress.

Even in deep sleep, part of him seemed aware of everything.

One, the clock announced in its somber voice.

Two. (The house creaking.)

Three. (A light rain began and ended within minutes.)

Four. (Night birds . . .)

Five. (Almost absolute stillness.)

At six, the clock's tone coincided with the sound of a newspaper hitting the front door. Michael's eyes opened slowly. He was not in the least groggy. There had been no dreams.

In his robe, he went downstairs to retrieve the paper, wrapped in plastic against the wet. A man sang softly and randomly in the side yard of the house on the left. Michael smiled, listening to the lyrics.

"Don't cry for me, ArgenTEEEENA..." The man walked around the corner and saw Michael. "Good morning!" he called out, waving and shaking his head sheepishly. He was in his early forties, with abundant light brown hair and a face indelibly stamped with friendliness. "Didn't disturb you, I hope." He wore a navy blue jogging suit with bright red stripes down the sleeves and legs.

"No," Michael said. "Getting the paper."

"I was just going to do some running. You knew Arno and Golda?"

"I'm taking care of the house for them," Michael said.

"You sound like they're coming back," the man said, pursing his mouth.

Michael smiled. "Arno appointed me executor of the estate. I'm going to organize the papers..."

"Now *that's* a job." The man had walked in Michael's direction, and they now stood a yard apart. He extended his hand, and Michael shook it. "I'm Robert Dopso. Next door. Arno and Golda were fine neighbors. My mother and I miss them terribly. I was married, but..." He shrugged. "Divorced, and I moved back here. Momma's boy, I know. But Ma was very lonely. I grew up here; my father bought the house in 1940. Golda and Ma used to talk a lot. My life in a nutshell." He grinned. "Your name?"

Michael told him and mentioned he had just moved in the day before.

"I'm not bad in the fix-it department," Dopso said. "I helped Golda with odds and ends after Arno died. I might know a few tricks about the place.... If you need any help, don't hesitate to ask. My wife kept me around a year longer because without me, she said, everything stayed broken."

"I'll ask," Michael said.

"Maybe we could walk or run together—whichever. I prefer running, but..."

Michael nodded, and Dopso headed down the street. "You were supposed to BEEE IMMORTal..."

Michael carried the paper into the kitchen. There, he ate a bowl of hot oatmeal and leafed through the front section. Most of the news—however important and ominous it might seem to his fellows—barely attracted his attention.

Then he came to a small third-page story headlined

CORPSES FOUND IN ABANDONED BUILDING

and his eyes grew wide as he read.

> The unidentified bodies of two females were found by a transient male in the abandoned Tippett Residential Hotel on Sunset Boulevard near La Cienega Sunday afternoon. Cause of death has not been established by the coroner's office. Reporters' questions went largely unanswered during a short press briefing. Early reports indicate that one of the women weighed at least eight hundred pounds and was found nude. The second body was in a mummified condition and was clothed in a party dress of a style long since out of fashion. The Tippett hotel, abandoned since 1968, once offered a posh Hollywood address for retired and elderly actors, actresses and other film workers.

He read the piece through several times before folding the paper and putting it aside. His oatmeal cooled in its bowl, half-finished.

The bodies might be a coincidence, he thought. As rare as eight-hundred-pound women were . . .

But in conjunction with a mummy, clothed in a party dress?

He called up the paper's city desk and asked to speak to the reporter who had written the piece, which had run without a byline. The reporter was out on assignment, he was told, and the operator referred him to a police phone number. Michael paced the kitchen and adjacent hall for several minutes before deciding against phoning the police. How would he explain?

He had to have a look at that building. Something nagged him about the address. Sunset and La Cienega. . . . Barely five miles from Waltiri's house.

He went to the Packard and retrieved the concert program, then checked the glove box in the Saab to find a city map. He took both to Waltiri's first-floor office, dark and musty and lined with shelves of records and tapes, and tried to locate

8538 Sunset Boulevard, the site of the Pandall Theater according to the concert program.

The address was less than half a block from the corner of Sunset and La Cienega.

2

Michael walked briskly up La Cienega's slope as it approached Sunset, breathing steadily and deeply, taking pleasure in the cool night air and the darkness. He could be anonymous, alone without all the handicaps of loneliness; he could be almost anything—a dangerous prowler or a good samaritan. The night covered all, even motives. To his left, the white wall of a hotel was painted with Mondrian stripes and squares. At the corner, he stood for a moment, looking across the street at the blocky, ugly Hyatt on Sunset, then turned right. His running shoes made almost no sound on the concrete sidewalk.

He passed the entrance of a restaurant built on the site where Errol Flynn's guest house had once stood and then spotted the Tippett building.

It rose more than twelve stories above Sunset, an aging Art Deco concrete edifice with rounded corners. Many of the windows had been knocked out, and black soot marks rose from several of the gaping frames. At ground level, it was surrounded by a chain-link fence. The lobby entrance had been blocked off by a chain-link and steel-pipe gate. A trash tube descended from the roof to a dumpster behind the fence.

The building made Michael uneasy. It had once been lovely. It stood out in this section of the Sunset Strip even now, in its present dilapidated condition. Yet it had been abandoned for over twenty years and, judging by the state of renovations, might continue that way for another twenty.

He stood before the gate and squinted to see the obscured address, limned in aluminum figures above the plywood-boarded doors: 8538. The 8 had been knocked askew and hung on its side.

The Tippet building stood on the site of the Pandall Theater. Having confirmed that much, Michael looked around guiltily and glanced over his shoulder at the lighted windows of the Hyatt.

There was a patched hole in the fencing to the left of the gate; with very little effort, he could undo the wiring on the chain-link patch and crawl under.

"Odd place, isn't it?"

Michael turned his head quickly and saw a bearded, sun-burned man with thick greasy hair and dirt-green, street-varnished clothes standing on the sidewalk a dozen yards away. "Yes," he answered softly.

"It's older than it looks. Seems kind of modern, don't it?"

"I guess," Michael said.

"Used to live there," the man said. "Don't live there now. Want to go in?" The man walked slowly toward him, face conveying intense interest and almost equal caution.

"No," Michael said.

"You know the place?"

"No. I'm just out hiking."

"Care to know about it?"

Michael didn't answer.

"Care to know about the two women found dead in there?"

"Women?"

"One big, a real whale, one a mummy. In the newspapers. You read about that?"

Michael paused to reflect, then nodded.

"Thought you might have."

"Did you find them?"

"Heavens," the man said, coughing into his fist. "Not me. Someone who didn't know much. An *acquaintance*. Dumb to stay in that building for a night." He wrinkled his face up, expecting skepticism, and said, "It's full of *things*."

"Why do you hang around, then?" Michael asked.

"Because," the man said. He stood about two yards from Michael, and even at that distance his smell was rank—urine and sedimented sweat. "You know what their names were?"

"Whose names?" Michael asked.

"The women. The whale and the mummy."

"No," Michael said.

"I do. My *acquaintance* found it on a piece of rock next to them. Gave it to the police, but they didn't care. Didn't mean anything to them. Do you know French?"

"A little."

"Then you'd know what one of the names means. Sadness. In French. And the other . . ."

Michael decided to try for an effect. "Lamia," he said.

The man's face became a mask between surprise and laughter. "Gawd," he said. "Gawd, gawd. You're a reporter. I knew it. Odd time of night to be out looking for facts."

Michael shook his head, never taking his eyes off the man. He had not yet tried to read someone's aura on Earth. Now was as good a time as any. He found a festival of murmurs, a bright little coal of intelligence, a marketplace full of rotted vegetables. He backed away from the search, having come out with only one fact: *Tristesse*. The second name. It suited the guardian of Clarkham's gate. Bringer of sadness.

Lamia and Tristesse. Sisters . . .

Victims of the Sidhe, sacrificed by Clarkham to guard and wait. . . . But how could they have found their way to Earth? And who had killed them—or *inactivated* them, since what life they had was dubious at best?

Abruptly and unexpectedly, Michael began to cry. Wiping his eyes, he glanced up at the Tippett building.

"Something wrong? I'm the one should be crying," the man said. "You're not a reporter. Relative, maybe? Jesus, no. None of them would have had relatives. Not the type."

"What do you care?" Michael asked sharply. "Go away."

"Care?" the man shrilled, backing away a step. "I used to *own* the place. OWN IT, God dammit! I used to be worth something! I'm not that God damn old, and I'm not so far gone I don't remember what it was like, having money and being a"—he lifted a hand with pinky extended, raised his eyebrows and waggled his head—"a big God damn citizen!"

Michael probed the man again and felt the sorrow and anger directly.

"Now everybody comes around here. God damn bank never does anything with it, never tears it down, never sells it. Can't sell it. Now there's people died here. Not surprising.

I'm going, all right. You figure it out. I've had my fill."

"Wait," Michael said. "When was it built?"

"Nineteen and forty-seven," the man answered with his back to Michael, walking away with exaggerated dignity. "Used to be a theater here, a concert hall. Tore it down and put this up."

"Thank you," Michael said.

The man shrugged his shoulders and waved away the thanks.

Michael put his hands in his coat pockets and leaned his head back to look up at the building again. High up near the top, one floor beneath a terrace, a faint red light played over a dusty pane of glass. It burned only for a moment.

Then, on the fourth floor, the red light gleamed briefly again in a broken and soot-stained window. All was still after that and quiet.

Michael shuddered and began the trek back down Sunset to La Cienega.

3

Magic like that worked by the Sidhe was more difficult on Earth; humans could not work Sidhe magic. This much Michael had gleaned from his training in the Realm, Sidhedark. But were these facts or merely suppositions? Breeds—part human and part Sidhe—could work magic; the Crane Women and Eleuth had demonstrated that much. Clarkham, a Breed born on Earth, had nearly bested the Sidhe at their own game.

Michael himself had done things in the Realm that had no other name in his vocabulary but magic. He had even channeled the energies of a Song of Power to destroy Clarkham. And in the year since he had returned to Earth, he had learned that he could still apply Sidhe discipline and invoke *hyloka*, the calling-of-heat from the center of his body, and in-seeing, the probing of another's aura to gain information.

For the time being, he was content not to test the other skills he had learned in the Realm. He had not used *evisa*, or out-seeing, to throw a shadow; there had been no need.

Each morning, he went through his exercises in the spacious back yard. He jogged around the neighborhood holding his *kima*, the running-stick, before him, as the Crane Women had taught him. Several times he jogged with Dopso, who kept up a panting stream of questions and observations. Despite the man's obvious curiosity about Michael, and nonstop talk, Michael liked him. He seemed decent.

Each day, Michael investigated another cache of Waltiri's papers and began to make a catalog of what he found. Within a week, he had worked his way through the garage and knew basically what was in each file box—manuscripts, contracts and other legal documents, and correspondence, including a wooden box filled with love letters from Waltiri to Golda, written in German. Even though he had studied German after returning from the Realm, he was hardly fluent, and that handicapped him. He thought about hiring a German-speaking student and acquiring the language more rapidly through in-seeing but decided to put that off for now.

He concentrated on the manuscripts. What little musical training he had acquired before he was thirteen—when he had put his foot down and refused to continue piano lessons—was of little aid in sorting out the Waltiri papers.

Michael recorded the names (if any), opus numbers and known associations of each musical manuscript. Most were scores for motion pictures; scattered throughout the four and a half decades' worth of work, however, were more personal pieces, even a draft of a ballet based on *The Faerie Queene*.

He spent hours in the garage and then began moving the sorted boxes of manuscripts into the dining room, where he stacked them along a bare wall.

There was no sign of a manuscript for Opus 45, The Infinity Concerto.

At night, he fixed himself supper and ate alone. One night a week he joined his parents for dinner, and the visits were enjoyable; occasionally, John would drop by the Waltiri house on one pretext or another, and they would share a beer in the

back yard and talk about inconsequential things. Ruth never
visited.

Michael did not tell his story to John, even with Ruth
away. John seemed to sense that the time was not yet right for
Ruth and that they should hear together when the time was
right.

All in all, with the exception of the discoveries in the Tippett Hotel, it was still a peaceful time. Michael felt himself
growing stronger in more ways than one: stronger inside, less
agonized by his mistakes, and stronger in dealing with the
ways of the Earth, which were not much like the ways of the
Realm.

What impressed him most of all, now that he had gone
outside and had a basis for comparison, was the Earth's sense
of solidity and *thoroughness*. Always in the Realm there had
been the sensation of things left not quite finished; Adonna's
creation was no doubt masterful, and in places extremely
beautiful, but it could not compare with the Earth.

While the Realm had been built to accommodate Sidhe—
and keep them in line—and while it contained some monstrous travesties, it had seemed in many ways a gentler place
than Earth. What cruelty existed in the Realm was the fault of
its occupants. Given Sidhe discipline, Michael had found survival in the Realm proper rather easy. He doubted if survival
would be quite so easy in similar situations on Earth.

The Earth seemed not to have been built for anybody's
convenience; those who had come to it, or developed on it,
made their own way and found and fought for specific niches.
The Earth never stopped its pressures. . . . Nor gave up its
treasures easily.

Michael acquired a videocassette recorder out of the sti-
pend paid by the estate and began renting tapes of the movies
Waltiri had scored. Watching the old films and listening to the
background music, he came to appreciate the old composer's
true skill.

Waltiri's music was never obtrusive in a film. Rather than
sweeping richly forth with some outstanding melodic line, it
played a subservient role, underscoring or heightening the action on the screen.

Again and again one day Michael played John Huston's
1958 film, *The Man Who Would Be King*, reveling the first

time in Bogart's Peachey Carnehan and Jack Hawkins's Daniel Dravot, the next in the fine black and white photography and the beautifully integrated matte paintings, and finally in Waltiri's subtle score, not in the least period or archaic but somehow just right for the men and their adventure. Michael enjoyed himself hugely; that one day seemed to put everything in perspective and set his mind aright. Suddenly he was ready to take on whatever might come, with the same impractical bravado of Carnehan and Dravot. He spent the next day gardening, whistling Carnehan's theme over and over again, pulling weeds and trimming back the rose bushes according to the instructions in an old gardening book in Golda's library.

As he trimmed, he thought of Clarkham's Sidhe woman, Mora, and of the way she had trimmed her roses, and of the rose turned to glass that she had given him, that still lay wrapped in cotton in a cardboard box in the guest bedroom.

His mood darkened the next morning, when again the newspaper proved to be a bearer of disturbing news. There was an in-depth article beginning on the left side of the front page and running on through section A for some two thousand words, describing waves of so-called hauntings in England, Israel and the eastern United States.

The phrase "intrusions into reality" occurred several times in the piece, but overall the tone was light. The conclusion was that the incidents had more to do with sociology and psychology than metaphysics. He read it through twice, then folded the paper over and stared out the kitchen window at the pink roses outside.

The phone rang. Michael glanced at his new watch—it was ten o'clock—and picked up the ancient black receiver. "Waltiri residence. Hello."

"Could I speak to Michael Perrin?" a woman asked, her voice crisp and resonant.

"Speaking," Michael said.

"Hello. My name is Kristine Pendeers. I'm with the music department at UCLA."

"How can I help you, Ms. Pendeers?" Michael said, assuming his best (and unpracticed) professional tone.

"You're organizing the Waltiri estate, aren't you? I've been talking with the lawyers, and they say you're in charge now."

"That's the way it's worked out."

"We have a project going here, rediscovering avant-garde music of the thirties and forties. We're interested in locating specific works by Arno Waltiri. Perhaps you've heard of them, or come across them . . . though I gather you haven't been working on the papers very long."

"Which papers?" Michael asked, though he hardly needed to; events were heading in a clearly defined direction: the dreams, the Tippett Hotel, the bodies of Lamia and Tristesse, the hauntings . . . and now this.

"You know, we haven't been able to find a single recording of the one we're really interested in, and our collection is extensive. And no scores, either. Just these fascinating mentions in memoirs and newspapers, and in this book, *Devil's Music*. That's by Charles Fort. Have you heard of it?"

"You're looking for Opus 45," Michael said.

"Yes! That's the one."

"I haven't found it."

"Is it real? I mean, it exists? We were beginning to think it was some sort of hoax."

"I have a concert program for the première," Michael said. "The music existed at one time. Whether it does now or not, I don't know."

"Listen, it's wonderful just having something about it confirmed. Do you know what a *coup* it would be to find it again?"

"If I find the score, what do you plan to do with it?"

"I hardly know yet," Pendeers said. "I didn't expect to get this far. I'm a connoisseur of film music, particularly from the thirties and forties. I must tell you that doesn't sit well with some of the music faculty here—in Los Angeles, of all places! Can we get together and talk? And if you find anything—you know, the score, a recording, anything—could you let me know . . . first? Unless someone else has priority, of course. . . . I hope not."

"No one else has priority," Michael said. "Where shall we meet?"

"I could hardly ask to visit the house. I assume it's not all organized yet."

Michael made a quick decision. "Frankly, I'm over my head," he said. "I could use help. Why don't I meet you near the campus, and we'll talk about having UCLA lend a hand?"

"Wonderful," she said, and they set a time and place for lunch in Westwood the next day.

Over my head, indeed, Michael thought as he hung up.

Kristine Pendeers was twenty-two, tall and slender with a dancer's build, and fine fair hair. Her eyes were green and eloquent, slightly hooded, one eyelid riding higher than the other as if in query. Her lower lip was full, her upper delicate; she seemed to be half-smiling most of the time. She wore jeans and a mauve silk blouse.

After less than fifteen minutes in her presence, Michael was already fascinated by her. His infatuations always came fast and died hard—the true sign of an immature romantic, he warned himself silently. But warnings seldom did any good.

They had chosen the Good Earth restaurant. She sat across from him in a double booth. A broad back-lit plastic transparency of a maple tree canopy hovered over them; since they were below street level, the effect was not convincing. Kristine had crossed her arms on the table, as if protecting the cup of coffee between them.

"My major problem is that I don't know much about music," Michael said. "I enjoy it, but I don't play any instruments."

She seemed surprised. "How did you get the position, then?"

"I knew Arno Waltiri before he died. We became friends."

"What did he plan to have you do with the estate?" Her eyes gave her the appearance of being nonchalant and interested all at once.

"To get it organized and take care of things as they came up, I suppose," Michael said. "It's not really spelled out. We had a sort of understanding . . ." Having said that, he wasn't sure how true it was. But he couldn't say, *I'm being set up for something bigger . . .*

"Did he ever talk to you about Opus 45?"

The waitress interrupted with their lunch, and they leaned back to let her serve it.

"Yes," Michael said. He gave her a brief outline as they ate, explaining about Waltiri's collaboration with Clarkham—to a point—and the circumstances after the performance.

"That's fascinating," she said. "Now I see why the music is

legendary. Do you think the score still exists? I mean, would he have . . . burned it, or hidden it away where no one would find it?"

Michael shook his head, chewing on a bite of fish. "I'll keep looking," he said.

"You know, this project I'm working on . . . it really goes beyond what I told you on the phone." She hadn't eaten much of her omelet. She seemed more inclined to talk than lunch. "We're—actually, it's mostly me. I'm trying to put film score composers back in their proper place in music. Many of them were as talented as anyone writing music today . . . more so, I think. But their so-called limitations, working in a popular medium, for mass audiences . . ." She shook her head slowly. "Music people are snobs. Not musicians—necessarily—but critics. I love movie scores. They don't seem to think—the critics and some of the academics, I mean—they don't seem to understand that music for movies, and not just musicals, shares some of the problems of scoring operas. I mean, it's such an inspired idea, full scoring for a dramatic perform- ance." She grinned. "I'll ride that particular railroad any time you let me."

Michael nodded. "I love movie scores, too," he said.

"Of course you do. Why would Waltiri let you handle his estate if you didn't? You're probably a better choice than most of the people in my department." She held up her hands, exas- perated at herself. "Look at this. I'm wasting food again. All talking and no eating."

"All singing, all dancing," Michael said with a smile.

She stared at him intently. "You have a very odd smile. Like you know something. Do you mind if I ask how old you are?"

He glanced down at the table. "That depends."

"I'm sorry. I'm intruding."

"No, not that," he said. "It's actually complicated . . ."

"Your age is complicated?"

"I'm twenty-two," he said.

"You look younger than that, and older too."

A silence hung over the table for several seconds.

"Have you gone to school?" Kristine asked.

"Not college, no."

She laughed and reached across the table to tap his hand

with her finger. "You're perfect," she said. "Everyone says Waltiri was an inconoclast. You're living proof."

"You've talked to people who knew him?"

"Yes. It's part of the project. I know a composer named Edgar Moffat. He orchestrated Waltiri's movie scores and acted as his assistant in the fifties. He's working in Burbank now on the score for a David Lean film. You'll have to meet him. I've interviewed him several times in the last few months. He was the one who told me about the Waltiri estate. He didn't know your name, but he had heard rumors."

"Did he say anything about David Clarkham?" Michael asked.

"That was all before his time, I think. He's only fifty-three."

"Why are you studying music?"

"I'm a composer," she said. "I've been writing music since I was a teenager. And you?"

Michael smiled. "I'm a poet," he said. "I've been writing poetry since . . . for a long time."

Kristine's expression was faintly dubious. "Have you ever had anything published?"

He shook his head. "In fact, I haven't even been writing much lately. Lots of things to think about, lots of work to do."

"Poetry and music," she mused. "They're not supposed to be that far apart. Do you think they are?"

How could he answer that without making her think he was either pretentious or crazy? What he had learned in the Realm —that all arts were intimately related, that underlying each form was a foundation that could be directed and shaped to yield a Song of Power—was not something a student of music at UCLA was likely to understand. "They're very close," he said.

"I've never been word-oriented," Kristine said. "It was a struggle just to get through English classes and learn how to write a clear sentence."

"And I don't know much about music," Michael said. "Two sides of a coin." That, he thought, might be a bit presumptuous.

Kristine watched him intently. "I think the music department has a place for Waltiri's papers," she said. "If the estate agrees, we could preserve them and help you get them organized. Maybe that would speed up finding the manuscript."

Such a move could also leave him without a job, or feather-bedding on the estate payroll after he was no longer needed. "I'll consider it," he said. Was that what Waltiri would have wanted?

Kristine pushed her plate away decisively and attracted the waitress's attention with a raised hand, then asked for the check.

"My treat," she said. Michael did not protest.

"When can we talk again?" she asked. "You can meet with Moffat at Paramount. . . . Tour the library, the music department. The department head could explain how we take care of collections . . ."

"I make my own schedule," Michael said. "Anytime."

She put down a generous tip and stood with check in hand. He accompanied her to the cash register and then outside. She said, with a hint of regret, that she had to return to the campus. Michael's car was in the opposite direction. For a moment, he contemplated walking with her anyway but decided not to be too demonstrative.

"It was a pleasure having lunch with you," Michael said. She cocked her head to one side and half-squinted at him.

"You are really very strange, you know," she said. "Something about you . . ." She shrugged. "Never mind. Give me a call if you find anything. Or just want to talk music, poetry, whatever."

She walked off toward the campus, and Michael strolled toward his car. On a hunch, he stopped off in Vogue Records and asked a dark-haired, slender male clerk with a prominent hooked nose if there were any recordings available of music by Arno Waltiri.

"Just the RCA collection," the clerk answered, eyes languid. "You have that already, don't you? Charles Gerhardt conducting?"

Michael said he didn't. The clerk emerged from behind the front counter and took him to the extensive movie soundtracks section and found the album for him. Michael scanned the contents: selections from *Ashenden, The Man Who Would Be King, Warbirds of Mindanao* and *Call It Sleep.*

"Have you ever heard of a recording of The Infinity Concerto?" he asked.

"We can look it up in Schwann, but no, I haven't heard of it."

A search through the paperback Schwann catalog revealed that the RCA collection was the only album currently available. Michael thanked the clerk and purchased it.

On the way home, he stopped at a stationery store and bought a blank book. He felt it was time to start working on his poetry again, if only to build up his self-confidence and put some conviction in his voice the next time he confessed what he was.

In the car, he removed the plastic wrapping from the book, wrote his name on the flyleaf, and then shuffled through the pages, as he always did when starting a notebook.

In the middle of the book, centered on an otherwise unmarked page, were the carefully typeset words

Give it up. Finding it won't do anybody any good.

He felt the raised ink with one finger and then slowly closed the book.

4

Michael's father came to the house the next day, a Saturday, ostensibly to finish looking over the woodwork and foundations and make sure everything was in order. He arrived at two in the afternoon, and Michael followed him as he made a circuit of the outside of the house, peering into the crawlspace vents.

"Your mother's worried about you," John said, using a small ballpeen hammer to sound out the wood immediately

within a vent opening. He crawled halfway into the vent, his
voice echoing. "She thinks this job might not be all that
healthy for you."

"I'm doing fine," Michael said.

John emerged and pulled cobwebs from his hair. "Seems
sound enough on a cursory look. Well, I'm worried about you,
too. I haven't the slightest idea where you were those five
years, but I'm wondering how much you grew up during that
time."

"A fair amount," Michael said. His father regarded him
steadily and got to his feet.

"It's funny, the way your mother won't talk about it. And I
suppose I'm funny, not wanting to hear unless she listens, too.
She hasn't even hinted that she's curious . . . to you, I mean?"

Michael shook his head.

"Wasn't something like William Burroughs, was it?"

"No. Nothing to do with dope."

His father's face reddened at Michael's light tone. "God
dammit, don't patronize . . . me or anybody."

Michael shook his head. "I don't think you'd believe me."

"I'm not a dullard. I have known lifestyles other than this."
He waved his hand around the neighborhood. "Hell, I've even
tried dope."

Michael looked down at the grass.

"Something you're ashamed of? Something . . . sexual?"

"Jesus," Michael said, shaking his head and chuckling. "I
did *not* run off to San Francisco and . . . whatever. You can
reassure Mom about that." He hated the edge of whine that
entered his voice just then.

"We didn't think you had. Believe it or not, we know you
pretty well. Not so well you can't surprise us, but well enough
to believe you didn't do anything self-destructive. We just
think it might not be good for you to stay cooped up in this
house all day, going through old papers."

"I've been getting out." He told John about the request
from UCLA and pointedly mentioned Kristine. "I also take
long walks."

Michael led him through the back porch into the house.
John inspected the water heater.

"Looks like the tank's okay, but I'd like to drain it and
remove the sediment, check the bottom and see if it's going to

rust out soon. Any problems elsewhere?" John paused and tapped his knuckle on the paneling covering a broad bare space between the heater cabinet and the pantry door.

So what could he ultimately tell his father—that he didn't think normal life was going to prevail, that something indefinitely enormous was approaching?

"I don't think so," Michael said. "I can call in maintenance people if I have to."

"Come on, give your old Dad a chance to feel needed. Is there any better carpenter in Southern California?"

"No," Michael said, grinning.

The door chimes rang. Michael went to the front door and opened it to find Robert Dopso shifting restlessly from leg to leg on the front porch. "Hi," Dopso said, stretching out his hand. "I saw you checking out the foundations. Thought I'd see if you needed some extra kibitzing."

Michael grinned. Three would make the conversation less awkward. "Sure. My father's here. We're looking at the service porch now. Come on in."

"Saturday boredom, you know," Dopso said. "Bachelor's lament."

Michael introduced them. "Robert grew up here," he told his father. "He and his mother knew Arno and Golda well."

"Speaking of my mother, she's invited you over for dinner tonight," Dopso said. "Another reason I came over."

John was still inspecting the wall. "Is there a closet or something on the other side of this?" he asked. The rap of his knuckles on the paneling made a hollow echo.

"No," Michael said.

"Odd to find an unused space this big." John looked down at the floor and kneeled. His finger followed a thin arc-shaped scrape in the linoleum just beyond the edge of the paneling. "Used to be a door here. I don't think Arno ever needed to hide skeletons . . . do you?"

Michael frowned and shook his head. Dopso bent down and ran his own finger over the join.

"I don't remember any closet here."

"Still, there was a closet or something, and now it's sealed up." There was a twinkle in John's eye. He winked at Dopso. "Would Arno take it amiss if we investigated someday, when you have time? Probably find nothing but spider webs . . . ."

"Probably," Michael said. He didn't want his father or Dopso involved, somehow. The discovery was both exciting and unnerving.

"Come on," John said, walking into the kitchen. "Where's your sense of adventure? An old house, a mysterious space . . . Maybe Arno hid his treasure in there."

"Maybe," Michael aid.

"That'd be interesting," Dopso said. "Something to look forward to in a dull neighborhood. Not that it's always been so dull." His glance at Michael seemed to be an attempt to convey some silent message. Michael hadn't the slightest idea what Dopso was hinting at.

After a few more spot checks, they stood in the foyer, and his father firmly invited him to dinner the next evening. "Let your mother lay out a feast for us. It's in her nature to worry, Michael."

"I know," Michael said, still uneasy. "Dinner tonight at Robert's, and tomorrow night with you and Mom. No lack of hospitality."

"Good. Six o'clock? And let me know when you want to pry loose some paneling."

After Dopso and his father had left, Michael returned to the service porch. He tapped the paneling, idly wondering whether he should feel for secret levers or buttons. It seemed to be nailed tight.

He found a flashlight and went outside to peer into the crawlspace again. Prying out the vent his father had replaced, he shined the light under the house and followed the contours of beams, braces, wiring and pipes. The light fell against a dark gray wall of concrete approximately under the service porch.

There was a basement.

Wiping his hands on his pants legs, Michael went to the garage and searched through a chest of tools for something with which to remove the panel. He found a pry bar and a claw hammer and carried them through the back door, setting them on the floor of the service porch.

When had the basement been sealed? He didn't remember any doorway when he had been a frequent visitor to the Waltiri house, almost six years ago, Earth time.

But he hadn't been in the service porch often, either.

Could the door have been sealed during the five years he

was away, after Golda's death? Or had Waltiri sealed it himself?

Here was his chance, he thought. He knew there was something unusual in the basement. When a man—or a mage—like Waltiri sealed a doorway off, there had to be good reason. At any rate, Michael could have his father witness the opening, see whatever there was to see, and perhaps then be prepared for the entire story...

But if the basement held something dangerous, then Michael did not want his father present. John could not throw a shadow or use any other tricks to escape.

He ran his hand over the panel again, feeling it carefully not for secret latches but to gather some sensation, a clue. He concentrated on what lay behind, closing his eyes and pressing his palm flat against the wood.

Nothing.

But then, the Crane Women had not gifted him with the boon of prescience or second sight. No guiding voices gave him clues, ambiguous or otherwise.

Taking pry bar in hand, he began to remove the trim from the panel edge, cringing at the squeak of nails being forced out. With the strips removed, he inserted the bar in the gap between panel and wall frame and shoved.

The panel held; he succeeded only in bruising his palms. He tried again, with no better result, and moved the bar to another vantage.

After several minutes of fruitless effort, he noticed that the panel was wobbling a bit in its seat and that the nails holding it fast had poked their heads a fraction of an inch above the surface. With the claw hammer, he removed one of the upper-corner nails and put the bar there, shoving against it with all his might. For this he was rewarded with a groan of wood and a half-inch of give, as well as several more nailheads ready for the claw.

In ten minutes, he had loosened the panel sufficiently to grip it with both hands. He pulled it suddenly free and fell back against the washing machine. Propping the heavy three-quarter-inch plywood panel in the kitchen doorway, he surveyed what was revealed: a door, pristine white, like virtually every other interior door in the house, with a brass knob instead of crystal and a perfectly innocent air.

There was a lock beneath the knob, and in the lock, a key.

Michael reached out and twisted the key and then the knob, and the door opened smoothly inward, revealing darkness. Dry, stale air wafted out, tangy with dust. There was also a sweet, flowery fragrance, somehow familiar, overlaid by an odor richer and less easily described. He pocketed the key.

On the right wall was a push-button switch. He flicked it, and at the base of a steep flight of stairs, a bare, clear bulb cast a dour yellow glow.

Michael walked down the first flight, turned the corner, and peered into the half-lit gloom below. At the end of a second flight of steps, at right angle to the first, was a cubicle barely four yards square, with a low roof. The cubicle was filled with boxes, some of them covered by a dark fabric tarp. To his right, cramped close to the steps, sat a large black armoire. Michael wondered how such a bulky piece of furniture could have been brought into the basement.

He descended the four final steps, his shadow falling huge across the boxes. The light was in such a position that he could see almost nothing in front of him, since his shadow obscured anything he approached.

He turned toward the armoire and opened one door. The interior, barely visible, was filled with small boxes stuffed with papers. He pulled out a drawer and found more papers: envelopes, packets tied with string, a small wooden cigar box stuffed full with what appeared to be letters. A small wine rack with three dusty bottles had been jammed in the lower corner.

Michael swore under his breath and ascended the stairs to get a flashlight. Returning, he played the beam over the contents of the armoire, seeing that most of the papers were letters, and most of the letters were in German. Curious, he removed a bottle from the rack and read the label, with some difficulty deciphering the fraktur lettering.

𝔇oppelsonnenuhr
𝔉einste 𝔊eistenbeerenauslese
1921

The label carried a sundial, the gnomon casting two shadows. Beneath the lettering was a rose and a cluster of red grapes. He replaced the bottle carefully.

On an upper shelf above the drawers, he spotted a black

looseleaf notebook, its spine rippled. The heavy sweet odor...

(And he remembered what that fragrance reminded him of—himself, whenever he had touched water in the Realm—the odor of the bearer of a Song of Power.)

...intensified as he opened the notebook. The paper within seemed to squirm under the flashlight beam, shimmering like a film of oil on water, the writing surrounded by warped dimples of oily red, purple and green.

It was a music manuscript. Holding his finger under the title on the first page, he was able to still the play of light enough to read:

> Das Unendlichkeit Konzert
> Opus 45
> von Arno Waltiri

Each turned page exuded a stronger, more clearly defined perfume, until Michael could stand no more. The cubicle seemed to close down around him, oppressing him with the mixed smells of sweet rain, decaying flowers, dust and endless abandonment. He closed the notebook and shook his head, snorting.

He doubted the notebook and the manuscript within had had these peculiar qualities when the music was first penned. Since that time, something had altered the very material on which the concerto had been written.

He shuddered and replaced the manuscript, closing the armoire doors.

In the clear April afternoon light in the back yard, Michael squatted on the grass and picked at a few blades, face crossed with intense thought.

Everything was laid out before him; he had only to choose what to investigate first. Which gate to take.

He did not have the luxury of not choosing.

5

Mrs. Dopso was in her mid-sixties, small and delicate. One of her blue eyes canted upward with perpetual concern, and a blissful smile lighted on her face frequently as she spoke. Robert invited Michael in and introduced them.

"Oh, I'm *so* glad we're finally getting a chance to meet!" she enthused, fluttering one hand as if shooing away moths.

They sat down to dinner within minutes of six o'clock, shadows lying deep in the old house, which was much smaller than the Waltiri home. Robert explained that his mother's favorite hobby was saving electricity. She lighted candles in brass holders on the table, her expression grave as she applied match to wick, then grateful as the flame grew.

"I'd rather let others have the electricity, those who need it more," she said. "Improve our country's productivity, pump it into big factories."

"She's a bit hazy on how the power net operates," Robert explained.

"Perhaps, perhaps," Mrs. Dopso said lightly. "I'm just so pleased to have Michael as a guest. We have so much to talk about."

"Perhaps not all at once," Robert suggested.

"My son. Have you ever heard such a son?" She hurried into the kitchen, hands twisting slowly back and forth at her sides, and returned with a bowl heaped high with steamed vegetables. Next came a cheese and tuna casserole, followed by a plate heaped high with uniformly sliced bread of virginal whiteness. "It's not a feast," she said. "It's just *food*, but the talk is more important than the dinner."

"Mother knows you're the caretaker for the Waltiri estate."
Robert scooped vegetables onto his plate. He handed the casserole to Michael, who took a generous portion. Thanks to his
upbringing—and a few months of deprivation—he had nothing against plain food.

"If we start talking now, we won't finish eating until midnight, and it will all be cold," Mrs. Dopso said. "So we will
...um...skirt around the main topic and just fill our
tummies. Then we'll...yes." She smiled and placed a modest
forkful of casserole into her mouth as an example.

They exchanged only light pleasantries until the meal was
finished. Michael felt slightly apprehensive. Mrs. Dopso and
her son were being politely mysterious, and that bothered him;
they behaved as if they were privy to knowledge that he might
find useful.

Robert cleared the table and brought out a bottle of wine.
Mrs. Dopso bit her lower lip as he held out the bottle for
Michael's inspection.

The label was similar to that on the bottle he had found in
the newly opened cellar. The double-shadowed sundial, the
rose and the red grapes, the fraktur lettering.

"This is our last bottle. We thought we would open it tonight," Robert said. "Mr. Waltiri gave it as a gift to my father
almost fifty years ago. You might have heard of the gentleman
who provided it to Mr. Waltiri."

Michael raised an eyebrow.

"His name was David Clarkham. He was a friend of Mr.
Waltiri's, although I gather they had a falling out before I was
born."

"Yes, dear, a year or two before you were born," Mrs.
Dopso reiterated.

"My father met Mr. Clarkham several times and was very
impressed by him. Mr. Clarkham was a connoisseur of wine.
He tended to talk about unusual vintages. German wines
mostly. Many of them my father had never heard of, and he
was himself quite a connoisseur."

"But all this," said Mrs. Dopso portentously, "is neither
here nor there."

"No. Father last drank one of these bottles fifteen years
ago, and judged it quite good, if unusual."

"Do you remember what he said?" Mrs. Dopso asked.

"Yes, 'A bit otherworldly, with a most unusual finish.'"

They seemed to expect a reaction from Michael. "I found several bottles like that today," he said.

"Good! Then this isn't the last. Notice there's no clue as to what kind of wine it is. Red, obviously—but what variety of grapes?"

Michael shook his head.

"What we're leading up to is that we're curious about that house. We've lived next to it for a very long time."

"One morning, very early," Mrs. Dopso said, her face almost radiant in the candlelight, "I got out of bed and looked over the cinderblock wall. It was foggy, and I wasn't sure I saw things properly. My husband was on a business trip, so I called out Robert—poor, sleepy child—to *confirm* or *deny*."

"I confirmed," Robert said. "I was eight."

"The house was absolutely *covered* with birds," Mrs. Dopso said breathlessly. "Large dark birds with red breasts and wing-tips. Blackbirds and robins the size of crows."

"She means, with the characteristics of blackbirds and robins, but crow-sized."

"And sparrows. And other birds I recognized. They blanketed the roof, and they lined up along the wall. All silent."

"Hitchcock, you know," Robert said with a grin. "Scared the daylights out of me."

"And when the fog lifted, they were gone. But that's not all. Sometimes we'd see Mr. Waltiri and Golda—dear Golda—leave the house in their car, the predecessor of the one you drive now—funny-looking thing—and after they had gone, when the house must have been empty—"

"We'd hear somebody playing the piano," Robert said breathlessly, leaning forward.

"Playing it *beautifully*, just lovely music."

Robert uncorked the bottle and poured the wine into crystal glasses. Michael sipped the deep reddish-amber liquid. He had never tasted anything like it. It was totally outside his experience of wines, which admittedly was not broad. The aftertaste was mellow and complex and lingered long moments after he had swallowed, succession upon succession of flavors discovering themselves on his tongue. The flavors stopped suddenly, leaving only a clean blankness. He took another sip. Mrs. Dopso closed her eyes and did the same.

"As wonderful as I remember it," she commented. "To my

dear husband." They toasted the man whose name Michael did not know.

"I think perhaps the only person who was not aware that something was going on," Mrs. Dopso said, "was Golda. Arno protected her *fiercely*. Nothing would happen to dear Golda while he was around. But you know ... after he departed, *died,* things became too much for her. A strain. She must have had some suspicions over the years. How could one not?" Mrs. Dopso sipped again and smiled beatifically. "We did not volunteer to tell her, because while we knew *something* was odd, we couldn't be sure. . . . Other than the birds."

"Now that you're living there," Robert said, "what do you think?"

Michael stared into his glass and twirled the stem reflectively. "It seems pretty quiet now," he said.

"Do you play the piano?" Mrs. Dopso asked.

He shook his head.

"*Somebody* does," she said dramatically. "We've heard it after you've driven away. And the music is not quite so lovely now. It's angry, I would say. Robert?"

"Heavy-handed, skilled but ... pounding," Robert said. "I'm not sure I'd call it angry. Powerful perhaps."

Despite himself, Michael shivered, and his arm-hairs stood on end. "I haven't heard music," he said, putting the glass down.

"It's so familiar to us," Mrs. Dopso said, "over all these years. We wondered if Mr. Waltiri—Arno—or perhaps even Golda—had a relative who stayed with them."

"An old hunchbacked cousin," Robert suggested with a hint of a grin.

"No," Michael said, smiling broadly. "I'm the only one living there." That much he could be sure of.

"Bring out the tape recorder, Robert," Mrs. Dopso instructed. Robert left the dining room and returned with an old Ampex reel-to-reel deck, the tape already looped and ready to play. He set it on an unused dining chair near the wall outlet and plugged it in. Then he turned it on and stood back.

Michael heard a piano playing. The sound was fuzzy and distant, but it was indeed powerful, pounding. There was no melody, as such.

"When did you record this?" Michael asked.

"Yesterday," Robert said.

"We're *very* curious," Mrs. Dopso said. "It's something of a mystery, don't you agree?"

Michael nodded, the dinner suddenly heavy in his stomach. "I can't tell you what's happening, though. I just don't know."

"The house is haunted by a spirit that loves music," said Mrs. Dopso, her expression again beatific. "How very appropriate for Arno's house. I do not think you're in danger in that house, young man." She took a deep breath. "But if you should find out more, do let us know?"

She went to bed shortly thereafter. Robert explained, chuckling, that his mother "Rises with the birds. Pardon our intruding."

"No intrusion," Michael said. "Has anybody else complained?"

"We aren't complaining; please don't think that. And no, nobody else has commented."

"If you hear it again, will you record it for me again?"

"Of course," Robert said. They shook hands at the door, but Robert escorted Michael to the sidewalk anyway. Dusk was deep blue above the shuffling black outlines of the neighborhood trees. "Thanks for speaking with my mother."

"My pleasure."

Michael returned to the Waltiri house, where he stood by the silent piano, tapping the rich black surface of the lid. "Arno?" he asked softly, the name again raising the hairs on his neck and arms.

No answer.

He hadn't expected one. Not yet.

A shaft of late afternoon sunlight warmed the hardwood floor beneath his feet. He sat in Waltiri's music library, the old black phone in his lap, surrounded by tapes and records and books, and dialed Kristine Pendeers's home number. A man answered on the third ring, his voice deep and indistinct. Michael asked to speak to Kristine. "Who's this?" the man asked.

"My name is Michael. She'll know me."

"She isn't here right now . . . Wait. She's at the door. Hold on." In the background, Michael heard Kristine and the man talking. There seemed to be a disagreement between them. The man's hand made squelching noises over the mouthpiece. She finally came on the line, breathless.

"I've found what you're looking for," Michael said.

"I was just coming up the steps . . . to our house. Wait a minute. I'm winded. I heard the phone. You've found what . . . 45?"

"I just opened a sealed basement door and found it among other papers below the house." He realized he didn't sound particularly happy about the discovery. Why was he calling at all? Perhaps to talk with her again, meet with her. Using the discovery as an excuse.

"That's wonderful, it really is. When can I take a look at it?"

He gingerly ran his fingers over the discolored, shimmering manuscript on Waltiri's desk. "It's not in very good shape. We'll need to copy it . . . maybe a copy machine will work, and maybe not."

"What's wrong with it?"

"You'll have to see it." *Dangerous, dangerous!* Simply staring at the manuscript was enough to bend a person's view of reality.

"Can you bring it here, or do I come over there?" She seemed to catch on that he was playing a game, and she didn't sound comfortable.

"I think you'd better come over here," Michael said. "Not tonight. I'll be busy. Tomorrow. In the morning, perhaps?"

"I'll have to be there early. About seven-thirty."

"Fine. I'll be expecting you."

"You sound strange, Michael."

"I just have a lot to do between now and then. We'll talk tomorrow."

"Okay." There was an awkward moment of termination and then simultaneous good-byes. He replaced the receiver and returned the phone to its niche on a bookcase. Then he held the manuscript up to his nose and smelled it. The sweet fragrance this time was fainter, like dried fruit.

Any world is just a song of addings and takings away. . . . The difference between the Realm and your home, that's just the difference between one song and another . . . So Eleuth had informed him in the Realm.

Was it possible, then, to create a song—a piece of music —that actively contradicted the song of a world and subtly altered the world?

He wished he knew how to play the piano and was better at

reading music. It was possible he had actually heard some of the music contained in the manuscript, when Clarkham's house and the replica of Kubla Khan's pleasure dome had collapsed in the Realm, but he couldn't remember what it sounded like now. The tune was elusive, and the orchestration had faded completely from memory

He slipped the manuscript into a manila envelope and placed it in Waltiri's safe. After memorizing the safe's combination, written in Golda's hand on a piece of masking tape attached to the door, he removed the tape, burned it in a metal cup on the desk and shut the door. Why the precautions were important, he wasn't sure.

(Perhaps it wasn't Arno—in any form—playing the piano when the house was empty . . .)

He had a lot to do this evening. He would not be back until early the next morning.

Just at dusk, as the moon-colored streetlights were coming on and a slight breeze sighed through the green leaves on the maples, Michael stood before David Clarkham's house. He had not come to this place since his return from the Realm.

The deserted house was in even worse shape than when he had last seen it. The lawn had gone to seed, a definite contrast to the green, well-kept grounds on both sides. The hedges were unruly, aggressing onto the driveway of parallel concrete strips, reaching out for the cracked white stucco walls. A FOR SALE sign still leaned at an awkward angle on the front lawn; either the realtors handling the property were not pushing it or the buyers were not enthusiastic, or the sign was a sham. There was no phone number attached, and Michael had never heard of the firm before: Hamilton Realty.

He closed his eyes and found the region nestled between his thoughts that controlled *evisa* and casting a shadow. It was not difficult to find, and the act was as easy on Earth as it had been in the Realm.

He left an unmoving and slowly fading decoy of himself by the curb. Anybody watching would soon lose interest and turn away; and if they didn't turn away, then the image would smoothly disappear among the shadows of the trees, and they would be none the wiser.

Michael approached the front porch with pry bar in hand. Best to begin at the beginning.

In four minutes, he had the door open. The house radiated something unpleasant; it was more than just unkempt, it was distasteful, as if the part of the world it occupied had been ill-used and now brooded resentfully. Michael didn't like the sensation at all, and his dislike went beyond mere association with the last time he had entered Clarkham's house.

He switched on his flashlight and closed the door to a crack behind him. The hallway before the living room was dusty and quiet; the living room itself was empty and drained and faintly melancholy, the back wall illuminated by square samples of the streetlight across the way.

Despite the unpleasant sensations, there was nothing magical or supernatural about the place. Michael could feel no hidden power or lurking residue. He advanced down the hall and checked the ground floor rooms sequentially, shining his flashlight into each, seeing only dusty floors and emptiness. He returned to the middle hallway and played the beam up the flight of stairs to the second floor. The carpeted steps exuded thin puffs of dust at each footfall.

At the head of the stairs, a hallway led past the three second-floor rooms, ending at the bathroom door. Clarkham's house in the pleasure dome had been laid out in just such a fashion; no surprise. Michael peered into the first bedroom. Nothing. The second bedroom was broad and empty, its windows draped with sun-tattered expanses of old cloth slung over bent curtain rods. Cupboards and drawers covered the far wall, reminding Michael of a morgue. "Nothing here," he said in a soft whisper. He was not afraid, he was not even particularly wary, but he knew that the preternatural sensibilities instilled in him by the Crane Women had brought him here for a reason and not just to satisfy old curiosities.

The final bedroom's floor was covered with a thin layer of dust, dulling the dark wood. So far, he had only taken two steps into the room. He played the beam back and forth across the dust.

Footprints interrupted the grayness in the middle of the floor. The prints led to the hallway and passed beneath his feet, where they were erased by his own shuffling. He knelt down and examined them more carefully. The dust around the footprints was undisturbed. Only one pair of feet—wearing moccasins or sandals, since the prints were unbroken by an arch—had made the prints, and the owner had moved without hesitation, beginning his journey (his because the pattern of the feet was large and broad) in the middle of the room

Michael knelt down and touched the nearest complete print. There was something odd about the amount of dust disturbed. He walked beside the prints, noticing that near the center of the room, where they began, they were quite clear. Toward the end of the trail, they became less distinct, disturbing the dust only slightly, as if the person had weighed much less.

He pointed the beam at the air above the floor where the prints began and saw nothing unusual. Felt nothing unusual. The house was otherwise undisturbed and normal. The sensation of earthly reality was seamless.

Still, Michael knew beyond any doubt that Clarkham's house had once again become a gate.

The Tippett Residential Hotel appeared regal and desolate and out-of-place against the ragtag architecture of the Strip. Its sad, sooted, broken windows and the trash chute attached to its face gave it a painful air, as if it were a victim of patchwork surgery, of half-hearted and ill-guided attempts to bring it back to life.

Through the chain link, Michael saw that the main entrance had been securely boarded off with big sheets of blue-painted plywood. Yet the former owner—if that was what the raggedy man was—had hinted that a few people still managed to get into the building, however foolishly. There had to be other entrances.

He had looped the short pry bar onto his belt, hanging it down inside his pants. A palm-sized flashlight rested in his jacket pocket.

On the building's west side, a broad patio and swimming pool were visible through the trees and shrubs pressing against the fence. Steps rose from the patio level to a terrace on the south side, overlooking the city. All this was dimly illuminated by streetlights along Sunset, and the general sky-glow reflected from the broken cumulus clouds above the city.

Michael glanced over his right shoulder at the lighted windows in the Hyatt across and down the street. Two instances of breaking and entering in one night. Superstitiously, he thought that might make things twice as bad as they had been after the night of his first passage through Clarkham's house . . .

He couldn't enter from the front without risking discovery. He strolled east on Sunset until he reached a side street and then walked downhill and doubled back to approach from the rear.

An open-air asphalt parking area, still accessible from the street behind, abutted a blank concrete wall on the hotel's east side. Michael saw there was no easy entrance from that direction.

On the west side, a garage in the lower depths of the building offered spaces for forty or fifty tenants. The entrance was blocked by a run of chain-link and a securely padlocked swinging gate. The iron-barred gate that had once rolled along a track on rubber wheels was no longer in place. Within, one space was still occupied by an old rusted-out Buick.

The rear doors and service entrances were covered over by sheets of blue plywood. He looked up to the top of the building. More broken-out windows.

With a sigh, he stood in the darkness, hands thrust into the pockets of his jacket, and closed his eyes.

How to get in . . . without noise, without drawing any attention . . .

No inner answers presented themselves. The mental silence of Earth prevailed; no Death's Radio, no supernatural clues, simply Michael Perrin, on his own.

He felt around the boards covering the rear doors. The pry bar would make a horrible racket pulling out these nails— would anyone notice?

"I thought you'd be back."

He tensed and immediately probed the aura of the speaker. Rotten vegetables—a supermarket full of dead produce, ancient thoughts, old dreams: the ex-owner. Michael could barely see him in the darkness; he stood inside the fence, at the south end of the footpath to the pool, little more than a gray smudge against the bushes beyond.

"I didn't think you were a reporter. You must have known them . . . the two women. But what would a young kid like you have been doing with them? I figure one was a circus fat lady, the other. . . . Who knows?"

"I'm just curious about the building," Michael said.

"It gets to you, doesn't it? So pretty. Like a pretty woman, and you're all optimistic, and you find out she's a real whore. Well, she's not a whore, but she's not what you'd expect. She was built well. She still meets earthquake standards. Work of craftsmanship and art. You want to get in?"

"Yes."

"Just look around?"

"Right."

"You seem okay. Not the kind to set fires or worse. Why don't you follow me. I . . ." The blur rummaged through a pocket with an arm. " . . . have a key. Old key. Maintenance entrance. Go back around to the lot"—he pointed east—"and jump that short wall, then crawl along the fence until you meet me here."

"You're not afraid to go in?" Michael asked.

"No. You're not afraid to go in with me, are you? I'm maybe not harmless, but I'm clean. Took the bus to my sister's in Venice, showered, cleaned my grubbies out, and not with Woolite, either." He chuckled dryly.

Michael did as he was instructed and soon faced the man on the path. There was no menace in him, only a crazy kind of hope, but hope for what, Michael couldn't tell. Old dreams. Rotten produce stacked yards deep. Dead ideas.

"Journalism used to be an interest of mine, writing, all that. My name's Hopkins. Ronald Hopkins. Yours?"

"Michael."

"No last name, huh?"

Michael shook his head; no last name.

Hopkins held up the key, barely visible as a gleam in the dim light, and motioned for Michael to follow him around the south corner.

The maintenance entrance was a wide, heavy double door on the west side of the building, set flush against the wall. Michael hadn't even noticed it in passing. Hopkins inserted the key and opened one door, pushing it against a runnel of mud. "No power," he said. Michael held up the flashlight and switched it on.

"What do you expect to find?" Hopkins asked, his voice a low croak in the darkness.

"I don't know," Michael said. He shined the light against cinderblock walls, water and sewage pipes on the ceiling, a flight of stairs at the end of the hallway. Through an open door on the right, he saw a huge hot water tank suspended high above a trash-littered floor.

"You looking for ghosts? A psychic investigator?"

Michael shook his head. While he was grateful for Hopkins's services, he much preferred acting alone in the darkness without having to take another's safety into account. (And did he think there would be something dangerous here? More red lights?)

"I should be quiet, right?" Hopkins asked. Michael turned the light on him.

"Right," he said. "Thanks for letting me in."

"Nothing to it. You going above the lobby level?"

"I think so," Michael said.

"I'll go that far. No farther."

"Okay." They climbed the stairs.

"Cops found the women on the eleventh floor," Hopkins said behind him. "But I still won't go above the lobby."

Michael tried the handle on the door at the top of the stairs. It was unlocked. They stepped out onto the darkened lobby. Hopkins eased the door softly shut behind them.

The air was heavy with decay. Mildew, dust, rotting carpet, stagnant puddles of water. Michael stepped over a pile of lumber and fractured sheetrock and played the light around the lobby. A long upholstered counter ran along one wall, its faded red leatherette ripped and scuffed and stained. The countertop— probably marble at one time—was gone, no doubt salvaged. The walls around the elevator and near the entrance had also been stripped, leaving mottled plaster and gaping holes for electrical connections.

Just beyond the elevator, a grand-ballroom flight of stairs led up to the second floor. The once cardinal-red carpet on the stairs was now dirty brown and black, water-stained and torn, coyly revealing concrete floor and rotten padding. Hopkins stood behind Michael, sadly surveying the ruin. "Brought it on herself," he murmured.

The elevator doors, half-open, showed a dark and empty shaft beyond. The polished aluminum door panels were gouged and marred and reflected Michael's light back with funhouse glee.

He sensed nothing beyond the melancholy and careless decay. There was nothing supernatural about such destruction. It was characteristically human; that which is not viable and protected is soon eroded by the passage of the desperate and irresponsible, the opportunists and the destructively curious. Humans had passed through here like water in a channel, wearing and grinding. Still, he felt a need for caution.

The Sidhe, Michael thought, would never engage in idle destruction for its own sake. However evil the Sidhe might become, they were never petty, never so *unstylish* as to vandalize.

"I'm going upstairs now," he said to Hopkins. "Will I need any more keys?"

"Nope," Hopkins answered.

Michael took the grand staircase, remembering Lamia at the top of her stairs, a huge bag of flesh, in Clarkham's first house in the Realm . . .

Which did he prefer—humanity in its idle and destructive carelessness, or the exquisite cruelty of the Sidhe, who could condemn a dancer and lover of ballet to become an obese monster?

"Be careful," Hopkins admonished.

The second-floor hallways stretched in three directions from the landing at the top of the stairs. Michael's light traveled only so far in the muddy darkness; he could not see the ends of the long hallways running east and west, but the south hall was short, with only one door on each side.

The water-stained walls were covered with markings, graffiti and scrawled names, and random gouges and scratches. A smaller stairway opposite the elevator door led from one side of the landing to the next floor. Michael climbed again; there was no sense inspecting every room.

On the fifth floor, he walked from end to end in each hall and found a broken, leaning door to one apartment on the east side. He kicked it open and grimaced at the destruction beyond. Anonymous green trash had drifted into the corners of the living room. The carpets had been shredded as if by iceskaters wearing razors for blades. Michael looked down at his feet and saw an ancient pile of feces. Nearby, yellow stains dribbled down one wall.

All of this, he thought, *from the descendants of those who struggled back to humanity—or something like it—across sixty million years*. The story was noble—yet as one of its end products, a human being had once defecated on this floor and urinated on this wall.

With a sudden flush of anger, Michael wondered to what extent human depravity could be blamed on the misguiding of the Sidhe acting in their capacity as gods—Tonn, who became Adonna in the Realm, portraying Baal and Yahweh, and how many other deities?

There was a puzzle here. He knew instinctively it was useless to blame others entirely for one's own failings—or to blame the Sidhe for the failings of his own kind. But surely there was some culpability. He had little doubt that the Sidhe had mimicked gods to restrain humans, to open a little more space for their own kind on the Earth they had abandoned thousands of millennia before.

He shook his head and backed away from the feces. Such profound thoughts from such miserable evidence.

And you, Michael? Withdrawing into cold intellectual splendor, knowing you are superior because of your knowledge, knowing you would never be so unstylish as to crap on the floor of a deserted building. . . . So you're superior to your own kind, more stylish; does that mean you have something of the Sidhe in you, then?

Suddenly, the crap on the floor and the piss on the wall became profoundly funny. In a way, that kind of fated animal indifference to the past had more style in it than any ordered Sidhe posturing. Michael's thoughts made a complete turnaround with dizzying alacrity.

The Crane Women, seeing the crap on the floor, would have drawn conclusions quite different from his own. They would have seen human flexibility—not just lack of dignity, but lack of restrictions.

He backed out of the apartment and returned to the stairs.

On the eighth floor, he vaguely realized what had drawn him here. There was a sensation in the air, as of a loosening or an *opening*. It was so faint as to be almost nonexistent, but he could feel it intermittently.

The higher he went in the Tippett Residential Hotel, the stronger the sensation became. There was nothing out of the ordinary here and now . . . but there had been, and there would be again. A breach in the mind-silence and the stolid yet ever-changing and infinitely detailed reality of Earth. He was feeling a tickle in an area of his mind once touched only by Death's Radio—the voice of Tonn . . . and the voice of Arno Waltiri. Yet the tickle came from neither of them.

It was the spoor of another place, lying nearby, separated by a much thinner wall here in the neighborhood where once The Infinity Concerto had been performed.

Michael felt a sudden exultation. His need for the bite of adventure.... Here, there was hope for more adventure, more tastes of the strange and dangerous and wonderful he had experienced in the Realm. Just a shadow away, across some sheer membrane ... punch a hand through and bring back mystery, wonder ... horror.

On the tenth floor, he felt an even stronger presence, quite different from that of the nearness of other worlds. He frowned, trying to analyze what the sensation was, draw it out from the back of his head and understand what it might mean.

Imprisoned music. Not The Infinity Concerto but something even stronger.

How was that possible?

The sensation suddenly confused him. He temporarily forgot who he was and why he was here. He glanced around the tenth floor landing and walked to the window overlooking the Strip. Wind brushed at him through a broken pane of glass. Somewhere in the building, a rush of air mourned for its freedom. Not remembering was exhilarating. Suddenly he could be anybody: murderer, vagrant, good samaritan, saint.

Michael Perrin came back to him in a gentle, nonerosive flood. And with the returning memory, he could feel through his skin, rather than hear, the music that was not The Infinity Concerto. His neck hair stood on end. It was sad, fated, vibrant yet losing energy. It was the sound of a world getting old, and of a world young and full of life, whose *situation* was growing old and rickety and dangerous. Put them together...

He climbed the stairs to the eleventh and last floor before the penthouse. Here there were no apartments, but meeting rooms, game rooms, broad empty rooms only lightly littered, slightly decayed.

In one of these rooms, Michael surmised, the bodies of Lamia and Tristesse had been found. He could not tell which room. If the police had laid down paint or chalk around the bodies, it was no longer evident, at least not in the dimming beam of his flashlight.

He shook the light and felt a small anxiety at its declining batteries.

The membrane between himself and the otherness was thinning. Michael was certain that at some time in the recent past, Sidhe had been here. What they had been doing, and with what purpose, he could not tell.

Someone or something had returned through Clarkham's house, a solitary return, not likely to be repeated because the house had felt inert. The eleventh floor of the Tippett Residential Hotel did not feel inert.

Sidhe were migrating to Earth. He had seen that much in his "dreams".

Soon, a gate would open here, and many Sidhe would emigrate through this building, perhaps on this very floor.

Possibly, at the beginning, Lamia and Tristesse had tried to block passage to the hotel. The Sidhe themselves had cursed them to assume the roles of guardian and gatekeeper, but when they were no longer necessary, in fact an impediment, the sisters—Clarkham's former lovers—might have been killed and cast aside by much stronger forces.

The door to the staircase going to the penthouse had been propped open with a crumbling rubber doorstop. Michael ascended from the eleventh floor to the twelfth, leaving behind the imprisoned music.

The penthouse apartment had once been surrounded by broad, floor-to-ceiling windows, fitted with heavy drapes. The drapes were gone, leaving only their broken and despondent fittings, and the glass windows had been shattered. Their shards crunched under his shoes. Wind blew through the empty suite of rooms, whistling but not mourning, for only the skeleton of the building restrained it on this level.

On the open deck, Michael stood with his hair flicking back and forth, looking out across the hills behind the Strip. Most of the lights in the Hyatt had been turned off. He walked around the deck to the opposite side and stared across the bright lights of downtown Hollywood and Los Angeles beyond. Dawn was the faintest suggestion of a lighter midnight blue in the east. The air smelled sweet and pure after the decay in the enclosed spaces below. He breathed deeply of it and stretched his arms out, jaws gaping wide, neck bones cracking with tension.

"What a night," he said. His voice was flat and vague in the wind-sound.

Something was very definitely going to happen. Whether
he was prepared or not, Michael didn't know, but he was
expectant, almost eager.

"Come and get me," he said, and then felt a chill. *But stay
away from those I love.*

Even at this hour, the city lights were a wonder and a glory.
Ranks of orange streetlights marched off to the horizon. High-
rise towers, far off in the clear night air, offered random
glowing floors as cleaning crews finished their night's work.

People.

His kind.

Shitting on floors.

Dreaming, growing old or sleeping in cribs with developing minds dreaming feverishly of vague infant things; working
late into the morning or tossing restlessly, coming up out of
slumber into an awareness of the imminent day; maybe somewhere someone killing a person, an animal, an insect, someone killing himself; someone being born; someone realizing
inadequacies, or preparing breakfast for the early-risers;
sleeping off a drunk or making early morning love; tossing
through insomnia. Mourning a loved one. Waiting for the
night to be over.

Just sleeping.

Just sleeping.

Just sleeping.

Unaware.

Having lived all their lives in the midst of mind-silence, in
the midst of stolid and infinitely detailed reality. Never knowing anything of their distant past except perhaps through vague
racial memories, bubbling up as fantasy or delusion.

Hoping for magic and change; hoping desperately for
escape; or simply clinging, unable to imagine something
beyond. Once in, never out, except through the black hole of
death.

"Jesus," he whispered on the deck above the city and the
hills. His mind was racing toward a precipice.

Every little fractured emotion, every grand exaltation, all
bred of Earth and nurtured by Earth and all without the com-
pensation of what Michael had experienced, the true and undeniable awareness of another reality, another history and
truth to match the grandest fantasies . . .

His neck-hair rose again. Some of the music he had felt

through his skin one floor below had insinuated itself through the building and found him again. A high, piercing chord of horns and strings blowing and bowing without relenting, a note of intermingled doom and hope (how was that possible?) conveying an

emotion unfelt for ages

Michael began to shake

the emotion that was the grandfather of all emotions, from which all human feelings had been struck off like shards from a flint core.

Michael heard a voice in his mind, neither Death's Radio nor Arno Waltiri, a voice he did not recognize, very old, conveying the word *Preeda*

that was its name, the emotion that burned inside of him, threatened to burn him hollow; the only true emotion, foreign to the Sidhe for sixty million years and almost lost to humans.

Michael reveled in the sudden breaking of the mind-silence, and simultaneously a muscle-twitching terror infused him through the burning *Preeda*.

Soon we will meet, the ancient voice conveyed.

Earth's silence had been broken.

Michael saw mapped across the back of his brain an infinity of shining scales and dark, murky water.

"Enough!" he screamed out across the city. "Please! Enough!"

The building became as dead and silent as the rest of the Earth.

Michael gulped back saliva to soothe his raw throat and wiped the flood of wetness from his cheeks and eyes. He might be hoarse for a week. Certainly he would be hoarse when he met Kristine Pendeers to show her the manuscript . . .

Everyday was back. Thoughts, concerns, schedules, plans.

Preeda was gone, but where it had been, its track was clear. And he had brought it on himself, by concentrating on the city and the people—the humans—living in it, by concentrating on their situation and breaking through to some sort of understanding.

The dissonant chord of horns and strings had also pushed.

Hopkins was waiting for him in the lobby, sitting on the top of the counter, heels kicking at the torn upholstery.

"See any spooks?' he asked.

Michael shook his head.

"Find any more bodies?"

"No."

"Now do you see why no one would live here?"

He slipped one hand in his coat pocket, then nodded. "Yes."

"Thought you might. You look the type that might understand." Hopkins's Adam's apple convulsed in his long neck. "Thank you for that, and amen," he said, and led Michael down the stairs to the maintenance door.

They separated in the dawn with nothing more said.

6

He did not sleep. By the time he returned to the house, there was less than an hour before Kristine would arrive. He showered and changed his clothes, then decided now was as good a time as any to do a load of laundry. He did not feel sleepy; the old patterns could be retrieved without effort, apparently.

He hauled his clothes in a wicker basket to the service porch, across from the closed basement door, and stuffed them into the washer, then poured in soap from a half-empty box of detergent. He hefted the box thoughtfully. Golda had used the first half.

Michael suddenly felt like an invader. Whether or not he had been invited, this was not *his* home; he did not have any real place on Earth now, and he had never found a place in the Realm. He had neither the achieved position of an adult nor the allotted circumstances of a child; what he had was a kind of mid-range sinecure.

But he was hardly so naive as to believe that Waltiri had arranged for the sinecure out of the goodness of his heart. "You'll earn your place," he told himself, dipping his hand into the spray of warm water in the washing machine.

He entered the library and looked around for things to straighten or put back in place, more out of nerves than necessity. The room was neat and quiet. Opening the safe, he removed the manuscript of Opus 45 and carefully slipped it into a manila envelope. The smell had dissipated, for which he was grateful. He carried the package into the living room and placed it on the polished black lacquer surface of the closed piano lid.

Letting everything take its course.

And when would he begin to *guide* the process?

At seven-fifteen, the door chimes rang. Michael answered expectantly and found himself face-to-face with a man in a brown suit, arms folded, carrying a zippered black folder tucked beneath one. The surprise on Michael's face must have been evident.

"Excuse me," the man said. "I'm Lieutenant Brian Harvey, LAPD homicide." He held the case under his elbow and produced a badge in a leather holder, which he suspended before Michael for several seconds, letting him examine it carefully. "This house belongs to—belonged to—Mr. Arno Waltiri?"

"Yes," Michael said. He suddenly felt guilty. The man's clear, steady blue eyes regarded him without accusation or any sign of emotion, but Michael's thoughts were already racing to find some explanation for the presence of a police detective.

"I'm sorry to be here so early, but I need to ask you some questions," Harvey continued. "Your name is Michael Perkins?"

"Perrin," Michael corrected.

"And you're in charge of Mr. Waltiri's estate."

"Yes."

"May I come in?"

Michael stood aside and motioned for the detective to enter. Harvey surveyed the hall and living room with eyebrows lifted. His receding fair hair had been cut to a close bristle on his scalp. His skin was pink and slightly puffy, but he appeared slender and in good shape. Michael did not even think of probing his aura of memory; it did not seem appropriate under the circumstances, and he was wary of what might happen if the lieutenant suspected he was doing something unusual.

Why so anxious? he asked himself.

He thought of Alyons, and of the Sidhe who had taken him into the Irall—his last brushes with appointed authority.

"We've encountered Mr. Waltiri's name under some unusual circumstances," Harvey said, standing before an easy chair. "May I sit?"

Michael nodded.

"Are you expecting somebody?" The lieutenant sat with the black folder resting on his crossed knees.

"Yes, actually," Michael said. "But if I can help you . . . "

"Maybe you can. I don't know. You made some visits to the Tippett Residential Hotel up on Sunset. Why?"

Michael's nerves suddenly calmed. Now he knew the direction the conversation was going to take. He immediately probed the lieutenant: a quiet, orderly room with stacks of paper awaiting methodic and concentrated attention. Michael liked the man almost immediately; he was no Alyons. Harvey was smart and cautious and thoroughly professional. Michael had no reason to hide anything from him but no immediate reason to divulge anything, either.

"I heard about the bodies found there," Michael said. "Maybe it was ghoulish, but I decided to go have a look."

"And Mr. Ronald Hopkins gave you access to the building just this morning. About four hours ago."

"Yes. He said he was the former owner."

"Did he tell you the place was haunted?"

Michael nodded. "Something to that effect."

Harvey smiled pleasantly. "Just happenstance, whim, that you went there, then."

Michael returned the smile.

"Do you know anything about the bodies found in the Tippett building?"

"Yes," Michael said. Harvey's eyes widened with interest, and he nodded encouragement to continue. "One was a very large woman, about eight hundred pounds, and the other was a mummy."

"That's all?"

"Hopkins said they were named Lamia and Tristesse. Sadness."

"You found that intriguing?"

"Yes."

"Did he tell you about the note found with them?"

"He said there was a carved stone tablet with their names on it."

"But he didn't see the tablet himself?"

"I don't think so. I don't know."

"Did you see the tablet?"

Michael shook his head.

"No, and neither did photographers from the papers, or anybody outside my department. I have photographs of the bodies. Could you identify them?"

Michael shrugged. "It should be easy to tell—"

"What I'm asking, Mr. Perrin, is whether you know of any connection between Mr. Waltiri and these women?"

"No."

"It's just coincidence that you're interested in the building at this particular time."

Michael said nothing. Harvey opened the folder. "You were missing for five years, right? Your parents notified the police five-and-a-half years ago, and when you returned, you didn't offer any explanations. Was this in connection with Arno Waltiri?"

"Yes," Michael said.

"But he was dead before you . . . left the scene. Did he give you any instructions, any last-will-and-testament-type requests?"

"Yes."

"What were they?"

"I am to care for his estate and prepare his papers for donation to an institution."

"Did he give you instructions before you left?"

Michael shook his head. Let the detective interpret that whichever way he wanted.

"Did you know these two women?"

The simplest answer, Michael decided, was none at all.

Harvey waited patiently and, when Michael didn't reply, sighed and said, "Do you know of any connection between them and Waltiri?"

"No."

"Then why was Waltiri's name on the stone tablet, along with theirs?"

"I don't understand."

The lieutenant produced a glossy eight-by-ten photograph from the folder and held it out with fingers at the top corners for Michael's inspection. Michael took the photo and sat down in the chair across from Harvey's. The depiction was of a block of stone, about ten inches square and several inches deep, judging from a ballpoint pen placed on the floor beside it for scale. On the tablet was carved:

Lamia
Tristesse
Guardians past need
Victims of Arno Waltiri

"Can you see why we might be suspicious, why we think there might be a connection?" Harvey asked. "One of my younger officers knew that Waltiri was a composer and that he had died. I took it from there. Eventually, you made the connection seem much stronger."

"How did they die?" Michael asked.

"We don't know. The mummy had been dead for some time. And if you're concerned about my not believing a very strange story, well, don't be. I'll listen to anything."

"I still don't understand," Michael said.

Harvey leaned forward, replacing the photograph. "The fat woman was shedding her skin. It was loose, like a sack. And the mummy . . ." He cleared his throat and looked troubled. "Had a very odd affliction. Too many joints. Some sort of freak. We thought they might be circus freaks. Were they ever in the circus?"

"I don't know," Michael said.

Harvey took a deep breath. "There's stuff you'd tell me, but—"

The chimes sounded again.

"Your visitor," Harvey said.

"Yes."

"Was it murder?" Harvey asked, staring at him intently.

"I don't know," Michael said.

"You're not holding something back because you're involved?"

"No, I'm not," Michael said. "It would be difficult to explain. Perhaps later—we can talk? If you'll tell me more, I'll tell you . . ." *No need to dissemble.* "I'll tell you as much as you'll believe. I don't want to hide anything. Their being in the building was a surprise to me."

Harvey took another deep breath and stood up. "Later today?"

"Fine."

"Four o'clock this afternoon, I'll call you here."

"Fine."

"You're not leaving town, Mr. Perrin?"

"No."

"Better answer your door."

Michael opened the door, and Kristine stood there, smiling and radiant and expectant. The contrast was so sharp Michael felt another brush with *Preeda*. Harvey stepped up behind him, said hello pleasantly to her, and then glanced at Michael as he walked in an S around them and out the door. "Four o'clock," he reiterated.

"Who's that?" Kristine asked. Harvey crossed the lawn and opened the door to an unmarked sky-blue car parked in front of the Dopso house.

"The police," Michael said.

Kristine gave Michael a sharp, discerning and altogether intrigued look. Michael smiled and invited her in.

"Are you in trouble?" she asked lightly, entering the house. She absorbed the interior with a series of slow, entranced sweeps of her eyes.

"No," Michael said. "I don't think so."

"This place is *wonderful*," she enthused. Then she glanced over her shoulder and gave him an unconsciously beguiling Mona Lisa smile. "I hope you don't think I'm starstruck, but could I have a tour?"

"My pleasure," Michael said. He conducted her through the first-floor rooms, deftly avoiding the service porch and the library, then took her upstairs. She absorbed everything quietly, as if she were on a long-overdue pilgrimage.

"I know so little about him," she said. "There's not much biographical material available—some interviews with his colleagues, and what I've learned from Edgar Moffat. In some ways, Waltiri was the quintessential forties film composer—don't you think?"

Michael hadn't given the question much thought. "I suppose so," he said. Most of his attention was focused on her, with an embarrassing concentration he hadn't felt since he had been alone with Helena in the Realm. (And where was *she*, now?)

Kristine examined the framed prints hanging in the upstairs hall. "From Germany," she said. "They're old—they must have belonged to his family."

Did Arno Waltiri ever have a family, or a true human past? If not, he had assembled the evidence scrupulously.

"You only knew him a few months?"

Michael nodded.

"And he sort of adopted you?"

"We were friends," Michael said. "My father built furniture for him—his piano bench, that sort of thing. He came to a party at our house, and I met him there. Golda, also."

"Edgar tells me Golda was a darling woman."

"She was very nice," Michael said.

"Where did he do his composing?"

"There's a music library downstairs. That was where the study was."

"And you mentioned a basement, where you found the manuscript?"

"Yes . . ." Michael said slowly. "I'd like you to see the manuscript first. And there's the attic—a lot of memorabilia is stored up there."

"You're being very mysterious, Michael." The glance she gave him was both intrigued and wary. It suddenly occurred to him that whatever childish pleasure he might derive from being mysterious could not possibly equal the pleasure of her continued company.

He would much rather be completely open with her.

"I don't know where to begin," Michael said, looking at the carpet. They were near the stairs, and he took the first step down. "So I'll start with the manuscript."

He had left it on the piano. They returned to the living room, and Michael removed the manuscript from the manila envelope, handing it to her. She glanced at it with some shock and reluctantly took it from him, holding it on the tips of her fingers.

"It looks as if it's been soaking in something," she said. She rubbed a finger across the shimmering surface experimentally. "This is the way you found it?"

"Yes."

"It *is* hard to read. What caused the paper to change?"

"Smell it," he suggested. She lifted it to her nose.

"Mmm," she said. "That's nice—I like that. Perfume? Soap or something?" She shook her head before he had a chance to answer. "No. Let me guess..." She sniffed it again, closing her eyes and almost hugging the manuscript to her. "That's really lovely. I could smell that all day."

"The scent was much stronger when I first found it," Michael said.

"Well, what is it?"

"It's the music, I think."

She gave him a hard look. "I'm not *that* starstruck, however much I admire Waltiri."

Her reaction took him aback. "I don't have any other explanation," he said. "Have you ever smelled anything like it?"

She wrinkled her brow in thought, then shook her head. "Maybe he brought the paper over from Europe. Were there any other copies—you know, performer's copies?"

"Just this one. After what happened, he may have had other copies destroyed."

"Okay. May I see the office and basement now?" With some reluctance, she returned the manuscript to him, and he replaced it in the envelope. Morning light through the arched front windows caught the envelope, and he saw a discoloration. The influence was passing from the manuscript to the envelope. "We can try to get it photocopied," she said. "If you trust me with it, I'll take it to the school..."

"I trust you," Michael said, "but I think I'd rather handle this copy. For the time being."

"I understand," she said.

The music library was dark and cool. Michael switched on the desk lamp and opened the shutters on the rear windows, admitting light filtered through the green clumps of giant bird of paradise at the rear of the house.

"All of his master tapes and records," Kristine said in awe. "This is *wonderful*. There must be hundreds of scores here." She passed before the cases filled with tape boxes and old, oversized lacquer master disks in bulky cardboard sleeves. "Have you listened to them?"

"Not to these, not yet," Michael said.

"Ohh . . . I wouldn't be able to wait, if I were you. This is priceless. We *have* to get them copied. These could be the only recordings."

"I've been thinking about buying new sound equipment and doing that," Michael said. "But I've really only just started getting organized."

"You're not a trained conservator," she said. "Are you?"

"No," Michael admitted.

"That's what this really needs. A musicologist and a conservator."

"I suppose it does. I'll take whatever help I can get."

"I think I can convince the department this is important. What's in the basement?"

"More papers, manuscripts," Michael said.

"I'd like to see them, too."

"I'll show you anything you want," he said. "It really isn't mine to conceal . . . if you see what I mean."

"No," she said. "What *do* you mean? Is there something all that mysterious about old papers and records and tapes?"

"Do you believe the stories of what happened when the concerto was first performed?" Michael asked, deciding to adopt her pointblank style.

"No," she said.

"Do you believe music has a power beyond notes on paper and sounds in the air?"

She frowned. Her face was not accustomed to frowning, that much was obvious. "Yes," she said, "but I'm not . . . gullible, I'm as much of a realist as a music-lover can be."

She had been a beautiful child, not so long ago, Michael thought. *Her mother raised her after divorcing the father early, and her childhood was reasonably happy, and she developed rapidly both in body and mind, she was independent—* He closed his eyes when her face was turned and abruptly cut off the probe. He was ashamed for having begun it. But what he had found made her even more enchanting.

Kristine Pendeers was a genuinely good person, without a hint of guile.

"The basement?" she prodded, catching him with a blank and inward-turned look on his face.

"This way."

He opened the service porch door and switched on the light, then went to find the flashlight. When he returned, she was still at the top of the steps, and she didn't look happy. "I don't like enclosed places," she said.

"We don't have to go down there," he said.

"Oh, I'll go. I just don't like the dark and the smallness. I can handle it." She preceded him, and he shined the light between the stair railings to fill in their shadows and show her the stacks of papers and the armoire. She took a deep breath and turned in the cramped space between the boxes and cabinet. Michael remained on the stairs.

"May I . . . ?" she asked, touching the armoire's left door. Michael nodded.

She opened the door and surveyed the letters on the shelves within. "Wine bottles," she said with a grin, tapping one lightly with her knee. "You haven't read the letters yet, have you?"

"Not yet. I found the manuscript in there and left the rest for later."

She nodded and lightly riffled a tied bundle of letters. Then she lifted up on tiptoe and tilted the bundle outward a few inches to see the topmost letter.

"Oh, my god," she said softly.

"What?" Michael descended a step, alarmed.

"This top letter . . . it's from Gustav Mahler. I only read a little German, but the signature. . . . Can we open this and look at the rest of the bundle?"

Michael drew a Swiss army knife from his pocket and handed it to her. She sliced the string carefully and returned his knife, then lifted the letters away one by one. "They're all from Mahler. . . . They're not dated. . . . But some have envelopes. These are worth a fortune, Michael!"

"Who are they to?" he asked.

"The first one says 'Arno, *lieber Freund*'. And the next, '*Lieber Arno*'. They're all to Waltiri."

"He was only a boy when Mahler was alive," Michael said. *Oh?*

"Maybe so, but they're all addressed to him." She handed him the stack. The letters at the bottom had been sent from Wien—Vienna; farther up the stack, from New York; and then the rest from München—Munich—and Vienna again. There must have been two dozen letters, some more than five pages long.

"That's a find," Kristine said. "That's a *real* find. If that doesn't convince the department, I'll just give up. Boxes and boxes of stuff . . . who knows how many correspondents, all over the world?"

"There's a manuscript of a Stravinsky oratorio up in the attic," Michael said. "And letters from all sorts of people—Clark Gable."

Kristine's face was flushed with excitement. "Okay," she said, raising and lowering her shoulders and arms like a fledgling bird. "Enough of this. This is too much all at once." She giggled and held her hand to her lips. "Sorry. It's just incredible. This whole house is crammed with treasure!"

"I really don't know why he put me in charge of it," Michael said, preceding her up the steps. "I don't know half what I should know. I only know of Mahler because Arno mentioned him to me."

"He chose you because he trusted you," Kristine said. "That's obvious. There's nothing wrong with that. He knew you'd find all the right people and straighten everything out. When you hear what has happened to other estates, to the libraries and papers of people even more famous . . . it makes you shudder. Sold off, auctioned, broken apart, rejected by big universities for lack of space. God. It makes you want to cry. But this . . . it's all here." Suddenly, standing in the service porch, Kristine impulsively reached out and hugged Michael. "I have to go now. If you can get the manuscript of the concerto copied, perhaps I can pick it up this evening?"

"I'll try," Michael said.

"There's a U-Copy place not too far from here . . . three or four blocks."

Michael nodded.

"That policeman said he'd be back this afternoon . . ." Kristine regarded him from the corners of her eyes. "What do you think?"

"About what?"

"Is he going to keep you busy very long?"

"No," Michael decided.

"Good. Then I'll call about six. Maybe we can have dinner?"

Michael's interior warmed appreciably. "That'll be fine."

He escorted her to the front door and watched her return to her car. Kristine's walk, like all her movements, was lithe and graceful, with an unaffected insouciance in the push of her legs and the angle of her shoulders.

Even after she drove away, Michael was reluctant to close the door. He felt ridiculous, standing there with the morning well along, but now that she was gone, there didn't seem to be anything very important to do.

All of his training, all of his discipline, could not keep him from feeling empty and confused in her absence.

"You're a mess," he whispered to himself and shut the door with a decisive clunk.

7

Michael carried the manuscript of The Infinity Concerto into the U-Copy and waited in line behind a broad, short woman in a dark wool coat. She fidgeted impatiently and patted her thinning black hair with a plump hand. Ahead of her, a middle-aged man with a bulbous nose copied a tax form dozens of times. When he finished, he smiled as if he had just solved the problems of the world, paid the clerk and walked out the door.

The woman in the dark wool coat knew nothing about copy machines. The clerk, a raw-boned girl with an open and pleasant face, tried to explain the operation but met with an obstinate stare and finally did the job herself. She glanced at Michael and smiled wryly. "This'll just take a sec," she said. That commission completed, she took a quarter from the woman, who grumbled and shook her head as she left.

"You know how to work the machine?" the clerk asked. She wore jeans and a man's white work shirt.

Michael nodded. "This might not be an easy job, though."

"Oh? What are you copying?"

He removed the manuscript from the envelope. "It's been soaked in something," he lied, trying to avoid other explanations.

"Hope it wasn't toxic waste," the clerk said, eying the manuscript distastefully. She sniffed. "Smells good, whatever it was."

She dialed the machine to a new setting. "This might work." Michael removed the green-corroded paper clip from the music sheets.

However its eyes was constructed, the machine saw none of the glistening, oily distortion. Each page came out in plain black and white from the machine, with faint edges of gray.

"Does fine, huh?" the clerk asked.

"Great," Michael said, surprised.

"Did you get the glass dirty?" she asked casually after he had finished the last page.

"No, I don't think so," he said.

"I'd like to know what it was soaked in, actually," she said. "Might appeal to my boyfriend."

Michael thanked her and carried both sets to the Saab. Simple enough, he thought. How long would it take the notes on the duplicate to transform the photocopy's fresh white paper?

He locked both manuscript and duplicate in Waltiri's library safe.

From the basement, he removed the open bundle of Mahler letters, found a German-English dictionary and sat on a patio chair in the back yard, warming nicely now in late morning sunshine, to make an attempt at translation. It was slow going. How much easier if there was a German speaker nearby; he could tap the knowledge, in-speak and translate effortlessly. He closed his eyes and let his probe go out through the neighborhood. There was no way of knowing how far he could reach. Before last night, he had never probed beyond a few dozen meters.

He seemed to be suspended in a dense leafy glade with neither leaves nor light. In this glade he found . . .

An elderly man whose mind was like banked coals, feverish with speculation on some topic he could not discern; the old man spoke only English and gutter Spanish.

A young girl home from summer school, in bed with a cold. She also knew rudimentary Spanish and was reading

Walter Farley books stacked six high beside her.

A woman cleaning a large and elegantly furnished house, her mind filled with strikingly original jazz. Was she black, Michael wondered? There was no way of telling; her thoughts were of no particular color, and whatever voices he heard in people's heads betrayed no accents. She did not speak German.

Housewives, handymen, a late middle-aged man with a mind like a musty bookstore typing on an old Royal, three young babies as selfish as three Scrooges, their thoughts incredibly sensual, nonverbal and as fresh as an ocean breeze . . .

He went back to the man at the typewriter. An article on guns was emerging from the antique upright Royal, an evaluation of a new Israeli automatic rifle.

This man spoke German fluently. He had <served as a guard at an American embassy in Europe during the fifties> <killed a dozen Asian soldiers in an empty grassy field> <married three times and shot his second wife on a hunting trip, but she recovered and did not prosecute, only rapidly divorced him, and he did not contest>

Michael pulled away from the middle-aged man as if stung. He did not wish to tap the man's language abilities if he had to face more of that sort of foulness.

Where did he live—and how far away?

He could not tell.

The shock of the man's frank evil had made Michael recoil drastically, throwing his probe out in a wide arc.

And he saw—for a brief moment became . . .

Eldridge Gorn, a horse trader. That was his euphemism for rounding up range horses and selling them to knackers. He had been in the trade for thirty years, starting in 1959, two years after he had been dishonorably discharged from the Navy.

He had come back to Utah and been received by his Mormon family with chilly aloofness. Eldridge Gorn had not lived up to his father's expectations. His father was a hard, unforgiving man, whom Gorn loved very deeply, and the rejection had hurt.

He had moved to Colorado, married and been divorced within a year. He had tried to take his life with a 12-gauge shotgun in a small motel room in Calneva; the gun had jammed, and he had spent twenty-five minutes laughing and crying and trying to get the gun to work. It wouldn't.

It appeared to Gorn that someone, at least, wanted him alive.

Shortly after that, he went to work on a ranch in Nevada and learned the trade of rounding up wild horses and selling them to slaughter houses. The money was marginal, and the last ten years—what with do-gooder animal groups and the ever-changing legal scene—had forced him to change his tactics, but he hung on. He knew he was a marginal man to start with, not worth much to anybody, the only sort of person who could seriously countenance turning range horses into dog food. And he liked the work.

He even liked the horses. Sometimes they outsmarted him, and he would laugh as he had when the shotgun had jammed, and wave his battered felt hat at them and whoop.

Gorn sat on top of the cab of his pickup, a light afternoon breeze patting at his face and hair. Sage scrub to the horizon all around, a cinder cone of a centuries-old volcano off to the east, and nothing but silence and twenty or thirty head of wild horses about three miles away.

Today he would just drive around them, count and look them over. Just possibly he could drive through the scrub and herd them into a small box canyon a half mile west of the cinder cone; but tomorrow would be better, when he had an assistant or two on horseback themselves.

He lifted his nose up and sniffed like a dog. Then he hawked and spat over the hood and sniffed again. There wasn't any storm or even a cloud in the mild blue sky, but he smelled something very much like cold and winter. He prided himself on his nose—he could smell mustangs from five miles away in a good straight wind—and what he smelled bothered him.

It didn't belong. It was out of season, that smell.

Winter. Snow and ice.

Something glittered by the cinder cone, like the flash from a circle of mirrors. Gorn began to feel spooked. His crusty burned-red arms itched, and his small hairs stood on end. He pinched his nose between two fingers, then blew into his clean white cotton handkerchief.

The breeze became something out of a musty old refrigera-

tor or freezer—not so much cold as having been kept still and
confined for a long time.

There were horses coming from the direction of the cinder
cone—twenty, thirty, maybe as many as fifty, galloping from
a direction where they couldn't possibly have been. What he
smelled now was enough to send him into the cab of his truck,
because the scent was fierce and electric and dangerous. He
started the engine and watched the new herd through the
windshield.

They were all gray, hard to see against the sage but for a
quality of irridescence more at home in an oyster shell than on
a horse.

And they were coming right for him, up the gentle scrub-
covered slope, faster than any horses he had ever seen, gray
blurs with long manes. Beautiful animals. If he could catch
them (who could possibly own such beautiful horses and let
them loose in this godforsaken country?) he could make a
good deal more money by changing his tactics, avoiding the
knackers and heading straight for the stock buyers in Las
Vegas or Reno.

A quarter mile from his truck, the herd began to divide.
His sharp eyes told him the animals were sinewy, tight-
muscled, oddly out of proportion compared to the animals he
had known all his life. They looked flayed, and their heads
were exquisite, more delicately featured than Arabians, wild
and energetic and maybe scared by something behind them.
Still at a gallop.

Suddenly, the five or six horses in the lead lifted all their
feet from the ground. They were barely a hundred yards from
his truck and Gorn clearly saw all four legs on each animal
curl up and spread out like those ridiculous hunting paintings
in rich men's clubs.

The lead horses became longer, leaner, flying over the
ground, not running, their hindquarters getting blurry, their
necks stretching out until their heads seemed level with their
shoulders—

"God *damn*," Gorn said under his breath.

Like bright streaks of Navajo silver, all five lead horses
merged with the sky and simply vanished.

And then the five behind.

In ranks, all of the pearl-colored herd took to the air near
his truck and were *gone*.

He did not see them come down again.

Gorn sat behind the wheel with the engine running for a quarter hour before he half-heartedly returned his attention to the ordinary animals still down in the middle of the sage scrub.

What he felt in his chest was something past all pain and feeling.

Loss. Bereavement. An agonizing sensation of beauty and one important thing long since fled from his life. Gorn did not know what it was.

But he knew he would spend the rest of that day, and perhaps the next, looking at the sky. Waiting.

Michael put the packet of letters aside and pressed the bridge of his nose between two fingers.

His life was dividing in two, and the division was fuzzing rapidly. How long could he keep the parts separated—and how long could he observe, and learn, without acting?

The sky was clear and bland overhead, an extremely self-assured sky, unlike the Realm's active and ever-changing blueness. Differences. *Contrasts are the direct path to knowing.*

He was becoming more and more aware of human variety; in contrast, the Sidhe had seemed almost uniform, lacking the physical and mental differences and distortions endemic to humankind.

The Sidhe were like thoroughbreds; their lines had been molded across tens of millions of years, with who could tell what kind of strictures and impositions? Humans, however, had re-emerged from the condition of animals (were animals still), with all the riotous multiformity of nature.

They would not mix easily.

Michael returned the packet of letters to the armoire in the basement and then fixed himself lunch, a cheese sandwich and an apple. Half an hour later, he returned to the back yard to practice *hyloka*, squatting naked on the grass, his skin glowing like a furnace.

"Salamander," he murmured, feeling the ecstasy of the unleashed heat subside. In such a condition, he realized, he could walk through a burning house unharmed; he would be hotter than the flames. He damped his discipline and got to his feet. Where he had been sitting, his legs and buttocks had left blackened prints in the grass. He was ravenously hungry again.

He ate a second lunch, much the same as the first, and replayed *The Man Who Would Be King* on the VCR. Halfway through, he found he was merely staring blankly at the TV screen, his mind elsewhere—with the horse trader on the rangeland, with the elderly woman in the old forest. . . . Mulling over the Tippet Hotel and Lieutenant Harvey, but most of all, thinking of Kristine.

At four o'clock, the phone rang. Lieutenant Harvey explained he was calling from downtown.

"I've had to put our mutual interest here, the Tippet Hotel case, on the back burner for the moment," he said. "But I'll want to talk with you in detail later. I doubt that you're a suspect, but if you'd feel more comfortable, you can have a lawyer present. I'm not looking for confessions or anything, you understand?"

"Yes," Michael said, aware the detective was telling the truth; learning more about Harvey perhaps than the reverse.

"But this is fascinating stuff, and I think you have some interesting things to talk about, don't you?"

"If you have an open mind," Michael said.

"Uh—HUH," Harvey grunted emphatically. "Keep us in the real world, okay?"

"No guarantees," Michael said.

"I have my instincts to rely on," Harvey said softly. "They don't fail me often. What they tell me now worries me. Should I be worried?"

Michael waited for a moment before answering. Eventually, Harvey would have to know. The dreams were spilling over into the real world. The division was fuzzing all too rapidly.

"Yes," Michael said.

"I can see it's going to be a cheerful week," the lieutenant said. "I'll get back to you in a couple of days. Sooner, if anything new comes up." Michael deposited the receiver on the hook. Logically, Harvey should question him as soon as possible. But the lieutenant was postponing unpleasantries for as long as possible. Michael couldn't blame him for that.

He walked up the stairs, pulled down the ladder to the attic and climbed into the musty warmth. Once, sitting in the attic while Waltiri looked through boxes of old letters and memorabilia, Michael had felt as if time had rolled back or even ceased to exist; nothing had changed there for perhaps forty years.

The attic still seemed suspended above the outside flow. He idly opened the drawer of a wooden filing cabinet and leafed through the papers within. So much accumulated within a lifetime . . . reams of letters, piles of manuscripts and journals and records . . .

He pulled out folder after folder, peering inside. Several letters from Arnold Schönberg, dated 1938; he put those aside for later reading. Schönberg had been a composer, Michael remembered; perhaps the letters mentioned the concerto.

Then he found the Stravinsky oratorio manuscript. Stravinsky had composed *The Rite of Spring* early in the century, and Disney had set the work to dying dinosaurs. Every adolescent knew Stravinsky.

Holding the oratorio was like holding a piece of history. He lightly touched the signature and the accompanying letter, savoring the roughness of the fountain pen scratches.

1937, the letter was dated. He could almost imagine, outside, a calm bright spring day, the cars parked on the street and in the brick driveways all rounded and quaintly sleek, like the Packard in the garage; silver DC-3s and Lockheed Vegas flying in to Burbank airport, tall palms against the sky, everything more spread out, less crowded, almost sleepy. . .

Michael looked up from the manuscript with a glazed, distant expression. Before the war. Days of the late Depression, easing now that Roosevelt was rearming the country.

Days of comparative peace before the storm.

Kristine seemed to regard Westwood as the center of the universe. She knew all the best restaurants there—"best" meaning good food on a slightly more than meager budget—and she had chosen a less crowded one this evening. It was called the Xanadu, which both discomfited and amused Michael. The decor was dark wood paneling inlaid with somewhat oriental, somewhat Art Deco scenes beaten into brass sheets. White silk canopies depended from the ceiling. Its fare was not Chinese food, but nouveau French, and Kristine assured him everything was very good despite the reasonable prices. "The chef here is young," she said. "Just getting started. He'll probably be gone in two or three months; somebody else will hire him, and I'll never be able to afford his cooking again." They were seated at a corner table by a wait-ress dressed in tuxedo.

Kristine gauged his reaction as the waitress wobbled away on high heels. "So it's not consistent," she said, laughing.

"Xanadu's an odd name, isn't it?" he asked. "For a restau-rant like this?"

She shrugged. "I suppose they intended it to mean . . . a pleasurable place, extravagant, not necessarily Chinese."

Michael felt a strong, all-too-adolescent urge to bring up his unusual familiarity with Xanadu, but he resisted. He would not impress Kristine by being any odder than he already was.

"Have you been reading about those hauntings?" she asked.

"Yes. In the papers."

"Aren't they strange? Like the flying saucer waves. Really spooky, though."

He glanced down at the side of his chair, where he had laid the envelope containing the copy of the manuscript. Time to change subjects completely, he decided. He brought it up to table level. "I made a copy," he said.

She glanced at the envelope, obviously aware of the gin-gerly way he supported it on his fingertips. "How did it come out?"

"You can look for yourself." He handed it to her.

"It's very clean." She pulled it halfway out of the enve-lope. "I didn't think it would copy nearly that well."

"We're in luck," Michael said.

"Thank you." She riffled the pages, returned it to its enve-lope with a broad smile and slipped it in her voluminous canvas purse. Her smile changed to concern. "Are you feeling all right tonight?"

He nodded. "I'm a little nervous," he admitted.

"Why? Is it the restaurant?"

"No. What will you do with the manuscript now?"

She shrugged, an odd reaction, as if it all meant very little to her. Then an excited smile broke through her nonchalance, and she rested her arms on the table, leaning forward eagerly. "I'll show it around the department. There are plans for a concert in the summer . . . July, I think. If we can get it pre-pared by then, perhaps we can perform it. And I'll show it to Edgar." The waitress returned for their orders, and Michael chose poached halibut. There were no vegetarian dishes on the menu; he felt less uncomfortable eating the flesh of sea-creatures but knew that a Sidhe would abhor even such non-mammalian fare.

Kristine ordered medallions of salmon. The waitress poured their wine, and Michael sipped it cautiously. He had drunk wine only once before, at the Dopsos's house, since his return, and he had reservations about how it might affect him in his present nervous state. He did not want to become even mildly drunk; the very thought bothered him. But the wine was agreeably sweet and light, and its effects were too subtle to be noticeable.

One evening, the soul of wine sang in its bottles . . .

Baudelaire. Why the line seemed appropriate now, he didn't know.

"I'm starting to have my doubts about this whole thing, about putting on a concert," Michael said, inching back into his chair.

"Why?" Kristine asked, startled. "Aren't you supposed to promote Waltiri's works? Isn't that what an executor does?"

"I'm not precisely an executor, I just manage the estate. I don't know." He opened his mouth to speak again, then shut it and shook his head. "I don't know what in hell I'm doing here. I'm giving you something you can't possibly understand—"

"Now wait a minute," Kristine flared.

He pointed to her bag, with the corner of the envelope sticking out. "When that music was written on the manuscript I made this copy from, the paper was white and pure. It wasn't soaked in anything between that time and now. It just . . . aged."

"I don't get you."

"No, and neither does anybody else." He felt his frustration suddenly rise to the surface. "I'm not in an enviable position right now. I'm pulled this way and that."

"How—"

"So—" He held up both hands. "Please. Just listen for a bit. You can say how crazy I am afterward. I know you're an expert on music, maybe even on Waltiri's music, but this is something else."

"I don't understand your doubts. You think—"

Michael's expression stopped her. She folded her arms and leaned back in her chair, glancing nervously at a patron walking past their table.

"You mentioned the hauntings. There's a connection."

"With this?" She dropped her hand to the envelope.

Michael nodded. "I don't know all the details. Even if I did, it wouldn't be worthwhile to tell you. Because you couldn't possibly believe."

"Jesus," she said. "What are you involved in?"

He laughed and looked up at the backlit white canopy overhead.

"That policeman. Is he part of it?"

"Not really. He's like you. And my father. And Bert Cantor."

"Who's Bert Cantor?"

"Somebody who knows. Whom do I tell? And how much? You all live in the real world."

"You don't?"

Michael sighed. "For a time, I didn't. I was missing for five years, Kristine."

Her brows knit. Then she leaned forward. "Because of the concerto?"

"It's part of the . . . experience. Yes." *And I ended up in a much better re-creation of Xanadu than this restaurant—* He severely edited what impulse would lead him to say. It was so difficult, wanting to tell the entire story and being constrained by practical considerations—belief, the impact the story might have on how she regarded him, his unease at what might seem self-aggrandizing.

"Okay. I'm listening." There was a look in Kristine's eyes then that only deepened his distress. She *was* interested. She was positively intrigued. He was something different in her life, and his attitude, his tone of voice, did not reveal him to be a nut or a liar.

Which compounded distress upon distress.

And stopped him cold before he could begin his next sentence. "I'm sorry." His face reddened.

"I said you were mysterious this morning," Kristine reminded him. "I don't know what I meant—"

"Okay," he said. "I'll tell you this much. I have been warned not to do any of this." He gestured toward the manuscript with an open hand. "I don't know by whom. I'm ignoring that warning, but I want you to be aware of the risk we're taking."

"Jesus," she said again, looking down at the table. They were served their salads. "Why didn't you tell me this earlier?"

"Because I'm an idiot." He touched his fork to the salad.

"You are *not* an idiot," Kristine objected, raising her eyebrows not at him but at her salad plate.

"Then maybe it's because I'm way out of my depth."

She regarded him shrewdly. "Then why are you doing this?"

"Because I find you attractive," Michael said, the editing function somehow completely deactivated.

Kristine didn't react for an uncomfortable number of seconds. "I'm living with someone now," she said.

"I suspected as much."

"I'd like to think we're both interested in the music."

"We both are."

"And I'd like to think you wouldn't use all of this as an excuse, just to see somebody you're attracted to."

"I haven't been. Not entirely."

"How old are you?" Kristine asked. "I mean, really?"

"I don't know," Michael said. "I was gone five years. It didn't seem like five years to me."

"I was thinking you might be older than you said."

"If anything, I'm younger."

"Then I'm really confused." She removed her napkin from her lap and laid it on the tablecloth. "And I'm not very hungry."

"Neither am I."

"You don't want me to do anything with the manuscript, then?"

"On the contrary. I *do* want you to . . . take it to the music department, look it over, get it performed. But I think you should be aware there could be trouble."

"Do you always cause trouble for women you're attracted to?"

Her question stunned him. *Yes.* "Not like this," he answered. "It's not me causing the trouble."

"What I think you're trying to say is, if we play this music again, the same things will happen as happened in 1939."

"Or something even more important."

"And I could be sued, as Waltiri was sued."

"I don't know about that. That isn't what worries me most."

She seemed absolutely fascinated by the idea. "That would be...interesting. But you're right; I find it all hard to believe."

"And you're only hearing the easy part," Michael said.

Again a pause, as she bit her lower lip and searched his face intently. "Let's talk about how you feel about me..."

"Please. It's embarrassing. I've said too much, and I've said it in all the wrong ways."

"No. I appreciate your honesty. You are being honest; that much is obvious. And you're not crazy. Believe me, I've gone out with enough crazy men..." She gazed off into the middle distance. "I like you, but there is this...situation."

"We shouldn't waste the food," Michael said.

"No." She picked up her fork, replaced her napkin and speared a leaf of lettuce from her salad plate.

"I mentioned the Mahler letters to Gregory Dillman. He's our department expert on Mahler and Strauss and Wagner. He's fascinated—says that none of the letters have ever been published, which is obvious, I suppose."

"Yes," Michael said.

"He's advising a fellow named Berthold Crooke on his orchestration of Mahler's Tenth Symphony."

"Oh?"

"Mahler died before he could finish the orchestration. Deryck Cooke orchestrated a version about twenty years ago, but Crooke has a different approach. They—Dillman and Crooke —would love to see the letters."

"We should get your librarians to work on them soon," Michael said. "Cooke and Crooke. That's funny."

"Right." She smiled. "Both with an *e*."

Their main course was served, and they concentrated on the food for a few minutes, though Michael was not particularly hungry. There was a hollowness of want inside him that had nothing to do with food. His mind was racing ahead, speculating, visualizing scenes he had no right to even consider now.

Kristine, without realizing it, had set the hook by confirming Michael's suspicions. She was not yet available; she might

even deny him. That made her infinitely more attractive. So it
had been with Helena in the Realm.

"Your situation doesn't sound good," he said on impulse.

Kristine twisted her fork around a fleck of parsley in a
small puddle of herb sauce. "Persistent, aren't you?"

"I'm just interested," he said. "Concerned."

"Well it doesn't matter. It'll work out," she said.

"I hope I didn't cause any trouble when I called. I thought I
heard an argument."

Kristine sighed and met his eyes. "You know, I must want
to talk about it, or I'd be angry with you now."

"I'm sorry," Michael said softly.

"I meet the strangest men. I really do. Maybe it's an occu-
pational hazard, part of being a woman. My mother says most
men are like wild horses. You can't expect all of them to be
Lippizaners. But mostly I think I'm just too young to have
much taste. You know. Can't tell the good wine from the bad
right off."

"So what am I—Lippizaner or mustang?" Michael asked.

"Oh Jesus, I don't know." She had finished her salmon and
laid the fork beside untouched broccoli spears. Her eyes narrowed, and she appraised him. "I don't know you well at all,
but you're no Lippizaner. You're not tamed, and you're not
trained. Not domestic at all. I think you must be . . . wild but
not a mustang. Some sort of fairy tale horse."

Michael raised an eyebrow and grinned.

"Well, we're going to be frank tonight, aren't we?"

"Okay."

"A white stallion maybe. Just something big and lean and
out of a dream. I don't know whether you're benevolent or
. . . not. I know you're not cruel, but—powerful. Somehow.
Oh, forget all this." She shook her head, hair drifting into her
eyes. As she replaced the strands, the waitress asked them if
they wanted dessert.

"Coffee," Kristine said. "I could have coffee. How about
you?"

"Nothing, thanks."

"Flying horses, silver-gray and lean. Maybe that's what
you're like. I had a dream about that last night. Maybe I was
thinking of you."

Michael felt his breathing stop, his insides tense, and then returned himself to some semblance of calm.

"Isn't that what a poet is supposed to be, powerful and ghostly inside, raise the hair on your neck?"

He had never heard it expressed quite so well before. He nodded. But—

. . .Once, poets were magicians. Poets were strong, stronger than warriors or kings—stronger than old hapless gods. And they will be strong once again. Adonna, Tonn, had told him that.

"So you're a real nightmare," Kristine said, smiling again.

"Better than being a nerd, I suppose."

"Tommy . . . he's the fellow I live with. We share a house with Stephen and Sue. A big four-bedroom place. We have a room and bathroom all to ourselves. Tommy's nice inside, but he doesn't know himself. He has no self-confidence. It makes him go off the deep end, like he has no real self-control." She held up both hands, one clutching her napkin, and leaned her head back as if looking for the right words to be printed on the silk canopy.

"If I left him now," she said, "he might just fall apart."

"Do you love him?"

To his distress, he saw tears in her eyes.

"Damn it," she said, touching the napkin to her cheeks. "You don't know me that well, to ask such questions. Let's get the check."

"I'm sorry. I'm just concerned."

"Oh, bullshit," she said, not unkindly. "You're on the make. No. I don't love him now. He's the albatross I get around my neck for having bad taste in men."

They split the bill, and Michael insisted he leave the tip. He expected Kristine to say good-bye and leave with the manuscript, but instead she began walking down Gayley toward Westwood, apparently expecting him to follow. He kept pace with her. "You know, maybe we could have a big concert in the summer," she said crisply. "Sort of the opposite ends of the early twentieth century German tradition—Mahler's Tenth and Waltiri's Infinity Concerto. Wouldn't that be an occasion? I'll mention it to Dillman. Maybe Crooke will have his performing version finished by then, and we can première it." She led them by a brightly lighted theater front. Michael automatically glanced at the movie posters on the side of the fourplex—a Blake Edwards romantic comedy called *Tempting Fate,* two theaters showing David Lynch's *Black Easter,* and a reissue of *The Black Cauldron.* The poster for *Black Easter* showed U.S. Army troops fighting demons around a city whose walls were made of red-hot iron.

Long lines of people waited behind ropes suspended from brass poles along the sidewalk. Michael feather-touched their auras automatically as he and Kristine walked past. The people were bright, expectant, full of the awareness that they were on a kind of social display; they were very much alive and enjoying themselves. Michael felt a fullness of love for them beyond immediate explanation.

"I'm an ambitious woman, Michael," Kristine said, walking ahead of him past the theater entrance. "Or didn't you get that impression already?"

"No, I didn't. I wouldn't use the word ambitious."

"Then I'm a dreamer. How's that?"

"That's a good word," Michael said.

"Jesus. All these fantasy movies." She looked back over her shoulder and shook her head. "Won't they ever go out of style?"

"Maybe there's a reason everyone's interested in fantasy," Michael suggested.

"What?"

"The hauntings. Dreams of wild horses."

"What about them?"

"Never mind."

She didn't press him. They came to a bookstore and looked in the windows. "Wouldn't you like to see your books in there, sometime?" she asked.

"I would," Michael agreed.

"And what I would like it to go by Vogue or Tower and see my music on CDs all over the windows." She laughed, but Michael saw her eyes were still moist. "Okay. I think it's time we went home. Tommy has the car tonight. I came here by bus. Can you give me a lift back?"

"Of course," Michael said.

Michael drove east on Wilshire, following her directions. The night was warm and the air relatively clear, with a few bright stars showing through low, orange-lighted clouds. Kristine stared up through the open sunroof. "I'm not really a complainer," she said. "My life is going along okay. I enjoy my work." She glanced at Michael. "Even so, I want to get away sometimes. Have you ever had that feeling? That you'd like to go away someplace far from everything, away from all the responsibilities and cares? That must be a common fantasy."

"I suppose," Michael said.

"Is that what you did? You said you were away for five years."

"I didn't get away from responsibilities."

"Can you tell me where you went? I've been doing all the confessing this evening."

He smiled and shook his head. "If I'm putting the make on you, then I mustn't scare you away by making you think I'm crazy, should I?"

"All right," Kristine said.

"But I will confess one thing."

"What?"

"From what you've said about Tommy, I don't think I like him very much. If he makes you unhappy."

"Michael, I'm the one who makes *him* unhappy. We make each other unhappy."

"Then why don't you leave him?"

"I told you. That's the street up ahead—South Bronson. Turn right." They entered a neighborhood of old, large homes, most in the California bungalow style. Kristine told him to slow down and pointed out the house where she lived. Two stories high, fronted by a broad porch with low brick walls and pillars supporting a second floor porch, it looked dark and ill-kept. Faded yellow paint peeled from the clapboard siding. An old black Trans-Am with gray patches of primer along its side and rear waited by the curb in front of the house, seats unoccupied, lights off and engine running. Someone stood in the shadow of the porch. Michael did not like the circumstances at all, but Kristine didn't seem alarmed.

"Tommy's back," she said. "You can just let me off here."

Michael stopped, and Kristine opened the door and stepped out. The figure on the porch came down the steps slowly, methodically, with an exaggerated cowboy walk. Michael quickly probed the man and found sullen anger, neat tidy rooms full of engine parts and tools, a flicker of light at the back of a long, dark hallway. The man crossed the street as Kristine shut the door. She leaned into the window. "Thanks for the ride. I'll call you about meeting Edgar and coming to the department. And we'll talk about having the library people take a look—"

"How cute," Tommy said, stopping several yards from the car. He was of middle height, black-haired, powerfully built and slightly bow-legged, his legs packed into faded jeans and his crossed arms revealed by a black T-shirt. "A Saab. Real powerhouse. College professor, right?"

"Tommy, this is Michael Perrin. He was good enough to drive me home."

"I'm sure. Pleased to meet you, Michael."

"Same here," Michael said.

"I've been waiting."

"You were gone when I got home," Kristine said. "I couldn't leave you a message. And you had the car." She looked back at Michael as she touched Tommy's arms.

"Fine," Tommy said. "Thanks for dropping her off."

Michael could not believe what happened next. The man reached out casually with one arm, as if to embrace her. She stepped closer, and he made a half-spin, striking her cheek with his hand. Kristine dropped to the street in a half-crouch, one leg stuck out to keep from falling over. Her purse hit the pavement, and the envelope slid out.

There was no thought involved in his reaction. He heard Tommy say something in a quiet voice to Kristine, and then he heard the Saab's door open. Michael stood on the street long enough to let the man know he was there, and then Tommy was on his back with his legs spraddled and blood pouring from his nose.

Michael had deftly lifted his leg and reached out with the toe of one running shoe to clip Tommy's face. Kristine had reached for the envelope and her purse and had not seen the blow connect. Now she scrambled across the pavement, dragging her purse, and knelt by Tommy.

"Bastard," Tommy said thickly. "Gib be a Kleedex."

"It isn't broken," Michael said with certainty, still calm but feeling the hot lava of angry reaction rising in a volcano tube to his head.

"Goddab," Tommy said, clutching her proffered scarf to his face.

"Are you all right?" Michael asked Kristine. The print of Tommy's blow was livid on her left cheek.

"I'm fine," she said. "He didn't mean to hit me hard. Oh, Jesus, what am I saying?" She seemed to be keening over him, repeating, "You idiot. You poor, stupid bastard."

"Leave be alode," Tommy said, pushing her away. She got to her feet. "You dod't go out with subwud else, dot without by dowing," he said.

"It was a God damned business dinner," she said. "Michael's in charge of the estate I told you about."

Michael probed Tommy as he stood, trying to predict what he would do next. Tommy's anger was now evenly mixed with shame, somewhere a small boy crying, light flaring red at the back of the dark hallway. Michael suddenly felt very sorry for the man and confused.

Kristine confronted him. "You're my protector, are you?" she asked, her voice level, her stare glassy.

"I apologize."

"That was sharp," Tommy said, grinning through the scarf. Black smeared his jaw in the orange streetlight glow. "That was do college professor's trick. Dod't get bad at hib, Kristide. I pulled a stupid studt, and he showed be. He showed be."

Kristine looked between them as if they were both crazy. Then she shook her head and walked to the house.

"Okay, Bichael," Tommy said, backing off the street and onto the grass strip beyond the curb. "You showed be. So dow leave us alode, huh?" He turned off the idling engine of the Trans-Am and followed her up the porch steps into the dark house, keys dangling from his hand, the other still clutching Kristine's scarf to his nose.

Michael stood in the dark living room, having walked unerringly on a path between the furniture to the piano, and with his eyes closed wept for a time, his arms trembling and his chest heaving as he tried to subdue the sobs.

The real world.

How far away the Realm seemed now, and how cut and dried most of its problems. With every breath, every choked-off sob, the real world exploded behind his eyes. Growing up, trying to fit into society, trying to decide who and what he was: the immediate reality.

Making mistakes. Taking actions in which there was no apparent right or wrong.

Hitting a man who was already deeply confused, hurting.
But he struck Kristine.

Justified or not, what Michael had done that night simply
tore him up inside. What made it worse was the knowledge
that as a hidden part of what the Crane Women had taught
him, he could have easily killed Tommy.

The impule had been there—raw indignation quickly
bursting into anger. He could still feel it in his gut: *The world
would be better off without Tommy.*

Something in his memory tickled. Something about Kristine. From the Realm. How was that possible?

All his emotions seemed to retreat like a fast sea tide. He
stood in the dark, made suddenly afraid by what he remembered, and wondering why he had not remembered before.

After the death of Alyons, Wickmaster of the Pact Lands,
at the outer border of the Blasted Plain surrounding the Pact
Lands, he had encountered for the second time the hideous
snail-like creature with the death's-head shell. With a
woman's voice, it had implored Michael, *"Take me with you.
Take me with you. I am not what I seem. I do not belong
here."*

"What are you?"

"I am what Adonna wills."

"Who are you?"

"Tonn's wife. Abandoned. Betrayed. Take me with you!"

*He walked in a wide circle around the creature. It made no
further move toward him.*

"You are a mage," it said. *"Take me where I might live
again. And I will tell you where Kristine is."*

"I'm sorry," Michael had said. *"I'm no mage. And I don't
know who Kristine is."*

He had crossed the border of the Blasted Plain, leaving the
skull-snail—Tonn's wife—alone and trapped, a victim of
Sidhe sorcery even more hideous than that used to transfigure
Lamia and her sister.

His back crawled. Tonn's wife had referred to him as a
mage. And by implication, something would happen to Kristine that Michael would have little or no power to prevent.

The Waltiri house seemed less and less a sanctuary and
more his own special kind of trap.

8

"I've opened that basement door," Michael told his father. They sat on the back porch of the Perrin house while his mother prepared iced tea and sandwiches in the kitchen.

"Oh? What'd you find?"

"A basement. It's crammed full of papers."

"John has something to ask you," Ruth said stiffly, laying a tray on the glass-topped table. She sat across from them, her face drawn. She had tied her long, dark red hair back in a bun.

"LAPD came by yesterday, in the form of a detective," John said. "He asked us questions about you, about your time away. We told him we'd rather discuss those things with you present."

"What did he say to that?"

"He smiled," Ruth said. "He said that was okay and that he had talked to you already. He said you were mysterious but seemed to want to cooperate."

"Then why did he come here?" Michael asked.

"I don't know," John said. "I suppose all this is linked with your disappearance."

Michael picked up a cucumber sandwich, examined it and then set it back on the plate. "I'm going to tell you everything," he said. "I don't care whether you believe me or whether you want to hear. I mean, I care, but I'll tell you anyway."

Ruth wrapped her arms around herself. John glanced at her. "I think it's about time, myself," he said. She sat beside him and nodded slowly.

"All right," she said.

Michael pulled a small cardboard box from his pocket and

opened it on the table. There, embedded in cotton gauze, was the glass rose given to him by Mora, Clarkham's Sidhe mistress.

And he related the story, much as he had spun it out for Bert Cantor, from the summer days he had spent with Arno and Golda to the few days in Clarkham's Xanadu; from the end of Xanadu to the opening of the basement and the discovery of the curiously altered manuscript of The Infinity Concerto.

The telling lasted into the evening, with a pause for dinner. There were many glasses of tea, and later of beer, and Ruth wept quietly once toward the end, whether for his sanity or in commiseration with what her son had experienced, Michael couldn't judge.

Twilight was deep blue above the trees and hedges in the back yard. Michael sat with his father while his mother went for a sweater in the house.

"It was always twilight in the between-place," Michael said.

"Where Tristesse waited for travelers," John said.

"It was odd in the between-worlds. Muddy, peaceful. I mean, the sensation of reality there was thin. It was more like a dream, or a nightmare. In the Realm, everything was sharply real, but it didn't feel the same as this, now." Michael tapped the table.

Ruth re-emerged with a pink silk and angora sweater draped over her shoulders. "Do things like that happen?" she asked her husband, matter-of-factly. John barked an astonished laugh.

"Damned if I know."

"I've always made myself be the practical one in this family," she said, face turned toward the fading blue in the west. Michael detected a falseness in her voice, almost a posturing. He realized she was playing a kind of role, using this persona as armor against something she felt threatened by. "John's the master at wood, and Michael . . . wordsmith, scattershot talents. I could never be sure what Michael would end up being." She glanced pointedly at her son. "You know I've always preferred Updike to Tolkien."

"*Witches of Eastwick?*" John asked with a small grin.

"It wasn't like Tolkien," Michael said.

"No, I suppose not. And this is the only evidence?" She touched the glass rose.

"There are several places I could show you. The Tippett Residential Hotel and Clarkham's house. Arno's basement could be first."

"I suppose the rule is, you'll have to show us three impossible things before breakfast," John said, picking up the rose gingerly to inspect it. It still kept a faint interior glow in the evening gloom. He sniffed it.

"Do you know what the hauntings in the newspapers mean?" his mother asked. Michael shook his head.

"Not exactly. I think I know what they're leading up to, though, which is why I'm telling you all this now."

"Is that why you're letting Kristine Pendeers get involved?" John asked.

"I don't know how I feel about all that." Michael stood and helped his father clear the dinner dishes from the table. When they were done, and the dishes had been stacked in the dishwasher and the table and counters wiped down, Ruth stood in the porch doorway with her arms folded.

She was crying. Her cheeks were shiny and drops beaded her sweater. "I just can't believe it," she said. "I've been saying this is all a nightmare for so long." Michael came to her, and she held him, running the fingers of one hand through his hair.

Michael started to say something, but John caught his eye and shook his head, no.

Later, after Ruth had gone to bed, Michael and his father sat in the back yard under the dim Los Angeles stars. "There's something she's going to tell us," John said. "She's had it inside her as long as I've known her. But it's never come out. Seems to me what you said tonight almost shook it loose."

"What is it?" Michael asked.

"I really don't know," John said.

"Is it important?"

"To her, it sure is."

Lieutenant Brian Harvey stood with Michael in the rear bedroom of Clarkham's house and peered at the footprints that began in the middle of the floor. "So there's no real estate company by that name," he said. "So there's no record of ownership for the house—no record of when it was even built. So this is supposed to be an empty lot. We're still trespassing."

"Are you worried?" Michael asked ironically.

"I suppose not," Harvey said. "It's a good trick, that." He pointed to the prints. "I can guess how it was done. Sprinkle dust around the floor—" He extended his jaw and rubbed his lower lip with his index finger.

"Your dad's an artist type, the kind that might enjoy this sort of thing, isn't he?"

"I suppose."

"You told them everything you've told me?"

"In more detail. There was more time. It took most of an afternoon and evening."

"Magic and ghosts and alien worlds," Harvey sighed. "Okay. So this Tristesse was transformed—is that a good word?—by the Shee."

"Sidhe," Michael corrected.

"I'll never get it right, and don't try to make me," Harvey grumbled. "They gave her extra joints and turned her into a mummy."

"She was a vampire," Michael said. "Did you look at her teeth?"

"No. Did you?"

Michael hadn't even seen her face. "What did her face look like?"

"I don't remember. A mummy's, I suppose. But you know, that *is* odd—I don't remember."

"Is she still in the morgue?"

"They were both cremated after nobody claimed them and the coroner's office couldn't prove homicide. I think they dumped the fat woman and the mummy just to keep from having them around. But I have photos on file. And in my car."

"Why are you still on the case?"

"Because I go in for weird things, Mr. Perrin. And I wanted to know what your connection was. What Waltiri had to do with it. I'm a mystery fan. There're so many unsolved crimes and so damned few *mysteries* in my work. Do you understand?"

"I'd like to see the pictures," Michael said.

"I thought you would. Tit for tat. You tell me the story,

show me around, and I show you the pictures. You've fulfilled
your end of the bargain."

Sitting in the unmarked police car, Harvey handed a file
folder to Michael. "They're grim," he said.

Michael opened the folder and took out the facial shots of
Lamia. There was a coldness to the black and white photography, and the way her flesh had slumped after death added to
the sense of unreality, of a poor cinematic makeup job.

He turned the picture over. The photo beneath it was
ruined; an oily, varnish-like stain had obscured the middle of
the print. Michael held it up for Harvey's inspection.

"Damn," Harvey said. "I'm sure there are other prints.
We'll get new ones from the negative."

"I don't think you will," Michael said. "She must have
been very beautiful, and very sweet."

"Why do you say that?"

"Because the Sidhe turned her into a monster and made
certain no one would ever really see her face again."

Harvey sat silent for a moment, holding the ruined print in
his hand. "Now you're spooking me," he said. "What in hell
are we going to do?"

Michael shrugged. "Wait, I suppose. Do you want to investigate this case any more?"

"What's to investigate?" Harvey said. "There's nothing
here that would mean anything to anybody in my profession.
Only the end of the world."

"It may not be quite that bad," Michael said.

"I'd be scared stiff if I were you."

"Oh, I'm scared," Michael said. *But I can't just stop everything in its tracks.* There was a process under way, of which
he was only a part—and how big a part, there was no way of
knowing.

A mage. A face in the blown snow.

What scared him most of all was the dawning realization
that his part was likely to be very big indeed.

9

Kristine called late the next morning. He answered the phone in the master bedroom upstairs and sat on the edge of the four-poster.

"Michael, I'm sorry about the night before last." She sounded tired; her tone was almost flat.

"So am I."

"Things haven't gotten any better. I'm not sure whom I can turn to."

"He hasn't hurt you any more, has he?"

"No. He's taken the car, and I don't know where he is. I've gotten this call . . . not from him. From an older-sounding man. He mentioned your name. And then he said terrible things were coming."

Michael looked down at his forearms. The hair was standing on end. "Did he tell you his name?"

"No. Do you know anybody who would do that?"

"I'm not sure," Michael said, his eyes closed.

"I was going to talk up the concert before the department chairman today. Now I don't know what to do. Michael, this man said the manuscript should be burned. He didn't have to say what manuscript. We know what he means, don't we?"

"Yes."

"He's some sort of crank, right?"

"I don't know."

"He made me angry. Everything's making me angry now."

"I think you should move out of there," Michael said.

"Oh? Move where?"

Michael didn't answer.

"Yes, well, I've been packing. Some of my girlfriends are

looking around for places. Rent is just crazy these days."

"You could move in here," Michael said, and immediately regretted it.

There was silence on the other end for a long time. "It isn't that easy, and you know why."

"Yes. But it's a large house, and—"

"I'll think about it. I'm at our house now. I'll take a bus to the university this afternoon and try to do some work." She seemed to be leaving an opening.

"We should get together later, then," Michael said. "No talk about the concerto or about anything important. Just small talk."

"That would be nice," she said, sounding relieved. "Michael, what happened in the street—"

"I am sorry—"

"No, it was stupid, it was all crazy, but I wanted to thank you. It was gallant, too."

They made arrangements to meet in front of Royce Hall on the campus at five. Michael opened his eyes as he replaced the receiver on the old black phone.

The footsteps in the middle of the dusty floor. The message in the blank notebook. He could feel the presence at the very fringes of the probe he had made throughout the call. There was something foul in the air, a sensation that made his stomach twist and his muscles knot.

Michael stretched and practiced his discipline for several minutes on the bedroom's hardwood floor.

David Clarkham had not died in the conflagration that had consumed his Xanadu. He had managed to escape somehow and was now in Los Angeles, or at least on Earth, and he did not want the concerto performed.

Beneath the tension and the anxiety, there was a calm place that Michael had only become aware of subconsciously in the last few weeks. The part of Michael Perrin that waited and grew within that calm place felt curiosity as to the lengths to which Clarkham would go to prevent the performance.

The brick facade of venerable Royce Hall dwarfted Kristine, who stood alone, hands clenched in the pockets of her brushed suede coat. Michael walked across the grass and concrete walkways toward her. She turned toward him and smiled with a bare edge of sadness.

There was no doubt about it now. He was very much in love with Kristine Pendeers. She hugged him briefly and then backed away. "I tried to call Tommy at the garage where he works. He quit the other day. They don't know where he is."

Michael damped the emotions Tommy's name conjured.

"I'm worried about him," she said. "He just has no control."

"What about your situation? I can help you find a place to rent."

"That would be nice. I have friends looking, too. I can't afford much on the pay of a teaching assistant." They walked to a bench and sat, Kristine crossing her booted legs and slumping against the back of the bench, leaning her head back until she faced the bright gray sky. "You know who called me, don't you?"

"His name is—probably—David Clarkham. He's very old. He helped Arno compose opus 45."

"How old is he?"

"Several centuries, at least," Michael said matter-of-factly. Kristine straightened on the bench and half-turned toward him. "I've told my mother and father, and I've told the detective, Lieutenant Harvey, about what happened when I was missing."

"I'm disappointed," Kristine said. "I would have thought you'd confess to me first." Michael couldn't tell how satirical she was being; her face was clear of guile.

"Do you believe what I said—you could be in some danger now?"

She nodded, staring at him. "Are you going to tell me?"

"Yes," he said.

"And we're still going to go ahead with the concert, if I can get it arranged?"

"Yes."

"I have a desk in an office in the music building. We can talk there. It's more private."

Michael agreed, and they crossed the campus, passing spare and modern Schöenberg Hall. Michael began the story before they reached the small office.

He had become more practiced in the telling now. He could complete the story in much less time, with fewer unnecessary details.

They ate dinner in a small pizza parlor in Westwood, then went to see a Woody Allen movie playing in one of the smaller theaters of a hexaplex. Kristine was obviously absorbing and digesting what she had been told; she didn't seem to pay much attention to the film. Michael felt her touch his arm on the rest between them, then grip it.

"You must have been terrified," she whispered.

"I was," he said.

"So you know what all the hauntings are?"

"I can guess."

"I thought you were dangerous," she said. "I was right. I'm not sure I need this kind of stuff now."

"In your situation," Michael prompted.

A middle-aged couple in the row in front of Michael and Kristine turned their heads simultaneously and delivered stern looks.

"Let's go," Kristine said. Michael vaguely regretted the fifteen dollars spent on tickets. Back on the streets of Westwood, Kristine took him through several clothing stores, pointing out dresses she would buy if she could afford them. She was still digesting the story.

"You're not crazy," she said as they left a boutique specializing in Japanese contemporary designs. "I mean, I believe you—in a way. But can you show me something, maybe this *hyloka* or whatever it was?"

"I'd rather not," Michael said. "The last thing I want is for you to think that I'm a freak."

She nodded, thought some more and then said, "I don't want to go home to the house on South Bronson tonight, and I'm not ready to make love with you. But I would like to go home with you. And maybe you could show me Clarkham's house? That might give me something solid to think about."

"All right."

"And when we're at Waltiri's house, I will not think you're a freak if you show me some magic."

Michael didn't answer. They doubled back toward the lot where he had parked the Saab.

Michael lay in his small guest bed, arms crossed behind his head. The tip of his finger still ached from the trick he had performed for Kristine. Using as an example what Biri had done in the Realm, Michael had taken a boulder in the back yard, applied his glowing index finger to the rock's surface and split it cleanly in four sections. Kristine had jumped back and then quietly asked to return to the house.

She slept in the master bedroom now. Michael knew she slept without probing her aura. His awareness in many areas now seemed to come without conscious effort. He could feel the sleep-breathing of many people in the neighborhood; he seemed to hear the world turning, and the stars above were almost evident to him through the house's ceiling and the cloudy overcast. Rain fell in a thunderstorm far to the east, over the mountains; he heard its impact on the distant roofs of buildings and in the streets, on tree leaves and blades of grass.

How much of this was imagination, he could not say for sure; he thought none. Michael was simply coming in tune with his world. His inner breath seemed to follow the respiration of the molecules in the air itself, whining in their manifold collisions. He felt he knew more about how those atoms operated than he had ever been taught in school.

He knew how each particle communicated its position and nature to all other particles, first by drawing a messenger from the well of nothing and sending it out, while the receiving particle dropped the messenger back into nothing once it had served its purpose. That rather amused him; no little scraps of telegrams lying about in drifts from all the atoms in the universe.

Yes, if he had designed this world, that would be an obvious asset.

Just before he let himself slide into sleep, he thought he felt the very singing of the vacuum itself, not empty but full of incredible potential—a ground on which the world was only lightly superimposed, from atoms to galaxies; it seemed as if it might all be swept away by a strong enough will. Or more probably, as if the ground of creation could be overlaid with another scheme, imitative but different in large details.

He composed a fragment of a poem, back-tracking over the words and editing several times before coming up with:

> Here makes real
> The weaver's weft.
> Lace-maker's bobbins
> Spin right, leap left;

Lift time's thread
Over atom's twist,
Bind such knot with
Death's stone fist.

Weave of flower
And twine of light
Must cross and thwart
By wilt, by night.

Michael mused for a time on how realities might be put together by those less than gods. Such thinking was so abstruse and farfetched, however, that he soon drifted back to more immediate concerns.

He was not disappointed that Kristine did not share his bed this evening. He was patient in his love. She already trusted him, though skittishly; she had given him an incredible gift by believing his story.

He smiled in his slumber. He was still thinking profound thoughts and still feeling Kristine's even, steady, sleeping existence. He would have gladly remained in that state forever, but he knew how fragile his contentment was.

Now he had told everybody who counted, who had the slightest possibility of believing him. If he had been secretive, if his courage had faltered and he had kept silent, he would have been playing along with Clarkham's plans.

Michael would not be isolated.

He suspected he had just purchased some extra time, at very little cost indeed.

Yet still, on the very fringes of his outermost perception: the foulness, the spoor of the Isomage.

Clarkham had one advantage over Michael still: a plan. Michael didn't have a clear idea of what he needed to do, or even of the nature of what was coming.

10

Downstairs, somebody banged on the door frantically. Michael broke out of a dream—dangerous, dreams, since they now pulled in his circle of awareness—and lurched out of bed, grabbing a robe and slipping it over his nakedness. In the hallway, he saw Kristine standing in the door to the master bedroom. She wore one of Golda's nightgowns, simple dark blue flannel. "Somebody wants in," she said sleepily.

Michael extended his awareness as he thumped barefooted down the stairs. The aura of the person beyond the door, a man, was very familiar and very welcome, though there was something subtly wrong . . .

He opened the door. A heavy-set bearded fellow in his middle forties stood outside, dressed in skins and furs like a trapper, with a cloth bag slung over his shoulder. His short gray hair jutted out in all directions. "Nikolai!"

"Thank God," the man said with a mild Russian accent. "I have been looking all over for this place. I am not used to Los Angeles now, Michael." He lay his cloth bag down on the step and hugged Michael twice, kissing him on both cheeks.

"How did you get here?" Michael was astonished; he had last seen Nikolai in the Realm, standing beside the Sidhe initiate Biri and Clarkham's mistress Mora at the outskirts of the imitation Xanadu.

"I walked," Nikolai said. Michael invited him in; Kristine watched them from the bottom of the stairs.

"This is a friend," Michael said to Kristine. "His name is Nikolai Kuprin."

"Nikolai Nikolaievich Kuprin, Kolya to friends." He returned to the porch for his bag, grinning sheepishly.

96

"Nikolai, this is Kristine Pendeers."

"Beautiful, beautiful," Nikolai breathed, staring at her with embarrassing concentration. "My pleasure." He shook her hand delicately; Kristine, Michael noticed, extended her hand to Nikolai in the feminine fashion, allowing him to grasp her fingers. "I have not seen a human woman in . . . ah, if I think about how long, I'll weep. Here, I have been staying out of sight, walking at night, because I would be conspicuous, don't you think?"

"How did you cross over?" Michael asked.

"It is very bad in the Realm now," Nikolai said. "I think perhaps Adonna is dead. Everything is uncertain."

"This is *that* Nikolai?" Kristine asked, her voice rising an octave.

"You've told her? Good. Prepare everybody."

"You still haven't answered my question," Michael said, too astonished and pleased to be exasperated.

"Because I am embarrassed," Nikolai said. "I took advantage of the Ban of Hours. I used the stepping stones in Inyas Trai." He crossed himself quickly as he said the name. "The Councils of Delf and Eleu have been dissolved—"

"You know about them?"

"Yes, yes—Eleu supports human participation in creating a new world, and Delf opposes . . . the Council of Delf sided with the Maln. But both are disbanded now, and even the Maln is in disarray. Tarax has disappeared. The crisis has divided everyone. Inyas Trai"—he crossed himself—"is full of Sidhe again, both sexes, all kinds. They are preparing the stepping stones for migration. Many thousands have left already. Exodus. And there are so many humans—more than I ever thought could exist in the Realm! Thousands. Where did they come from? I do not know! But I separated myself from those captured in Euterpe. I had to get back to Earth and warn you. I used a stone not yet open for the journey. I'm not sure I did the right thing." He looked around the house, face filled with wonder, mouth open. "So familiar. So beautiful. Like my parents' home in Pasadena."

"Why wasn't it right?" Michael asked, sensing again something wrong in Nikolai's aura.

"I don't feel very good. Sometimes everything seems like a painting on glass. I can see through. Perhaps the stone hadn't been . . ." He shrugged. "I am tired. May I sit?"

They entered the living room, and Nikolai lay down on the couch, then craned his neck back to look at the piano. "A beautiful instrument," he said. "Is it yours?"

"It belonged to Arno Waltiri," Michael said.

Nikolai stiffened despite his exhaustion. "Do you know about Waltiri?" he asked.

"He was a mage," Michael said. "I know that."

"Mage of the Cledar." Nikolai returned his gaze to Kristine, and his drawn, dirty face seemed to light up from within as he smiled. "The birds. The musical race. He worked with the Council of Eleu, on Earth mostly. There was a rumor that the Maln collected humans from Earth, like Emma Livry . . . so much confusion, so many rumors."

"I haven't told Kristine everything," Michael said. "Where are the Sidhe migrating?"

"I attended the last meeting of the Council of Eleu," Nikolai said. "The Ban requested the presence of a human, and I was the most convenient. The Ban became part of the Council, but what her intentions are now, I don't know. I have no idea what is happening in the Irall. The Maln do not enter Inyas Trai."

Kristine shook her head, completely lost. "He's talking just like you," she said.

"Do not doubt my friend's word," Nikolai advised solemnly, leaning toward her from his recumbent position. "However crazy he might seem. Michael is a very powerful fellow. He bested the Isomage and destroyed him."

"Clarkham isn't dead," Michael said. "Where are the Sidhe migrating? Please answer me, Nikolai. It's important."

"Back to the Earth. They have not the power to go anywhere else. Adonna built the Realm close to the Earth on the string of worlds. They can only return."

"The hauntings?" Kristine asked.

"I thought as much," Michael said.

"The stone I took is a direct route to Los Angeles," Nikolai said. "Nobody explained why. It was certainly convenient. If I haven't done a mischief . . ." He fell back on the couch pillow and closed his eyes. "Do you have aspirin?"

Michael brought a bottle of aspirin and a glass of water. "Where did you come out in Los Angeles?" he asked, stooping next to the couch and dropping two tablets into Nikolai's hand.

"Hollywood," Nikolai said after swallowing the tablets and draining the glass. "A tall building on Sunset. Very bad shape inside, filthy."

"Are you hungry?" Kristine asked. Nikolai regarded her as if she were a saint.

"Very hungry," he said.

"Then let's have breakfast." She went into the kitchen. Nikolai smiled weakly at Michael.

"She is very nice," he said. "You have been well since your return?"

"Healthy, getting stronger," Michael said.

Nikolai appraised him shrewdly. "Stronger, as in arm-strong, leg-strong?"

"That, too," Michael said.

"I surprised you, no, by coming back? I'm not a great magician, not even of much concern to the Sidhe, yet I made it home, or nearly so. What year is it—truly, I mean? I look at the city and think perhaps centuries have passed."

"It's 1990," Michael said. "May the twelfth."

Combined grief and dismay crossed Nikolai's face. "Not as bad as I expected. So many changes! I am Rip van Winkle now, true?"

Michael nodded. "There doesn't seem to be any link between time in the Realm and here," he said. "I was gone for only a few months, yet five years passed on Earth. And you . . ."

"It is good to see you, very good," Nikolai interrupted. "My brain swims. I cannot think clearly now. Perhaps some food."

Michael spread his hands out beside Nikolai and frowned. The man's aura was extremely weak, almost indetectable. The way the morning light from the front windows played on Nikolai's eyes was also subtly wrong—the reflections seemed bland, lackluster.

Nikolai got to his feet and wobbled, shaking his head. They joined Kristine in the kitchen and sat at the small table. She complimented Michael on the larder he had stocked. "You're pretty self-sufficient. Most bachelors act as if their mommies were still around to do everything for them."

"Most women I know would have freaked out long before this," Michael said.

"'Freaked out,'" Nikolai repeated, chewing on a slice of

toast he had slathered with butter and marmalade. "That means go crazy, perhaps?"

"How long has he been gone?" Kristine asked.

"Sixty, maybe seventy years," Michael said.

"Sixty-seven years," Nikolai said. "You would have made a fine dancer, Miss Pendeers."

"My hips and legs are too heavy," she said.

"Not at all. It is strength that is important, and grace. You have grace, and the strength—" He slowly lowered the last scrap of toast to the plate. "Oh, Michael, it is not good. It is not working."

Michael could not detect his aura at all. Instinctively, he reached out to hold Nikolai with both arms.

"I am going back!" Nikolai bellowed, standing and rocking the table. He held his hands up to the ceiling and moaned, clutching at the air. "Please, not—"

His last word ended in a high-pitched squeak. The table rocked on its pedestal, upsetting jars of jam and cups of coffee. Kristine screamed and backed against the sink. Michael had taken hold of Nikolai's skin jerkin and felt the material squirm between his fingers as if alive.

The table settled, and a cup rolled to the floor and shattered. Where the man had stood, the air was wrinkled by a heat mirage. That also faded. Nikolai was gone.

Kristine began to cry. "Michael, what happened to him?" She wrapped her arms around herself, leaning backward over the sink.

Michael stepped away from the table and stood with his arms hanging by his sides, clenching and unclenching his fists helplessly.

"What happened?" she asked again, more quietly.

"I think he's back in the Realm," Michael said. The eggs that she had begun frying now smoked in the iron skillet. He lifted the skillet from the stove and carried it carefully around her, lowered it into the sink and filled it with water. She watched him as if hypnotized.

"Nobody's joking, right?" she asked. "This is serious?"

Michael nodded and took her hand, sitting her down in the chair he had occupied. He righted Nikolai's chair and ran his hand over the seat as if to search for a trace of the vanished friend. Kristine sat in silence for several long minutes, not looking at him. Her breathing slowed, and she swallowed less often.

"Do you still want to go on with it?" he asked.

"The performance?" She shrugged with a sharp upward jerk of her shoulders. Her arms were shaking. "Yes. This is frightening. It's . . ." Michael squeezed her hand and looked at her intently. "It's not like anything I've experienced. I mean, that's obvious, but. . . . It's incredible." She was high from terror and excitement. "I want to go on with it. Oh, yes!"

"Why?" Michael asked, his tone close to anger. "You saw what happened to Nikolai. It's no game."

"What do you want me to say, then? That I'm going to give up? I don't understand you."

"I'm angry at myself," Michael said.

"That's your privilege," Kristine said. "I think I'm doing rather well."

Michael laughed and shook his head, then sat in Nikolai's chair. "You think it's an adventure," he said.

"Isn't it?"

"Do you understand the danger?"

"Is Nikolai dead?"

"I don't think so."

"Will someone try to kill me? Us?"

"Very likely," Michael said. "Or worse. The Sidhe can turn people into monsters, or they can lock them away in limbo."

Kristine's face was bland, seemingly peaceful, as she considered. "When I was nineteen," she said, "I thought about committing suicide. Everything seemed cut and dried. Art and music were fine, but could they explain anything? Could they tell me why I was alive or what the world was all about? I didn't think so. And ever since, I've lived a compromise; I wouldn't try to kill myself, because there was always a chance something would happen to explain everything."

Here was a depth to Kristine he hadn't begun to reach. He could feel, without probing, a melancholy and rootlessness in her words that shook him.

"When I listened to your story, I had a crazy hope that it was true and you weren't just crazy or putting me on. Even if the world was a wall of paper and everything I had learned was wrong. Because it meant there was something behind everything, some purpose or greater . . ." She gestured with the fingers of her right hand. "Something. Life is such a mess most of the time, and everything that's supposed to be important—love and work and all of it—can be so petty and senseless. Now I've seen a man just vanish, after confirming your story. And . . ."

There were tears on her cheeks. "God dammit," she said, wiping them away hastily. "I'm so God damned *grateful*, and scared, and excited. There *is* something else, and maybe I'll learn, maybe I'll be really important."

Michael smiled. "You're very courageous," he said.

"Why do we *have* to perform the concerto?" she asked, expressing no doubts about the project but simply requesting a reason.

"I wish I knew."

11

Kristine stayed in the Waltiri house only two nights. She then found a small studio apartment, sharing with an older woman geology student who spent most of her time on field trips in the Mojave Desert. No mention was made of Tommy; there seemed to have been a clean break. Nor did Kristine speak of Nikolai again; her almost panicked enthusiasm of that day had apparently subsided.

She kept up a feverish activity arranging for the concert, but whenever the possibility of something more came up— something more intimate—she backed away. A look came into her eyes. As tempted as he was, Michael did not probe. His own emotions seemed to have slipped into neutral. The times they met and discussed the performance, he felt more relaxed and open, unpressured. But as interested as they were in each other, their relationship did not advance. It was necessary for Kristine to reevaluate, and for Michael as well.

Students from the university came to the Waltiri house and carted away truckloads of papers. For a week, Michael simply kept out of the way of a group of musicologists and librarians who spent the hours from eight in the morning to six at night cataloging, rerecording and safeguarding Waltiri's recordings. They worked mostly in the music room.

Two weeks passed. He experienced no further visions or revelations, and there was nothing overtly unworldly in the news. Twice Michael inspected the Tippett Residential Hotel, and once, late at night, he revisited Clarkham's house, but all was quiet.

The quiet times would end soon.

He began sleeping in the master bedroom in late May. Kristine's occupation of the room had dispelled some of the groundless tabu Michael had felt about the marital bed of Arno and Golda. He found he slept more peacefully there; it was quieter even than the rest of the house. His sleeping awareness was sharper in that room.

It was on an overcast, drizzling night in early June that Michael dreamed of the reoccupation of Earth's oceans by the Pelagal Sidhe.

He floated just above the level of deep-ocean waves, cresting at thirty and forty feet. On the horizon, a wickedly glorious sunset was approaching its climax, tipping each wave with red and gold. Columns of clouds advanced east from the squat red sun, each wearing a cap of fading glory and resting on a base of shaded slate-brown. Rain fell in sheets to the north. Michael could feel the freshness of the ocean wind and the cold of the sea spray; he could smell the salt and the fresh rain. He had never felt more alive, and yet he knew he was asleep and that his sensate body was nowhere near his point of view.

The west was darkening, and all the clouds had gone to gray and dark brown with edges of green. He seemed to look up at the zenith, rotating his nonbody somehow, and felt rather than saw a discontinuity in a massive gray cloud high overhead. Water began to fall, not rain but salty and brackish, copper-colored like the sea beyond Clarkham's Xanadu. Michael thought of water breaking during birth. A radiance of blackness ate away the bottom of the cloud, and out of the blackness, an entire ocean fell, not in drops, but in solid columns dozens of yards wide. In the columns, Michael saw deep sea-green male and female Sidhe riding the fall with webbed feet pointed down, arms held high over their heads and fingers meeting in a prayer gesture, eyes trained down, huge bubbles flowing around them from air trapped between the columns and the Earth sea below.

The ocean was a mass of foam for miles around, and the air filled with a noise beyond the capacity of ears to hear, even had he listened with ears. Waves surged outward from the fall in immense rolls.

The sky closed up, and the cloud dissipated.

Michael's point of view shifted, and he now looked down on the roiling Earth sea. The surface was lime-green with breaking bubbles. Fog and salt mist hid the horizon on all sides.

A dozen, then a hundred, and a thousand, a myriad of the Sidhe breached the surface in graceful lines, ordered themselves in cylindrical ranks beneath the waves and swam from the site of the fall.

Michael came awake abruptly and lay on the bed, his body cold as ice. After a few moments of *hyloka,* he warmed again.

The mass migrations were beginning.

Kristine parked at a lot across from the studio's Gower Street gate. "Edgar's very busy now. He's doing sessions on the score for Lean's new picture—a real break for him, you know. Lean has always used Maurice Jarre."

Michael nodded, more intent on examining the studio than the names. The bare tan outer walls seemed more appropriate for heavy industry than a dream factory.

Kristine crossed the street and opened the glass door for him, pointing to a reception desk on the left side of a small sitting room. Behind the desk sat a woman in a blue and gray security uniform, appointment book and computer terminal before her. She smiled at Kristine.

"Betty, this is Michael Perrin," Kristine introduced. "Betty Folger. She keeps out riffraff like us most of the time, but..."

"Mr. Moffat?" Betty asked, smiling. She referred to the screen, then to the book. "He's logged you in for eleven-fifteen. It'll take you five minutes to get to recording studio 3B. If you start now, you'll be right on time." She held up a map, but Kristine waved it off.

"I know the way," she said. "Thanks."

Michael followed, impressed by the quiet and sense of order within the studio. Kristine led him down a corridor lined with offices and out of the building, across a small grassy park shaded with olive trees and then between two huge hangar-like sound stages. Beyond one rank of sound stages and before a second, nestled between backdrops imitating sky and rocks, was a quaint western town, quiet now except for a repair crew and a blue Ford pickup loaded with paint and supplies.

"It's magic, isn't it?" Kristine enthused.

Michael agreed. He had never visited a studio before, not even on the déclassé Universal tour. He knew the basics of motion picture production—location shooting, interior sets built within the sound stages, special effects and opticals, but the actuality was still magic.

They skirted a shallow, dry basin covering at least two acres, with a rough-hewn wooden pier jutting out to the middle. On the sound stage immediately behind the basin, a monumental blue sky and clouds had been painted. A line of painted dead palm trees hid the foundation of the sound stage.

"3B is back around that way," Kristine said. "We're taking the long route. I wanted you to see the sets. No tour complete without them."

They entered a long, white two-story building across from the studio fire department, passed down yet another cool, darkened hall lined with framed photos of studio executives, composers and movie sets and stopped before a door marked "3B—Authorized Only." A red light above the door was not glowing. Kristine knocked lightly on the door, and a dark-bearded young man in a *Black Easter* T-shirt and jeans answered.

"Frank, this is Michael Perrin—Frank Warden."

Warden shook Michael's hand and returned to a bank of sound equipment covering an entire wall. 35 mm spools unloaded their tan recording tape through a maze of guides and heads, while rows of lights blinked nearby and dB meters bounced their needles in reaction to sounds unheard. "Edgar's listening to the playback now. Might as well go in. We're about to dump a flighty saw man and do it all digital." He gave them both a stern, meaningful look: rough session.

"It's a different world from Waltiri's day," Kristine commented softly as they took the right hand door into the control room. Edgar Moffat—in his early fifties, balding, with a circlet of short-cut gray hair—sat in a leather swivel chair before a bank of sliding switches, verniers and three small inset computer screens. Compact earphones wrapped around his head played faint, eerie music. Through the glass beyond the controls, Michael saw two performers in a soundproofed recording studio, one clutching a violin and the other an elongated band of flexible steel. They were exchanging bows with each other and trying them out, in complete silence, on the bandsaw and the violin. Moffat removed his earphones and shook his head, then punched a switch. A squeal of vibrating metal invaded the control room.

"Gordon, George, it's still off. Take a break and get your shit together. We'll want it right next time or we synthesize it. One more blow against performers, right?"

The musicians nodded glumly and set their instruments down.

Moffat swiveled to face them with a broad smile. "Kristine, good to see you again. It's been weeks since you last slummed from the heights of académe."

"It's been busy. Very busy. Edgar, this is—"

"Your new boyfriend. You dumped that Tommy bastard, right?"

Kristine gave him a pained look. "This is Michael Perrin. He's executor for the Waltiri estate."

Moffat's expression intensified, and he stood up. "Sorry, but he wasn't worthy of you, and you know it. Michael, glad to meet you. Kristine told me about the situation. I worked with Arno in the fifties and sixties. You might say he gave me my start. Tough old bird." He raised a bushy white eyebrow as if hoping for a reaction. Michael calmly shook his hand. "Kristine says you've found 45."

"We're going to perform it, if I have my way," Kristine said proudly.

"Christ, I always thought it was a myth. I talked with Steiner once—he said he was there, at the Pandall. He plugged his ears with cotton. Now I ask you, is that to be believed? Others weren't so lucky, he said. Friedrich, Topsalin—where are they now? Topsalin sued, so the legend goes."

"It's all true," Michael said. "That's what Arno told me."

"Well, Arno never talked about it to us. Not even to

Previn, and he was really intent on making Previn a protégé. Previn resisted, unlike me, and look where he is, and look where I am." He held out his hands, smiling ruefully. "Arguing with a man playing a blunted cross-cut tree-cutter."

"I brought a copy along," Kristine said, unzipping her bag. She handed him the manuscript. He motioned them to sit in worn but comfortable chairs crammed into a corner, then put on a pair of glasses and peered at the pages.

"Mm," he said on the third page. "I heard once that Schönberg liked this better than anything else Arno had done. Heard that from David Raksin. More legend. Arnold and Arno. Arnold kept accusing Arno of doing nothing but Hollywood." He briefly assumed Schönberg's Viennese accent. "'45 is not Hollywoody. Finally!' I can see why he said that. I wouldn't dare put a score like this in front of a bunch of union musicians. This is difficult stuff. The piano . . . Jesus, how to mangle a good instrument. Brass bars on the strings, a microphone hook-up . . . hell, he was asking for an electric piano. Cosmic honky-tonk." He spent several minutes leafing through the first third of the concerto, then closed it and sighed. "Absolutely insane. You can't even call it discord. It's wonderful. So who'll perform it?"

"I was hoping you could make recommendations. We have a good orchestra, but—"

"You need seasoned folks. You know, a lot of pros would give their perfect pitch for a chance to perform a legend."

"You have the contacts," Kristine said. "If you could put out the word . . ."

"Have you tried to reach David Clarkham?" Moffat asked.

"He disappeared in the forties," Michael said.

"Why should we talk to him?" Kristine asked, tensing.

"If he's still alive, he might have something to say about this. He's almost as legendary as 45. The dark man of Los Angeles music. I could tell you stories . . . secondhand, of course . . . the man was certifiable. Why Arno worked with him I'll never understand, and of course he never told me, except to shake his head once or twice and wave away the questions."

"What kind of stories?" Kristine asked, forcing herself to relax with a small shiver.

"Steiner told me once, before he died, that he met Clark-

ham. Clarkham confessed to Steiner that he was the figure in
gray who commissioned Mozart to write his requiem.
Hounded Mozart."

Michael's eyes widened. "He might have been," he said
simply. Moffat narrowed his eyes and cocked his head to one
side.

"Don't mind Michael," Kristine said. "He's full of mystery, too."

"At any rate, combining both of their talents in one
work . . ." Moffat returned the concerto score with some reluctance to Kristine. "It'll need reorchestration. I can already
pick out passages that simply can't be played."

"Arno would want it exact," Michael said.

"I'm sure he would," Moffat replied, lifting his eyebrows.
"He could be as bitten by the serial bug as any of us. But he
knew as well as I that a score has to be looked at realistically.
Some things inevitably have to be changed. And I think we
can do it *better* than it was done in 1939. The notation
here . . ." He reclaimed the manuscript and opened it to the
middle, pointing out long black jagged lines, half-circles and
maltese crosses. "I may be the only person who can decipher
some of this now. Arno's special symbols. I decoded from his
four-staff scores when I orchestrated for him."

"I knew we'd need you," Kristine said.

"Okay, but where's the funding?"

"I'm working on that. When will you have time to re-
hearse?"

"Starting on the thirty-sixth of June," Moffat said ruefully.
"Depends on whether or not Lean and I see eye to eye on this.
He insists on waltz beats in the strangest places. I love Maurice dearly, but those two have worked together entirely too
long." He reached his hand out and gripped Michael's
shoulder. "You know music, young man?"

"Not very well," Michael said. "I've been teaching myself
for a few months now."

"Not the way to go about it, believe me. You seem concerned about . . . what? Duplicating the effect of the original
performance?"

Michael nodded.

"You want to get us all sued?" Moffat smiled wolfishly,
knitting his gray brows. "Well, I'll take the risk. There's not

much adventure in this business. I'll need all the notes and journal entries you can find on this . . . and correspondence, anything where Arno might have revealed his intentions. He was never the most precise composer. It'll be doubly difficult not having him here to make final decisions."

"There's a special study crew from the UCLA music library going through all his papers now."

Moffat released Michael's shoulder and patted it gently. "I will await further instructions, then. Honestly, I should have the recording wrapped up in three weeks. I can start rehearsal after I get back from Pinewood. Shall we aim for something in a month and a half?"

"Not unreasonable," Kristine said.

"Good. Now go away, and let me harass my sessions people. Michael." He held out his hand, and Michael shook it firmly. "Far be it from me to nudge, but this woman . . ." He indicated Kristine with a nod and a wink. "She's something quite special. You could do much, much worse."

"Edgar . . ." Kristine warned, lifting a fist.

"Out! Work to do." Moffat opened the door and showed them back through the recording room to the hallway, then shut the door abruptly. The red light came on.

Kristine and Michael regarded each other in the hallway for a moment. "All right," Kristine said. "Now you've met him. I think he's essential. Don't you?"

"Yes," Michael said. "Especially since I don't believe Arno left many instructions or very many clues. I've looked through a lot of papers and letters in the past few weeks. The manuscript is all I've found."

"Can't hurt to look again, though," Kristine said. "Now. If you'll drop me off at the campus . . ." She marched down the hall ahead of him, turned and cocked her head. Michael remained by the door smiling at her.

"Coming?"

He caught up, and they left the building. "Moffat's a touch pushy, isn't he?"

"More than a touch," Kristine said. "He only met Tommy once, for just a few minutes, and— Well. Not worth talking about."

"We haven't had lunch in a long time," Michael said hesitantly.

"No time, not today," Kristine answered crisply. He did not persist. Even without a probe, he could sense her uncertainty and pain. She glanced at him as they climbed into her car. "Patience, Michael. Please."

He agreed with a nod and put the car in gear.

Michael watched as a librarian and a team of students hauled the last papers from the garage into a campus van. The attic was empty; the music room had been processed the week before, leaving little more than the furniture. Now, with the removal of the last of the material from the garage, the house seemed less protective and himself more vulnerable, but vulnerable to what he couldn't say. Clarkham's inroads, perhaps.

But Michael couldn't believe Clarkham was the greatest of his problems.

> I am dark!
> Awaiting sight
> Formless wave
> Guiding light

Again his poems were short and enigmatic, as they had been in the Realm, but they offered no answers to his questions; there was no Death's Radio infusing his art.

He was on his own, whatever he had to face.

The van drove away, and Michael shut the garage door on the aisles of empty metal shelves and the old Packard. He paused at the latch and lock, frowning.

Confusion. Carpets of dirty car parts arrayed in dark halls. And over all—a nasty, sickening foulness of the mind.

"That's a beautiful old car."

Michael turned and saw Tommy at the end of the drive. "Isn't it?" he said. "Pity it's too expensive to drive."

Tommy shrugged that off. "Belonged to your friend, didn't it? Waltiri?"

Michael nodded. "What can I do for you?"

"Leave her alone."

"Kristine? I haven't heard from her in two days." He swallowed. "Besides, she left you weeks ago."

"Just two days. Great. You're right. She left me weeks ago. I'm partly to blame. You're the main reason, though."

There was a repulsive foulness in the man's aura that Michael found all too familiar. He began walking down the brick drive toward Tommy, acting on instinct again. The situation felt dangerous.

"You know a fellow named Clarkham?" Tommy asked, backing up a step and then standing his ground as Michael approached.

"Yes."

"He knows you. He's been watching you and Kristine. He told me all about you. How you badmouth me. A poet." Tommy laughed as if he had just seen a pratfall on TV. "Jesus, a poet! You look like a God damned athlete, not a poet."

"Looks deceive," Michael said, sensing that Tommy had a gun, knowing it was behind the jacket, held by the left hand stuck through a hole cut in the fabric of the side pocket. The jacket could open, and he could fire in an instant. Michael was five yards from the gun.

"He said you're as bad for her as I was. You hit her more than I did. He says you take her to . . ." His free hand swung back and forth, and he nodded his head deeply, twice. "Parties. Get her in that scene. Do lines of coke. Shit, I would never get her involved in that." The hand stopped swinging. "Hollywood shit."

Whatever native intelligence Tommy had once possessed had been corroded by Clarkham's discharge of foulness. Michael could feel the Isomage near, if not in space then in influence, watching through this pitiful and extremely dangerous intermediary.

"He's a liar," Michael said. "You don't want to believe him."

"No, I don't, really," Tommy said. "I didn't know she was like that. I was bad enough for her. I just loved her too much, and I'd get jealous, you know?"

Soon; it would be very soon. Two and a half strides. He could judge the size of the gun. It was a .45 automatic, and it was loaded with hollow-core bullets. It could cut him in half. Clarkham had sent him a missile loaded with death, much as the Sidhe had sent Michael to Clarkham.

It would be useless trying to stop Tommy. If Michael cast a decoy shadow, to give himself time to find shelter, it was entirely possible that Clarkham would have prepared the man for such an eventuality, even equipped him with a means to see through the deception. Michael's thoughts were sharp as razors, cutting quickly at this hypothesis, then at that.

He felt Robert Dopso nearby—a definite complication if Dopso or his mother came out of the house now. Michael's senses rose to a higher level of acuity.

"It's not that I hate you," Tommy said, smiling, the arm in the jacket pocket twitching. "You're just like any other son-of-a-bitch. Her body." Pain crossed Tommy's face. "That's all you care about. Me, I really *cared*. I wanted her to be everything she could be." His voice was hoarse. He was shaking.

"We're friends, that's all," Michael said calmly. "No need to be upset."

"My needs and your needs aren't the point, are they?" Tommy said. "Don't come any closer. He warned me, but he didn't need to warn me, did he? I remember." He touched his nose.

"Clarkham is a liar," Michael reiterated. "He filled you full of bad things . . . didn't he?"

A light of recognition appeared in Tommy's eyes. "He touched me when we were talking."

Something built rapidly in Michael, a shadow different from the ones he had cast before, different even from the one he had finally sent spinning to trap Clarkham in Xanadu. This was a variety of shadow he had not been told about, and finding it within him frightened him almost as much as Tommy did. He tried to hold it back but could not; his augmented instinct told him there was no other way.

But Michael did not want to believe that. He did not want to believe he was capable of defending himself in such a way.

The part that thinks death is sleep. Lose that part. The part that seeks warm darkness and oblivion. Lose that self. He will embrace it. He desires rest and escape from the pain.

The voice telling Michael these things was his own.

Dopso walked down the sidewalk before the driveway, saw Tommy and Michael and smiled at Michael. "Hello," he said. Then he frowned. "What's—"

"No!" Michael said. "Go back!" Whatever choice he had had was now taken from him. Tommy would kill Dopso and anybody else who walked by. Clarkham's missile was not precise, could not control itself, could not discriminate.

Across the street, a middle-aged woman in a pink dress sauntered by, taking her schnauzer for a walk.

Tommy jerked the jacket open, revealing the dull gray gun.

Michael sent. The shadow that went forth was not even visible. It did not mimic Michael's form. It simply carried another self away, a self he did not need and could use to advantage.

Dopso and the middle-aged woman saw Tommy lift the gun, turn halfway, twitch and apply the gun to his own head. There was a sleepy look on his face; this would have happened anyway, but nevertheless—

Michael screamed inside.

The gun went off.

Tommy's hair lifted obscenely on the opposite side of his head, and he dropped as if kicked by a bull. Michael closed his eyes and heard the dog barking and the woman shrieking. He opened his eyes and saw the dog dragging the woman back and forth in a space of a few yards. Dopso had turned away, arms held up against the sound of the shot. Splashes of blood covered the sidewalk and grass by his feet.

Even knowing there had been no other choice, Michael felt sick. He forced himself to look at the body. Clarkham's deposited foulness had eaten away the dead Tommy almost instantly. What was left was not recognizable. It was covered with a shining blackness and had slumped inward, wicked witch style, only the gun unaffected. In seconds, there was little more than a pile of tattered clothing and evil-smelling dust.

The woman had stopped shrieking. The dog sat on the sidewalk, tongue hanging. "Are you all right?" she called out to Michael, her voice hoarse. Michael was too stunned to answer.

"God," Dopso said, eyes wide, staring at the dust.

"What happened to him?" the woman asked sharply, her voice on the edge of a scream again.

"He's dead," Michael said. "I'll call the police."

"He shot himself," Dopso said. "But he's . . ."

Michael nodded and looked at the ridge of the roof on the house directly opposite. A large crow-like bird with a red breast perched there.

The woman crossed the street, dragging the dog on its leash behind her back, her eyes glazed with anticipation of disgust. She stepped up on the curb, staring fixedly at the pile of debris. "He's not there," she said, amazed. "What happened to his body?"

"Please go home," Michael said. Gently, he gave her a forgetfulness, this time hardly even aware he was exercising an ability for the first time. Absentmindedly, he extended the forgetfulness to the dog. The woman wandered off, silent and calm.

The bird on the roof had flown away.

He did not want Dopso to forget. He was close enough to the action to need to remember and understand.

"Michael . . ."

"Do you want to know what happened?" Michael asked.

"I don't think so," Dopso replied, his voice fading. He shook his head.

"You'll have to know sooner or later."

"But not now. . . . Where did he go?"

"He was sent here by David Clarkham."

"Yes . . . ?"

Michael could tell now was not the time to reveal all to Dopso.

"I'm going to call the police," Michael said.

He entered the house and walked into the kitchen, slumping into a chair. He picked up the phone receiver and dialed the number Lieutenant Harvey had given him. Harvey's assistant, a young-sounding man, answered. Michael gave him few details, just saying that the lieutenant should call him immediately.

"I'll tell him when he comes in," the assistant said dubiously.

Michael hung up and returned to the clothes and the gun. No other people had stepped out of their homes to investigate. Dopso had gone back into his house. Michael could feel him sitting in a chair inside, ignoring his mother's questions.

The woman and her dog had walked out of sight. Everything was quiet again.

The clothes themselves had disintegrated. The gun's grip had turned rusty brown and ash-gray. Michael held the gun butt between two fingers and carried it into the house.

The wind was already blowing what was left of Tommy down the sidewalk, onto the grass and the bushes at the edge of the driveway.

12

"I think I'm more upset than you are," Michael said, sitting across from her in the cramped apartment. Rock-climbing tools hung on the small dining nook wall like pieces of art; knapsacks, tents and metal shelving covered with rocks filled the hall to the bathroom and bedroom. Kristine's living there seemed to have hardly made an impression. Aside from a three-tier fold-up bookcase beside the couch and a stack of blank ruled composition sheets, the roommate's presence dominated even in her absence.

Kristine did not speak for a long time. She took deep, even breaths, looking out past the hide-a-bed and through the sliding glass door at the courtyard beyond. "You're sure he died. He didn't just disappear."

"He died, and then he decayed," Michael said bluntly.

"I don't know why you should be upset," Kristine said, still not looking at him. "He threatened you, and you lived. You won. Poor bastard."

"He was used," Michael said for the third time.

"Did he feel what he was doing—did he know?"

"I think so," Michael said. "I can't be sure, though."

"This fantasy of yours is real ugly, you know that?"

Michael didn't understand.

"This macho fantasy world. Men do so like to kill each other." Her soft voice dripped venom. "I *do* care. I loved him. I said I didn't, but . . . I didn't need you to protect me from him. I don't care what I said."

"No. He didn't go to you after Clarkham—"

"Just shut up about Clarkham. About everything. Jesus, Michael, it's so convenient. He didn't even leave a body.

115

What did your police lieutenant think about that?"

"I haven't talked to him yet. It's only been two hours. He's supposed to call me back."

"Trying to be legal and above suspicion. Good move." She had not cried at all, but her eyes appeared puffy. "I'm not excited now about the strangeness. I was. It seemed fantastic, people disappearing, fairies coming back to Earth, old sorcerers battling it out with music. Now it just seems like maybe the Middle East. Terrorists. Murder. No different."

"It's not a fantasy," Michael said. "It's deadly serious. Nobody escapes for long." His last four words sounded ominous even to himself. Kristine looked at him directly for the first time since he had told her what happened. She squinted.

"Are lots more people going to die?"

"I don't know."

"You're talking about a war, aren't you?"

Michael shook his head.

"But you didn't really kill . . . Tommy."

"I made him kill himself. That's close enough."

"You didn't murder him because he would have killed you. Self-defense isn't murder. Clarkham filled Tommy with lies. That means *he* killed Tommy. What do you think about that? Don't you *hate* Clarkham now?"

Michael considered for a moment, then shook his head. "Does me no good to hate him, or anyone."

"But you'll kill him if you get the chance?"

Michael considered some more, then said, "I'll kill him."

Suddenly, everything about Kristine seemed to soften and relax. She closed her eyes and drew in a shuddering breath, letting it out with a moan. "I cut him out of my life weeks ago. Isn't that strange? When you build up a dependence on people, knowing you can't possibly ever see them again—because they're dead—that's like having it shoved in your face. It means you'll die too. Am I making any sense?"

Michael nodded. Alyons, Lin Piao Tai, Clarkham, and now Tommy. Directly or indirectly, three deaths and one failed attempt. That wasn't what Kristine meant, but the sensation was the same—he felt his own mortality acutely.

"I'm supposed to be on campus at two," Kristine said. "I'll wash my face." She stood.

"Kristine, if I could have done it any other way, I would have."

"I don't blame you, Michael," she said, two steps from the table.

Michael stared at her until she turned away.

"There should be something more between us. Don't you feel it?" he asked.

"Yes."

"And it's just not working out."

"That's putting it mildly."

"I'll go, then."

"Not that I don't want it to work out," Kristine said. "But we're partners in something else, aren't we?" She primmed her lips in a defiant, hard line.

"Yes?"

"We're partners in the concerto. Clarkham doesn't want it performed. That's enough to convince me. And you?"

"Yes," Michael said. "That's enough."

"Then let's move on with that and let the other stuff work itself out in due course."

"Okay."

"Let me know what the lieutenant has to say. And I'll let you know what Moffat thinks about the new orchestration."

They parted outside the apartment's main gate, and Michael returned to the Saab. He sat in the car with his hands on the wheel, certain about nothing and guilty because he was hurting, not for being a murderer, but simply because he was no longer in Kristine's presence.

In truth, everything had been so much easier in the Realm, so much more clear-cut.

13

Harvey led Michael down the hallway, his scuffed brown Florsheims clacking, every sound both of them made seeming hollow as it echoed from the ranks of stainless steel doors. An assistant coroner in a pristine white lab smock followed a few steps behind.

The unofficially-named Noguchi wing of the Los Angeles County Morgue had been added three years before, after years of overcrowding, and was seldom filled to capacity. The last tagged stainless steel door was on a corner with an as-yet unfinished corridor stretching to the left for another dozen yards.

Harvey gestured at the door, and the assistant placed an electronic key against the code box. The door popped open with a slight hiss, and the chamber bed slid smoothly out. Within the translucent bag on the bed was a blue-green body at least six and a half feet long. The assistant unzipped the head of the bag and pulled the material wide for Michael to see. Other than Alyons, Michael had never seen a dead Sidhe before.

"Do you know what it is?" Harvey asked.

"It's an Arboral female, I think," Michael said.

"And what is an Arboral?"

"A Sidhe that lives in forests. Is a part of forests. Controls the wood." The Sidhe's face was composed, peaceful. Michael intuited a kind of postdeath discipline at work; the Sidhe had self-control even after life ended.

"Okay," Harvey said. "I've never seen a human being with skin that color. Even dead. Or with a face that long. Do you know her?"

118

"No," Michael said. "I never knew any Arborals." He had only seen Arborals twice, the first time when they had delivered the gift of wood to him near the Crane Women's hut in the Realm. That had been at night, and he had not seen them clearly. The second time had been in Inyas Trai, just a glimpse of them tending the Ban's library-forest.

"Now after this, I ask you, should I be surprised at what you've told me about this Tommy fellow?"

Michael could not turn away from the blue-green face. "I suppose not."

"Because I believe you." Harvey nodded to the assistant, and he zipped the bag up and sealed the chamber. "Thank you." The assistant walked back up the hallway without a single backward glance. "He may not look it, but he's spooked. Twelve years in this office, and he's spooked. Everything's changing now. We found this," he indicated the body, "in Griffith Park, not far from the observatory. It was backed up against a tree. Somebody had shot it. Her. Just once. This is the third unexplainable body found in Los Angeles in the last month.

"I'm going to ask you a question." Harvey stared up at the fluorescent fixtures on the ceiling. "What in hell are we supposed to do to prepare for this? Wetbacks from beyond. Jesus."

"I don't think you can prepare," Michael said.

"There are going to be more of them?"

"Yes."

"How many more, and where?"

"I don't know how many more, and I don't know exactly where they'll arrive."

"The Tippett Hotel?"

Michael nodded. "That's going to be a major gateway."

"And if I tell my department we have to surround the hotel —if they believe me and don't let me out on a stress-related discharge—will that do any good?"

"No," Michael said.

"They can be killed, though."

"Arborals, maybe even some Faer, but I don't think you could kill some of the other types that will be coming through. I wouldn't advise you to try."

"'Wouldn't advise me to try.' Jesus. Maybe I should just

resign and take up throwing ashes over my head and wearing
hair shirts?"

Michael smiled.

Harvey appeared disgusted. "You're not doing me any good
at all," he said. "And it wouldn't do either of us any good to
have you arrested. There's a witness that Tommy committed
suicide. This Dopso fellow. Whatever you say about self-
defense, that's all that matters. I presume there's going to be a
missing persons report. I'll try to take care of that. But what
are *you* going to do?"

"Wait. Try to be patient. I'm not in control, Lieutenant."

"Is anybody?"

"Perhaps."

"Anybody human, I mean?"

Michael hesitated, then shook his head, no.

14

He walked for miles along the fire trails through the hills,
feeling the growth within him and trying to come to grips with
what he was, and what he was becoming. This time, the development was internal; it had been triggered by the Crane
Women's training but was not now controlled by anybody. He
had no specific assigned task. If anything, Michael Perrin was
a rogue, an unexpected product of Sidhe and Breed ingenuity.

Somehow, he was able to work powerful magic on Earth.
Forcing a man to kill himself had to be very powerful magic
or the word lacked any meaning.

The sky was clear and hot and dusty blue. Sparrows and
mockingbirds sparred through the scrub bushes. The hillsides
were already turning brown and gray after less than two weeks
of no rain and only a few hot days; they reverted so easily to

their accustomed state, almost uncomfortable in the luxuriance of a wet spring. Michael wished he could do the same. His last faint hopes of normality and a reasonably peaceful life had fled.

He would never sit in a fine old house in Laurel Canyon and write poetry and worry about brush fires. That dream had never been particularly well thought out, but he had recently been placing Kristine in the middle of it nevertheless. He was still an adolescent in many respects. His visions had not yet been completely tempered by reality.

And why should they be? Which reality?

Such considerations made maturing all the harder.

How much magic could he do, and how ambitious could he be? He hardly wanted to test the abilities (not yet skills) he felt within him, but he was impelled to do so. More important than knowing how he had acquired or developed these abilities was deciding how to use them in the coming exodus and the merging of the Realm and Earth.

He stopped and shaded his eyes against the sun, looking south over the city, the tall skyscrapers of downtown Los Angeles faint in the hazy distance. Then he hunkered down and picked up a stick, using it first to break the crusty dry soil of the fire trail into a finer powder, then to write in the powder: "Protect this city from harm."

He had no idea whom he was addressing, or what. He scratched out "city" and replaced it with "land," then scratched that out and replaced it in turn with "world." He would have to start thinking on a much broader scale. Even now, he resented the forced expansion of perspective. He had known boys and girls—now men and women—who relished the larger realities, who kept up with the news and held opinions on issues that did not immediately affect them. Michael had always felt himself different from these people, dreamier perhaps, more fascinated by the inner world than the outer.

In the Realm, some of that inner-directedness had been dusted out of him. The last shred, after Tommy, had a very weak hold indeed.

He hardly felt he had an identity any more. The old Michael had not existed for some time; the new one was not yet fully formed, and was not sure he liked himself.

15

Moffat's studio office resembled an especially broad hallway, about three times deeper than it was wide. Moffat had
placed his desk at the end opposite the door. A Synclavier
occupied one corner near the door and beside it, a cello in its
black leatherette case. On the carpeted floor under a broad
glass window showing the false-front tops of the Western set
buildings, Moffat had spread printouts and sheet music and
scribbled notes on tiny squares of adhesive-backed yellow
paper. More printouts had been pinned to the opposite wall,
with Xerographic copies of storyboard sketches taped beside
the appropriate sections. Beside his desk was a small laser
audio disk recorder on a rolling cart. Wires trailed from the
unit to a jury-rigged stereo system.

"Welcome to confusion," Moffat said. "The Lean score's
recorded, and I am free to contemplate this monstrosity"—he
pointed at the copy of opus 45 on the desk—"at some leisure.
I've already worked some of it through on the Synclavier."

Kristine wore a gray silk dress with billowing sleeves and
silver-gray nylons. Michael had never seen her so formally
attired. Her behavior was also strictly business. He took the
second chair at Moffat's invitation. Moffat sat in his black
leather executive seat behind the desk and looked from one to
the other.

"It's in five movements," he said. "I'm sure you're both
aware of that. Clarkham's instructions—they must be his,
since they're in English and are not in Arno's handwriting—
say that the movements should not be rehearsed together, that
movement four should be left out until the actual performance.

Rather like assembling the bomb without the explosives." He smiled, but Kristine and Michael did not. Moffat's smile faded, and he shook his head. "Bit chilly in here, don't you think? Maybe we should open our *mouths* a little bit and let out some air, warm the place up?"

"I'm sorry," Kristine said. "We've got other things on our minds."

Moffat swiveled on the chair to look at Michael. "No comments?"

"No," Michael said. "But I think you should follow Clarkham's advice."

"Oh, I will, if only for authenticity's sake. The game is part of the pleasure, don't you think? Do it just as they did it fifty years ago. Now. I've managed to put together a fair string section. I have the two pianos required and a fellow I trust to play one of them. I think I can get another pianist within the week. Two oboes, two bassoons—a celeste. That might be considered overkill, three percussion keyboards, but I'm going to be authentic. In 1939, Clarkham suggested a theremin. I'll substitute something which seems to suit Waltiri's requirements better—my Synclavier. That makes four keyboards. Since overkill is what this piece is all about, who will complain? Not I. The other instruments I can get out of the sessions pool in a couple of weeks. No problem. Now, as for *paying* these people—"

"The university is going to pay scale for a week of rehearsal and two performances," Kristine said.

"Labor of love, is it? Well. It's not the busiest season now. Everybody needs work. Okay. We'll manage. My agent will wince, but we'll manage."

"You're doing it for the challenge, aren't you?" Kristine asked.

Moffat looked pained. "Challenge isn't the word for it. Arno was always the type to ask for sixty-fourth notes out of the French horns. But in the time I worked with him, he was positively *restrained*, compared to when he wrote opus 45. Some of it is clearly impractical. Nobody human could play a few of the measures, so to accomplish what the score demands, the Synclavier will be programmed to do some of what he's asking for. Not exactly live, but then, neither is most music today. I want to go over the movements with you

—you too," he added, glaring at Michael, "and see if my plans match your expectations. Remember, this is very humble of me."

"We'll remember," Kristine said with a hint of a smile.

"That's it. No gloom. This is a lively piece."

He handed copies of the manuscript to both of them and went through the movements one by one. The first movement began in A minor, crossed into C major, then returned to A minor. It was labeled *allegro con brio*. "A quick intro, with six very odd half-notes tacked on just after it should end," Moffat said. "Beat of eight to the measure. Fast, fast. First piano does most of the hard work here, *mezzo forte*. That's good. Mutilated piano comes into its own in the second movement."

"We have a campus engineer building the brass piano baffle," Kristine said.

"I'm anxious to hear it. I can't make anything out of the instructions—what is it supposed to do to a piano?"

"We don't know," Michael said.

Moffat raised an eyebrow. "Good. I like surprises."

The second movement in C major-minor was in common time and introduced entirely new themes, which gradually blended into a much slowed and much softened reprise in A minor of the first movement. The third movement was a dialogue between an unspecified but closely described instrument—originally a theremin, now to be the Synclavier—and the "mutilated" piano. "Not easy," Moffat commented. "Full of traps. It would take a small army of spiders to play some of the passages."

The fourth movement was a torturously slow *adagio* in F major, again blending at the end into a reprise, transposed to B minor, of the original theme. This was the "explosive," Moffat reiterated, not to be rehearsed with the other pieces, not to be played together with the other four movements until the actual performance. The fifth movement, in A major-minor, was a sweeping, romantic *ländler*, a country dance. "Very Mahler. Brisk, not as fast as the first movement, but coming to a cheerful conclusion—and *then*—" He shook his head. "An abrupt switch to C minor. I cannot 'hear' the last hundred measures. I've been reading scores for four and a half decades now, but I can't hear those notes. That's odd, and maybe it's magical, too. But I've played them on the Synclavier and on a piano, and they're quite interesting."

"It sounds confused," Kristine said. "All those abrupt key changes."

"Oh, it's worse than that," Moffat said. "It's downright chaos. There's no way in hell it should work. Psychotropic tone structure or not, it reads like Korngold and Mahler take a vacation with Schönberg and end up on Krakatoa with a gamelan."

"You mean, it's *bad?*" Michael asked, feeling as if the last firm foundation was about to be pulled from beneath his feet.

Moffat smiled up at the ceiling and closed his eyes. "Not at all," he said. "It's impossible, but it's wonderful. The few sections I've played—masterful. Demonic, but masterful. Liszt with his hair in braids and on LSD."

Kristine laughed, the first time Michael had heard her laugh in weeks. She glanced at him and pursed her lips primly, then shook her head. Serious. Subdued.

"I'm sure you two are keeping things secret from me," Moffat said. "I wouldn't want to guess what. Scandal? The Society of Musicians is about to picket us for trying to play this piece again?"

Kristine leaned forward. "I couldn't have chosen a better conductor," she said.

Moffat sighed. "What makes you think *you* chose me?" he asked. "Maybe there are forces at work here of which you wot not of, or whatever." He was puzzled by their silence. "That was a joke."

"A stunningly bad one," Kristine said softly. "There are a few more details to arrange at the university, and then we'll get the hall scheduled for you—"

"Which hall?" Moffat asked.

"Royce Hall."

"That fossil?"

"It meets the requirements perfectly," Kristine said. "It's about as close to the old Pandall Theater as we could possibly come."

Moffat smirked and then held up his hands. "So be it. We're still on for a double-bill with Mahler's Tenth?"

"I'll be firming that up this afternoon," Kristine said.

"What a night," Moffat said, rubbing his hands. "We'll knock 'em dead."

Walking to the main gate, Kristine put her arm around Mi-

chael's and squeezed his hand. "It's really going to happen,"
she said.

"You didn't think it would?"

"I had my doubts."

"Why?"

They passed the guard and waited for traffic before crossing Gower to get to their cars. "Because I've been getting
phone calls," she said. "Someone's still trying to stop us. He's
not succeeding, but he's trying."

"Who?"

"Clarkham, I presume," Kristine said almost lightly. She
glanced at Michael.

"He's been talking to you directly?"

"He hasn't called you?" Kristine countered.

"No," Michael said.

"Maybe he's afraid of you."

Michael snorted. "I don't think so."

"You say you beat him once."

"Yeah, with all the Sidhe behind me."

"But you *did* beat him."

"And he survived. Apparently."

"Why does he feel threatened by this performance?"

"I'm not sure he does. He hasn't been able to stop it, and
he must be a hell of a lot more powerful than..." Michael
shrugged. "Than my beating him would lead you to believe."

"You think he *wants* it performed?" Kristine asked. "He's
running all this interference just to make us follow through?"

"I don't know."

Kristine unhooked her arm from his and backed off a step.
"I don't know any magic," she said. "What will I do if things
really get rugged?"

Michael had no answer. That made him acutely miserable.

"I suppose you'll protect me?"

Michael felt his eyes smart and then a rising warmth behind them. Whether she was baiting him or not, he decided to
give a completely serious and sincere reply. "I'll try," he said.
"I'll do my very damnedest."

"You know, I'd like to be self-reliant, but failing that..."
She smiled at him. "You'll do. I have to go now—I'm meeting Berthold Crooke at two. The fellow with the new orchestration of the Tenth."

They stood awkwardly two steps apart. Kristine moved in

quickly and kissed him on the cheek. Michael blushed as she backed away. "You'd think we could talk about normal things sometime," she said.

"I'd love to."

She cocked her head to one side. "It'll happen, Michael. I'm pretty sure of that."

"I wish I was," Michael said.

"Got to go. You'll be at the library tomorrow?"

"Signing papers. Yes."

"We'll talk then." She walked to her car.

You can spend the most important parts of your life on a street, Michael thought, and unlocked the Saab's door. His whole body seemed to be breathing in and out, restless and ebullient at once.

16

The next day, at eleven in the morning, two Jehovah's Witnesses proselytizers came to the door of the Waltiri house, and Michael did not have the heart to simply send them on their way. The elder of the two was middle-aged, gray hair carefully groomed, dressed in a brown suit with a narrow gold tie; the younger, a trainee about twenty years old, wore a black suit and a red tie. Both carried satchels.

Michael listened wearily to their prophecies and Bible quotations, and they kept him at the door for half an hour. When he managed to convince them he was not really interested, he shut the door and stood with his back against the dark wood, eyes closed, almost sick.

They preached the Apocalypse. He knew it was coming— but not as they visualized it.

He could practically *smell* the poisoned Sidhe-imposed ignorance, the most modern incarnation of the thousands of years of Tonn's attempts to play God for humans. Some of the poisonous philosophies had been transmuted by humans despite the best efforts of the Sidhe—but how many hundreds of millions of humans still wholeheartedly embraced the blindness and cruelty and the shackles? He stood up straight but kept his eyes closed.

"No way," he said softly. "I'm just a kid. No way I can understand how to lead so many different kinds of people. I don't want it. I reject it." He opened his eyes and blinked at the framed prints in the hallway.

The silence demanded, *who asked you to lead?*

But Michael could feel it as surely as he could hear the ticking of the grandfather clock. That was what it was all leading toward: his growth, his maturation, the challenges and the apocalypse.

He shivered and then convulsed, dropping to his knees. His arms shook until he clenched his fists, and he felt the inner abilities—*nothing from outside all inside all from within*—course through him like power through an electric line, let loose for a moment, set free and exulting at its lack of restraint.

For a moment, he nearly died. And even after he had regained control of the power and had wrapped thick steel bars of his will around it, it took him hours to realize how close he had come to simply disintegrating, much as Tommy had done, but for different reasons.

He walked slowly upstairs and lay down in the Waltiri bed, not tired but stunned, for the first time fully aware of how sensitive he was and how dangerous his sensitivity could be.

Tiger by the tail.

Michael—and what he contained, generated, not by his conscious self but by something within him that didn't have a name—Michael was his own tiger. Losing control, he would eat himself alive.

"Who in hell am I?" he whispered harshly, wiping sweat from his eyes.

In mid-July, Kristine drove Michael to Northridge to meet Berthold Crooke. Crooke lived in a complex of condominiums at the edge of a broad empty field of dry yellow grass. He taught music in a local junior college and had received little attention until the publication of his orchestration of Mahler's unfinished Tenth Symphony.

Crooke was a lanky, hawk-faced man with blue-black hair and a perennial shadow of beard. His eyes were his most remarkable feature, large and vaguely horse-like. His teeth were also large and prominent. He was slow of speech and quick to smile, pulling his lips back over his broad white teeth in a way that would have seemed menacing but for the obvious gentleness of his eyes. His manner was self-deprecating but also obviously confident. Michael liked him immediately and felt no need to read his aura; however, to his mild jealousy and chagrin, he saw that Kristine also liked Crooke.

They sat at Crooke's kitchen table and went over the arrangements point by point. After an hour of discussion, Crooke served coffee and doughnuts and stood behind Kristine, looking over her shoulder as she compared the orchestral requirements for the concerto and the symphony.

"They're not really all that different," she said, shaking her head in some surprise. "We can use practically the same players. Edgar told me the concerto was lush with orchestra, but..." She glanced at Michael. "Mahler isn't known for his spareness."

"No indeed," Crooke said. "You mentioned Moffat had the orchestra assembled—I don't need to approve them or anything, but—"

"You'll have equal time for rehearsals," Kristine said. "The university hasn't done anything this ambitious in years. I think it's starting to catch on. Nobody in the department is complaining about costs, and *that's* a miracle."

"What I meant," Crooke said, smiling sheepishly, "is that I haven't conducted that large an orchestra. Only college orchestras. I'll need the rehearsal more than the musicians."

Kristine patted his arm reassuringly. "We have faith," she said. "It's going to come together just fine."

Crooke made a face and slumped in his chair with a sigh. "Makes me almost wish I didn't start the whole thing..."

"How *did* you start it?" Michael asked.

Crooke knitted his fingers together. "When I was sixteen, I heard a recording of Rafael Kubelik conducting the only portion of the Tenth orchestrated at the time—the *adagio*, the first movement. I was playing the record in my room, away from the rest of the family. We had a huge ranch house in

Thousand Oaks, halls and bedrooms all over—like a maze.
Even six kids rattled around in it. The music seemed very sad,
a slow and discouraged dance, and then toward the conclusion
of the movement, there is this discord—trumpets shrilling in
A, the orchestra seeming to scream or cry out . . ." He shook
his head. "It devastated me. I had never heard anything like it.
It was . . .all the oppressed, all those in pain, breaking their
bonds and looking *up*. It was revelation, and it was death, too.
It really affected me. I started to shake and cry." The sheepish
smile returned. "I knew there had to be more. I found Deryck
Cooke's orchestration and listened to that—Eugene Ormandy
conducting. It was beautiful, but it seemed to be missing
something. The symphony became an obsession for me. I
thought if only the piece could be orchestrated the way Mahler
would have done it, had he lived, then . . ." Crooke lifted his
hands. "Bingo. How to express it? It would be the greatest
piece of Western music ever written. or at least the most powerful. There were times when I simply couldn't listen to the
pages after I finished orchestrating them. I couldn't even play
parts of the four-staff score on the piano."

"Some people say you've succeeded in doing it just as
Mahler would have done it," Kristine said. "How do you feel
about that?"

"Oh, yes," Crooke said, his expression suddenly stiff and
serious. He straightened up and cleared his throat. "That's the
way it had to be. This sounds silly . . . perhaps even a bit insane . . ." His index finger tapped on the table top nervously.
"But sometimes it felt I had Mahler helping me." He laughed
nervously, shaking his head. "Have you ever heard it before?"
he asked Michael. "Any of the other versions?"

"Not all the way through," Michael said.

"It is sublime, even incomplete."

Michael nodded. The discord, the trumpets sounding a
shrill A, all that was very familiar to him. He had heard it
while exploring the top floors of the Tippett Residential Hotel.

Late July in Los Angeles was a procession of cloudy days
held over from June, broken by a week of the more usual
summer weather, the temperature climbing into the eighties
and the sky clear of overcast, if not of haze.

Michael did not attend the rehearsals. Kristine reported on

the progress to him every two or three days. Otherwise, they did not see each other.

He spent most of his time exercising in the back yard or jogging. Dopso no longer ran with him. Since the incident with Tommy, Michael had heard nothing from the Dopsos. The mystery had become all too specific for them, apparently.

At night, in the house, Michael sat before the fire in the living room, practicing his discipline.

On July 16th, at one in the morning, after six hours of steady concentration, Michael reached into the Realm with one hand and brought back a leaf and a translucent red insect, much like a ladybug. The insect quickly died, and the leaf shriveled into a brown husk.

He had barely reached the level of Eleuth. But with just his hand in the Realm, he had sensed a discontinuity that was most unsettling. If reality could be described as a kind of heat or warmth, then his body—sitting on the oriental rug in Waltiri's house on Earth—was in the middle of a kiln, reality invading everything with a bright white glow.

In the Realm, everything was cold. The fire was going out.

The real fire before him was dying into embers as he thought about this. His eyes closed, and almost of their own volition, his arms rose from his sides, and he spaced his hands some five inches apart. His palms tingled, and something passed between them, a silvery extension of his discipline and of the primal emotion *Preeda.* He tried to bring them together and could not; startled, he opened his eyes and saw a pearly thread stretched between and strung on the thread, a glowing sphere. He could feel the sphere's qualities through the skin of his palms and along his arms; it was *enfolded,* and it embodied some of the requirements he had outlined in his poem about reality knots.

But what was it? He slowly pulled his hands apart, and the thread snapped. The sphere swung to his left palm and clung there for a moment before vanishing.

In early August, the rehearsals neared completion on both the concerto and the symphony. Advertisements were placed in the Sunday *Los Angeles Times* Calendar supplement, four days before the first of the two scheduled performances. Flyers were mailed out and posted on bulletin boards around the campus. Kristine did much of this work herself.

On Thursday evening, she appeared on the front porch of the Waltiri house, dressed in an exquisite dark blue-black gown, smiling, holding two tickets in one gloved hand.

"An occasion," she said. "Shall we go, partner?"

17

The dusk sky above Los Angeles was a cloudless, clear sapphire blue, complete with evening star. Kristine drove down Wilshire toward UCLA, talking about the last-minute preparations, why she had been a few minutes late—having to reassure a nervous Crooke by phone that all would go well—and generally expressing her own reservations about the evening. She became quiet as they approached Westwood, glancing at him with one eyebrow raised slightly, lips drawn together.

"Something wrong?" he asked.

She laughed and shook her head. "My whole world has changed since I met you, and you ask if something's wrong. I don't know how I've managed to lead a normal life after. . . . Your friend disappeared. What happened to Tommy. I should be terrified. I really should."

"Why aren't you?"

"Because you're with me."

"Not much assurance there," Michael said softly, turning away.

"Clarkham called again this evening," she said, "just after I got off the phone with Berthold."

Michael felt a deep barb of anger and quickly buried it under the rising inner warmth of *hyloka*. "What did our ghost have to say?"

"He says if the performance takes place tonight, he'll be seeing you."

"That's all?"

"Yes. I'm not afraid of him now, Michael."

"You should be. We should be."

"Don't you feel it, though? Tonight is going to be a *fine* night. Because of us."

He shook his head. "I just feel nervous."

"I'm the one who should feel nervous, but I don't. I don't even believe I'm awake now. I think I've been dreaming since I met you." She swung the car into a reserved space, pointing out Moffat's BMW and Crooke's ancient, battered Chevy Nova on either side. "Everybody's here. The cast is assembled. Let the dream reach its climax." She shut off the car motor and twisted in her seat to face him. "This has been difficult for us, especially difficult for you, I think," Kristine said. "You've been . . . not 'patient'. That sounds so prosaic. You've been . . ." She shook her head vigorously. "Tonight, after the performance, we have to go out with everybody to Macho's and celebrate."

" 'Macho's?' " Michael asked, incredulous.

"It's a Mexican restaurant in Westwood. We have reservations. And afterward—listen carefully, because this is important—we are going to go back to the Waltiri house, together, and make love." She stared at him intently, biting her lower lip. "If you want to."

"I want to." His need mixed with the warmth of *hyloka* and made an indescribable echo through his abdomen.

"That is as important as anything else that happens tonight," Kristine said. "To me, it is. Being involved doesn't come easily for me. I'm cautious, too cautious. You've noticed."

He didn't answer, simply returned her stare.

"You are so *unreadable*," she said, smiling faintly. "Let's break through it all tonight—the music, this world, all the walls and the shams." She opened her door and got out, and they walked side by side across the grass, heading toward Royce Hall.

UCLA at night was more attractive than by daylight. Floodlights and the lighted windows of buildings produced magical areas of brightness and pitch-dark. A few students were walking quickly between buildings, on breaks from their night classes or hurrying to the library.

In front of Royce Hall, the crowd standing in line before venerable pillars and brick Romanesque arches was encouragingly large. Michael spotted his parents in the line and introduced them to Kristine. Ruth was very pleased with her but kept glancing at Michael with raised eyebrows. John became debonaire and witty and inquired whether they would all be able to get together after for a celebration. "If we're still here," he added ominously.

"We have an appointment for a kind of orchestra party," Michael explained. "But maybe tomorrow . . ."

Ruth held John's elbow and said that would be fine. "Go on now. This is your night." John raised his eyebrows. "Don't mind him." Michael smiled and hugged them both.

Kristine then led him around the side of the building and up a flight of concrete steps to a double door, where a male usher in a crewneck sweater and white pants examined her pass, gave them programs and let them in. They took seats in the center, fifth row back.

Michael cleared his throat and opened the pamphlet. "Do you think we should be sitting this close?" he asked, only half joking.

"All the better," Kristine said, "that the perpetrators should face the brunt, don't you think?" She patted his arm and opened her own program.

"They've got this wrong," Michael said, pointing out a passage on the second page. "Clarkham didn't get sued—he left before the lawsuits began. Arno faced the reaction alone."

"Hm. Let's hope our audience isn't litigious."

The curtain rose, and the players whose instruments were not already on the stage carried them to their seats. In Clarkham's instructions, the orchestra was enjoined to make itself conspicuous and to exhibit the process of the performance as openly as possible. That instruction was reproduced in the program booklet, in Clarkham's original handwriting.

The crowd grew quiet as the lights dimmed. Mahler's Tenth, the giant of the evening, was to be performed first, followed by an intermission of only five minutes and finally the concerto.

Berthold Crooke came to the podium, with the orchestra already assembled and waiting. Crooke tapped lightly on the podium and motioned for an oboist to play an A sharp. The orchestra tuned to that note and then went off on its own, instrument by instrument. Again the oboist played an A sharp, and again the orchestra tuned. Finally—on the verge of over-kill—the Synclavier keyboard performer produced a perfect A natural, and the orchestra tuned to that. All of this had been ordained by Clarkham's instructions, not Mahler's or Crooke's. When the pleasant cacophony was over, Crooke tapped again, and there was silence.

He raised his baton.

The first movement of the Tenth was an elegiac *adagio* in F sharp major-minor. Michael fell into the music despite its intense anxiety and sadness. The weave of the music was hypnotic, swinging from domestic tranquility to ominous warning. What ensued was almost painful in its intensity—a dissonant clash of the orchestra, topped by a solo trumpet blaring a high A note—death and destruction, shock and dismay. The *adagio*, now concluded, seemed complete in itself, and it left Michael almost empty of feeling, drained.

The second movement, a *scherzo*—the first of two—was a complete contrast, beginning with a heavily satiric taunt in changing rhythms and tempos and then transforming the theme of the first movement into a happy country dance. It concluded joyously in the major key, leaving Michael with an overwhelming sensation of hope.

That sensation was tempered by the third movement, titled *Purgatorio*. In B flat minor and 2/4 time, it drew its own conclusions after seesawing between anxiety and hope, sun and cold shadow . . . and those conclusions were dark, declining.

"'Oh God, why hast thou forsaken me?'" Kristine whispered.

"What?" Michael asked.

"That's what Mahler wrote on the original score."

The beginning of the second *scherzo* nearly lifted him from his seat—a shrill blast from horns and strings and then back to the dance with life and hope, decline and death.

"The poor, sad German."

"I was not responsible for Mahler. Or for his child. That was not my work at all."

The *scherzo* brought to mind that long-past snippet of conversation between Mora and Clarkham under the Pleasure Dome.

"Did Mahler lose one of his children?" Michael asked Kristine.

"A daughter," she said. "His other daughter was incarcerated in a concentration camp during World War II," Kristine added softly, leaning to speak into his ear.

"He was dead then," Michael said.

"Maybe he could tell what was coming. Seeing what the old world would bring."

Michael felt a thrill run up his spine. *Yes. . . .* Old world passing into new.

More anxiety after a rich, romantic interlude. Horns, xylophone accents, clarinets and French horns—that hideous solo trumpet again, intruding into the anxiety, presaging a delicious, horrible revelation.

Michael was frozen in his seat. He could hardly think about what was occurring within him. *Old world into new.*

Yet all this was accidental—the matching of the Tenth—

Unfinished. Interrupted by death.

—with The Infinity Concerto.

Uplift, again the anxious strains, and back to domestic normality, the world and social life and children—

Mixed with a foreboding of disaster to come—

Of change and trauma and anticipation, foresight—

Harbinger of a new age, of fear and even disaster—

Then quiet, skeletal strings, thinning out the fabric of reality, extending the cold from his stomach to his head. Drums pounded unobtrusively, ominously.

On the stage, the largest drum—an eight-foot-wide monster—was assaulted by the drummer with one shattering beat.

The coldness vanished, leaving him suspended in the auditorium, hardly aware of seats, orchestra, walls, ceiling. He could feel the sky beyond. In his left palm lay a pearly sphere. He closed his hand to conceal it.

Camouflage. Everything had been camouflaged to mislead, misdirect. The Infinity Concerto was not by itself a Song of Power. The similarities had seemed merely coincidental.

Mahler's Tenth was leading the way, closing out the old world, describing the end of a long age (sixty million years! or just the end of European peace—or merely the tranquility of one man's life, blighted by the death of a daughter . . . perhaps feeling what the second daughter would have to suffer in a new world gone twice mad) and expressing hope for a time beyond. Rich, anxious, neurotic, jumping with each tic and twitch of things going awry, trying to maintain decorum and probity in the midst of coming chaos.

The beats of the huge drum accented a funeral dirge. Again the skeletal tones, this time from muted trumpets . . . and then heralding horns, a light and lovely flute song of hope developed by the strings . . . becoming strained again, overblown, life lived too hard, tics and twitches—

Drum beat. A tragic triad of notes on the trumpet.

Drum beat. Low bassoons vibrating apart the seconds of his life. Michael still could not move.

(Deception. Camouflage. Misdirection.)

The tempo increasing into a new dance, new hope—recovery and healing—and yet another decline. Michael was growing weary of the seesaw, but only because it was too close to the everyday pace of his life. Life in this world, world passing.

Rise to triad and . . .

A disaster. The entire orchestra seemed to join in a dissonant clash, trumpet holding on the high A again, matched by more horns, another clash that made his head ache, reprise of the theme of everyday life. . . . And then the trumpet, released somewhat from its harsh warning role, was allowed a small solo. The triad reoccurred on other instruments, in a major key and hopeful, not shattering, and then domesticity.

a segue, connective tissue old to new

How much like what had happened recently, the weirdness mixed unpredictably with Earth's solid reality and inner silence of mind. There seemed to be a rise in intensity to some anticipated triumph, thoughtful, loving and accepting . . . but not acceding. Quiet contemplation.

Michael could move again. He glanced nervously at Kristine to see if she had noticed. The symphony was coming to a conclusion, and he felt his inner strength surge.

Triumph. Quiet, strong and sure—overcoming all tragedy. Triumph.

The last notes of the Tenth faded, and Crooke seemed to reappear on the podium, and the orchestra seemed to become real again.

The audience was silent for an uncomfortably long time.

"You're sweating," Kristine said, handing him a handkerchief from her purse.

"Thanks." Michael wiped his forehead. Sweat had dripped into his eyes, stinging. The hall seemed very warm, even stifling. He glanced at his hand. The pearl was gone.

Finally the audience reacted with strong but not overwhelming applause. They had heard, appreciated, but they had not felt, or if they had, they had ignored what they felt. A few stood and applauded vigorously, as if to make up for the rest. Michael glanced back but could not see his parents.

Crooke appeared exhausted but happy. He bowed and then continued with the structure of the program by taking a microphone handed to him and announcing that the interval between pieces would be very short. Some in the audience grumbled.

"Stand, stretch our legs?" Kristine suggested.

Michael stood beside her and discreetly windmilled his arms, tensing and untensing his legs. His lungs felt as they once had when he had accidentally breathed dilute fumes from a spill of nitric acid in a chemistry class—tight, but not constricted.

"That was wonderful," he said, sounding doubtful even to himself.

"I'm very proud," Kristine said softly. "Everything's turning out fine. Even the audience."

The air suddenly seemed much improved. He was calm again, prepared.

Mahler's Tenth, properly orchestrated, was itself a Song of Power. It codified the old world, harsh and demanding, lovely and lyrical, unyielding and fickle.

An old rose, fading and growing thorny. How had it avoided being pruned by the Sidhe? Then again, it had not—Mahler had died before finishing it. Other attempts to fulfill the promise had not succeeded . . .

Edgar Moffat came to the podium. Michael, on impulse, kissed Kristine lightly on the cheek, then caressed her bare shoulder with one hand. She smiled uncertainly at him, then sat and focused her attention on the podium.

The baton went up and lowered slowly . . .

The first movement began rapidly, the unmutilated piano jumping in almost immediately. As it played, a deep, resounding tone came from the double basses, ascending in pitch through the strings, almost harsh, moving from cello to viola to violin to be drowned by drums, low and rumbling. A sharp rise of French horns glared and did battle, fast, fast, dancing, dissonant and yet perfect, a rousing gallop of ghost horses that faded into whispering strings.

Sea-grass propelled by moonlight.

Horns sketched out a vast unease, brooding. They lost all musical tone and *whooshed* like the wind, a soft winter storm coming.

A passage of unfilled graves, herald of change and nightmares from unlived childhoods, from an infinity of lives never occupied by the moving strands of an infinity of souls.

Michael blinked back tears and held Kristine's hand. She, too, was responding, and her cheeks were wet.

Lives lived and lost. *Tommy.* The others.

Eleuth.

If they let go, he seemed to understand, they would lose each other. She moved against his shoulder and shivered.

"Is this what they heard?" she asked.

Michael swallowed. "No. Everything was different then. It's the same music, but it's in its proper time now."

"How do you *know* that?" she asked.

He shook his head. "It resonates."

"Will people vanish tonight, or later?"

"Not from hearing this," he said.

The music increased tempo and surged forward on horns, harp and strings, the second rank of violins plucking furiously. The musicians seemed obsessed, and Moffat directed them with a minimum of motion, baton describing the beat and left hand barely indicating emphasis; he was giving them their lead and letting their concentration carry them through.

At no point did the music let up. When the piano rejoined the flow, the beat, the pulse, was in a fractured and disjointed waltz time. The pulse became even more ragged, jazzed, with unpredictable and violent bursts from the drums and horns. Then it smoothed and mellowed.

Gentle, heart-beat sounds, lulling, pierces of ragged dance fading, recurring but polished, and then slowing.

As gently as could be imagined, the prelude ended. Without a moment's pause, the second, mutilated piano began a quiet and persistent solo, staying in the middle register, its tone odd and almost harsh, not disturbing, simply biding its time. And the music did something Michael had never heard before.

It described waiting. While not long in itself, the piano

solo was covering thousands, perhaps millions of years.

He glanced at Kristine. Her eyes were wide. She was enchanted, uncritical, absorbing all. Waltiri's magic—evident in his movie scores—was here unbridled.

The orchestra leaped in behind the piano. Time was still at issue—and growth. Michael no longer paid attention to the mechanics, the key or the structure or the way the sounds were created.

He had caught on to the underlying beauty of the piece. He saw it in relation to *Kubla Khan,* to the pleasure dome even in its incomplete, unsuccessful form; he saw it in relation to the symphony just played. They were all similar songs played in different worlds, to accomplish similar purposes. Subtle variations in the underlying patterns could lead to widely disparate results.

Mahler had once written a song-cycle/symphony called *Das Lied von der Erde*—the Song of the Earth. The name had been applied, perhaps, to the wrong piece. His Tenth was a Song of the Earth, of Earth as it had been.

The Infinity Concerto was heralding the Earth to come.

And Michael felt himself *in* it. He was described there—not personally, but in his role. Growing, mutating, uncontrolled, all potential and little achievement. It frightened him. The music was not gentle now. It was complex, demanding, full of discord.

Dischord.

Discard.

Start again.

Renew.

Unite. (How?)

Create. Create what?

The audience was becoming noisy, even above the now-loud music. There was something unresolved, and they sensed it almost in mass.

Decline to quiet, persistent but soft, demanding but muted . . .

Strings played on their bridges—skeletal—horns muted—breaking time down. The celeste tinkling behind all. Apprehension . . .

What happened next, Michael could not describe, nor could members of the orchestra. The music suddenly denpended on the fourth movement, *adagio, which had not yet been played,* and that fore-reference *worked* because he—they —understood what would happen in the fourth movement.

Kristine was smiling ecstatically. The audience fell silent. The tension had been impossibly resolved.

The second movement ended. The third began without more than a few seconds' pause. The Synclavier and the mutilated piano involved each other in a philosophical discussion. The third movement passed, and Michael did not remember its passing, or even what it was. It was played, but it added a nonmemorable subtext to everything around it. It was a movement and a bridge in itself, effective only as a commentary.

The fourth movement was upon him. Kristine's face showed irritation or pain. The pain changed to dismay.

The fourth was not the same movement referred to in the second. There were in fact *two adagios,* but only one was being manifested. The other existed as a creation solely in the minds of the audience, a phantasm of music, yet Michael had no doubt that both movements had been minutely composed and scored by Waltiri.

He began to fear what the fifth movement might bring.

The fourth, as played, was slow, primitive, spare, even deliberately inelegant. It was a new world unresolved, the shape undefined, though with all the elements present, coalescing. Instruments played to different rhythms, slowly coordinating, then fading, then coming to agreement again, themes weaving in and out, with then a reprise of the original theme transposed to B minor. Moffat had called this the "explosive," yet it seemed anticlimactic.

The normal piano began to dominate, with its precise laying down of individual notes and chords, no glissandos, no slides, simply sketching what was to come.

Then, entirely unearthly, the Synclavier mocked the piano. It created the slides and linked the sketched-out harmonies. It played them back upon themselves and created canons and reversed them in ways only a machine could manage.

This was the *human* contribution to the music. The Sidhe would never have countenanced a Synclavier, or anything similar to it—not even a simple theremin. What Waltiri had requested was something only humans could add to music. Through technology, they were performing music the Sidhe could have created only through magic.

Humans had found their place in the world to come. They

had lived in this universe long enough to master it not with magic, but on its own terms. Not with outside skill, but with skills taught by the hard, unyielding nature of reality. And they had turned those skills into devices for creating wonderful, impossible music.

But this isn't music any more, Michael thought.

"What is this?" Kristine whispered.

The Synclavier had made its point and did not belabor it. Sounding almost abashed, the orchestra resumed its dominance, but the normal piano was done for. It played no more in the fourth and not at all in the final movement. The final movement was home for the mutilated piano and the Synclavier.

Michael shut his eyes. It seemed as if all his hopes and concerns were about to be examined. The fifth movement would be *himself*. And he knew Kristine was feeling the same thing—that it would be about herself.

The music, a sweeping, demanding dance, was now a training ground for a new world.

In 1939, before its time, opus 45 at this point in the score would have sown the seeds for a translation into the Realm. Other music had accidentally achieved this effect; Clarkham, and perhaps Waltiri as well, had deliberately designed The Infinity Concerto to work in such a way.

But Waltiri had woven in something else. With time, the effect of the music would alter. It would not translate; it would prepare. The audience was being made aware of the world they would ultimately have to face.

The music vanished into its own purpose.

Only in the last part of the fifth movement did the adjunct Song of Power rise up and show its medium again. The music became light and beautiful, consciously showy and rich with melody. The melody switched to C minor.

"Jesus Christ," said a man behind Michael, loudly.

Out of the last hundred measures—the measures Moffat had confessed he could not "hear" while reading the score—came quiet assurance, not disturbance. The bomb was being carefully, elegantly defused. The worlds would meet, pass into each other . . .

They would not destroy each other.

The concerto reached its conclusion. (But the unplayed

fourth movement echoed; perhaps it would never stop. *Das Unendlichkeit Konzert.)*

The music faded.

The hall was as quiet as empty space.

Kristine shut her eyes folded her hands as if in prayer. "They're going to like it," Michael reassured her.

The audience exploded. Everyone stood at once. Applause, shouts of "Bravo!" and exclamations of amazement both crude and ecstatic. Michael stood and looked around anxiously, seeing a few people still in their seats, limp, eyes glazed. But gradually they, too, stood and applauded, returning to the hall from wherever they had been. Moffat took his bow and called out Crooke from the wings. The applause redoubled and did not diminish as the soloists were brought forward. Michael glanced around apprehensively as he applauded.

He didn't know what he expected next. Whether the sky would come crashing down and the air would be filled with flying Sidhe, whether Clarkham himself would appear ringed in fire, whether Waltiri and his birds would fill the hall. . . . Anything seemed possible. The Song had been played through. How long would it take to accomplish its task?

The crowd surged out of the hall, forcing Michael and Kristine with it. It stood on the grass and sidewalks outside, shouting and arguing. Kristine was beaming. "It's like when they played Stravinsky and Milhaud," she said. "It's really happened!"

"I thought they threw the seat cushions around for Stravinsky," Michael said.

"Our crowd is much too liberal to do *that*," Kristine said. "Let's find Berthold and Edgar."

The gathering at Macho's was crowded and noisy. Michael stayed on the sidelines, letting others enjoy their triumph; he had really had so little to do with it. Crooke was flushed, a beer in one hand and a glass of sparkling water in the other, sipping from them alternately and smiling at a short, very shapely woman who had attached herself to him. Moffat held court from a large round table, regaling his audience of students and formally dressed alumni with tales of Hollywood in the fifties.

"Maybe everything's going to be all right, hmm?" Kristine suggested as she passed Michael in one of her orbits. She made frequent eye contact with him, smiling reassuringly each time. It suddenly occurred to Michael that she was uncertain about his reactions, even a little afraid he might leave without her.

Little chance of that. Even Songs of Power and the sway of dying and birthing worlds seemed pale compared to what he anticipated.

He ordered and drank a beer, enjoyed it immensely and almost immediately regretted it; his *hyloka*, held at a constant simmer under all his careening emotions, fluctuated wildly under the influence of the alcohol. He felt excessively warm —as he had for a time during the concert—and looked for ways through the crowd to a restroom in case things got out of control and he had to doff his clothes.

But the *hyloka* settled down, and he felt a simple, direct sensation of well-being. Everything had gone *beautifully*. Clarkham—wherever and whatever he was now—had failed again.

Kristine hooked her arm through his on her next orbit and took him with her. "Let's find a door," she said. "It's getting late."

They went to the Waltiri home, and Michael took Kristine into the upstairs bedroom. As he held her warmth closely, still fully dressed, he felt that nothing could possibly go wrong, ever. She was nervous; he could feel her tension, and he eased it away expertly with his fingers, drawing a line down both sides of her spine, searching for and finding the physical centers of her anxiety and releasing them.

More things he had not known he could do.

More growth.

She started to undo the eyes and zipper of her dress, and he finished the task for her, pulling it away from her shoulders, letting it slide past her hips. He lowered her half-slip a few inches with his index fingers and kneeled, rubbing his cheek against her stomach, feeling the warmth and softness of her skin.

They made love as if they were lost deep in woods, and nothing mattered or could interfere. There was nothing improper or suspect, nothing to hold him back or bring an edge of dismay to his enthusiasm, nothing tragic.

The crescented outline of Kristine beneath the sheets was

more beautiful than anything he had ever hoped to see, much less have. He propped himself on one elbow and stared at her as she lay in the ghost-glow of the window. Her eyes were half-closed, drowsy; she was content as a tree is content after a day full of sun. He probed her aura gently and found a smooth continuity, near slumber, mellow.

He lay back on his pillow. He would sleep with her tonight. They would dream beside each other. For the first time in a great many months, he would be merely a young human being, not in the least important.

The unplayed fourth movement came back to haunt him just before sleep, making a cold, hard circle at the center of his contentment. In the silence of the old house, in the darkness, the music was almost audible.

The bomb had not gone off.

Not yet.

But

18

Michael.

A voice in his sleep. He cannot struggle up out of slumber, and he feels as if all his senses have been smothered in thick clouds of wool. He struggles without moving or waking.

I've been right here for weeks.

He feels the hidden foulness. It fills his mind like a mist of sulfurous gas and ammonia.

Waiting.

The wool lifts but not enough to allow him to awaken or put his discipline to use. He cannot sense Kristine beside him.

I've taken her. But that isn't enough. You must go as well. You've become entirely too dangerous, too skilled. Look to your ancestry, Michael.

The words fade.

Look to your ancestry. And calm, assured laughter.

Downstairs, a few sharp measures from the second movement of The Infinity Concerto are pounded out on the piano,
then more laughter. Michael tries to struggle up out of sleep,
but he knows he is much too late. He has let his guard down;
he has been happy, and he has let his happiness and his wish
to be normal obscure all the defenses the Crane Women had
instilled in him, overtly and otherwise.

Clarkham has been in the Waltiri house, or very nearby as
worlds are concerned, for weeks. Has played the piano when
Michael was out; has perhaps even used the house phones to
call Kristine. The house has been Clarkham's base of opera-
tions.

Michael feels all of these awarenesses fading. He opens his
eyes in time to see everything in the bedroom suffused in
sepia. When the sepia brightens, he—

19

—felt a pang of grief so sharp it made his stomach twist.
Another morning, another day of living with the loss and the
sheer misery of his aloneness and vulnerability.

He closed his eyes and silently rolled his face into the pillow, trying to keep from weeping.

No.

He rolled back and took a deep breath, letting it out slowly.
Through the still curtains over the open window he heard
nothing outside, no cars, no birds, only a steady low whine of
wind. The sounds of a desert outside. Sun faded in and out in

the room, as if clouds were passing by. He glanced at the opposite side of the bed and saw pillows still wrapped in the comforter, sheets and blankets undisturbed except by his tossing.

Michael Waltiri

—*no*—

got out of the bed and slipped on his boxer shorts and pants, white Arrow shirt with button-down collar, slinging the suspenders over his shoulders with both thumbs. Wide-cuff baggy pants riding high above his hips. Wool socks and black patent leather shoes. Sports coat slung over the back of the chair before the vanity, the chair where just weeks before Kristine had put on her makeup, her rayon stockings, her dress and hat.

NO!

And taken the Packard to the bank. Wifely errands.

He parted the curtains and leaned out the window. Warm yellow sun fell on him. Clouds drifted overhead, rounded and puffy, regular and sheep-like.

Taken the Packard to the bank and . . .

He shut his eyes and bent down to tie the flapping laces on his shoes. Everything was wrong. The world was topsy-turvy.

She was gone. Quick as that. Just as his parents were gone. They had gone down in a Dakota near Guam, along with other entertainers, all out to

—*the war's over, Michael; it was over before you were born*—

give the troops a little amusement. And here he was. 4F. Useless. An orphan and a widower. Dead to the world, whatever world there was outside.

He went downstairs and made himself a pan of oatmeal, mechanically lacing it with oleo and Karo syrup. He ate it mechanically, mind blank and uncritical simply to avoid the pain.

When he was finished, hall chimes clanged together, and he went to the front door and opened it. His father's partner, David Clarkham, stood on the porch with hat in hand, wearing a very natty camel hair coat and matching pants, with a wide sky-blue tie covered with regular puffy clouds, sheep-like. Michael stared at the clouds and watched them move across the tie.

"Checking to see how you're doing, Michael," Clarkham said, concern crossing his smooth, young face.

"As well as can be expected," Michael replied. "Want to come in? Can I offer you a drink? Some wine?"

"No, thank you. You shouldn't be drinking, anyway. There's a lot of work to be done. Organizing your father's papers, settling things down at the studio. I spoke with Zanuck yesterday. He wishes me to pass along his condolences, both for your parents and . . . Kristine."

"Fine." Numb. Pain pushed back by an effort of sheer forced blankness. "Thanks. Tell him . . . yes."

"I'll take over the work on *Yellowtail*. Your father would have wished that."

"Fine."

"Is there anything I can do for you, Michael? At the studio, perhaps? Need legal matters resolved?"

"No. The lawyers are taking care of all that."

"Your parents were such fine people, Michael. They would have wanted to go together. But there is nothing sensible to be said about Kristine. So much death overseas . . . it seems doubly senseless here. Trivial accidents."

"Yes. I know." He wanted the man to go away. He wanted to shut the door again and block out the sun and the sky and the regular sheep-like clouds and the faint whine of the wind.

"I'll go now. Just checking." Clarkham smiled, and for a moment Michael felt a black depth of corruption behind the smile that made him dizzy, that almost brought back—

"Thanks for your concern." He shut the door and returned to the kitchen, where he poured himself another cup of tea. As he sipped it, he frowned. Why feel such antagonism toward his father's partner? Just a symptom of his general condition: a wreck.

He considered exercising in the back yard and decided it was not worth the effort.

A blackness descended over Michael Waltiri then, numbing his senses even further, discouraging him from making any plans or thinking too deeply about anything. He loved Kristine very, very much, and they had had so short a life together (How long? Hours? Non

sense)

that his own youth and upcoming three score and ten years

of life seemed to conspire against him, offering a bleak desert of endless and unfilled hours, days, years.

Michael Waltiri felt as if he had been sentenced to prison. He would live it out; that was all he could do.

20

Days and weeks passed, and he ate and slept and worked in the garden in the back yard, keeping the roses trimmed. He patched and rehung the Chinese paper lanterns strung from the trellis to poles in the back yard, and he wiped down the white-enameled wrought-iron table on the brick patio. He disliked the back yard—it gave him the creeps—but he worked there nonetheless, making sure it was tidy, because (it must have been so, though he couldn't remember specifics) he and Kristine had spent time there.

He remembered someone wearing a fancy dress sitting behind the white table at one time. That must have been Kristine. Not her style (certainly not Golda's—his mother's—style), and why was he so aware of having been frightened by her in the dress? Everything was jumbled by his grief.

Days and weeks. He shaved with a French razor and played records on the Victrola, Toscanini and Reiner and Strauss and Stokowski conducting on 78s. Endless hours of music, over and over again.

The grief and numbness refused to fade.

He never saw anyone, and nobody called him on the phone. He read the newspapers and occasionally listened to the radio. None of it seemed right, but what could he do?

Michael felt as if he were in hell.

21

He finally gathered up enough energy to take a long walk.
He started out at dusk, as the empty sky was a dull and dusty
blue, when the twilight seemed willing to last forever, and
walked along the empty streets, past the white plaster and
stucco Spanish-style homes the neighborhood favored and the
ranch-style and the California bungalows. He stopped with a
frown and watched an electric streetlight come on with the
deepening of dusk and a brown-leafed maple droop its
branches over the light as the wind whined. The stars came
out and whirled like fireflies on strings and then settled, and
the sky became a gelatinous black.

Michael walked to La Cienega and followed its course,
seeing people on the other side of the street, or walking some
distance ahead or behind him, but never passing them or seeing them up close. All the shops and restaurants and even the
bars were closed. The war, he decided. Not enough to go
around.

Not even enough people.

The street narrowed as he approached the hills. He looked
both ways on the corner of Sunset, at the houses on each side
and the shops, all closed and dark, and then at the old theater
rising above the roofs to his right. He headed toward the theater.

In round neon letters, the neon turned off, the name of the
theater stretched around the marquee and up a tall radio tower
mounted on a silver plaster sphere.

P
A
N
D
A
L
L

PANDALL

The doors were boarded over. The wind whispered between the plywood and the locked glass beyond.

The place was dead. Its hold on reality seemed tenuous, as if it were merely a memory. He didn't like it. He walked away, glancing back over his shoulder. Someone dark was following him, and that frightened the wits out of him. He turned onto a side street and tried as casually as possible to shake the pursuer: a tall white-haired figure in a black robe.

Michael came home and shut the door.

He felt as if he had been suspended in a jar, some museum specimen, all life drained, time and blood replaced with formaldehyde.

22

At some point he began to write poetry, though he had no memory of having ever written poetry before. He wrote about what was on his mind all the time: Kristine.

Who goes in me
The one who pulls my

Lost mind into dawn is
Innocent of guile

From cold dreams to fire at
End of day she crowds a zoo
All my animal thoughts She

Is innocent of guile Does
Not see my labyrinth More
Than flesh in space words on paper

In me she lives Once
She lived her own

Now alone in me she goes

And after a day sitting quiet in the dark upstairs bedroom,
he took out a pencil and wrote on a paper napkin:

Watch him developing!
But where's his knowledge?
See that bright little pinpoint? That's it.
And his maturity?
Coming along slowly.
I see a dark spot, too. Someone missing?
He's lost someone.
Looks like he's trying to replace
   the dark spot with the bright.
*He thinks he may be able to bring back
   the lost.*
Can he do it?

And no answer; the pencil stopped at the end of the napkin.
The next day, he could not find the napkin, or any of the
poems he had written, and there was an odor of something
like ammonia and sulfurous gas about the house that drove
him outdoors.

He sat before a clump of gladioli, squatting on the sidewalk with nobody to see him—nobody visible, anyway—and
held a leaf in his hand, concentrating on it.

Focus. Detail. Clarity. Sharpness.
Detail.

He could not concentrate on the leaf. It seemed to shy

away from him, all its innermost details fuzzing and his attention drifting with them. That was not right.

The anger he felt was quickly damped by his dark mood.

Have to get over this. Can't think straight.

He stood up and wiped his hand on his pants for no particular reason. He was always clean; he did not sweat and had not
taken a bath since

When?

He looked down the street and saw the white-haired figure
in black watching him. It raised its arm, and Michael ran back
to the house. Even behind the door, however, he knew he
could not escape this time.

Mixed with his horror was an inexplicable spark of hope. If
what he saw was his death, coming for him, then it would take
away the burden of this dreary life, this grief-bound hell.

He stood two steps from the door, waiting.

A light, almost casual knuckle-rap sounded on the door.

Michael swallowed back a substanceless lump in his throat
and reached for the doorknob. Before his hand reached it, the
lock clicked, the deadbolt slid aside and the knob turned. He
retreated three steps.

The door swung open. He recognized but did not know the
man standing on the porch. He was tall, slender but very
strong-looking, of indeterminate age, face long and somber,
hair white and fine as mineral whiskers from a cave. The
collar of the robe was the color of old dried roses, cut from
dusty velvet woven with floral details that seemed to blow in a
wind quite different from that whining even now outside. The
man's eyes were the color of pearls, and his skin was pale as
the moon.

"Michael Perrin. Do you know me?"

His voice was like a sword drawn across folds of silk.
Michael shook his head, then nodded. He could feel power
radiating from the man.

"Do you know where you are?" A stinging pity came to the
man's face, mixed with mild contempt.

"No. I'm not at home."

"You are *loghan laburt,* loss-cursed. You cannot see
through your pain. You have been wrapped in a large but
poorly conceived *almeig epon.* A bad dream."

"Your name is Tarax," Michael said, feeling something rip
in the back of his head, a shroud around his thoughts. But the

name brought him no comfort. He began to shiver.

"I am indeed. I can bring you out of here, but you must do something for me."

"I don't remember clearly. I can't think straight."

Tarax narrowed his pearl-silver eyes, and Michael felt another parting of the shroud, letting in some memory. "Music," Tarax said. "The songs of worlds breathing in and out."

"Before I was here."

"Yes?"

"Nothing is right here. Where is Kristine?"

"She can be part of our bargain."

"Is she dead?"

"She might as well be," Tarax said, "unless you pull yourself from your self-pity and think clearly."

"She's not dead." The veil lightened and dissolved. The grief withdrew its dark wings and flew up and away from him.

"You were trained by the Crane Women," Tarax said. "They are gone now, and nobody replaces them. I need their function. You can fulfill that function." Tarax's smile was distant and ironic; that he should come to a mere human child with such a proposal . . .

Michael said nothing, simply reveled in the clarity of his mind and the relief he felt. He listened closely.

"I have a daughter," Tarax said. He stepped inside, and the door swung shut behind him, without making a sound. "My only offspring. She is of age for training in the discipline. She will attend me as a priest of the Irall, so long as it lasts, and on Earth after that."

Mention of the Irall drove away his relief and brought back a new dread.

"You have the heritage of the Crane Women within you. You can—you must—train my daughter in their ways. If you agree to that, I will tell you how to leave this dream and return to your world."

Michael nodded once, signifying not agreement but that he was still listening.

"If you succeed in training her, then I will reveal to you where this female called Kristine is trapped, much as you are trapped here."

"We are enemies," Michael said. "You hate me."

Tarax raised his hand, long fingers pointing, and tossed

those words away. "I hate nobody. We have cooperated in the past, and you have been aware of that. And there is the Law of Mages, which must be observed."

Indeed, they might have cooperated; Tarax might have been part of the conspiracy to nullify Clarkham. But what was the Law of Mages? "We failed, then. Clarkham is still alive."

"Not precisely alive," Tarax said. "The struggle isn't over."

"I've been warned never to trust a Sidhe," Michael said.

"Do you have any choice? At the very least, you will return to your world."

Michael considered. "What could I possibly teach your daughter?"

Tarax betrayed his only sign of uncertainty at this question. "What the Crane Women have willed, I presume."

"You'll take the risk that I might not be able to pass on the discipline?"

"Yes."

Michael faced the Sidhe and stood erect, saying, "Then I agree."

"You can take yourself back to Earth now. You know how. Simply use what you know. Ask yourself where you are." Tarax turned, and the door swung open. The Sidhe reached out with his long fingers and ripped the door apart, letting it drift in dusty shards to the floor. The wind ceased its whine.

"How?" Michael asked, frightened again.

Tarax faded, and then he was gone.

Michael trembled and stared at his hand. Already he could feel the memory of this experience slipping away and the dreary grief returning. He looked upon the house as a refuge, a place where he could grieve in comfort; it seemed suited to him, since he had lost everything.

He bit his lip and wriggled his fingers. "Where am I?" he asked. He thought of the floorplan and the

There was no piano in the house. This was not Waltiri's house, and Waltiri was not his father.

brick patio and white wrought-iron table, which Kristine had never seen, much less sat behind, and the figure in the flounced dress, Tristesse, that had been somebody some*thing* else.

It was so simple. He reached his hand through the air—not

across but through the intervening space—and tore aside the dream. Then he stepped through the descending ruins of Clarkham's trap.

And stood (shadows slipping away from him)

In the middle

(dust on the floor, a single track of footprints)

Of the upstairs room in Clarkham's house.

Rare summer rain fell on the roof, a sound so simple and soothing that he closed his eyes and listened for almost a minute before walking down the stairs and out the front door.

He had not been trapped in Clarkham's house; that much he knew almost immediately upon returning. Clarkham had created a crude and simple world for him and held him there. The house had not even been an integral part of it; where he had lived had seemed a mix of the Waltiri house, Clarkham's, and even parts of the house next door to Clarkham's.

Michael walked slowly up the walk to the Waltiri home, exhausted but inwardly reveling, each breath he inhaled like an intoxicating liquor.

How long had he been away?

"Finally home!" Robert Dopso stared at him from his own porch.

"How long have I been gone?" Michael asked.

"Long enough, believe me. Just long enough for everything to go to hell. Your folks have been by here several times, talking to Mother and me . . ."

"Kristine? Have you heard from Kristine Pendeers?"

Dopso frowned. "Nobody else. . . . Your parents mentioned a somebody-or-other Moffat. No women. I've got your newspapers here—those that have been delivered. The city's a shambles. Nothing's on time or reliable now."

"Why?"

"Haunts," Dopso said, shaking his head. "It's been at least a month since we saw you last."

Michael unlocked the door and entered, hoping vaguely that Kristine might be waiting, but the house was empty. Forearmed now, he probed deeply for signs of Clarkham, physical or otherwise, but found no evidence of him.

Dopso came up to the open doorway with an armful of newspapers. "Where should I put these?" he asked. "And your mail, too. Not much of that."

Michael indicated the couch. Dopso deposited the pile and stood, wiping his hands on his pants. "I've been thinking," he said, "that maybe it's time you give Mother and me the full story. I've had time to sort a few things out—that fellow who shot himself and disappeared. We both decided that if anybody knows what's going on, it must be you. We'd be very grateful if you'd let us know."

"All right," Michael said. "Let me catch up, and I'll come over this evening. What time is it?"

Dopso checked his watch. "Five-thirty."

"Make it eight."

Dopso nodded, stood for a moment with his hands in his pants pockets, as if waiting to say something more, then shrugged his shoulders.

"Oh." He stopped halfway down the sidewalk, raising his voice so Michael could hear. "You might want to clean out your refrigerator. The electricity isn't on all the time now."

23

He read the papers voraciously; there had been no news at all in Clarkham's dream-trap, of course. What he read both horrified and exhilarated him.

The Sidhe were reappearing all over the world, in the hundreds of thousands, if not millions. Apparently, large migrations from the Realm had resumed just days after the performance. He thumbed through the papers, tearing pages in his haste. England, of course—and Ireland and Scotland—: appearances by the hundreds. Whole sections of Ireland were now closed off by impenetrable and immaterial barriers, erected by the Sidhe; there was no way of knowing what kind of Sidhe. The editorials and reports he barely glanced at; they were, of course, not informed, and their guesses were ludicrous, if very twentieth century: aliens from space, high-technology terrorist actions.

They had no idea what was happening.

In other areas—India, China, the Soviet Union—news reports had stopped, and all travel had been banned. There were hints of enormous disruptions and even battles.

In Los Angeles, the "invasions" had centered on the Tippett Hotel, through which hundreds of "tall, strangely dressed" individuals had passed in just the last two weeks. The building was now surrounded by National Guard troops, but (Michael whooped and shook his head) that did not stop individuals from *flying* off the roof, some riding gray horses and others without apparent aid, vanishing into the sky.

The Sidhe were returning to find Earth a hornet's nest. How many had died, both Sidhe and humans, so far?

There was an enormous amount of work to do. First, he had to meet with his parents.

And then—Kristine. He had no idea how to find her. He wanted to pound the walls with frustration; his fingers gripped the pages of yesterday's *Times* until the paper curled up as if in pain.

When would Tarax send his daughter—or could he believe anything from Tarax's lips? Michael had found his way back —that part of the bargain had been carried through. But anything else . . . "I am so God damned IGNORANT!" Michael yelled, throwing the papers from the couch. He walked stiffly into the kitchen, face red with frustration, and tried to comb his hair back in place with his fingers as he punched out the number of his parents' phone.

Ruth stared off across the living room, eyes focused on something far beyond the opposite wall. John regarded his son directly, his face almost slack, eyes tracking with little jerks.

"Everything that's happened here since you left, it's been more than a nightmare for me," she said. John leaned forward and took her hand. "The world is real," she continued. "These things don't happen. But they did, and now they do again."

Look to your ancestry. Michael sat stiff as a wooden dowel in the familiar chair, in the familiar living room. His father's maple, oak and rosewood furniture surrounded them, and from the TV and stereo stand, the VCR clock blinked on and off, in bright turquoise numerals, *12:00, 12:00, 12:00.* It had not been reset since the last power outage.

"She's never told any of us," John said softly. "I tried to get it out of her over the years."

"Now, I'm going to tell," she said. "Look at your hair, Michael."

"That's rather hard to do," John said, smiling. "You'd have an easier time of it, sweet one."

Ruth tapped his extended hand with her fingers but did not grasp it. "It's the color of my great-grandmother's hair..." She sighed. "In West Virginia, back when it was still old Virginia, before the Civil War, my great-grandfather took a Hill wife. That's what he called her. In the family Bible, her name is Underhill. Salafrance Underhill."

Michael had read the names and always thought that one strange and beautiful, but he had never been told anything about his relatives so far back.

"She was a tall woman. Some said she was a witch. My grandfather always said she died, but my grandmother said she just went away, around the turn of the century. Great-grandfather never married again. And my grandfather, before he caught sick and died, asked that my parents keep my hair cut short always, and when I was grown, marry me off right away, because 'In our family a woman is a curse.' That's what he said. And my father always obeyed his father without question. I would dream things at night, and in the middle of the night, Father and Mother would come into my room, and Father would tell me what I dreamed was bad—he *knew* what I was dreaming—and he would beat me."

Her face had gone soft and her eyes large. She looked as if she were crying, but no tears came.

"I would dream of forests, and of Salafrance Underhill living in the Virginia woods, deep back where the great maples and oaks could sing their own songs when the wind blew through them. And her eyes were the color of old silver dollars. That's what I would dream of, and when I dreamed, I knew she was still alive...but not on Earth. She had gone back with her people. She had left my great-grandfather with two babies to care for, one a girl that died young. I think he killed her. And one a boy. My grandfather. And they beat the dreams out of him early."

John patted the chair arm rhythmically with one hand.

"So from what you say," Ruth went on, "my great-grandmother must have been a Sidhe, and that makes you and me Breeds."

"Lord," John said hoarsely. He cleared his throat. "This is a day, isn't it?"

"I left Virginia when I was fifteen and went to work in Ohio. I met your father in 1965, and it took me three years after we were married to decide to have a child. Your father pestered me year after year, but I was afraid, and I couldn't tell him why. I didn't know what I'd do if I had a girl. What I'd tell her."

"Do you have powers?" John asked, matter-of-factly.

"I've never tried to find out," she said. "Outside of stuff that could get away with being called intuition. But Michael. . . . He's always had a way of seeing, a sensibility. Even though he was male, I've feared for him. All his poetry and his thinking. He had something. So now there's this. Now people might believe about Hill women and fear and cutting hair short to stop something not right, not Christian. When he went away . . . I *felt* where he was, and I couldn't tell even you, my husband. I couldn't believe it myself because so much time had passed, and everything was hazy. I'd blocked it for so many years—the beatings and the dreams. My mother looking so scared and not knowing what to do."

She lifted both her arms, and Michael came to her, and she enfolded him and asked, "What are you going to do?"

"I don't have any choice, really," he said, voice muffled against her shoulder. She opened one arm and motioned for John to join them, and they sat on the couch, as they had after Michael had returned, all together, silent.

"Will they ever go away?" Ruth asked. "The Sidhe?"

Michael shook his head. "I don't think they can," he said. "They wouldn't be coming back to Earth if they could avoid it."

"And you love this woman, Kristine."

"Yes," he said.

"She loves you?"

"Yes."

"She's a hostage, then."

"I don't know why he's keeping her."

"Can he hurt you?" Ruth asked.

Michael lifted back and looked into her eyes. "Not any more," he said. "I don't think so."

"Be very, very careful."

"Whatever happened to your grandfather?" he asked. "And to your father?" He could not simply ask if they had the immortality of the Sidhe.

"Grandfather was killed in a wagon accident," Ruth said. "Father just disappeared a year after I ran away from home."

He left the house, stunned and thoughtful. How many times would everything cast itself in a new light? Had anybody else besides Clarkham—apparently—known he was a Breed? The Crane Women, or Waltiri himself? *How many Breeds were there on Earth now?*

Theoretically, because of Aske and Elme, most of the human race could have some Sidhe blood; he had accepted that much months ago. But to be so close to the Sidhe himself —almost as close as Eleuth—was a shock he was not prepared for.

It explained a great many things, however.

Mrs. Dopso sat in her overstuffed chair, the light of the reading lamp missing her face and casting a warm glow on her lap, which held a Bible opened to Revelation. Robert sat on a dining room chair next to her; Michael sat on the couch.

"Then the house *was* haunted," Mrs. Dopso said, seeming to derive satisfaction from the confirmation.

"In a way, yes."

"But it doesn't matter much now," she went on. "The whole world's haunted."

Michael nodded.

"I've been reading the Good Book," Mrs. Dopso said. "I'm afraid it doesn't give me much comfort."

Michael, remembering the debate with the Jehovah's Witnesses, said nothing.

"Will there be a war?" she asked. "I mean, will we drop bombs on them?"

"Not that kind of war, I don't think," Michael said. The old woman nodded. Dopso moved his chair forward.

"Should we move out of the city?" he asked.

Michael shook his head. "No. I don't recommend it."

"What are you going to do?" Robert pursued.

"I have a lot of . . . tasks. Jobs. I'm not sure where I'll start."

"Maybe you'll be a diplomat," Mrs. Dopso suggested.

"Maybe."

"So young. Everything has become serious, so serious for somebody so young." She closed the Bible. "Will Christ come to Earth again?"

"Mother . . ." Robert said with only mild disapproval.

"I need to know. Is this the Apocalypse? I don't think you could be the Antichrist . . . but is it Clarkham, then? Or one of the . . . what did you call them . . . the Shee?"

"I don't think so," Michael said softly.

"But everything will change," Robert said.

"Everything will have to change."

"I don't believe it." Robert stood up and stretched his arms out. "The world doesn't work this way. It's a delusion."

Michael could think of nothing to counter that. "I owed you an explanation," he said after a silent moment went by. "And I'm telling you what little I know. I presume I'll have to tell others also. I don't know how many will believe me. There are probably thousands of people out there trying to cash in on what's happening. My story won't be any less crazy than theirs."

Robert shook his head. Mrs. Dopso simply placed her hand on the Bible in her lap.

"Godspeed," she said.

That evening, lying in the downstairs bed but not sleeping —he might never sleep again—Michael wondered if he should offer his help to those dealing with the Sidhe. As a mediator, a diplomat, or simply an advisor. Lieutenant Harvey might appreciate such guidance.

But it was immediately obvious to him that he could not. Becoming involved in the confusion might be brave, even noble, but it would ultimately be futile.

The *enormity* of the confusion was awesome. Billions of people becoming aware of a new reality almost overnight. . . . He could not encompass such an upheaval. Some would welcome the change, taking it as an adventure—the disenfranchised, the disillusioned, those who yearned for apocalypse, whether it be Christian, nuclear or any combination thereof. Others would opt out, ignoring it or simply drawing up their barricades, in effect, becoming crazy, unable to face a reality they had never been prepared for. Facing the change realistically, Michael realized, would be almost impossible, for the humans of his time had been enmeshed in status reality for so many thousands of years . . .

If he tried to involve himself directly, he would be swept away in the hurricane of disruption, no matter what his powers.

But there was another less overtly courageous approach. He would go behind the scenes, doing what he had to do— finding Kristine, fulfilling his pact with Tarax, finding and eliminating Clarkham—and at the same time, he would work toward an understanding of the major problems.

When he was prepared, he would take whatever role was best suited for him.

"Coward," he whispered in the darkness. He unfolded his senses then, impetuously answering that self-accusation with an immediate act.

And felt:

The city, spread across its hills and shallow, wide valleys, vibrating, moving like a sluggish river this way and that in its tide of individual thoughts, disturbed like an anthill by a stick brought down from some direction it could not comprehend. Children having nightmares, having seen not airplanes not kites or gliders not even flying saucers, but Amorphals, wraiths and ghosts, or having been told about them not just by other children but by grownups on *television* with pictures.

Thousands contemplating their sins and the inadequacies of their lives, their inability to face unforeseen change, contemplating suicide.

He focused:

On a pregnant woman not more than five blocks away, radiant with health, holding her full abdomen as she lay in bed next to her sleeping husband, wide awake, mind suffused with a shadow *I decided to have it and now look now look what it will be born into.*

On:

A boy, fourteen or fifteen, mind twisted like a wrecked ship, thoughts caroming without pattern, full of anger, trying to feel his way through instinctively to a method of dealing with the little he did know, wondering if his dead father was coming back with the ghosts to punish him. Walking a city street—Santa Monica Boulevard—alone, armed with a small pistol, daring something weird to pop up in front of him yes he could deal with *that* images of a dozen movie screens and

big guns and Max Factor blood, flying acrobatic martial artists, and finally of drawn-faced priests pulling forth huge
crosses and *losing* to the devil.

On:

Faer, huddling beneath a city bridge, weak and exhausted,
waiting to cast shadows should they be discovered, their
magic much weaker here; their horror and confusion matching, if not exceeding that of the humans they had met.

Umbrals, dark and brooding and powerful; they had dug
holes for themselves in the ground beneath the trees in Griffith
Park and waited for the night; or they had lingered in
shadows, dazzled by the sunlight, whispering softly to each
other as the long day passed. Now they were abroad, trying to
find a niche for themselves in this unfamiliar world.

The Pelagals had already set up liaisons with the creatures
of the sea and swam with whales and sharks and huge wide-
finned mantas in the sparkling moonlit waters beyond San
Pedro harbor.

He extended his range and focused once more on humans.
There was something he had to acquire, a *sense* about the
world. The sweat started again on his skin. The effort was
almost painful, but he stretched the range of his probe and the
breadth of its sweep, until he could feel himself extended high
up into the sky, and deep into the Earth and across the city for
miles around. Then he drew in the height and depth and
seemed for a moment to cup the land in his hands, touching
lightly upon a million, two million, five million minds.

The richness of flow was overwhelming. He drew back and
became selective again, but over a much wider area.

sleeping city dark and nervous
This is what humans are
to work all day work for wages hope for gain and all this
comes this nonsense fall behind expected expected this is the
way life is it gets you you don't watch it and it creeps up on
you Oh yes Daddy says Mommy says meanness meanness
don't touch the cat that way I should have listened and not
taken that position before the board Satisfaction in that the
world is falling apart and still I have peace in the garden with
the thick crumbling soil works into my fingers and sprinkle
the bone meal think this was an animal once a cow I suppose
now it's garden that's what we'll be garden stuff walking meat
and bone meal for Earth's garden Yes it was sex and I don't

know what to do it comes up it sneaks up I must answer like an animal not an angel ape not angel wish for self-control but what the hell Pills and such death and simple joy in a bottle so hard so hard to be good when what feels good to me kills me a bit at a time *what did she say in sleep she comes to me just stares with that look she always had when she was alive I wonder is it really her and she's talking in my sleep to me?* Shot strategy all to hell all that work all that dedication and now it doesn't mean shit well I'm free [tomorrow back to the struggle act like it's all the same but it isn't it's a nightmare out there] *Thick waves oily and blue-green up around my sleeping ankles I can wake up before it covers my head I know I can but what if I'm not asleep same dream this has happened before but I can feel it cold and know it's rising I can see the moon overhead full drawing it up over my head and those people on the shore, they see the seaweed around my ankles, they know the knife is dull* Ceiling blank and dark spackle landscape it's like a joy that doesn't let me sleep he loves me and it doesn't matter all else Stupid goddam kikes every year stronger hate them so much liars and niggers and their women breeding and the brownies from the south and now *this* shit who can take care of it maybe they'll all kill each other and what's left over will be mine ours

Take it then take it and be damned CROSSING OVER yes God is with me and I can cross over swift river river of sinners *Listening!* Must pray Jesus for a drink Wait for the sun stretch out my outrageous arms and warm them in the sun sleep in the dumpster tonight listen for the trucks in the morning mustn't drink all this tonight or I'll sleep through the truck will get me eat me What can I teach them now it's all changed have a hard enough time anyway who wants to take a test when ghosts walk the streets and oh God I'm scared what must they be feeling just young kids faced the bomb now this

Kill him Shouldn't have eaten that Kill him Damned dog cleaned it up Pray Pray *Prey* Walked all over Like frogs on lily pad staring at each other oh it hurts I want to love Lust for nirvana that's it make them lust for enlightenment Breaking down everything Can't say it what I feel it's been twenty years we're together and she's everything and I'm so afraid of her for her for me Tomorrow I might be dead and no worries then it's getting close what can I expect five years maybe six

The grownups don't know nobody knows what do I tell my

sister *Growling stomach* Filth filth and degradation Kill them
Kill them *Whistling* I can't go on just being hungry and the
children that bastard kill him Why won't they let me be *Listening! Somebody listening! Feel—*

He expanded the range of his probe. It seemed an effortless
maneuver, but he scrambled to become more selective—

And nowhere Kristine

Beautiful women in bed making love and not thinking of
love and the men not thinking some thinking of cars High
glass and steel Lord could use a sniff a line how much I
wonder call Marge no turn in script tomorrow Kill them Meeting Immigration car lawyer card car card lawyer My baby my
baby [Emptiness, hollowness, grief close to bliss it has burned
so deep] The way the paint muddies when you use those
colors Bad mix Station nulls out that way six antennas got to
save Utah from 50,000 watts I'll remember and tomorrow
River flows river deep moon wide in my loins the blood
dances with the moon I hate her for what she did but I hate
everybody they hate me I know How do I convince them they
are so bored they might as well be dead

[Pain so intense and prolonged it makes him flinch]

Interruption.

Something searching *for* him not Clarkham not Tarax, long
and dark plying the waters of the Earth, a huge and ancient
sinuosity, inwardly human.

He tried to withdraw, but it was upon him, gripping him
with unbreakable gentleness, leaving a message:

Soon we must meet. Our time is coming.

Then releasing him.

And Michael, still and cold in the downstairs bed, eyes
stinging, deduced, knew, what it was that had reached out
several times to touch *him:* the oldest living being on Earth,
even now that the Sidhe were returning; the only representa-
tive of the first humans, alone of his kind cursed by the Sidhe
to remain sentient after all the rest had been transformed into
shrew-like animals. Alive and thinking and remembering for
sixty million years under that curse.

The Serpent Mage.

He pulled back within himself, head aching, and struggled
to reduce the pain with his discipline. He had overextended;
he had been met, matched and exceeded.

24

The Tippett Residential Hotel now stood at the center of an evacuated no man's land about three long blocks in diameter. Helicopters patrolled above the Strip and the Hollywood hills in the early morning darkness, spotlights searching the curfewed streets. Soldiers waited nervously beyond their sandbag and brick barricades. They had been awake, most of them, all night.

Michael walked casually down Sunset toward the barricades. Police cars were parked diagonally in a line across the street before the Hyatt. Highway patrol and LAPD officers stood with arms folded, talking with each other. They paid him little attention. Gawkers had been around for days.

He reached out and skimmed across their thoughts, taking in all that had been happening—all they thought had been happening—and distilling from the different viewpoints a reasonably clear picture.

The hotel had become particularly active about two weeks before. Hundreds of Sidhe had appeared in the building and exited, most from the ground floor, vanishing into the city. A few had flown from the roof on *epon*, the Sidhe horses. Amorphals and Faer, at least, had joined in the exodus through the Tippett. Other varieties of Sidhe—the Pelagals in his sleeping vision, for example—had taken other routes, using other gates.

It would not be difficult for many of the Sidhe to doff their clothes, find or steal or even buy others and merge with the human population. With a few simple illusions—cosmetic touchups in their appearance—the Faer, at least, could pass.

Now, however, the gate through the Tippett was blocked, at least on the ground. Michael had to go back into the building and find out what the situation was. If a backlog of refugees was building up, something would have to give, and that meant more people—and perhaps Sidhe—would be hurt or killed.

But that was not his main purpose. It was possible the gate was two-way—or that he could use the presence of a one-way gate to enhance his own abilities and cross over into the Realm. And perhaps there, someone could tell him where Kristine was . . .

Tonn's wife.

He did not feel easy relying on Tarax, at Tarax's leisure, to regain Kristine.

The line of squad cars and police was easy to penetrate. He threw a shadow of himself walking back up the street and moved casually past them, unnoticed. A sandbag emplacement blocked the street a dozen yards beyond, with three armed National Guardsmen sitting behind it, weapons aimed toward the Tippett Hotel. They had their backs turned to Michael. He suggested that if and when they turned, they would see—and recognize—another guardsman. None of them turned.

The side walkway of the hotel was hidden from view. Michael climbed the battered front fence quickly and found the side door open a few inches. Pausing to close his eyes and concentrate on the service hallway beyond, he took a deep breath. Nothing. The hallway was empty, as was the first floor—empty, that is, of anybody or thing he could probe. He knew he could not necessarily locate Sidhe.

The lobby of the hotel had changed little since he was last there. The elevator doors reflected a muddy, distorted view of the light coming through cracks in the freshly-boarded entrance. Bullets had penetrated the wood and left the remaining glass in pale diamond scatters on the faded and torn carpeting.

Michael walked up the stairs slowly and paused on the landing, glancing over his shoulder at the lobby now half a floor below. Indefinite emotions, memories, hung in the air like evidence of a passing cigarette: not good emotions, and not human.

It took him a moment to recognize the mental spoor of frightened Sidhe.

On the second floor, he saw a piece of fabric cast aside in a corner opposite the elevator door. He bent and picked up the cloth, holding it loosely in both hands. It was a jerkin, dark amber, embroidered with vivid brambles . and unfamiliar thorny flowers. The jerkin smelled like a winter forest. He laid the fabric down, disturbed by it, and saw another piece of clothing and a wooden staff on the stairway, the staff lying along one step.

The higher he climbed, the more discarded articles of clothing and accessories he found: bits of polished and engraved rock, even viewing crystals similar to the ones he had peered into in the Crane Women's hut, but dark and empty; a long full robe the precise color of a thunderstorm; several pairs of slipper-like shoes; and gems that would command a fortune in normal times.

On the fourth floor, Michael stopped. The spoor was strong enough here to tighten his stomach. The thought of powerful and noble Sidhe knowing such fear, almost panic, was frightening in itself.

On the fifth floor, he felt rather than heard a movement in the shadows. The dawn light did not relieve the gloom much. He walked between a thin forest of creeper-like electrical conduits hanging from the ceiling. The interior walls had been torn out long ago, leaving the entire floor open but for the elevator and stairwell.

The floor undulated and crawled as Michael slowly approached the rear of the building. His feet brushed soft objects, and he stopped; the objects soundlessly huddled and bunched away from him.

His vision adapted with uncanny quickness.

"Birds," he whispered. The floor was carpeted with sparrows, pigeons, robins and blackbirds. They all watched him warily, without menace but also without fear, and silently; not a single coo or chirp among the thousands of them.

On the porch, beyond shattered and leaning sliding glass doors, a single much larger bird, about two feet tall, perched on the edge of a concrete rail. Its feathers ruffled in a passing breeze, and it turned to face him. It appeared corvine, but with a blood-red breast and beak; its eyes were small black

jewels lined in white. Michael thought it might be the same
bird that had watched from the roof when Tommy came.

The large red-breasted bird stabbed its beak toward the
upper floors and nodded three times, making a tiny *gluck*
sound in its throat.

"Arno?" Michael asked. The bird preened itself, ignoring
him. Then it smoothed its feathers and pointed to the upper
floors again.

Michael backed away from the carpet of silent birds and
resumed his climb. There were no more abandoned articles of
clothing; if anything, the stairway and halls of each floor
seemed less cluttered than when he had last been there, as if a
group had made some pretense at cleaning and inhabiting the
empty rooms.

As he approached the eleventh floor, he could feel the presence of an intrusion quite strongly. The gate was still open.
And someone was standing before it. . . . That much he could
sense but no more. He paused by the elevators, staring down a
long, dark southern hall, all its doors closed. The end of the
hallway was darker than it should have been—a rectangle of
subterranean blackness. Standing before the blackness was a
white-haired figure in dark clothes.

Michael's heart was subjected to two separate moments of
alarm and shock. The first came when he thought the figure
was Tarax. He had half-expected to find Tarax here, and perhaps his daughter as well, but this individual was neither. As
his eyes probed the gloom, he saw that it was long of arm and
leg and short of trunk, which gave him his second shock; he
thought it was one of the Crane Women. Then it approached
him.

It was indeed an old Breed female, but it was not Nare,
Spart or Coom. Her long white-blond hair hung down to her
shoulders. Her lips were full, pink, even luxurious, but her
skin was nearly as pale as her hair. She regarded him suspiciously with small, bright blue eyes sighting along a thin nose.
She wore a man's black suit, which hung loosely on her, a
stiff, starchy white shirt (also baggy) and a narrow black tie.
"I've been here two days," she said with a mild Scottish
brogue. She did not touch his aura to learn what language to
speak. "The Serpent told me to wait for you and bring you
back with me."

"Who are you?" Michael asked. Why did such a simple question seem so clumsy? Because he already knew the answer, had known without even asking. "You're his attendant," he said.

She nodded. "The Serpent expects you. You are a candidate."

Then she motioned for him to follow. "This is not the path the Sidhe take from the Realm," she said, waiting for him to approach only two steps behind her before she reached with one hand toward the cavern-dark rectangle at the end of the hallway. "That is closed temporarily, but its power is here, waiting for those who know how to hitch on." The Breed pushed her hand into the blackness and passed through, briefly filling the hallway with blinding daylight. The blackness closed around her, leaving only her left hand suspended in the gloom, long finger curling, curling, urging him on.

The daylight flashed around him this time, and he stood on the barren shore of a broad slate-colored lake. The time was early afternoon. Thick clouds hovered over the lake and the adjacent brown hills. Nearby, gnarled pines encroached upon the rocky shore. A mist drifted across the far shore, obscuring more hills and a small peninsula sparsely fletched with more pines. The air was chill and moist but not cold. The Breed female stood near the still edge of the lake a few yards away. "Do you know where you are?" she asked.

Michael sniffed. "East," he said. "England . . . or Scotland."

"Have you been here before?"

He shook his head.

"Do you know why you have been called here?"

"No, not exactly."

"You've heard the tale . . . of the War, and the fall, and the loss, and the rise again, the flight and the return?"

"Yes," Michael said.

She nodded, and then she was gone. In her place stood a tree stump, its roots covered with algae below the water's murky line. "Thank *you*," he said with mock brightness. Then he sat on a rock and waited, feeling curiously patient. Only the gnawing thought of Kristine's captivity disturbed an extraordinary peace that settled over him.

This was finally the time, and it was sufficient in and of

itself. What he felt was akin to pride, but he was not prideful.
He was worthy to meet the Serpent Mage, but did that convey
any honor? Yes, and no. If Michael thought as a human might
think, then yes. If he thought as a Sidhe, it conveyed something else entirely. A fitting into the flow, a final integration
into the overall story.

Late afternoon lengthened imperceptibly into dusk. He was
neither bored nor anxious. He simply waited, his *hyloka*
throbbing, heating and cooling him like another kind of
breathing. Michael did not think much, nor did he daydream
or doze. The hour approached. He would feel apprehension
and even terror when it arrived; he was not above his origins.
Transcendence, perhaps, but not aloofness.

He had come a long way to be here. Distance in space was
the smallest component of that long, difficult vector. He had
learned many disturbing things about himself, about the world
and about his family. He was no longer the same Michael
Perrin he had been when he had first entered Clarkham's
house, passed through and around and entered the house next
door, to find Tristesse's backyard and alley and the gate that
gave access to the Realm.

The water of the lake—the loch—rose in a glassy, swell-
ing hump in the middle distance, then smoothed again without
waves. The hump reappeared halfway toward the shore, this
time disturbing the water with the faintest iridescent ripples.
Night was falling rapidly, and the mist was thickening, bead-
ing his shirt and light jacket.

*The oldest living creature on the Earth, or perhaps any-
where else. Older even than Adonna called Tonn.*

The air warmed. Michael surveyed the nearby waters. A
very long black shape—perhaps twenty yards from beginning
to end—lay curled just below the surface of the loch about ten
yards offshore, taking advantage of the decline and deeper
water beyond.

Slowly, it unwound and moved toward the shore, sine-
waving from side to side, sending out oily ripples in beautiful
whirlpool patterns. Its head broke the surface in the shallows,
and Michael felt its dark gaze on him.

The Serpent Mage was ugly. It looked dangerous, with its
smooth black skin dimpled all over like a very old catfish or
electric eel, its filmed eyes tiny, its fins small and barbed,

dorsal fin little more than a ridge of thorn-like stickles in the middle of its back. It was a yard and a half wide and squat in cross-section, as if oppressed even in the water by its freight of time.

Michael shivered. The head slithered up the shore, cresting sand and gravel before it. Then it rested, careened slightly to one side, still watching him, silent on all levels.

Its mouth was a wide, round-gummed crescent recessed behind the blunt two-lobed snout. The mouth opened an inch or two and shut, then again. Recessed deep behind the gums were crescents of sharp, tiny teeth, no larger than Michael's, but far greater in number.

Michael dropped his legs over the side of the rock and approached the Serpent, hands held out before him. His fingers trembled.

But for a tiny, final thread of noctilucent cloud, the last light had gone out of the sky, He was seeing the Serpent by all of his new senses, and in that seeing, the Serpent was suddenly wrapped in cold fire. Mother-of-pearl stripes retreated down its length from its snout. Its eyes became sullen blood rubies. Then the decorations passed away, and it lost all character but its length and its width. It sat on the shore as black as polished obsidian, blacker than the turbid loch water and the mist-shrouded night air beyond.

"You called me," Michael finally said.

"Yes, I did," a voice issued from the long form. It spoke human words but hardly sounded human. There was too much age in it, too much time wrapped in solitary contemplation.

"I don't know why you called me."

"We must discuss what you're going to do," the Serpent said. "The world is remaking itself."

"I'm ready to listen," Michael said, stopping three strides from the Serpent's head.

"I am not here to give instructions," the Serpent said. "The most I will do is suggest. The rest is up to you. Do you know what you are now?"

"The Breed woman who brought me here said I was a candidate. I assume that means I'm a candidate to be a mage."

"And how do you feel about that?" The Serpent rolled slightly and inched back and forth on the pebbles, as if scratching.

Michael shook his head. *Not much different from any other job interview,* he thought. "It seems ridiculous. I'm weak and ignorant and unprepared."

"What is required of this new mage?" the Serpent asked.

"I'm not sure," Michael said. "I assume to offer leadership and help bring humans and Sidhe together, to live in peace."

"Do you know that such a thing is possible?"

"No. But I know it's necessary, or we will all die."

"I have been listening to humans for sixty million years, give or take a few million, and I've listened to the Sidhe also. I've reached around the world, and beyond the world, and felt lives. When our kind was incapable of thoughts much deeper than planning for the next meal, or the next coupling, I waited. I saw their dreams increase in subtlety and power and watched them struggle back to awareness. The seed of rebirth I planted in them began to bear fruit. But time still dragged.

"I have been alive and carried in this body much too long. I have lived so long that I have gone crazy, and outlived my insanity, thousands of time. Each time I slipped back to savagery, I fought my way out of the tangle, even though savagery and insanity were more comfortable, because I knew this time would come. I suspect other mages have also known. But unlike other mages, I could not participate in the preparations. And during my lucid moments, I planned what I would say when a new candidate appeared."

Rain started to fall, and the loch sang and hissed under the passing storm.

"I swam the oceans of the world, and found deep passages beneath the land and came to these inland bodies of water to rest. Once, not very long ago, Elme brought me to her garden, and for a time I taught the children she had made with Aske, and the others who had gathered there. When Tonn reigned as Yahweh, our time in the garden became a legend, then a lie, and I swam the deep reaches for a thousand years, sick at heart and crazy again. I hated all living things. I thought the past, before the War, was lost forever. Even now, human life seems to me largely a dance of ignorance and hunger. What light there is is rare, and when discovered, usually snuffed out. Do you know who most often does the snuffing?"

Michael considered for a moment, water dripping from his face and steaming from the heat coming off his body. "Tarax and the Maln," he finally answered.

"They are the latest, yes. Do you know why humans have had to struggle against such odds in the past thousands of years?"

"Because of interference from the Sidhe."

"Yes. Do you hate them for their interference?"

Michael considered again, then shook his head. "It wouldn't do any good," he said.

"Wouldn't it be best to free us all by destroying the Sidhe?"

"No. We need them."

"Do they need us?"

"Even more."

"You know of some of the actions taken by the Sidhe. But the conspiracies have gone much deeper than you suspect. When you think of the finest human achievements, practical and artistic, names occur to you. Whom do you think of immediately?"

"Leonardo da Vinci, I suppose," Michael said. "Shakespeare, Beethoven. Einstein. Newton."

"Yes, and hundreds of others, east and west, most lost to history. I hope you do not leave out Bach . . . not very long ago, listening to his music helped me return to my present clarity. In your culture, these giants seem preeminent, do they not? But they are not the peak of human potential. They were *safe* enough to be ignored by the Sidhe. Some were ignored for a time, and when, unexpectedly, they began to worry the Sidhe, their lives and careers were plagued or cut short. But the finest, the preeminent—the ones I could feel even in the womb, radiating their genius—were snatched away by the Sidhe before maturity, or before they could accomplish their work. Almost all of the finest have been stolen away for ten thousand years, and *still we have matured and progressed.* The Sidhe have failed again. But they have come close to crippling us."

Michael said nothing, simply listened and waited.

"Now, only in the past few centuries—the wink of an eye —have some of the Sidhe come to their senses. Plans have been made, and factions have struggled with each other. And you have survived and come here to listen to me. So listen closely, for this is the most important information of all.

"The worlds are coming together. Adonna's Realm has failed. It lacked the mastery of prior creations. And here, in our universe, all have forgotten the art of making worlds. The true masters died during the War or were turned into animals and died not long thereafter. Since that time, this world—our world—has not been maintained. Few even remember that once, making worlds was the grandest craft of all—and the most necessary."

"Somebody made this world—the Earth?" Michael asked, incredulous—yet it felt so right! Answered so many inner questions . . .

"Not just the Earth. The universe."

"But it's *huge*," Michael said. "I don't see how humans or even Sidhe could have made something so enormous, so complex."

"Complexity is not always desirable. Enormity . . . yes. It always had a potential for growth. But it has gotten completely out of control now. Hundreds of creators, dozens of mages, worked to make this the grandest world of all . . . and succeeded. But the War ended cooperation. Now only I remember those times."

"People once lived only in universes they had made?"

"Why should it be otherwise?" the Serpent asked. "You are a child of your times. Do you not build your homes and live in them, in preference to staying out in the wind and the rain?"

"But that can't be quite the same thing. I thought that the Realm was like a growth, a polyp or something, on our universe."

The Serpent growled. For a moment, Michael began to tremble again, until he realized it was laughing. He did not expect such a human response from the monster stretched out before him, but then he realized how ridiculous that was. The Serpent was more human than *he* was. Age and transformation did not cloak its humanity.

"That was all Adonna managed," it finally said. "An admirable effort, but ill-conceived. The Sidhe had destroyed or transformed all the mages and peoples who might have helped Adonna succeed. His was the ultimate conceit."

"How can this universe be controlled again?"

"It can never be controlled again. If you leave a garden untended long enough, it is no longer a garden but a wild forest or a jungle, and it cannot simply be trimmed back and weeded and replanted. Our world has grown far beyond our power to control. It has merged with other worlds, cross-pol-

linating and taking on their qualities. That is part of the enormity you see—we are now a polyp on the worlds of creators
beyond our reach or understanding.

"Besides, your people—my children—have evolved in
this garden-turned-jungle. You have learned some of its ways,
and you are attuned to its character, however much you struggle against it. The world has turned cruel and harsh against
you and made you tough and creative and resilient. The Sidhe
cannot hope to match your creativity, whatever magic they
wield.

"Human discipline, on Earth, is now stronger than theirs.
And strongest of all, in potential, is the discipline of the
Breeds. Those who cross the barriers between Sidhe and
humans hold the heritage of both peoples."

"I'm a Breed . . ."

"You are still more human than Sidhe. You are not immortal, and you have that miracle called a soul."

"What . . . what is that?" Michael asked.

"Curious that you think I would know," the Serpent said.

"You don't know?"

"I only discovered how to destroy the soul, not to understand it. It is perhaps the final mystery, forever closed to those
who live in universes. Those who do not need to dwell in
shells, who stand out in the final sunlight and the final rain-
storms, the weather beyond all worlds, perhaps they understand souls. Or perhaps that is what our souls mature to
become . . . independent, free."

"The Sidhe will never have souls again?"

"No. My work was final."

"No wonder they hated you. You were worse than they."

The Serpent rolled back again, and Michael felt its clouded
eye on him. "More evil, more willful, and more creative. I
have had long enough to contemplate my excesses."

"Then they're doomed."

"No. There is a way to save them. Not in the individual—
only in the race. And they must sacrifice their racial purity to
do so."

"They must join with humans."

"Yes."

"But they hate us."

"Many of them both hate and fear us. We are the vital ones

now. They are the elegant and stylish ones. They have maturity and experience. We have anger and compassion and creativity. Now they come to Earth and hide. They feel hunted; they feel lost. They fear retaliation when humans discover what the Sidhe have done to hold them back."

"Humans will take a long time to accept what I've learned," Michael said. "It wasn't easy for me, and I saw things with my own eyes."

"Now they see things directly too. The Earth will not be the same. The Realm will not just vanish—it will leave its mark when it finally disintegrates. And no one surviving that cataclysm will doubt the new reality."

Michael squatted on the sand, then sat back on his butt and took a deep breath. "Why always disaster?"

"Because our universe has lost its safeguards. The garden has become filled with lions and scorpions. The gardeners are dead or, like me, ineffective, most of their skill sucked away."

"I had a safe and peaceful life until just recently," Michael said. "I still wonder about being a candidate for anything as important as a mage. I suppose I'd be asked to tie worlds together and to help create new ones."

"Ultimately," the Serpent agreed, "that would be your task. Why do you think you are inadequate?"

"I've done silly things," Michael said. "I've gotten people killed. My magic is comparatively weak. I'm young, and I feel very stupid most of the time. And . . . I don't *want* to be powerful and important." So he had finally said it.

"No person in his right mind ever wants to be a mage," the Serpent said. "It is a greater sacrifice and a harder life than any other you could choose or have forced upon you. No, those who *want* to be mages can never be true candidates. Clarkham, for example. His desire corrupts him."

"But I have been *stupid*," Michael cried out. "In the Realm, there was a Breed woman who loved me. She sacrificed herself for me—for nothing—and I . . ." He stopped, gulping rapidly, and found he couldn't say any more. He shook his head and wiped tears from his eyes.

The Serpent watched him without responding.

"Now, I've put another woman in danger. I have to find her. I don't know what I'll have to do to save her."

"You'll do what you must, obviously," the Serpent said.

"Conflict is part of your existence. Why are you ashamed of your mistakes?"

"There's no excuse for being stupid. I was blind. Ignorant."

"Do you think you committed a sin?" the Serpent asked.

Michael was a little shocked to have the word he had been avoiding brought forward so abruptly. "I suppose I have."

"Do you know what a sin is?"

"Doing something stupid you can avoid. Being vicious or selfish. Not thinking of others as living, thinking beings."

The Serpent growled. "Sin is refusing to accept things as they are and refusing to learn from them. Sin is acting out of deliberate ignorance. Did you act out of deliberate ignorance?"

"No," Michael said. "But I was acting in my own self-interest. I didn't think about Eleuth . . . I used her."

"That is a very youthful thing to do."

"It was still wrong."

"She chose to sacrifice herself, did she not?"

"Yes, and she didn't tell me it would kill her, but I should have known."

"Adonna, when he play-acted as God, implanted a very inadequate and corrupt notion of sin in human minds. He said sin was a violation of God's law. That is the philosophy of a tyrant, not a creator. He wished to keep all humans subjugated and ignorant. Human growth was anathema to him. He wished to keep us in ignorance and darkness. There is no God's law. Why should a god impose arbitrary limits? There is only growth and understanding. Through growth and understanding, there is love. Where there is no understanding and no growth, only ignorance, there is no love. That is sin. But to grow is to commit mistakes. To learn sometimes requires trial and error. It should be apparent to you now that all sins are youthful transgressions. All evil is youthful. After a few thousand years, thoughts of evil become ineffably boring, like the posturing of ill-mannered children."

"But I've *felt* evil. In Clarkham . . ."

"Poor Clarkham. Ambitious, inadequate, very talented but flawed clear through. Adonna was once like Clarkham. And that is how Clarkham was ultimately defeated, by those who could reach back into their own pasts and understand him.

Clarkham is only a few hundred years old. Adonna and the members of the Maln and the Councils of Eleu and Delf are tens of thousands of years old."

"But what they did to him—filling him with evil."

"Clarkham brought that upon himself. He made a trade when he was young. Magic for corruption. It is a way to gain power—a short-sighted and foolish way. When he had his power, he wished to stay the way he was, forever. And that means he cannot grow or learn. Such temptations are often placed before candidates. If they succumb, they are marked forever and easily detected."

"I haven't been tempted that way."

"Not yet," the Serpent said.

"And even if I should become a mage, it would still be possible for me to sin, wouldn't it?"

The Serpent rolled and rubbed itself on the stones.

"I mean," Michael continued, "you sinned . . . in the War."

"I fought. We all sinned."

"But you took away the souls of the Sidhe."

"And it was not enough. I would have destroyed them utterly if I could have."

"Why?"

"Because they chose to destroy my people. I was a mage, and I was sworn to protect my people."

"Then evil breeds evil."

"Around you is the result. Conflict. Confusion. Horror. And also . . ."

Michael waited, but the Serpent's voice had simply trailed off. It did not continue.

"Beauty," Michael finished for it.

The Serpent growled. "I have listened and watched for so long that I am beyond weariness or astonishment. I have lived far too long, but I cannot die. If you succeed, then perhaps I can be released."

"But you still haven't told me all that a mage does."

"A mage cares for his people. He—or she, for some mages have been female, though not many—smooths the path. A mage must understand his people. Do you understand yours? Humans, I mean."

Michael shook his head.

"Now think deeply, don't answer quickly. Do you know the character of humans?"

"They surprise me all the time. How can I know them?"

"Then you already understand that humans are surprising. Sidhe rarely are. Sidhe are deliberate. How else do humans and Sidhe differ?"

"Humans don't have magic," Michael said.

"But some can work magic, no?"

"Breeds."

"Michael, you are mostly human; what Sidhe there is in you is not enough, by itself, to convey magic if magic was the talent of the Sidhe alone."

"Then I was lied to."

"If you do not believe you can work magic, then you cannot work magic. Simple and effective; another link in the chain the Sidhe forged thousands of years ago. Adonna taught humans that even if magic can be worked, it is evil, a sin. How have humans compensated?"

"By working with matter. Science and technology."

The Serpent seemed to purr deep in its throat. "Yes. A surprise. Using the wild fruits of the untended garden. Adapting to a universe, rather than tailoring a universe to fit them. Listening to the echo of the long, complicated song the world has become and accepting it, not circumventing it. A novel idea. The Sidhe have not done it; they have worked their magic, but in a way, magic is a denial of reality, not an acceptance.

"So humans are makers of tools, forgers of iron, builders of metal wings and artists of plants and animal flesh. Such work seemed a crude and futile quest to the Sidhe, thousands of years ago; they were much more worried about your artists and musicians. They did not discourage your scientists. They could not understand them. Now, the quest of human science has been so successful, it is often more powerful than its masters. And in the twentieth century, it has become more powerful than the Sidhe."

"But scientists can't make universes."

"Not yet," the Serpent said. "Given another hundred years or so—a very small amount of time—and they will. If it is necessary. It may be necessary. But they will not do it through magic. And really, even the Sidhe can no longer create successful worlds. Adonna was the best, and his Realm is failing even as we speak. But we have gotten away from my question. What are humans?"

"Humans are animals," Michael said. "They think they aren't, but they are."

"True, but not in the way you mean. Humans are like animals, because many animals—even cockroaches, Michael!—were once people, long ago. The Sidhe forced me to turn my own kind into animals. And they transformed all their past enemies. You know of the Cledar and of the Spryggla. Their descendants are the birds and the mammals of the sea."

"I mean, so few humans can think beyond their immediate concerns."

"That may lead to tragedy, but could they have survived with any other attitude? The universe is no longer kind and nurturing."

"But some of them are cruel."

"And some Sidhe are cruel. How are they different?"

Michael was confused. "I don't understand what you want me to say."

"Do you detect similarities between humans and Sidhe, at the very bottom? Similar capacities for evil?"

"Yes," Michael said.

"Our kind, and the Sidhe and the others were all one, once. Have you thought about the origins of those who lived in the original tailored worlds?"

He hadn't. "Where did they come from?"

"They had no beginning. They were never created."

Michael wrinkled his nose. "That doesn't make sense."

"We are eternal. We change, we die, we return, and the combinations and permutations go on forever and ever. And slowly, we progress. Ever higher and higher. I imagine that long ago, we were simple vibrations in nothingness, small songs, each individual differing only in subtleties. How long the simple songs lasted, who can say? But they became more complex and more involved with each other. The songs joined and withdrew. Again and again they found patterns together, and the patterns broke down to make new patterns. New collections of songs, new styles, new addings and takings away. At times, what might seem setbacks—even disasters—happened, but across the greatest spans of time, there was progress. You must draw back before you can leap.

"And finally, that progress has come down to us. But there was no beginning. There shall be no end. Only variations on a theme, never repeating, always improving."

"Sidhe and humans were once one species?" Michael asked, still incredulous.

"It must have been so, once. One comes before many. And there are similarities."

"Yes . . ."

"Deep similarities. Though thousands of millennia have passed, the descendants of the original Sidhe can still mate with re-evolved humans. The songs even now beckon to each other."

"Why all the fuss, then?" Michael asked.

The Serpent growled quite loudly and rolled back and forth on the rocks. Michael backed away in some alarm.

"Why all the fuss, indeed! Do you imagine I have all the answers?" it finally said when it could control its laughter.

"You should," Michael said resentfully. "You're old enough."

"I should indeed. But my life as a serpent has not been an unbroken and rational continuity. As I said, I've spent much of that time being little more than a senseless sea monster, loving shadows and deeps, only rarely stumbling back into something like sanity. Fortunately, this season I am reasonably lucid. But . . . not entirely. Once I knew much more than I do now. Perhaps even the answer to the profound question, 'Why all the fuss?'"

"Maybe I shouldn't ask any more questions," Michael said, disgruntled.

"Not at all. Continue. There is much more to talk about. . . . But I should warn you. Even the answers I have given to you—*they are not certain*. They may not be entirely true. I am too old by far to be sure what the truth is. My own fantasies and dreams. . . . They could be more real to me than memories."

They continued talking until morning light suffused the mist. The Serpent withdrew into the water for a time, leaving Michael alone on the shore while it made a circuit of the loch. Then it asked him to swim, and Michael stripped down and waded into the murky water. Not once did he touch the Serpent but simply treaded water while it slithered in wide circles around him, head breaking the surface like the end of a weather-smoothed log.

Every few hours, the Serpent would illuminate itself with some fabulous design—lines of jewel-like swellings along its body, large and ornate fins, shimmering scales. But usually it was black or mud-colored, dimpled and ugly, ageless.

With the sun high, directly overhead, and the mist burned away, the dreary landscape around the loch took on a bright, desolate beauty. Michael lay on the rocks and sand to dry himself. The water had tasted sharp, like weak tea.

The Serpent crawled half its length up on the shore and rolled on its back, revealing a pale blue stripe running the length of its belly. A series of rune-like symbols were carved in the stripe. Michael crawled closer to the Serpent to examine the symbols. "What are those?"

"The terms of my imprisonment. The list of my crimes."

"I thought the Sidhe abhorred writing."

"They abhor the casual use of writing. They abhor book-keeping or the pinning down of history. For poetry, or for magic, writing is sometimes essential. These symbols are my prison."

"What do they say?"

"I don't know," the Serpent replied. "I can't see them. If I knew, I could free myself. And no one can reveal them to me."

They lay silent in the sun for minutes.

"Who was the last human you spoke to?" Michael asked.

The Serpent became a volcanic line of glowing red and then darkened into dying embers. "I haven't conversed with a human, face to face, for almost two thousand years," he said. "It is not pleasant to discuss."

"Why?"

"Because the last human candidate was deluded into thinking of our conversation as a temptation. He was extraordinary. He could have been a mage of the highest order, but he had attracted Adonna's attention as a youth. He had something else within him . . . something that went beyond the limits Adonna had set for him. Something above and beyond all these conflicts, very beautiful, without hatred, without greed. Still, he carried Adonna's mark . . .

"When his philosophy touched people on a large scale, it perverted and destroyed as much as it comforted and enlightened. There have been others like him since, but not nearly as strong. I have spoken with none of them."

Michael was tempted to ask more, but the tone of the Serpent's voice dissuaded him. After a while, when his clothes were dry, he stood and stretched. "I don't have much time," he said. "I have to find Kristine."

"We have wandered far with words, haven't we?" the Serpent asked. "How much have you learned?"

"Some. Not a great deal," Michael said.

"Then you know that what must be learned cannot be taught with words."

Michael felt a chill.

"You must sacrifice yourself now."

"I don't understand."

"You pride yourself in your individuality, your personal memories and accomplishments. But if you were to place all you have thought and been and done on top of what I contain, your mere two decades on my millions of years, you would be lost."

"Yes. Probably."

The Serpent growled softly. "That is what you must do."

Michael stared. "Why?"

"You cannot be a mage as you are now. You must have experience. You must learn."

"I don't want to be a mage," Michael said softly, shivering again.

"Do you have a choice?" the Serpent asked.

"Is this what you offered the last man you spoke to?" Michael asked. The Serpent did not answer. "Is it?"

"Yes."

"And he refused?"

"He had the mark of Adonna."

"Do I have the mark of Adonna?"

"You do not," the Serpent said. "You shed the mark in the Realm."

"And you want me to carry your mark?"

Again the Serpent burned lava-red, and the water around his submerged length bubbled and steamed. "You must combine worlds. You must create new worlds. You must unite the races."

"Yes, yes, somebody has to do that! I know."

"And you are a candidate. Perhaps the best candidate."

"But why must I submerge myself in . . . in you?"

"I have the experience. The memories. I cannot use them. You can."

"You have something else," Michael said, hardly believing

what he was feeling, what he was about to say. A voice inside him fairly screamed that he was being childish and stupid. Who was he to challenge the oldest living human? But another, stronger voice compelled him. Both voices were purely his own. This choice was his. "You carry the horrors of the past. If I absorb you, and lose myself, then I *become* you. And you were as evil and willful as Adonna."

"I have contemplated my excesses," the Serpent reiterated, its length obsidian-black.

"But would you commit those excesses again...to save your people?" Michael put on his clothes again.

The Serpent withdrew a few yards into the water. "If I were given no choice, I would."

"When you tried to destroy the Sidhe, did you really have no other choice? Or did you hate them?"

"I hated them," the Serpent admitted.

"And you would try again?"

"They are weak now."

"Would you try to destroy them?" Michael felt a surge of defiant horror. "You could, now that they're weak. You could finish what you started."

Only the last three yards of the Serpent's trunk and head protruded onto the shore now. "I hope I would not do that."

"But you might...anyway."

"I might," the Serpent conceded.

"I can't become you," Michael said, crying out again. "I can't be the kind of mage you were. If I can be any sort of mage at all..."

"You are very young."

"I wish there was a way I could learn from you, learn what is necessary, without the risk. If that is possible..."

But the Serpent withdrew into the loch without another word. The ripples stilled along the shore, and Michael was alone. He turned toward the tree trunk where the Breed female attendant had faded away.

She stood there again, her white hair dazzling in the sun, her baggy black suit and starchy white shirt and narrow black tie just as he remembered them.

"Follow me," she said. She tore away a part of the landscape beyond the tree trunk and stepped into inky darkness. Michael crawled through the hole after her.

And returned to the eleventh floor of the Tippett Hotel.

The Breed woman was a translucent shadow ahead of him, halfway down the hall. "You have failed," she said, her voice as weak as her image. "You are no longer a candidate. Go home and weep for your people and your world."

25

Michael stood in the hallway, alone and angry and as still as the marred plaster walls around him. *Why did I do that?* he asked himself, relaxing his clenched fists and arm muscles. *Because I am a coward? Afraid to submit to a higher personality?*

"No," he said. He felt his strength returning—that strength which had been growing, unaided, since he had returned from the Realm, since he had dropped out of the complex picture of machinations between the Sidhe and Waltiri and Clarkham. The strength returned, but not his confidence. The talk with the Serpent Mage had been so *interesting*—and for it to come to such an unexpected and painful end, because of his own rebellion, was agonizing.

In a way, he had been waiting for just such a conference for months.

"I'm a renegade," he said. If he was out of the picture completely, with no hope of returning, then he was free to act as he chose . . .

Which was what he seemed to be doing anyway.

He turned to look at the rectangle of darkness. When he had first passed through, following the old Breed female, he had felt the nature of the region beyond as a kind of tingling against his palms. He could feel that same tingling now. The unspecific gate led to *nowhere in particular*—it was an open

exit with no fixed destination. To someone with no training
whatsoever—the soldiers and police in the streets below, for
example—it would be simply a blank wall, darkened as if by
a polarized filter. For someone with inadequate training, it
could be very dangerous. It could put Michael into a between-
world as complex and delusive as a nightmare. . . . Or it could
take him where he wished to go.

To the Realm.

To seek out Tonn's wife, the skull-snail, if she was still
alive.

*Toh kelih ondulya, med nat ondulya trasn spaan nat
kod* . . .

So Eleuth had told him in the Realm, before bringing back
a beetle from Earth. "All is waves, with nothing waving
across no distance at all."

"*The Sidhe part of a Breed,*" she had explained, "*knows
instinctively that any world is just a song of addings and takings away. To do grand magic, you must be completely in tune
with the world—adding when the world adds, taking away
when the world takes away.*"

Did he feel that instinct clearly? When he had last stood on
the top of the Tippett Hotel, looking out over the city, he had
felt in touch with the inhabitants of the Earth for miles around
—and he had felt even more in touch later, lying in bed in the
Waltiri house. But the inhabitants were not the world itself.
He needed to make that final link.

It was certain no one else would do it for him. He was
working alone now, without support from any faction or
quarter. He had to lift himself up by his bootstraps.

For an instant, he felt a sense of despair and defeat that left
him dizzy. How inadequate he was, how ill-trained and ignorant . . .

And yet . . .

And yet, he was capable. He had the means to do what
needed to be done. Clarkham, the Serpent Mage, Adonna,
Tarax, even Waltiri aside, Michael felt the strength within
him. The product of a long year's discipline.

For a moment, the hallway ahead of him seemed to vanish,
and he saw nothing but waves of darkness shimmering against
each other. Addings and takings away—risings and fallings.
Peaks and valleys. He felt the hum in his palms, the singing of
all reality, and closed his eyes to tune himself to that.

With Tarax's suggestion, he had broken free of Clarkham's weak trap-world.

Now—

He turned to the dark rectangle. He remembered the *tune* and *timbre* of the Realm. He made the distinction between Earth and the Realm. Their wave-trains separated, and he could feel the distinct hummings. He reached out with one hand, feeling the buzzing in his palm, and pressed against the darkness.

Adding.

Taking away.

The darkness became potential. For a moment, he felt a hideous between-world beyond his fingers, and he wanted to pull back, but he held himself there and tuned an interval higher. Closer. Another interval.

His index finger drew a gash in the darkness, and sunlight beamed through onto his feet. He clawed the opening wider and felt it resist him, trying to close again.

The Realm was distinct and real beyond the darkness, but hardly stable. The tune and timbre were in fact fluctuating even as he tried to break through. He ad-libbed a tremolo to the song. The darkness faded.

He stepped through.

And stood on a grassy dell, with thick, green forest beyond. Overhead, in the dusk of a failing day, stars were twirling like fireflies on short leashes, and the moon was cutting a trail of crescents in a pearly band across the sky.

The Realm.

For the first few hours, Michael reveled in the clean, cold sensation of air that had blown across scattered patches of snow and through miles of uninterrupted forest. He reached out to the auras of any within his range and found only a few lone Arborals—and a hint of others in the direction of the setting sun. He then settled into a cold evening, warmed by his *hyloka*.

Wherever his probe extended, it met an undertone of disruption. In one direction, he actually felt a cutting-off of the Realm—an edge, beyond which lay something distastefully like the Blasted Plain that had surrounded the Pact Lands. As the evening lengthened, he felt more such edges. The Realm was now cut through by swaths of decay. He did not know whether he could cross such a discontinuity or whether the Realm would last long enough for him to find Tonn's wife, but he felt a nervous contentment nonetheless. He was actually doing something to locate Kristine. For the time being, it was all he could do.

Until, of course, Tarax came forth to present his daughter. When—and if—that happened, Michael would change his plans accordingly. But the thought of waiting for Tarax's move had eaten away at him. This was much better, if no more certain.

Michael had never suspected himself to be such a rebel. He had trained under the Crane Women with a bare minimum of argument, accepting the situation and the necessity of their discipline. Now he was ignoring Tarax, who was almost certainly more powerful, and he had defied the Serpent Mage, who was beyond doubt wiser.

But tainted. If the wisdom of the past came with all the patterns and mistakes of the past built in, then surely there was another and better way.

He ruminated on these thoughts until dawn, which came much sooner than he had expected, even given the Realm's erratic time scales. Everything was shifting.

Then he set out in the direction of the murmuring crowd of auras, more certain with each mile he ran and walked that there were humans among that group—a great many humans. This gave him another hope, that he could rescue the humans he had left behind in the Realm. That was something he had never felt right about. However weak he was, he should have tried to help them. . . . But he had not been his own individual then. He had been carrying out somebody else's mission.

And what if that's what you're doing now, and you don't even know it? The nagging doubt was his own; it came from no outside source. He was of so little importance now, so rejected and ignored, that nobody in all the Realm felt it necessary to cloud his mind with messages.

Not even Adonna, who might be dead . . . though that was hard to believe. What could kill a god-like Sidhe? Nothing, perhaps, but the end of his greatest creation. If Adonna had fashioned the Realm out of himself, then the Realm's death would be his own.

Within two of the irregular days and nights, he stood on the inner edge of the forest that had once surrounded the Blasted

Plain. Nearby, the river still flowed, and the bitter, corrupted circle of the Blasted Plain itself still stuck out like a festering sore. But where the Pact Lands had been, where the villages of Euterpe and Halftown had stood and the house that had once belonged to Clarkham, there was desolate emptiness. The Blasted Plain had half-heartedly moved in to fill the emptiness.

There were no humans, no Breeds, and certainly no Sidhe nearby . . . with one exception. Michael probed cautiously, unwilling to intersect with the minds of the Children, if any still existed.

But the Children were gone, too. They had been expunged by the Sidhe who had carried away the humans and Breeds and resettled them, perhaps in the direction in which Michael sensed a large group of humans.

He thought of Lamia, the last inhabitant of Clarkham's house. The house and the decaying field of vine stumps behind it, on a bank above the sluggish river, were gone.

Michael blanked his thoughts of all cross-connections and associations, searching for the trace of one aura: Tonn's wife, transformed into the skull-snail.

He found nothing. Concentrating, reaching out again, he refined his sweep. Again nothing—and still no sign of the Children or anything else alive—or quasi-living—in the Blasted Plain.

And then he came across a wavering pinpoint of awareness, almost too weak to be perceived.

Without hesitation, he stepped from the forest into the Blasted Plain, his feet raising puffs of bitter dust.

Within an hour, he came upon the hulk of the skull-snail, its hideous shell stuck fast between two leaning pillars of rock the color and texture of clotted blood. In the orange light of the dusty sky, he walked around the hulk, examining the desiccated remains of the beast within the shell. The skin had hardened to tough leather on the trunk and tentacles; the lantern-like protrusions at the ends of the arms were dim and opaque.

Yet Tonn's wife was not dead. He reached deep into the hulk, touching the weak aura directly.

Sun. He kills me finally.

—I've returned, Michael signaled.

The boy. . . . Seeking now?

—You said you knew where I could find Kristine.
You did not even know who Kristine was then.
—No, I hadn't met her. How did you know?
A mage's wife has many skills. I taught Tonn a great deal.
Magic is transferred through the female.

Michael wondered about that but decided to let it pass. He
did not think Tonn's wife would live much longer.

—Where is she?
I knew then. I knew where she would be . . . . But you have
changed things. The answer is less clear now.

—How did I change things?
You did not concentrate on Clarkham. You thought he was
defeated forever, when he was only removed from the immedi-
ate concerns of the Sidhe. What I saw was that Tarax held her,
to force you to train his daughter as the Crane Women would
have. But Clarkham may also have taken her now. The picture
is not clear.

The leathery appendage emerging from the "nose" of the
skull-shell twitched and slid a few feet in his direction. Michael did not move to avoid it. She had no power to harm
him.

Please. You must call the Arborals. I am dying.

—There are none close now. The Realm is being evacuated.

Then it is over. I will be released even from memories.

—If Clarkham has her, where would he keep her?

Practicing. Mock-ups, dreams, failed attempts to be a
mage.

—He would keep her in another incomplete world, as he
kept me?

There was no answer.

—Which world? Please—describe the song, the timbre.

A world built to contain his evil. A slippery, hardsided
world, a trap for all, even him. She does not know.

—How will I find it?

By teaching Tarax's daughter. Or by . . . you are strong
now, much stronger.

The hulk shifted between the rocks.

If the Arborals cannot come, then I will not wait. The last
pinpoint of awareness winked out, suddenly and finally. The
hulk was empty and useless to him.

Michael stood for a few moments by the remains, filled

with an emotion between pity and indignation. From what he had felt in his probe, he could tell that Tonn's wife—he didn't even know her name!—had once been nearly as noble a Sidhe as the Ban of Hours. So what had she done to deserve such punishment? What had Lamia and Tristesse done? He could understand the action taken against the Serpent Mage, but why so much undirected and senseless cruelty?

As he recrossed the border of the Blasted Plain, Michael saw the sky and the sun slew to one side, then spin. He fell to the ground and crept toward a tree. The shadows of the forest recessed wildly, then steadied. He looked up, eyes wide, then got to his knees. All the directions had changed.

His skin itched, and his hair stood on end. Fundamentals in the construction of the Realm were decaying, that much was clear.

But which direction would he take now? He couldn't follow the sun—it seemed to have been smeared into a constant glowing haze above the land. He walked into a clearing and shaded his eyes against the warmth and glare of the entire sky. He would have to travel rapidly. There was very little time left.

Calling upon all his discipline, he took several deep breaths and began to run through the forest and across the open fields, following now the much weaker and confused beacon of that mass of human minds. He did not run far.

The land ahead had abruptly separated, leaving a chasm several miles wide. Michael slowed to a walk, frustrated and more than a little frightened. He had never seen such a feature in the Realm before; it was new, and it looked very dangerous, certainly uncrossable without aid. The edges of the chasm were crumbling away, the clumps falling off into nothingness with majestic slowness.

Michael came as close to the edge as he dared, crawling out on a lip of solid rock, fingers seeking any sign of tremors or instability. Far below, he saw the foundation of Adonna's creation roiling and rainbowing in opalescent mist. And nothing else.

The chasm appeared to extend in both directions forever. It cut him off from the human murmurings. It even separated him from the distant sensation of Inyas Trai and the Irall.

If he could not cross, then he could do nothing more in the Realm. He retreated from the lip of the precipice and walked

back into the forest a safe mile or so, to rethink his plans and
see if another way presented itself.

"Why do I feel so *good?*" he asked himself, standing beneath an enormous conifer, at the center of a circle of half-
melted snow. "Everything's going wrong..." But he already
knew. It was because he was back in the Realm. The Realm
had a beauty, even now, that he had deeply missed after returning to Earth. Beauty—and horror and sadness, much
more concentrated than on Earth. Every sensation felt here
was at once more intense and more stimulating.

The inexplicable horror of Adonna's wife; the surreal nastiness of the Blasted Plain; the ever-changing days and seasons.
The lushness of the forest, with its wild orchards. Inyas Trai.
The cursed territory of Lin Piao Tai. How would the Sidhe
feel, forced to return to Earth after their centuries here?

How could a mage take the demanding variety of Earth and
mix it with the intensity of the Realm?

He closed his eyes and spread his palms. He could *see*
everything through his skin. The Realm vibrated and sketched
itself across his eyelids. He could almost feel its deep structure, catch the secret of Adonna's creation...

"Man-child."

Michael opened his eyes and saw a Sidhe horse approaching him. An image of Tarax—clearly not the Sidhe himself
but a shadow—guided the *epon* through the trees with one
hand cupped under its chin. The shadow smiled. "Play-acting
at magic?"

Michael stumbled over his words and finally, face flushed,
just nodded.

"We have an appointment," the shadow said. "You obviously can't make your way across the Realm unaided. Even
most Sidhe have difficulty now. Adonna can spare one of its
epon for your journey. We will meet beneath the Testament of
the Irall."

The shadow faded. The horse stood, tail flicking, long
foreleg pawing the grass and humus, with its eyes fixed patiently on Michael.

"Hello," Michael said.

The *epon* tossed its head and turned sideways to allow him
to mount.

26

The Sidhe horse, eyes blank as ice, silver-pearl skin blinding in the diffuse sky-glow, leaped from the crumbling edge with legs extended fore and aft. Michael clung to the mane, his heart racing, and cried out, *"Abana!"*

The chasm, the separated sections of the Realm, the mist of Adonna's creation far below, all skewed and tumbled. The horse screamed and was surrounded by a coma of fire that broke away like shards of glass behind them. The cold was so intense that Michael nearly froze before he could increase his *hyloka*. The horse's lips curled back from its teeth, and its muscles tensed hard as stone between his legs. Michael's head seemed about to explode.

The journey was an agony. It hadn't been this way the last time. The Realm no longer accommodated such rapid travel without protest. They skimmed the ragged, bleeding borders of the Realm and the Earth and a thousand between-worlds. The Realm was an open wound, and the Earth beyond cut deep as a knife, defending itself. Michael could stand no more when the journey ended, and the horse threw him and fell on its side, kicking and shrieking.

He rolled across a flat, abrasive surface and leaped to his feet instinctively, bruised and scraped on his arms and knees but otherwise intact. *That's more like it,* he thought. He had seldom spent more than a few hours uninjured during his last visit to the Realm. The horse, shivering but apparently unhurt, clambered upright and regarded Michael resentfully.

They were on a dark stone road flanked by shiny black pillars, each pillar filled with tiny flaming glints like eyes around a campfire, watching, enjoying his predicament. At the end of the road, squatting under the brilliant, hot, milk-white sky like a monstrous gray seed-pod, was the Irall. At the opposite end of the road, behind them now, the color of incandescent marble, was Inyas Trai, the city that the last of the Cledar has designed for the Sidhe ages past.

He was alone on the road. The horse calmed under his caressing hands and allowed him to remount.

Michael's enthusiasm for the Realm had declined considerably. The sky was hotter here, abusive in its brilliance. The Irall stood in sharp contrast, its inward-leaning outer towers rising black as coal from a dome of silky gray. Its black central spire rose to a haloed needle point that could hardly be seen against the dazzling whiteness.

The last time he had entered the Irall, it had been involuntarily, surrounded by Sidhe coursers.

He was not so sure that this time was much different.

Michael stopped the horse and surveyed the land around Inyas Trai and the Irall. The city seemed empty—a quick probe found no sign of Sidhe, Breeds or humans. Perhaps most of them had been evacuated through the customized stepping stones Nikolai had mentioned. Another probe into the Irall itself, cautious and tentative, revealed that it was also deserted.

He tried to find the direction of the massed human auras again, and when he did, he sensed a great body of water and mountains between. The humans were on the other side of *Nebchat Len,* in the mountains where the Sidhe habitually trained their initiates. Michael received some of the captives' emotions—and made his first good guess as to their number.

There were far more than Euterpe had ever contained; as many as five thousand of them. Some were fearful, others calm and expectant. He did not have time to find the individual auras of people familiar to him—Nikolai or Helena. If he did not take Tarax at his word, perhaps even Kristine waited there.

Michael urged his mount forward into the gate of the Irall, barely wide enough to allow three horses entry abreast. He remembered the cupped dark walls beyond, like a glacial cave suddenly converted to stone. The floor was littered this time not with dried flowers, but with the leavings of panic and flight—shreds of clothing, muddy bare footprints, broken and powerless wicks; not unlike the stairs of the Tippett Hotel.

The tunnel broadened but remained dark, without its prior greenish luminosity. The walkways to each side were empty; there were no longer enslaved Breeds in the Irall to serve Adonna, or Tarax and the Maln.

The walls spread into an immense chamber, its limits lost in darkness. Where before there had been smoke rising to its heights, now there was simply cold, stale air. The beehive chamber beyond was flooded to the horse's hocks with rusty water, hiding the sunken amphitheater at its center. He rode the horse around the perimeter and into a tunnel carpeted with swaths of electric blue mist. That, at least, was the same; they were nearing the Testament.

Thus far, they had only passed through chambers within the wall of the temple. They emerged from the tunnel into the central hollow of the dome. The air smelled of dust and decay and sour, poisonous blossoms. Yet Michael was not afraid. He had been more nervous meeting the Serpent Mage.

Long minutes passed while they crossed the interior. All around, the blue mist mocked them, rising in animated sworls and snake-like curls, beckoning and striking, reminding Michael of the blueness that had emerged from a single flower to destroy Lin Piao Tai. (Was all magical power simple and interrelated, like combinations of letters in a remarkably small alphabet?)

Finally, before them appeared the stone table flanked by tall stone chairs. No amphitheater crowded with Sidhe appeared out of the mist this time to surround the table, and the chairs were empty.

"Where do I go?" he asked nobody in particular, except perhaps the horse. He patted its shoulder. It glanced back at him, eyes unfathomable but calm, and flared its nostrils. Then it led him past the table, and Michael knew where he was going. The horse would take him to the pit at the center of the Irall.

They were going to the spinning brass cylinder above the mist and beneath the Realm proper.

And so it was.

Down the rocky shaft, past the thick upper layer of rock and the lower layer of blue translucent ice, now cut through with milky fractures, toward the spot of rainbow-colored light and finally out the bottom of the shaft, the horse's hooves straining for solid ground and finding none, its mane and tail streaming, lips revealing tiger teeth biting the empty air ahead—

Under the rugged ice belly of the Realm, above the chaos of the mist—

Toward the spinning brass cylinder, perhaps a mile wide and two long—

And into the hole at the center. The last time, he had been struck unconscious by the errant hoof of a horse. Now he saw it all. And still he was not afraid.

The horse flew him past bent and twisted platforms mounted on girders that vanished into dusty darkness. The cylinder did not seem designed for any practical habitation; it might have suited a community of anchorites, each sitting on a platform separated from the others, contemplating verdigris decay and endless rotation about the hollow axis. Michael probed ranks upon ranks of platforms his dark-adjusted eyes soon saw, half a mile deep to the wall of the cylinder. Each platform was empty, collecting only dust. *Why all this?*

He thought of the graveyard near the opposite end of the cylinder, where thousands of Sidhe and Breed and human skeletons were chained to a free-floating network of brass bars. Had Adonna truly demanded so many sacrifices? Or had the corpses been criminals captured and executed by Tarax?

The horse shuddered, and Michael turned it away from the center as they saw the graveyard ahead, still filled with dust and captive dead. They flew in a spiral around the cluster of bones. He saw the platform from which Tarax had addressed him when Michael had found himself chained among the corpses. The horse stretched and flew around the platform and then moved inward toward the axis again as the graveyard receded into a lattice of brown points.

Repeating journeys. Ringing changes on the same themes.

This time, however, Michael knew he had some measure of control. Tarax needed him—or at least behaved as if Michael was necessary.

The solid, closed end of the cylinder loomed, streaked with black and green stains radiating from the center to the edges. Then a pinprick of light appeared in the center, widening, its edges glowing and sparkling. Beyond, an unknowable distance below—if distance meant anything there—was the mist, chaos and potential, a vortex of pastel rainbow colors run through with painful ambiguities. Michael would not allow himself to turn his head away. He would have to face such—

If he wished to become a mage. Did he? What sort of mage, without the support of the Serpent? Ignorant and weak? A renegade mage. Something young and powerful and unexpected.

He shook his head slowly and grinned. His every thought betrayed how foolish he truly was.

The hole stopped growing, its edges solidifying into fresh-polished brass, as if a giant drill bit had recently pushed through. Two figures floated at the center. Michael recognized Tarax. Beside him was a Sidhe female, tall and slender. The horse shivered and accelerated, neck muscles writhing.

From a hundred yards, Michael could see Tarax's patient, weary face surrounded by a drift of fine white hair. He wore the same robe he had worn when he had last sent Michael into the mist to meet Adonna: gray stripes floating above black fabric, intertwining to form knot-like designs.

You don't even have the necessary clothes to be a mage, Michael admonished himself. Tarax observed the faint smile on his lips. The horse turned and slowed barely five yards from the Sidhe father and daughter. They all might as well have drifted in emptiness above the mist; without looking back or toward the distant reflecting edges of the hole, the only sign of the cylinder's presence was a sensation of vast silent motion.

"You've matured, man-child," Tarax said. "You're no longer a mere tool, an aimed weapon."

Michael examined the daughter. Her face was sternly beautiful, in the way he had never quite grown used to among the Sidhe; long, sharply cut, with large pale eyes and dark red hair. He could not tell how old she was; her figure betrayed some maturity, but was by no means voluptuous. She wore a white blouse with the sleeves rolled and tied back above her elbows, and knee-cut riding pants. Her boots were long and black and came to mid-calf. Her gaze was steady and calm. Beyond the Sidhe resemblance, Michael could detect neither Tarax's nor any other heritage in her; she could even have passed as a Breed. She was taller than Michael by three or four inches, if height could be judged in the weightlessness above the mist.

He thought of walking beside her on an Earth boulevard, through a human crowd. She would pass—but barely.

"I'm puzzled," Michael said. "This is your daughter?"

Tarax nodded. He had not even bothered to probe Michael, nor had Michael tried with him. Mutual respect. "Her name is Shiafa." That, Michael knew, would be the extent of the introductions. "What puzzles you, Man-child?"

"The last time we met, you wanted me dead. You were very disappointed when Adonna spared me."

"I was even more disappointed to learn you had survived your encounter with the Isomage."

"Yes. Well, you saved my life, and now you bring me here on one of Adonna's horses—which I presume I will not be arrested for stealing—and treat me with civility and even respect, though you keep calling me Man-child."

"My apologies. All humans are children to me. Shiafa is a child, and she is three times older than you, by Earth time."

Michael shrugged. "All right. I don't understand why your attitude toward me has changed."

"Sidhe take advantage of fortune and misfortune alike. My misfortune—that you have survived and matured—is also my daughter's fortune, for the Crane Women are gone—"

"Dead?"

There was a hint of the old Tarax in the Sidhe's long, patient silence and slow blink. "They are gone," he repeated, "and my daughter needs to be trained. Only you can pass along the discipline of the Crane Women."

"What about Biridashwa—Biri? He was trained by the Crane Women."

"He is a Sidhe. You are a Breed. It is necessary that Breeds train."

"Why?" Michael asked.

Shiafa had hardly moved during this exchange. Now she pushed away from Tarax and, without a word, mounted behind Michael.

"There is subtlety in Breed discipline," Tarax said. "That subtlety is necessary for an initiate to the Maln." Michael sensed this was not the complete truth.

"Is there still a priesthood? I've heard Adonna is dead and the Councils are dissolved."

"Adonna is dead," Tarax said. "The creation is sundered

and will soon die. But there is still need for a priesthood. Train my daughter, and you will learn where the Isomage keeps your woman."

"What will I teach her?" Michael asked, looking back over his shoulder at Shiafa.

But Tarax was already fading. The Sidhe's black robes smeared like paint in water. His face and hands and feet lengthened into blurred lines. A billow of mist flashed and danced around him, and he was gone.

"I will be first priestess to the new mage," Shiafa said, her voice husky and musical and enchanting. "My father." She gripped Michael's hips with her long-fingered hands. "You will train me on Earth—"

"I'll train you where I damn well please," Michael said, reacting with anger to his arousal at her touch. "Whatever I'm going to teach you, I'll start in the Realm. We have work to do."

The new mage. Michael brought the horse around and urged it back along the cylinder's length.

"Our first job is to undo all your father and the Sidhe have done with humans in the Realm," he said. "If you refuse to help, then I'll cut you loose here and you can return to Tarax."

"I will help," Shiafa said without inflection. Michael glanced back at her with some surprise. Her eyes were closed to slits. "You are the master of discipline. But we will not have much time. My father will dissolve the Realm any day now."

"Heir to Adonna, eh?" Michael asked, as the dusty wind beat at them from around the floating graveyard. Shiafa said nothing.

The ice beneath the Realm was cracked and veined and calving into huge, drifting spikes and bergs. With some difficulty, Michael found the shaft leading back to the Irall, and they rose to the surface of the Realm.

27

The night of the failing Realm was impenetrably dark. The ribbon of moon that had once stretched across the sky, and all the twirling stars congealing into a fixed night canopy, had gone. There was nothing but cold wind and the soughing of the grass around their campfire.

Michael had started the fire by extending his *hyloka* to one finger and igniting a small pyre of dried wood and leaves. Shiafa watched him with some interest and then experimented on her own pile of leaves. She, too, was able to light a small blaze, which she then heaped on the bigger fire. She turned her large pale blue-green eyes on Michael and blinked.

"I'm not sure there's anything I can teach you," Michael said. "My skills are crude."

She said nothing, but went to the horse and removed a comb from her pack, then began currying the animal's short, tight-packed fur swiftly from neck to withers.

"There are people here—humans," Michael said. "I know some of them. I'd like to get them out of the Realm before it collapses."

Shiafa nodded.

"Do you have any suggestions?"

"The Ban of Hours defies my father," she said. "You might consult with her."

"Is she still in Inyas Trai?"

"No. The city is empty."

Truth so far, he thought.

"She's protecting the humans?"

Pulling back from a long stroke that made the animal shiver with pleasure, Shiafa shook her head. "I do not know."

202

"You speak English well," Michael said. Neither Tarax nor his daughter had resorted to in-speaking. "Where did you learn it?"

"From my *Mafoc Mar*," she said. "My Bag Mother. She attended the Mab on Earth before the final flight to the Realm. The Mab had dealings with English and Scots. And my father has been to Earth since."

"Your father still hates humans."

"Yes," she answered matter-of-factly.

Michael sighed and stared into the crackling flames. "If he becomes mage, the new world he makes won't be suited to my people, will it?"

She did not answer. That much was self-evident.

"This is crazy," Michael said. "You're probably a better magician, just by instinct, than I am."

"No," she said. "That is not so. You defeated the Isomage. My father was unable to do that."

"I had some guidance," Michael said. *And an element of surprise.* "What does your father plan to do with the humans here?"

"I do not know."

"Is he at war with the Ban of Hours?"

"I do not know."

Michael wrapped his hands together and cracked his knuckles, something he hadn't done in years. Shiafa's voice was having an effect on him he did not relish. He increased the level of his discipline and fought back the attraction.

"You don't sleep, do you?" he asked.

"No."

"Do you eat?"

"I eat what food the teacher thinks necessary."

Now was the time for the big question. "If your father is unhappy with the way I train you, he won't tell me how to find the woman I'm looking for, will he?"

"I do not know," Shiafa said.

"Are you keeping track of me for him? Spying?"

"I will not communicate with my father until the training is finished."

"Honestly?"

Shiafa betrayed her first sign of irritation. "Humans may find Sidhe untrustworthy," she said. "But I have never lied in my life. Neither has my father."

"Some Sidhe haven't been allowed that luxury," Michael said, thinking of Biri and Clarkham's Sidhe woman, Mora. "Do you hate humans?"

"You are the first I've ever met."

"Do you sympathize with your father?"

"I have had little contact with my father."

"And your mother?"

"Since my birth, I have never met her." Not knowing one's mother was the reverse of the usual situation for Sidhe, Michael thought.

"I'm going to close my eyes and rest," he said a moment later. He lay back and banked his *hyloka* until he was enveloped in warmth. After some hours had passed, he opened his eyes and saw Shiafa sitting on her slender haunches by the fire, face peaceful, staring into the darkness.

Wary thoughts tickled him. *Magic is passed through the female.*

Dawn came as a sudden steely grayness and a teeth-grating vibration that set the grass shivering. The vibration passed quickly, but it left Michael disoriented and uncertain of where he was and what he was doing. Shiafa was also discomfited.

"Morning has never been that bad," she said. "We must hurry."

Michael had composed another string of questions, but thinking about what he had learned last night—not much of any use—he kept his silence. They mounted the horse. He spread his probe out across the land and felt for the human sign, but his disorientation persisted.

"Everything's changed location," he said. "Nothing is where it was yesterday."

"Dead gods have bad memories," Shiafa said behind him.

"I thought your father was taking Adonna's place."

"He is not stronger than Adonna was," she replied. "And he would have to be much stronger and more clever to hold the Realm together."

Michael concentrated all his effort and fanned his probe in a broad circle, as he had done on Earth. The result was remarkable. For the first time, he felt the *edges* of the Realm—not the chasms paring it like a badly cut pie, but the borders it shared with the between-worlds and the Earth. They were not linear borders, nor even areas of boundary—they were spaces of demarcation, hard to visualize and even harder to think about. *I can learn from witnessing a world falling apart,* he thought. *Learn what, though? How to be a mage?*

Within the borders, still at about the same distance but in a new direction, he found once again the massed human auras. Overall, they seemed little changed from the day before. He bent down to the horse and began to whisper in its ear, then jerked back with a start.

"Is this your horse—the one you'll have to—?"

Shiafa shook her head. "Tarax will bring that one to me. A special horse."

"Then I can impress myself on this horse?"

"You can try," she said. "Not all of Adonna's mounts are so cooperative."

He frowned and reapplied his lips to the naked, warm interior of the horse's ear. "You are my soul, I am your body." The horse shook its ears and twisted its head to stare at him. Again there was that icy, resentful, half-lidded eye, filled with light like a frozen man's dream of fire. "Okay," Michael said. "Unimpressed."

Shiafa smiled, and Michael quickly looked away from her. Very dangerous, a smile on that long, lovely face.

"So we only borrow this horse," Michael said. He stroked its neck and then felt under its ear, along the deep line of its jaw. Through his fingers he passed a kind of out-seeing or *evisa* for the beast. The horse trembled, then trotted across the grass in the direction he had requested.

Michael had decided against any more precipitous *abana*, at least for the time being. The last such journey had not been pleasant; he thought it best to rely on the horse's higher talents only in an emergency. He was even wary of prodding the horse into the spectacular flying gallop its kind could execute so easily. So they moved at a measured pace across the inconstant landscape, passing within hours through areas where both spring and winter ruled.

They found another chasm when they crested a hill and looked across a broad, sparsely forested savannah. Within the chasm, an island tens of miles long—carrying a mountain on its broad back—had pulled away and wobbled ponderously. Chunks office several hundred yards wide hung without support near the island.

"Were you born in the Realm?" Michael asked.

"Yes," Shiafa replied.

"But you've never been to Earth."

She shook her head when he glanced back at her. "My father has been telling me about it recently."

"What do you know about magic? About *lengu spu,* for example—in-speaking."

"I know only the basics," Shiafa said. "Only from one to one. Not to spread wide."

"Can you feel me broadcasting?" -

He allowed her to draw the meaning of that word from his own memory. "Yes," she said. "Like standing before the sun."

"Do you know the three disciplines of combat—*isray, vickay, stray?*"

"I know of them," she said. "Sidhe females are not always trained in those things. The *Mafoc Mar* have other defenses for us to learn."

Michael suddenly realized that he could not train this female the way the Crane Women had trained him. He could use very little of their instruction, in fact . . . because they had trained him as a male. He had no idea how to train a female Sidhe. Shiafa would have to guide him . . . student leading the teacher. "Do you know how to throw a shadow?"

"Yes. We have many kinds of shadow. There is the shadow preparatory to birthing—given out before we are born, to carry away all illness and malformation. That shadow is taken and disposed of by the *Ban Sidhe.* We do that instinctively. And there is the shadow before mating and the shadow of motherhood."

"That's all you know?" Michael asked facetiously.

"It is not," Shiafa said, slightly indignant. "When women fight, we spin shadows like webs to confound our foes—"

"And you know how to do that?"

"No. That you must teach me."

Jesus, Michael thought. "I'm not sure why your father thinks I can train you."

"Nor am I," Shiafa confided. "But he does, and you must."

So be it.

They rode until the quick evening, then set up a temporary camp. In the darkness, they ate a few pieces of overripe fruit from a withered copse of trees.

As the evening lengthened, there was once again a discontinuity, and all locations and directions changed—but this time to their advantage. Michael sensed that the humans were much closer. The next morning, he directed the horse again, and they traveled across another, much wider savannah of emerald grass.

"I think we are near the *Chebal Malen*," Shiafa said. "Can you smell the snow?"

Michael sniffed the air but could not. "It's a little colder," he said. "That might be the seasons changing again."

"I don't think so," Shiafa said.

At the end of that day, they came across the nearly empty basin of what had once been a huge lake, perhaps fifty miles wide and as much as a mile deep, with scattered ponds of water glistening green and stagnant at the basin's bottom. *"Nebchat Len,"* Shiafa said.

"Someone once described this to me as a sea," Michael mused, rubbing his cheek with one finger. "I wonder what drained it . . .?" Then he shook his head and grinned. "I think I know. The Pelagals lived here, didn't they?"

"Here, and in the brazen ocean at the edge of the world," Shiafa said.

"I think most of them are on Earth now. They crossed over in a cataract."

"You saw that?"

He nodded. "Why haven't all the Faer left the Realm yet? Many are already on Earth."

"You are the teacher," Shiafa said quietly.

"That means you don't know."

"It means I don't know."

"All right. We travel around the lake, across the forest called *Konhem*—am I right?—and after that we'll find the *Chebal Malen*, the Black Mountains. And somewhere in the *Chebal Malen* is the *Sklassa*, the fortress of the Maln." He drew his brows together and reached out again to feel for the humans. His heart sank. Beyond any doubt, that was where they were being detained. "We'll have to go there," he said.

"That is not wise. There may not be time, and it is very difficult to reach the *Sklassa*. It is protected." The emotion in her voice went beyond caution. For the first time, Michael detected unease in Shiafa.

"Nevertheless, that's where we're going," Michael said. "That's where all my people are being held. Have you been there?"

"No," she said. "I was raised in Inyas Trai and the Irall."

"What sort of difficulties can we expect to find there?"

"You are the teacher," Shiafa said, somewhat forcefully.

"But you *do* know," Michael persisted.

"I am not supposed to know."

"What does that mean?"

Shiafa turned her eyes away, and an odd, defiant expression—chin outthrust, eyes narrowed—crossed her face. "When I was a child, I listened to the *Mafoc Mar* when I was not supposed to. They were talking with each other about the *Sklassa*. It is not a place for young Sidhe."

"But you're Tarax's daughter," Michael reminded her.

"It is not a place even for me."

"Somehow, I doubt that," Michael said. "What are the difficulties?"

"I cannot tell you."

"I am your teacher," Michael prodded.

Shiafa's eyes widened, and her mouth became a tight, thin line. "We will learn them together, then," she said.

Michael shook his head and smiled. Beginning of the discipline, he thought. Rattle the student, the initiate, and strip away preconceptions. Ultimately, terrify her. That's what the Crane Women had done to him. But who was rattling whom?

If Tarax's daughter was worried by the thought of going to the *Sklassa*, then what should his own attitude be? Michael started the horse on the long journey around the drained basin of *Nebchat Len*, uncertain now whether they could keep up such a torturously slow pace—or whether they would have to use the horse's erratic talents again.

"Perhaps we should hurry," Shiafa said an hour later.

He sighed, then squinted at the empty blue sky. "I agree," he said. "Are you prepared to *aband?*"

"Anything," Shiafa said nervously. "You are the teacher."

"Teacher asks you not to say that any more." Michael leaned down. "Hang on." He whispered in the horse's ear, "*Abana!*"

This time, the ride was much worse.

* * *

They rested in the shadow of a rock overhang, the horse breathing heavily and trembling, its eyes half-closed. Shiafa had collapsed on her side, and Michael had sat down heavily beside her; they had not moved in an hour. "Next time, we'll just try the gallop." Even speaking was a chore. With an effort of will, all his muscles protesting, Michael finally stood and walked out into the glare. Shading his eyes with both hands, he turned toward the black rock of the lower slopes of one of the mountains of *Chebal Malen*. There were no foothills, no gradual ascent to the peaks beyond; the *Chebal Malen* began abruptly as huge, jagged black monsters, mottled with snow up their sides and capped with solid sheets of snow and ice, partly hidden in clouds dipping and wheeling like huge gray and white birds.

"The *Sklassa* is on the opposite side of the *Chebal Malen*, isn't it?" Michael asked, as he stepped back under the overhang.

Shiafa rolled over on her side, head weaving slightly, and said, "Yes."

"We're closer to the Stone Field on this side, aren't we? Where male initiates are taken to be trained."

She nodded.

The *Sklassa* was where he had instructed the horse to go; obviously, it had been unable to comply. So one could not simply *aband* into the fortress of the Maln. He doubted that the horse could make such a climb by galloping, however miraculous an *epon's* gallop could be.

Worse, he could not feel the human auras; he had lost them totally since the last *abana*. "We don't have time to climb the mountains," he said. "And we don't have time to go around them, that's for sure. I don't think we should try to *aband* again."

Shiafa sat up and crossed her legs. "No."

"Any suggestions, then?"

She simply looked disgusted.

Her reaction dismayed Michael. "I've never been here, either," he said. "It's obvious we've run into one of those barriers you mentioned. If you can't tell me what the barriers are, then—" He stopped himself and shook his head vigorously. "This whole stunt is ridiculous. Your father must be a fool."

Shiafa continued to stare at him.

"So how do the Maln get there? A password, specially bred horses? A secret path? A stepping stone?"

Still no reply. Michael paced angrily, then sat on his knees and closed his eyes, feeling, thinking, reaching out to their surroundings. Again he could sense the borders of the Realm inexorably closing in. They had a few days, at best, and toward the end, time would be uncertain.

"All right," he said. "Now is as good a time as any to begin your training. Come with me." Shiafa followed him onto a patch of snow that had filled a shallow, narrow canyon. The black rock reached to twice his height above the snow on each side; at the end of the canyon, about a hundred yards beyond, the walls met in a V.

"What do you think Sidhe magic is?" Michael asked her, taking a stance two paces in front of her, arms folded.

"We all learn that. It is putting yourself in synchrony with the Realm. When your thoughts breathe in, they should match the breathing of the world."

"What if the world isn't so cooperative?"

"You mean, the Earth?"

"Yes."

"Then magic is more difficult, but not impossible."

"Is it impossible for humans to work magic?"

"I do not know. They are not known for being magicians."

"But I'm mostly human. There's some Sidhe blood in all humans by now. So is it necessary to be a Sidhe?"

Shiafa shook her head, unsure.

"Obviously not. But Sidhe, even Breeds, would like to keep humans in their place. And the humans who come here —or who have been brought here—are deliberately kept in the dark. I've come to the conclusion that it doesn't matter what you are. Concentration is the key, and seeing without preconceptions. Do you have preconceptions?"

"I must," Shiafa said, all too reasonably. He had expected some youthful bravado, but then he remembered: she was three times older than he was.

"I certainly do. I believe I'm weak. That makes me weak. I believe in things being a certain way, and they are. Each time I truly break through..." He smiled. He was formulating thoughts heretofore scattered and unorganized. Teaching was also learning, or at least *realizing*. "Each time I break through my preconceptions, I dare something new. Sometimes I succeed. I gain a new ability." There were no flowers nearby. He stooped to pick up a rock the size of a golf ball. "Sidhe dislike casually written words. Writing fixes reality and creates stronger preconceptions. It's dangerous. But any language involves preconceptions. Any communication. That's why words are powerful—they convey the thoughts of others. And the thoughts of others can get in your way." He opened his palm. "What is this?"

"A rock," she said.

He closed his palm . . . trying something he suspected the Crane Women had used on him . . . and opened it again. She smiled at his legerdemain. The rock was a butterfly.

"And what now?" He opened and closed his palm again. His powerful *evisa* seemed to impress her no more than a child's toy.

"A rock," she said.

"Do you know how to be a butterfly and remain a rock?"

"I cast a shadow."

"I'm going to attack you," Michael said abruptly, standing back from her half a dozen paces. It was time to discover what she was capable of. Shiafa was starting out substantially more sophisticated than Michael had been. "No other warning. Prepare yourself."

Shiafa stood, hands hanging at her sides, head lowered slightly. She was still a little woozy from the *abana*. Fine, he thought. Jerk her up out of her uncertainty, just as the Crane Women had done to him.

Suddenly, there were five Michaels surrounding her. She looked from one to the next, turning, raising her hands. One Michael moved in toward her; the next seemed ready to send a sharp probe in her direction; and the next began to circle, grinning. "You can't predict humans," all five said. Then, one by one in the circle, "They're dangerous that way." "They don't know the discipline." "They don't know magic, and they have all the guile and unpredictability of the weak and fearful." "They have emotions even they are not aware of." "They can become angry in a flash. Some are ill-trained and ill-educated, and because of that they are underprivileged, and that makes them vicious." "They can turn on you without warning. I imagine even a few Breeds won't miss a chance to take revenge on you." "And some Breeds know the disciplines. They can assault you with magic." "Humans and

Breeds may join forces to hunt you down. When you go to
Earth, that's the way it could be—hard and bitter times."
"Especially when humans find out their real history. No
mercy. No style, no dignity. Just revenge." "Are you ready for
that?"

"No," Shiafa said, facing the shadows one by one. They
closed in on her.

"Which one of us will you fight first?"

"The real one," Shiafa said.

"How will you fight the real one?"

She shook her head, agitated.

"Think," the shadows intoned together.

"What purpose is this?" she demanded. "I have told you I
do not know how to defend myself."

"I think you do," Michael said.

She frowned and bore down hard with a single probe—
aimed at a shadow. The effort seemed to exhaust her. She
shook her head and made a weak probe at another shadow.
She had wasted her energy by making the first probe too
strong. She should have feather-touched the entire circle in
one sweep, as if politely in-speaking for an item of information, something Sidhe did all the time by instinct. Instead, she
had panicked.

Michael considered probing *her* at this weak moment,
breaking through whatever personal barriers she might have
set up and taking the information he needed about the *Sklassa*.
He would have been justified; a great many lives were at
stake, and as Shiafa had stated repeatedly, they had little time.
But he did not. The shadows continued to move in, a step at a
time, menacing her.

There was something deeper, stronger, far below the surface of her exhaustion and youthful inadequacy. He could
sense it without probing. She was Tarax's daughter. . . . And if
he could get her to reach that far down, *he* might be the one to
learn a lesson.

She straightened. "You are not going to hurt me," she said.
"You are a teacher, not an enemy."

There! He had it. A strong preconception. One of the
shadows turned black as coal and swung a long, night-colored
swath at her from shoulder-level. The swath wrapped around
her head. She struggled to tear it away. It was soaking up her
breath. Michael could feel her discomfort. It was not wrong

for a teacher to inflict discomfort on a student; it was wrong, however, not to share the discomfort. *The Crane Women felt all my pain when they trained me, and all my confusion and fear*, he realized. *They did what I am doing now when they left me under the path of the Amorphal Sidhe*.

Shiafa was genuinely afraid. She could not breathe and she was close to fainting. "Come on," Michael said under his breath. "Dig deep."

She cried out, her voice muffled. Michael felt faint himself and had the urge to run to her and tear away the veil. Then something snapped within her. There was nothing animal within the Sidhe to be unleashed, since they had never been animals, but there were deeper and more primitive layers of Sidhe-ness. Shiafa reached down into one of those layers to perform instinctive magic that—he now knew without doubt —had once been the common heritage of all peoples.

She left a shadow-self wrapped in the black veil and stood outside the circle of Michael's shadows. Lightly, swiftly, she probed the remaining figures and located him. She then reversed the black shadow's net and shot it toward him, tinged red with her own anger.

Michael dodged the veil—but just barely—and dissolved his shadows. They stood facing each other across the snow. "Your feet are cold," he said. "Bring up your *hyloka*."

She fell to her knees. Her cheeks and neck were flushed. "Why?" she asked, her voice harsh.

"Did you feel your strength?" he asked, reaching out to help her stand again.

She did not look at him for a long moment. He had given her a scare. "I felt something . . ."

"That's where we have to begin. You have it in you. It's closer to the surface than it was in me. You have to find it and make it yours. It's like an *epon*. You must impress it."

He led her back beneath the overhang and watched her closely as she sat and controlled her energy levels. Her normal skin color returned.

There was hardly any time to bring out her talents and train her, even less time than the Crane Women had taken with Michael. He had to play with an even more delicate balance, between the trust, or at least respect, necessary between teacher and student and the harsh techniques urgency required.

"Since you won't tell me how we can get into the *Sklassa*, we'll go to the Stone Field. We'll try putting the horse into a gallop. We'll leave as soon as you've recovered."

"I feel it now," Shiafa said, looking at him with wonder. "It's within me. It burns. I wonder I never knew it before."

"Good," Michael said. At the center of his stomach, he felt slightly ill.

At a gallop—if it could be called that—the Sidhe horse was much slower than during an *abana*, but the effects of the Realm's disintegration were much less apparent. They half-rode, half-flew through the passes of the *Chebal Malen*, looking for the trail that would take them to the Stone Field. The horse could not simply scale the tall peaks at a single bound; its flight relied on stable ground in a way Michael could see but not yet understand. The Sidhe horses had flown away from the Tippett Hotel on Earth; they had lifted from the prairie before the startled horse trader. But they could not simply rise tens of thousands of feet up sheer rock precipices.

Shiafa genuinely did not know where such a trail was, or even if one existed. Michael tried again to search for the human or Sidhe auras, but the mountains from this angle seemed absolutely barren of life. There was only monotonous black rock and snow, under the pale sky gone curiously cold in this region.

During their pauses to rest, Michael instructed Shiafa in the proper fine control of her *hyloka*. At the end of the second day, when they had traversed thousands of miles through and around the *Chebal Malen* and still had not found a trail, he guided the horse to ground beside an ice-glazed stream of snow-melt. "Get down," he told Shiafa. His patience was at an end.

She dismounted and stood beside the horse.

"Something has to give," he said, squinting up at the sky. "Some*one* has to give. We're all carrying honor and honesty a bit far. And we're getting nowhere. We can't even reach the Stone Field. I've lost the sense of human auras I felt from far away."

Shiafa looked down at the undisturbed snow around her feet.

"Do you have any suggestions?"

She shook her head.

Michael swore under his breath. "Then that's it," he said. "We go back to the Earth. You've defeated me. We leave the humans here; I doubt the Maln will bring them to the Earth with them. So they'll die in the Realm. All because of a young Sidhe's honor." He thought of Nikolai, of Helena and Savarin and all the others in Euterpe. And he thought of the thousands of humans selected from Earth over millennia, kept in the Realm—humanity's finest. Not even his discipline could quell his anger and frustration. He leaned over to bring his face closer to Shiafa.

"Damn you and your father," he said. "I was an idiot to think there was any possibility—" He couldn't express himself through his anger.

"You will not teach me?" Shiafa asked evenly.

"Hell, no. You can stay here and freeze. I'm going back to Inyas Trai. Maybe I can find a stepping stone there . . . in the few days I have left."

"There is a stepping stone here," Shiafa said.

Michael stared at her.

"You cannot get into the *Sklassa* or the Stone Field from the passes below. You must return to Inyas Trai through the stepping stone, and then you can take a stepping stone to the fortress. Now there is no other way to enter Inyas Trai. The city is forbidden."

"Why are you telling me this now? Why not earlier?"

"Because I need to be trained," Shiafa said. "Whether I die or not is unimportant, but I need to be trained by you. Your training me is more important than my betraying knowledge I should not have."

Michael sniffed and rubbed a sudden itch in his nose. His anger had not yet subsided; he still had half a mind to leave her and go off on his own. But that would have been desperation. "Will you give the horse directions to the stepping stone?" Another idea formed in his head: they might not need to go to Inyas Trai.

"I will," she said.

"Then please do so and climb back on."

She stood by the horse's head and touched it behind the jaw, as he had done, out-seeing the location of the stepping stone. "It is at the edge of the *Chebal Malen,* below the *Sklassa*," she told Michael as she remounted behind him. "It was used long ago, but not recently."

Within hours, they stood on the steps of the largest stepping stone Michael had ever seen. It rose from the floor of a broad rocky valley, at the head of which glowered an immense wall of ice; he could not tell if it was a glacier or something else unique to the Realm. The stepping stone itself was fully a hundred yards wide, circular, with two obelisks positioned beside a twenty-yard-wide slab of white marble at the center. The obelisks were square prisms, featureless and ancient. Drifts of snow formed crescents on the surface of the larger stone.

They crossed the expanse on foot.

Michael climbed the steps to the white slab and stood there with hands extended, hair blowing in the freezing wind. He advanced slowly, feeling for the gate. He passed between the obelisks and turned to look at Shiafa, still standing by the steps. "Nothing," he said. "It's closed."

"I did not know that," she said. "Though perhaps I should have. If the city is forbidden..." If she had been human, Michael would have predicted she was about to cry. But she did not cry.

He balled up his fists and kicked aside a limb of snow from a perfect crescent. More time wasted. *Dig deep.* He let his hands relax. *No sense even thinking about it. Just dig deep and do it.*

He stared down at his hands. The limits of the possible, of his ability.... What were the limits? In the palms of his hands, he could feel the quality of the Realm as a singing tingle. With the exception of his unsuccessful first attempt to reach into the Realm and his escape from Clarkham's near-Earth nightmare, he had used gates made by others, or adapted pre-existing gates for his purpose. Now... to simply create an opening between one spot in a world and another ... he had never done that.

Not the greatest task ever performed. Simple for a very accomplished Sidhe or Breed. In a way, the horses do it when they aband, *and they're just animals. Don't even think about it. Dig deep. Last chance. Do it.*

"Come up here," he told Shiafa. "And bring the horse."

She obeyed and stood beside Michael between the obelisks. He closed his eyes, listening with his palms, feeling the different parts of the song that was the Realm, now discordant, its melody weak and wandering.

Just what you forced Shiafa to do. Find the resources within.

But he had never dug so far into his dark, untried potential. He had never thought it necessary; indeed, he had never known there were such depths to be found. "I'm learning a lesson," he told Shiafa.

"What lesson?"

"Whether you succeed or fail, you are what you dare."

And if I dare to be a mage, against Tarax and Clarkham and all the others?

For an instant, no more, he had absolutely no doubt that he could open a way to the *Sklassa*, completely avoiding the Stone Field, whatever the barriers and defenses. He would simply invert the song, play it back upon itself, add where normally one would find a taking-away, and then take away during the adding . . .

Nonsense.

But it worked. He tore aside a piece of empty air and widened it for the horse. Shiafa stared at his face, radiating heat and power, then at his hand, glowing like a white-hot iron, and passed through with the horse. Michael stepped into the rent and closed it up after him.

As when he had let his *hyloka* run wild, he felt a sense of giddy exaltation. He wanted to skip and dance and shake his hair in the breeze. But their surroundings immediately sobered him.

"The *Sklassa*," Shiafa said, her voice filled with wonder and fear.

28

There was the Spryggla touch about the fortress of the Maln. Michael and Shiafa stood on top of a broad, thick wall of polished black stone. The curved wall was a petal of a huge, squat black flower blooming from a mountain peak. No snow sullied the *Sklassa's* perfect surfaces. Although their images were reflected in the stone beneath their feet, the hot-milk sky was not, and in the depths of the wall, stars gleamed. The flower-fortress might have been carved from a block of space itself.

Between two huge petal-walls hung a spider's bridge of silvery lace. It began barely ten yards from where they stood and ended at a single small wooden door. "This is incredible," Michael said. "It looks simple from here."

"We are not inside yet," Shiafa reminded him.

He could feel the presence of humans very close, but he could not tell how many. "Did Adonna build this?" he asked.

"My father built this," Shiafa said, without pride or any other emotional inflection. "A Spryggla designed it, and Adonna approved the plans, but Tarax supervised the construction."

"A multitalented Sidhe, your father," Michael said lightly. "I assume the only way in is that bridge."

Shiafa nodded. "From what I heard, even that way is uncertain."

Michael was feeling very assured now. He walked toward the near end of the bridge and motioned for Shiafa to follow. "We'll leave the horse here. It's on loan anyway; presumably someone will take care of it if . . ." He smiled at her. "If. I'll cross first. You follow after I've made it through the door."

The span, Michael realized as he touched the guy rope on his left, was a taut and very fancy rope bridge. Its strands, woven into intricate patterns of starbursts, leaves and flowers, gleamed with an inner light, combining the qualities of silk and milk opal. He pushed one foot forward and tested the tension. To his surprise, there was no give; the bridge might as well have been made of iron. Cautiously, he rapped on a guy rope with his hand to see if it would shatter. It did not.

"Nothing ventured, no pain," he said, mixing adages. He put his entire weight on the bridge. Then, slowly at first, he made the crossing. When he stood before the wooden door, he examined it closely, bending down to run a finger along its intricately carved surface. The wood was dark and well-worn, polished by centuries of touch. The carvings, contained in four panels forming a compacted Maltese cross, were of mazes and whorls. At the center of each panel was what appeared to be a schematic flower representing the *Sklassa*. There was no knob or latch.

"Open sesame," he muttered. He tried to grip a panel and pull the door outward, but it was fixed. His palms tingled faintly, and he heard a tune playing under the rhythm of his breath. He brought the tune forward to his lips and whistled it softly. The door recessed a few inches and swung inward. Beyond lay a corridor illuminated in a wedge by the milky daylight outside.

Michael entered the corridor, then turned and called for Shiafa to cross. She did so without mishap. "We need some light," he said. "Do you know how to turn up your *hyloka* and make your hand glow?"

She shook her head. "But I know how to see in the dark."

"Good enough," Michael said.

"Can you?" she asked.

"I can certainly try." He tried and found that with some effort, he could indeed see down the hall as if through a night-vision scope. The hall's green, ghostly image shimmered like a heat mirage. "Will wonders never cease?"

"You do not seem serious," Shiafa observed.

"I do not feel serious," Michael said. "I have had just about enough of Sidhe wonders and portents. This place is incredible. It's beautiful, it's weird, it's powerful—and I don't really care any more. I want to get my people out of here and return to the Earth. And I'm hungry. I'd love a plain old hamburger right now." He glanced at her apologetically. "Pardon my savage heritage."

"Flesh of beasts?" she inquired.

"You got it."

She shuddered. "Will humans stop eating meat if the Sidhe live among them?"

"That's a good question," Michael said. "I don't know the answer."

"That will cause . . ." She touched his aura lightly. "Friction."

He grimaced and chuckled. "I'll worry about it later." The presence of humans was much stronger. Michael tried to determine where they were. "I think we're very close," he said. "I can feel my people everywhere, all around." The hallway ended at a circular shaft about twenty yards across, with a spiral staircase winding around its walls. "Down," Michael said. But he held her shoulder before they descended. "If push comes to shove, are you still committed to your teacher— even against Sidhe?"

"Do not doubt me," Shiafa said in the dark. "Without discipline, I am nothing, and you will teach me the discipline."

They came to the bottom of the shaft. Throughout their time in the *Sklassa*, not once had Michael felt any sign of Sidhe. This lack of sign carried no information to him. The *Sklassa* was a place of unknown qualities, and the Sidhe within it were bound to be watchful, protected—as Shiafa had told him, without being specific. And they would have good reason for protecting the humans now held prisoner within the fortress and for wanting to keep them away from Earth. *There might be hundreds of potential mages here,* Michael thought, not without a tinge of worry. His newfound desire to be a mage rankled like a burr. *Why a mage? Because of the challenge. Because the alternate candidates are so undesirable. And is that all?*

Because of the power. Wouldn't it be something?

The hallway ended abruptly. One moment, Michael was looking at what appeared to be a bend in the hall, and the next, it was a blank wall. He touched the wall tentatively— cold stone. Nothing more. He turned. Behind Shiafa, there was another wall.

"No," he said. "This will not do." He extended his palms

and squeezed around her in the cramped space. "This is one trap you didn't know about?"

She shook her head, her breath coming faster.

"Control yourself," he said. "The air might give out." *And it might not.* Everything... *vibrated* suspiciously. He smiled and felt his power again, like stroking an internal dynamo. It seemed to expand within him, taking its own kind of breath.

"If I were to design the *Sklassa* to be impregnable," he said, turning back to the other wall, "with the power of the Sidhe at my disposal, how would I do it? Would I build physical traps? That seems too obvious. No, I might go for something more ornate, more devious. More a credit to the style and ingenuity of the designer." Concentration was the key to this prison. Shadows could take many forms.

Blue flower, yellow flower. Black flower.

The flower fortress was not real. "We have to close our eyes and clear our thoughts," Michael said. They did so. After a few moments, Michael opened his eyes and touched Shiafa's arm.

They stood at the end of the hard silk bridge, on the flower-petal parapet. The horse blinked curiously at them. The black flower-fortress was losing definition, powdering in the air, the powder swirling and assuming a new shape.

This new shape was less artistic but much more ominous. They now stood on a cliff edge, with the same bridge before them, but the *Sklassa* had become a broad, many-leveled castle. Its walls were rounded like water-worn rocks, and its towers were blunt, squat and featureless, upper surfaces polished gun-metal gray, vertical surfaces streaked with black and rusty brown.

The bridge led to the same wooden door, now embedded in a metallic wall below one of the faceless towers. Michael squinted, his palms still tingling. Shiafa said nothing, watching him with a studied patience he found faintly irritating.

"Why is the door made of wood?" Michael asked.

"I do not know," Shiafa said.

He frowned at her briefly. "Do you believe this shape?" he asked, pointing to the castle.

"I have my doubts," she said.

"So do I." Concentration. Palms extended. The designs could be arrayed like bars, bells and fruit on a wheel inside a slot machine. Any one of them could be real. Choosing one that was not real could result in their being lured into a dream of imprisonment and even death. They might or might not be able to escape from the trap of each false design.

And, of course, it was just as possible that the true *Sklassa* would have traps of its own.

"Adventure," Michael said under his breath. "This part's like a game of Adventure. I never liked that game."

Think it out.

"Here's an exercise for you," Michael said. "I assume you're as ignorant as I am about which design is the real one."

"Yes," Shiafa said. "I have nothing to conceal now."

"If you were building a fortress that would have to be assaulted in a dozen or a hundred different ways, what design would you choose for the actual structure? Thinking like a Spryggla—or a Sidhe overseeing a Spryggla."

Shiafa stared at the gun-metal castle. "In the Realm, the only purpose fortifications would serve would be to defend against a mage. No Sidhe or Breed—much less a human— would think of acting against Adonna."

"That's—" Michael stopped. "Hm. No mages here but Adonna and possibly Clarkham. Did they fear Clarkham? I don't think so. But they must have feared somebody. Who? Waltiri? The Serpent? Did they think their magic would fade?"

"It has," Shiafa said. "The Realm is failing."

Michael was confused. He brushed the confusion aside. In the time remaining to them, they could not afford to speculate endlessly. "No physical barriers would prevent a mage from entering a fortress. These walls and towers are ridiculous. Any other fortress design is equally ridiculous. I don't believe there's a fortress here at all. I think . . . it's a place pleasant to the Sidhe of the Maln. It's the opposite of the Irall, the opposite of cold and dank and hard."

He took his hand and spread it against the image of the castle and then smoothly, with substantial mental effort, wiped the image away like so much dust on a sheet of glass. Shiafa stepped closer to him, and he passed on to her what he saw through gentle *evisa*.

The shining silk bridge now crossed a rushing stream of clear water and green, flowing reeds. Across the bridge lay a meadow of tall blue-green grass and flowers. At the center of the meadow rose a Boschian tower seemingly carved from red coral. The tower was at least as tall as a good-sized sky-scraper, ornately embellished in a style Michael could easily recognize. A Spryggla had designed that tower; it seemed obvious that a Spryggla had sketched all the illusory forms of the *Sklassa* as well.

He crossed the bridge, and she followed. The horse again remained behind, but this time there was some grass on the cliff top for it to crop.

At the sprawling base of the coral tower, covered with vines bearing huge coral-red berries, they found a broad gate carved from transparent crystal and flanked by what looked like ivory posts. Michael pushed gently on the gate, and it opened inward. Between the posts poured a virtual flood of human sign; thousands of humans, and only a few Sidhe.

But among those Sidhe, there was no mistaking the aura of the Ban of Hours. He began to have a glimmer of understanding; the Ban's opposition to the Maln continued, even after the Maln's dissolution. As Shiafa had said, she must be in the *Sklassa* to protect the humans the Maln had gathered over the centuries, and perhaps the humans of Euterpe and the Breeds of Halftown. But where were the other Sidhe of the Maln? Surely there were more than a handful . . .

Overhead, the sky changed abruptly to anthracitic blackness, overlaid by an oily smear of spectral red, green and blue. It was more than a precipitous nightfall; it was the end of the Realm's sky.

The meadow and tower were surrounded by penumbral gloom. All around, the flowers withdrew, and the grass withered. Then, just as the darkness became oppressive, the tower began to gleam from within, a warm and welcoming glow that belied all Michael had heard about the Maln and made him wonder if he had stumbled into yet another illusion.

Even villains would enjoy paradise, he told himself.

"I never knew of this," Shiafa said. They stepped through the crystal gate, between the ivory posts, and stood on a white-tiled floor beneath a broad blue dome mimicking the night-skies of Earth. Each star was a glittering jewel, and thousands of stars were set within the lapis firmament.

Michael looked down from the jeweled sky. A young male Sidhe stood before them, wearing the full black and gray of the Maln, with a red robe beneath. His face was a mask of discipline. For a moment, Michael didn't recognize him.

"You are not expected, man-child," the Sidhe said, smiling faintly. "We thought your work was done here."

"Biri!" Michael said, startled. Biridashwa—with whom he had shared the Crane Women's training, who had attempted to infuse him with poisonous Sidhe philosophy, and who had then contemptuously watched Michael be jerked back to the Earth after the destruction of the pleasure dome. The one-time initiate's red hair had been cut to a skullcap, and his eyes seemed hollow and haunted.

"We have no need for you here," Biri said, advancing on them a step. He held out his right arm, and a wick grew into it, starting as a green branch and ending as a sharp-pointed pike.

Michael looked over the haggard Sidhe with a touch of sadness. "I bring Tarax's daughter—"

"Tarax is no longer of the Maln," Biri said. "He is in the isolation of becoming a mage. His daughter is not our concern."

Michael glanced at the wooden doors set into the circled wall of the chamber. "The Ban of Hours is here. She is protecting some of my people."

"You are a Breed. You have no people but Breeds," Biri said. Michael could almost smell his desperation—and his fear. Stronger than both, however, was the acid hatred that etched the depths behind his blue eyes.

"Nonsense," Michael said almost casually. His assurance was seamless; he was moving over the border into arrogance. Catching himself, he backed away from that danger and smiled politely. "I am here to take my people home."

"Their sentence is absolute," Biri said. "We will not allow you to return them to the Earth."

"Why?"

"You are still a man-child if you do not see."

Michael folded his arms. *Arrogant gesture*, he warned himself. *Don't underestimate this Sidhe. He's fooled you before*.

"I'm sure the Ban of Hours would want to speak with me," Michael said. "Surely you wouldn't deny her that?"

"She is here by pact. She remains with the humans until we all die."

"Who ordains this?"

"I do. I have replaced Tarax as chief of the Maln."

"I didn't know the Maln still existed."

Biri's face paled ever so slightly, giving his skin a mother-of-pearl iridescence that was quite beautiful. "It exists in me," he said. "The Councils are dissolved. Their work is done."

"Now that Tarax is going to be mage."

"Now that the succession is assured."

"They opposed Adonna?"

"In the end, Tarax opposed Adonna. The Councils agreed with his judgment that Adonna was failing."

"So whom are you sacrificing yourself for?" he asked.

"For *my* people," Biri answered.

"By letting all these humans die—and Breeds, and yourself—you think you'll make the Earth safer for Sidhe?"

Biri's jaw was outlined by clenched muscles.

"It's a useless gesture, then," Michael continued. "The Sidhe are overpowered on Earth. Their magic can't win them dominance. They'll have to parley. Killing these humans won't affect that outcome—because my people have already won."

Shiafa stood a step behind Michael, stiff and silent. He could not detect her emotions without lifting his concentration from Biri, which he did not dare do. The wall of discipline behind which Biri stood was strong and only grew stronger under Michael's pressure. He did not want to fight Biri—not yet. *But you'll ultimately have to defeat Tarax, defy the Serpent, deal with Clarkham . . .*

"Is this true?" Biri asked Shiafa.

"As far as I know," Shiafa said.

"There are no strongholds on Earth?"

"Science beats magic," Michael said. "Not for subtlety, perhaps, and not at magic's highest levels—but in the long haul, and with my world as it is now. . . . That's why the Sidhe finally withdrew from Earth."

"There is war on Earth?" Biri's dignified demeanor slipped a little. Clearly, he did not relish the thought of dying—especially without good reason.

"I don't know what's happening on Earth now, but yes, very likely Sidhe and humans are dying. I would like to prevent more deaths. I can't if I'm stuck here."

Biri considered this at some length. "You must leave," he concluded. "The decision is not mine to make."

Biri's defenses, from the moment of his appearance, had

been focused on Michael. They were weak in Shiafa's direction. Michael took his own arrogance and frustration and drew from the center of his *hyloka* as much power as he could spare and remain alive. He held this mix for as long as he dared and then echoed the virulent shadow off Shiafa. Shiafa reeled and barely kept her footing. Biri's eyes widened as the darkness oozed through his defenses and enveloped him. He struggled, but Michael's strength seemed to reverbrate through him; the more anger and frustration Michael felt, the more stymied and impatient, the stronger the shadow became. Within seconds, Biri fell to the tiles.

Michael probed the Sidhe, not knowing precisely what to look for, but knowing it was there. A glowing thread. A cord. The link which held together Biri's discipline.

Someone buried deep within Michael was almost hysterical. *Jesus! Stop doing this! Stop it now, before you eat yourself alive!* But he did not listen. He cut Biri's cord of discipline. Michael glanced at Shiafa, who had slipped to her knees, and then at Biri, who lay on the tiles as weak as an unstringed puppet.

"My apologies," he said to Shiafa.

She did not bother to use English. *"Yassira bettl striks,"* she hissed. "You fight unfairly."

"I suppose there's fairness in smudging out thousands of innocent lives?" Michael asked, shaking his head. "The hell with Sidhe honor. I apologize for using you without asking. There wasn't time."

She stood and looked down at Biri with wide eyes. "He was chief of the Maln. He had great power. . . . Hidden ways of discipline are given to the chief."

I am a bomb again, Michael thought. *More powerful, more of a wild card, every minute. Someone will have to stop me before this is finished, or I'll—*

He shook his head slowly and probed for more Sidhe. There were two others, and one of them was the Ban. He did not think there would be any more opposition. The Sidhe of the Maln had deserted their own fortress, probably to return to Earth— leaving behind only Biri. They had not expected anyone to reach this far into their defenses.

Michael delved into Biri's aura for knowledge of which door to take. The Sidhe rolled over on the tiles and gasped, still in the shadow's grip. Michael considered lifting the shadow, then decided against it. *Don't press your luck.*

He walked across the chamber toward the proper door. Shiafa ran to catch up with him.

"I am afraid of you, Teacher," she said in a harsh whisper. "You do not know all that you do."

"Amen," Michael said. After so many months in the Realm as a helpless pawn, he felt fierce joy at being able to convert his uncertainty and even his fear into weapons. How far could he just glide, stacking victory upon accomplishment? "It's about time the Sidhe face a real challenge on their own territory. I am sick of duty masking cruelty and of hatred and envy disguised as Sidhe honor and purity. The hell with all of you."

He felt a hint of the Serpent's deep rage there and, to negate that, touched the door with unnecessary gentleness, as if caressing Kristine. The wood was rough and unvarnished. As he had half-expected, it spoke to him. "Welcome, Man-child." The voice was familiar to him; that he had not expected. It belonged to the attendant of the Ban whom Michael had met in Inyas Trai while traveling with Nikolai.

"Ulath?"

"I am honored you remember. The Ban awaits you. She is in her chamber."

"Are you dead?" In his experience, only dying Sidhe had their thoughts pressed into wood.

The voice laughed. "No! This door carries only a shadow. There are so few of us here and so much to be vigilant against. Enter, man-child."

29

The door swung inward, and Michael passed through. Shiafa did not. "She stays outside," Ulath explained.

"Why?" Michael asked, though he was relieved not to have her tagging along.

"Please, no questions. You must move quickly."

The floor-plan of the dark, quiet rooms beyond the domed chamber was like a cross section through a lump of pumice. Ulath's voice guided him from one round bubble-room to another, and it took him some effort to remember the path and keep track of where he had been. The floors were covered by resilient carpets in tessellated patterns, brilliant in sun yellow and coral red. Throughout the rooms, translucent silken curtains dyed in leaf, floral and geometric patterns were suspended from bars reaching wall to wall.

This was not at all what Michael had imagined the fortress of the Maln to look like. There was a feminine sensibility and elegance to the place that completely contrasted with the Maln's age-long activities.

"Stop," Ulath's voice gently commanded when he stood at the center of another large, domed chamber, very much like the first. Overhead, however, was a sophisticated mimicry of day, with soft cloud-patterns weaving back and forth and a gold-leaf stylized sun at zenith, its rays spreading out like branches from an incandescent tree.

Through a door on the opposite side, a Sidhe female in a cream-colored robe with red trim entered. Michael recognized the warm brown skin and black hair, the full lips and eyebrows wryly askew: Mora, who had once been Clarkham's consort. She smiled warmly, but with an edge of guilty tension, and approached Michael slowly, her gown trailing.

"You surprise us all," she said. "The Sidhe thought they were done with you. Even the Ban."

Michael nodded. "I had to . . . fight Biri to get in here. Subdue him."

She did not seem distressed. "Then you've grown remarkably strong. Biri is not easily overcome." She sensed Michael's unease at her lack of sympathy. Biri, he had learned during his last few minutes in Clarkham's Xanadu, had been her lover, and she had served Clarkham only in the interests of the Sidhe. "I have been sequestered here, away from Biri, that I might not endanger his accession." Her eyes searched him for any further response, but he kept his reactions under tight control. "Why have you returned?"

"I'm here to bring the Realm's humans back to Earth."

"If you can do that, you will have our cooperation. The stepping stone gates to Earth have been closed; we are not sure by whom."

"Perhaps Tarax," Michael suggested.

"Perhaps. At any rate, Ulath tells me we should arrange a meeting with the Ban, and with Mahler, with whom you are, I believe, familiar."

"I've heard some of his music," Michael said. "Waltiri met him . . . knew him, once. They corresponded." His eyebrows lifted. "He's *here?* Alive?"

"Yes. We also have a human named Mozart. . . . He and Mahler have quarreled some in the past. Debated is perhaps a better word. Mozart was astonished when the Ban allowed Mahler to confer with a human on Earth."

"When was this?" Michael asked.

"Recently. Days or weeks or months past on Earth. The conspiracies have not even begun to spin themselves out, Michael. Plays of power and flights of intrigue. Mahler can convey your plans to the others kept here."

"How many are there?" Michael asked.

"Five thousand and twenty-one. Artists, writers of poetry and fiction, storytellers, composers, potters, dancers, dreamers . . ."

"All . . . recent?" *Days, months . . . centuries?*

"Heavens, no," Mora said, laughing lightly. "The Maln has

been collecting them for ten thousand years, ever since the end of the *Paradiso*. The Ban was appointed by Adonna to watch over them."

"Then . . . Emma Livry was not the only one brought here."

"No. Not at all. She was a special case, because of her suffering. The Maln allowed the Ban to bring her to the Realm, even though she was no longer a danger to them—and of no use to their archrival, Clarkham. Other humans whom the Maln ignored until they proved to be a threat were the most unfortunate . . . Mahler and Mozart among them."

Michael shook his head in wonder. "And the prisoners from Euterpe?"

"They are here."

"Nikolai?"

"After his brief venture on Earth. His journey alerted Biri, who may or may not have acted under Tarax's orders in shutting down the stepping stone in Inyas Trai reserved for humans."

"Then the Ban was going to return them to Earth."

"Of course. They cannot stay here."

"So you are all prisoners . . . and Biri is your guard?"

"There are other guards," Mora said, with a delicate shudder. "The Realm has become much more . . . creative, let us say, since Adonna's passage. The Maln has taken advantage of this. Leaving will be much more difficult than getting in."

I should have thought as much. "I'd like to see the Ban now," Michael said.

Mora nodded once and withdrew. Michael took a deep breath and prepared himself; at their last meeting, the Ban had been in complete control—time had seemed to stop, and his memories of her had emerged only after hours of contemplation, emerged in just the right order to convey what the Ban had wished him to know: that he was a pawn.

Her magic was of a peculiar kind, he could see from this more experienced perspective. It was not an active magic; it was passive. It did not assert and create and destroy; it nurtured and cherished and allowed development. She was none the less powerful for that.

And she had not followed her sister, Elme, in defying their father, Tonn, mage of the Sidhe. She had remained loyal to Tonn—later Adonna, God of the Realm. In return, Adonna had granted her a place and position in Inyas Trai and had supported at least some of her efforts to help the humans in the Realm. *Then had she really differed from Elme? In tactics, perhaps, but not intent?*

He heard and felt her approach. Her aura was broad and comforting—and also, more than a little deluding. He penetrated the delusion and found warmth beneath. He also found something that drew tears to his eyes and a fullness to his throat.

The Ban of Hours stepped through the doorway, followed by Ulath. The daylight dome seemed to come alive with a greenhouse heat. She was tall, dressed in a gown the color of clouds covering the sun, with silver and gold trimming the sleeves and hem. She moved silently, gliding across the floor with the ease of a dancer—*Kristine is almost that graceful*—and smiling at him. Her eyes were the only cold thing about her, as dark and intensely blue-green as the ice beneath the Realm, but the coldness was enhanced by contrast rather than detracting. She was nurturing, but she was not to be trifled with, her eyes said.

And she was using none of the tactics she had used on him during their last meeting. She was not greeting him as a pawn or a weak supplicant.

Her gold-red hair was restrained by a white scarf that trailed down her back. She held her hand out to Michael, and he took it, bending automatically to kiss it.

"Welcome," she said. "Friend of Nikolai and one-time weapon of the Councils, now burst his bonds and turned rogue." Her smile was dazzling, conveying gentle humor and no hint of superiority.

She's treating me as an equal . . . or an ally, Michael realized. *Even though I don't yet deserve it. She nurtures what is in me.*

"Thank you," Michael said quietly. "I am honored to be in your presence again, Mother." The honorific surprised him some, but it seemed completely appropriate.

"Unfortunately, there is little time to discuss matters, and not even we can hold back the death of my father's creation. Not even if we join hands and concentrate all our combined power."

She held out her hands, and he took them. The sensation that passed back and forth was stunning, an echo of some of the abilities he had felt springing unwilled and unknown from within him. In the Ban, however, these abilities, though weaker (!), were controlled, fully realized. "Not even then," she added softly. "How will you save our humans and Breeds?"

"I'm not sure yet," Michael said. "I have to know what guards the *Sklassa* and whether I can open a path to Earth big enough, or for a long enough time."

"You already advance beyond me, if you contemplate such acts," the Ban said. "Only the tribal sorcerers—and my father, of course—could do such things, and they are nearly all on Earth now, with their people."

"What I have . . . what I am . . . is not developed, Mother," he confessed. "I do not know my limits. I might be dangerous."

"Oh, yes, you are that. But you are the last chance we have. You have seen the true *Sklassa*, I assume?"

He nodded. "It is not what I expected."

"The illusions of fortresses and horrors . . . something of a joke for my father, I fear. He ordered Tarax to create this refuge that he might bring Sidhe males and females together in harmony. The Maln administered this fastness. Here they brought Sidhe of all races from around the Realm, to reconcile . . ." She was suddenly sad. "We have been declining for millions of years. The *Sklassa* was kept secret because it was not a center of raw power, but only of hope. And the hope was not fulfilled. Few children were born here. Not even Tarax's daughter, though he took a wife in the *Sklassa*. The wife is dead now. Most of the women who came here did not live, or wished they might not . . ."

There was a darkness in the Ban at that moment that chilled Michael to the bone. The Sidhe were a dying race. Even the Ban had given up hope for them.

"You have brought her with you, have you not?" she asked. "Tarax's daughter, Shiafa?"

"Yes."

"And she will come with us to Earth, should you succeed?"

He nodded. "I'm her teacher, for the time being."

"Yes. She will teach you much," the Ban said. "Now it would help you, I think, to see the quarters of your brothers and sisters, to look over our preparations for the end and to meet our Mahler. He can tell you more that could be useful."

The Ban dismissed him with a distant smile. Ulath took

Michael's hand and led him through another door. "The Ban is very tired," she explained. "Adonna's death and the difficulties since have taken more than even she can give."

"How did you come to be here?" Michael asked. "And where is the rest of the Maln?"

"The Ban insisted that she stay with the humans when Tarax brought them here from Inyas Trai and other refuges in the Realm. Adonna was still alive then and had some influence, though waning. The Maln disbanded shortly thereafter, that the tribal and racial sorcerers might focus on the problem of the dissipation."

They walked through a sinuous corridor, passing many wooden doors with names scratched on them in Roman and other alphabets.

"Dissipation?"

"When the Realm finally breaks up, it must dissipate. Since the Realm is not far from Earth as worlds go, its end will have an effect."

"I haven't given much thought to that."

"It will change Earth's reality, and much time will pass before the influence of the surrounding reality of Earth will stabilize things."

At the end of the corridor, Ulath held open another thick wooden door for him. Beyond lay a vast ruined garden, rising to hills crested by dying trees and rugged upthrusts of black rock and falling into what might have once been leafy glens. Michael experienced a sharp disorientation; where was the tower? Behind them was only the door in a low cylindrical brick structure like a squat silo. And the sky was not oily slate but a dusty dark gray-blue, like the twilight of the between-worlds.

Across the garden, strolling singly or in groups, were men and women—humans—dressed in Sidhe garb, white *seplas* and long gray robes. The nearest man, a middle-aged oriental, looked on Ulath and Michael with some interest but did not approach.

"Our humans," Ulath said, smiling. "The Ban has come to think of them as her children—and indeed, she is in a way their aunt."

"Where are we?" Michael asked.

"We are still in the tower. The walls themselves have out-seeing pressed into their fabric. The Ban and Adonna designed this thousands of years ago, that Sidhe might court and find peace. It has not been tended of late."

"I see that. It's sad."

"We are a sad race," Ulath said lightly. They followed a stone path weaving through the hills. Here and there, houses much like the hut of the Crane Women rose in the middle of spinneys of skeletal trees. "Some have chosen to live here, some in the tower."

"And outside the tower?"

"Biri gathered Adonna's abortions and placed them in the grounds around the tower. No one goes there."

Ahead, standing alone on a hill overlooking a lead-colored lake, was a house unlike the others, small and square, surrounded by a rickety porch. The house had apparently been recently assembled in some haste and lacked the ancient stolidity of the other buildings.

A door was half-open on the side facing away from the lake. Ulath knocked lightly on the frame.

A small man, thin and slightly stooped, opened the door and stared at Michael and Ulath over pince-nez glasses perched on a blade-sharp aquiline nose. His gray-unto-white hair flowed back from a high forehead, topping almost emaciated features; he radiated an intensity that Michael found fascinating.

"This is our savior?" the man asked in English with a soft Viennese accent.

"This is Michael Perrin," Ulath said. "I believe you are acquainted with Gustav Mahler."

Michael hesitantly extended his hand, and Mahler looked down on it with a frown, then grasped it with both hands and shook it vigorously.

"Please come in," Mahler said. The room beyond was sparely furnished with wicker and wood. There was a small writing table and chair beneath a piece of tattered gray and black floral-patterned Sidhe fabric. The table held layers of dozens of sheets of handmade paper, creamy and rough-edged, covered with hastily scrawled musical notes and blots of watery ink. A goose-quill lay near one of the fresh blots. On the opposite side of the room stretched a narrow wicker cot covered with a richly woven red rug. The walls of the room were bare but for dead branches strung up in the corners, reaching out like withered hands.

Michael hardly knew what to say. Mahler had supposedly been dead for eighty years, yet this man matched the pictures Kristine had shown him, though he appeared some years older. Remembering the extraordinary music in Royce Hall increased Michael's awe.

With the Ban of Hours, he had stood before a magical presence, an age-old personality enhanced by inhuman power and the mystique of the Sidhe. Mahler was human—not even measurably a Breed, as Michael was—and his accomplishments had been purely human, and mortal.

"Did it go well? Were you there?" Mahler asked.

"I'm sorry?"

"The performance. The new orchestration of my symphony, my Tenth."

"Yes. It went very well," Michael said.

Mahler rubbed his bony hands together. "Ah! Good," he said almost as one word. "Ah yes good. The *Jungling* Berthold Crooke was skillful. I came to his dreams. I hinted, pushed, and he was kind enough to listen. It was frustrating not to be there *incarnatus*, but then, I am a ghost, no? A muse.

"I don't know much about the Earth now. What I was shown in the past . . . discouraged me. But it still has music. My music is still listened to. More . . ." He took a deep breath. "More popular than when I was alive, I understand. And all the ways you have to listen to it . . . !" Abruptly his face, which had assumed a mask of angelic enthusiasm, paled and stiffened. He glared at Michael and gestured for him to sit on a second wicker chair. He then pulled out the desk chair and sat on it, hunched forward with elbows resting on his knees, hands clasping each other. "Can you return us to Earth? Bring us all to life again?"

"I came here to try," Michael said.

"Is my . . . is my daughter still alive? Is Anna still alive?"

Michael glanced at Ulath. "I don't know."

"After I was taken, after I *died,* your . . . they put her through such *hell.*" Mahler shook his head furiously, face flushing. "I vowed I would never have anything to do with Earth after I was shown, after the Maln . . . Tarax, the damned son of a whore, after he showed me."

"I don't understand," Michael said.

"They convinced me to work for them," Mahler said. "The

Maln let me see what was happening on Earth. Alma! She I
could understand and forgive, though that Werfel fellow..."
He shook his head sadly. His emotions flashed like shadows of
clouds passing over a landscape. "But my last daughter! My
only daughter!"

Michael was still puzzled.

"You do not know about them, the camps, the guards, the
ovens? They made my daughter conduct music for human
monstrosities. They made her play music to entertain the ones
who could have killed her, who were killing all those around
her. I saw this, and I *hated*. I *hated* my own countrymen. I
swore I would never..." He stood up and leaned on the desk,
facing away from Michael. His gestures were stage-dramatic,
but his strength of feeling was beyond question.

Michael gently probed the man and emerged with a confusion of horrifying images: the concentration camps constructed by Germans in Europe before and during the Second
World War. "The Maln showed you these things?" Michael
asked, incredulous.

"Yes. Jews. Gypsies. Catholics. Children. Old men and
women. My entire *world*, consumed by wars! I blessed the
day I was taken away from the foulness of the Earth."

Mahler's cheeks were wet with tears. He suddenly straightened, pressing his hands into the small of his back, and stared
at Michael with a sad, dreamy expression. "They wanted
songs from me. Songs I wrote for them. But nothing like the
symphony, my Tenth. I am not of Earth now, and my strength
has always been in the Earth. *Erde*. My mother, mother of
skies and fields and woods." He held up his hands and nodded
forcefully, thrusting his long chin forward.

"All right. Here is what they told me. They said my music,
my Tenth, was a Song of Power. They said if performed properly, it could let this Realm die gently and pass into the Earth
without destroying it. It could harmonize the two worlds. So I
worked in the dreams of this young man, this finisher of a
symphony I was not allowed to complete because of the Sidhe
in the first place!" He smiled ironically, and despite himself,
Michael smiled along with him. "They will all tell you. I am a
bastard to work with. A perfectionist. Not unreasonable, but
demanding of perfection. I could not expect perfection, direct-
ing the young man like a puppet master with half the strings
cut. But I could expect *power*, and apparently . . . that is what

I have gotten. Without my music . . ." He threw his hands out, fingers spread. "Without that, the Sidhe would return to our world and find themselves crushed not long after by the death of the Realm."

"The Maln explained all this to you?" Michael asked. He was piecing together an impression of the Maln very different from the one he had picked up on his first visit.

"They never lied to me," Mahler said solemnly. "They have treated all of us well. . . . Once we were brought here. Their only torture was to show us what was happening on Earth. Our children and grandchildren killed, cities burned, madness and madmen. 'This is your humanity,' they said."

Michael felt a sharp tickle of anger. "Did they show you other things? Humans conquering disease, trying to work against plagues and famine? Going to the Moon?"

Mahler shook his head as if that did not matter. "What they showed was the truth." He gave Michael a hard look. "Going to the Moon?"

Michael nodded. "Landing on the Moon."

Ulath spoke. "Your people were shown only what the Maln considered appropriate, and only in special cases."

Softly, dreamily, Mahler said, "They claimed Sidhe had been to the Moon, and beyond, by magic . . ." He sat again. "I was shown machines that play music, writing it down— recording it. The Sidhe can do that too. They can conjure an entire orchestra out of thin air . . ." He snapped his fingers. "They wanted me to understand that everything on Earth, everything done by humans, they could do as well. So confusing."

Michael pushed back his anger and followed an inner thread of thought, unwinding so rapidly he could hardly keep up. He saw things rather than traced their progression: the Realm's edges meeting the boundaries of the Earth and smoothing out across the landscape—the mental landscape, the physical landscape.

Even with Mahler's Song of Power in effect, the Realm's death would change the Earth's reality. Everything remaining in the Realm would be destroyed. But there was no way he could open a gate for five thousand people. That might not be the best method, anyway.

Again Michael felt the cold dagger-twist of uncertainty. He closed his eyes for several seconds and fought back his fear.

What I am thinking of doing . . . not thinking, seeing myself do. . . . You are what you dare. Succeed or fail.

He stood and gripped Mahler's extended hands. "Can you improvise a composition?"

A large black man entered the cabin, saw Ulath and Michael and deeply bowed toward the Ban's attendant with hands folded before him. "Excuse me," he said, his voice deep as a drum. "Gustav, the committee is meeting in the tower. Bes Amato and Hillel ask that you be there. Again they want to move 'Die Zauberflöte.'"

Michael easily read the man's aura. He was—or had been more than two thousand years ago—a soldier in the army of the Mauretanian king Bocchus. Michael did not know enough about this period to make much sense of the man's memories. He seemed to have been a storyteller, a singer and an archer.

"This is Uffas," Mahler explained. "He is superintendent of our pageant."

"What pageant?" Michael said.

"Music, drama, dancing," Mahler said. "To celebrate our release by death from captivity. Uffas, the committee should know we may not have time to put on the pageant. This man is here to save us."

Uffas regarded Michael with a mild, almost placid suspicion. "We've planned for many months," he said.

Mahler placed his arm on the huge black's lower shoulder. "Uffas, how long have you been here?"

"Centuries. I do not know."

"And what did you do?"

"I sang and told stories for the Sidhe."

"Like my daughter," Mahler said quietly, eyes on Michael. He looked at Ulath, tall and still. "Like Anna, playing for the monsters. Tell the committee nothing. Let them plan. Perhaps there will be time, and we will celebrate something else. Living."

Uffas left, and Mahler closed the door behind him. "I am sorry. What were you asking me before Uffas came?"

"Can you play music on a piano, new music, without a score, without composing ahead of time?"

Mahler's eyes became languid. "Not well," he said. "But I know one who can."

"Who?"

"Wolferl," Mahler said. "Mozart. He excels at that sort of

display. Why is this talent necessary?"

"I'll need music to save us," Michael said. "An extemporaneous Song of Power."

Mahler smiled broadly. "Mozart has been bored, you know. Like me, like most of us, he prefers the drama and pain of Earth to this limbo. I hope the Ban does not think us ungrateful.... But that is the way it is. Mozart and I have argued much in the past. But I think he will agree to try."

Michael told Ulath what would be necessary. "And bring Shiafa here," he added.

"The Ban does not want her in the *Sklassa*," Ulath said.

"Tell the Ban I will need her," Michael said firmly. His *hubris* led him to defy even the Ban of Hours! He turned again to Mahler. "Where is Mozart now?" he asked, the back of his eyes again warming with an inexpressible wonder. *Mozart!*

"Follow me," Mahler said. "If he is not talking or playing music, he will be in his room in the tower."

30

Wolfgang Amadeus Mozart, who had allegedly died on Earth at the age of thirty-five of typhus, had left the wooden door and curtain of his chamber open. Mahler knocked lightly on the coral wall and then held his hand to his lips and turned to Michael. "He is napping," he said, almost reverently. "We will not—"

"We don't have a choice," Michael said. The three of them entered the room. Mozart lay on a wicker couch covered with a single brown blanket. He wore a gray robe embroidered with black leaves. The robe was obviously meant for a Sidhe and fell below his feet. His paunch was clearly outlined by the finely woven cloth. Michael stood over him and bent down to touch his shoulder.

Mozart opened his eyes and glanced up at Michael, then turned his head to see Mahler standing in the door. "Ah, God, Gustav, not now," he said in German. "I'm sleeping. We'll talk about the pageant later." He returned his gaze to Michael and half-sat in the bed. "You're in my room," he said shortly. "Don't gawk."

Mozart resembled a very wise, sad child. He might have been thirty, or he might have been forty—his apparent age had settled at some indefinite point, leaving him suspended between middle age and late adulthood. His large eyes protruded slightly but seemed sympathetic even when he was irritated. His thinning brown hair was cut short and carefully combed back.

No wig, Michael thought. "We need you," he said. "We're going back to Earth."

Mozart blinked and then smiled. "Mahler, too?" he asked.

"All of us."

"If Mahler's going back, I don't want anything to do with it."

"Wolferl," Mahler chided. "We argue," he said to Michael, "but we are friends."

"The hell you say." Mozart kept his gaze on Michael, exploring his face like a landscape. "Who are you?"

"I'm from Earth," Michael said. "Recently."

"Yes, but *who* are you?"

"My name is Michael Perrin," he replied. "If that's any answer."

"It isn't," Mozart murmured.

"We must hurry."

"Is this correct?" Mozart asked Ulath, who nodded once. "All right," he said grudgingly, sitting on the edge of the couch. "Good riddance to this *Ort.* Any way out. It's all been a mighty pain in the arse."

Michael turned to Ulath. "Is there a large hall here, where everyone can be assembled?"

"Yes. At the top of the tower. The arena of the skies."

"It's reserved for the pageant," Mozart said. "Is the pageant canceled?"

"Please tell the Ban that everybody in the *Sklassa* who

wishes to return to Earth—who wishes to live—must be assembled in the arena soon. You have a piano here, don't you?"

"Yes," Ulath said. "And other human instruments—we brought them with us, with the Maln's permission—"

"For the pageant. Such singers assembled for my opera! The Ban herself to play the Queen of the Night, and Uffas—did you meet Uffas? To be Monostatos—"

"Just a piano. Please have it placed in the arena."

"What *is* all this?" Mozart asked indignantly.

"You know that music can send humans to the Realm?" Michael asked.

"Yes." Mozart smiled, baring uneven teeth. "I wrote quite a bit of that sort of music. So I'm told." He favored Ulath with a wink.

"We're going to try the reverse. You must play music that will transport us to Earth. You must play the finest and the most enchanting music you've ever played."

Mozart gaped at Michael. "You put him up to this," he accused Mahler.

"Can you do it?" Mahler challenged.

Mozart shrugged. "Let me get dressed. No rehearsals?"

"There isn't time," Michael said.

"Of course I can do it," Mozart grumbled. "I'm surprised nobody asked me earlier. '*Wir wandeln durch die Tones Macht, /Froh durch des Todes düstre Nacht.*' Do you know that?"

Michael said he did not.

"'We walk with music as our might /In cheer through Death's own darkest night!' Pity, if the pageant is canceled, you won't hear that sung. We have the most *engelgleich* voices here. But despite that, I've spent some very dull decades in the company of nothing but Faeries and arse-head geniuses. Very trying." He swung his legs off the cot, stood, stretched his arms out and spun around. "What shall I wear?"

"Formal attire, I suggest," Mahler said.

"Yes. My best. Now please leave, all of you."

Michael returned to the outer courtyard to check on Biri's condition. He found him as he had left him, still helplessly bound by the shadow. Biri regarded him through the shadow's dark strands with the calmness of a trussed pig, resigned to slaughter.

"What are we going to do?" Michael asked him. "Do you still oppose me?"

Biri said nothing.

"You told me never to trust a Sidhe. But I've been told by the people here that the Sidhe never lied to them. I think . . ." He knelt to bring his face closer to Biri's. "I think you've been used as much as I have by the Maln and all the others. Mora was used, too. You've been sacrificed. That much should be obvious to you by now. They left you here to die."

Biri turned his face away and stared at the tiles.

"Well, you've failed. But you shouldn't have to die. One way or another, if we succeed, you'll be coming back with us. I'll ask the Ban to watch over you. I may keep you wrapped in this shadow. But you're going to Earth."

"I am disgraced," Biri said. "Better by far to kill me."

"Nonsense," Michael said. "There's too much work to do. We have to help your people on Earth. I'll certainly need assistance. I think the time for lies is over. Will you help?"

Biri's face had gone pearly-ashen in color. "You say we are all pawns."

"And we're moving into the end-game. Most of the powerful pieces are gone. Pawns are very important. We're marching across the board. Do you play chess?"

"The Sidhe do not play human games. I am aware of its rules."

"Then you know that a pawn can become a very powerful piece if it crosses the board."

"Yes, but it cannot become a king."

Michael shrugged. "Rules change. Would I be stupid to trust you now?"

Biri looked directly into Michael's eyes.

The shadow dissipated at Michael's touch. "We're gathering in the arena," he said.

At the top of the tower, they could see across all that was left of the Realm. Chasms had absorbed huge sections; the territories around the *Chebal Malen* had been pierced by upthrust needles of ice. All around, the land seemed in constant motion, heaving and quaking in a slow, spastic dance.

Michael stood at the edge of the arena, beneath the glistening black sky, watching the five thousand humans file through the central doors around the stage. The arena had been designed to hold perhaps four thousand; the performance would be crowded, but all would get to hear.

Shiafa approached him along the walkway. Her hair had grown unkempt and stringy. Michael thought she had the aspect of an ill-treated human adolescent; he realized, with a pang, that she was as frightened and unhappy as any Sidhe he had ever met. She thought they were all going to die soon, and she no longer trusted her teacher. "Why do you need me here?" she asked. "I am not welcome. They think my father has tainted me."

"Magic is passed through the female," Michael said. "I don't want your magic for myself, but to help us go to Earth. There's no time to do it subtly, so I'll have to . . ." He shook his head. "I can't even describe it. When we're done, you'll know your potential, and you'll need much less training."

"Do you know what you're doing?" she asked.

"No," Michael said. "Not exactly." *It might kill us all*.

She looked out over the mountains. From where they stood, they could see the deserted Stone Field and the empty basin of *Nebchat Len*. "My father does not know you," she said. "You do not think like a Sidhe. Nor do you think like a human."

Michael nodded, not really listening. He was absorbed in some inner dialogue which he could only follow in part; a dialogue between the various parts of himself, all his voices coming together. They could not stand apart within him now. When this was done, he would no longer be able to isolate a part of himself and sacrifice it as a shadow; the only shadow he would throw would be the one attendant upon his death. He would lose this neophyte ability. *You've already lost Michael Perrin. Where is he, among all these voices?*

"I don't think the Realm has more than an hour remaining," Michael said. He could feel an almost nauseating vibration in his palms.

Three people pushed their way through the crowd in the upper tiers of the arena. They broke into the clear and climbed the steps to the walkway, approaching Michael and Shiafa. Michael saw Nikolai first among them and smiled broadly, then hesitated as he saw Savarin and Helena trailing him. But

there was no bitterness left in him now. He had sacrificed
those shadows long ago.

Nikolai ran toward Michael and hugged him vigorously.
"We're all here!" the Russian enthused, his face red from ex-
ertion. "Ah, all that has happened since I tried to escape! But
we're here, all of Euterpe . . . Emma Livry and the others . . .
and you!"

Helena smiled nervously, hanging back. Michael extended
his hands to them as Nikolai stepped aside. "Friends," he said.
Helena swallowed hard and took his hand firmly in hers. Savarin nodded solemnly and did likewise. Nikolai removed a
handkerchief and loudly blew his nose. There were tears in
their eyes, he saw with another pang. In the middle of his
interior preparations, he could not feel such strong emotions.

"So wonderful," Nikolai continued. "We will all be together when it ends."

"It isn't ending," Michael said. "We're returning to Earth.
We're going back the same way you came."

"There was a rumor . . ." Savarin said. "Mozart is going to
play. . . . And the pageant is canceled. Is that true?"

Michael nodded.

Helena glanced over Michael's shoulder at Shiafa, her eyes
narrowing. Helena had aged noticeably—she appeared to be
thirty or older. Michael doubted that so many years had passed
in the Realm.

"You should find your seats now," Michael said.

"You will not believe who is here with us!" Nikolai enthused. "Besides Mozart. People we've never heard of, but
wonderful artists and—" He saw Michael's concern and
clasped his own hands together before him. "Later. We talk
later." He ushered Savarin and Helena down the steps to seats
below the walkway.

The faces of the crowd filling the arena were as varied as
the leaves on an autumn tree. Michael saw all races repre-
sented, and with some surprise—would he ever be beyond
surprise?—he realized that more than half, perhaps three out
of four of the humans assembled were women.

These were the best, the ones the Sidhe had thought the
most likely to imperil their position as the supreme people on
Earth. They had been gathered by the Maln across thousands
of years and brought to the Realm . . . and most of them were
women.

Magic is passed through the female. Was that adage, or something like it, true for both Sidhe and humans? And did the proportions of the crowd filling the arena explain a major curiosity about the arts on Earth—the predominance of men?

A single broad aisle without seats was left mostly clear. Michael and Shiafa descended the steps between a few standing humans dressed in Sidhe garb and makeshift styles from their own eras. They watched Michael and Shiafa pass without a word, and from them Michael felt that thing he had always assumed was the difference between humans and Sidhe: a strong sense of reserve and style, of discretion. He also felt the strength of their personalities and saw the clarity of their eyes, whatever age they had finally settled on in the Realm's odd scale of time, and the expressions of calm anticipation. There was fear, but no panic; concern, but no hysteria. They all fully expected to die soon, but they were prepared and self-possessed.

Michael and Shiafa came to the center of the arena, an elliptical stage about sixty feet wide in one direction and thirty feet deep. The ponderous black grand piano was already on stage, its lid opened.

Could the Song of Power be played with just a piano? Waltiri's concerto and Mahler's symphony required complete orchestras . . . but then, they had been patterned for many instruments. Mozart's playing would not be so patterned. Scale was not the secret—it was the subtlety of design. And if the music was not enough. . . . Then Michael would engage his own power, and Shiafa's.

But there had been an expression in Mozart's protruding eyes. . . . There was more to magic than could be encompassed in Sidhe disciplines.

Michael looked around the inner circle of benches and saw Ulath and the Ban of Hours seated nearby. Ulath regarded him with calm expectation. Beside the Ban sat the delicately beautiful dancer Emma Livry and her odd, thin woman companion. Emma was not looking in Michael's direction; she was waiting for Mozart, her rapt attention fixed on the stage.

Mahler was nowhere to be seen.

Michael's impatience grew. He probed for Mozart and found the composer waiting in a small dark room beneath the stage, talking quietly with Mahler. Mozart's mental state was unperturbed, almost casual, but the energy within was enormous, and his confidence was a wonder to feel. *He doesn't doubt he will succeed*, Michael realized. *You are what you dare*.

Already, time was beginning to play tricks. As the Realm condensed and collapsed, fragments shredding and rotting away, even within the *Sklassa* he could feel the deep tremors of each moment straining to pass, each second shuddering with a kind of pain.

Mozart took a deep breath and left the small room, climbing a short flight of steps onto the stage. He wore a sky-blue coat, short white kneepants and high stockings, and a powdered white wig. The Ban smiled upon seeing him, and Michael realized that Mozart, like Livry, had been one of the Ban's favorites.

Michael probed his memories, saw a ghostly figure in gray commissioning Mozart to write a requiem . . . and the Maln moving in to end his career on Earth before he could finish the requiem—

Clarkham! The figure in gray, as Moffat had heard, could have been no other. Mozart had almost certainly been Clarkham's first victim, even before Coleridge.

Once again the emotion he felt toward Clarkham lay rich and heavy in him, not precisely anger, but a kind of *necessity*.

Michael's thoughts came to an abrupt dividing line. He looked across the stage, where Mozart was even now sitting at the piano, as casually as if he were alone.

Beneath the oily black sky, with time's heartbeat fluttering in his palms like a wounded dove, Michael felt tears running down his cheeks.

You'll kill yourself. Say good-bye to everything you've ever been. There's a sixteen-year-old boy still buried in you who wants nothing more than a normal adolescence. You'll kill him; he is you. A new person starts here, not normal, weighed down with impossible responsibilities. He thought of the key and Waltiri's note and the door through Clarkham's house. If he had simply left that avenue untraveled, would any of this have happened? Would he have involved himself in this incredibly convoluted, beautiful, horrible nightmare? It seemed that all of reality had changed when he entered that door.

The Jehovah's Witnesses, with their crazy and unshakable convictions about history and prophecy, about the way the universe was. . . . Were they any crazier than he, with his new knowledge? Perhaps not.

But they were weaker.

The most frightening realization of all was that *he* could be master of this particular nightmare. He could swing worlds one way or another, creating paradise or hell or simply continuing the monstrous progression of the past.

Mozart applied his fingers to the keyboard without hesitation.

I am the key. A few realize that now. But I am not even sure who I am or what I am going to do. Michael tried to recall the self-confidence he had felt earlier, the undoubting assurance of what had to be done. He could not. Something like that assurance was necessary, but he had disliked himself, feeling thus.

Still, he did not have the luxury of long introspection.

Mozart sat at the piano with head cocked to one side, listening to the music before his fingers drew it from the keys. Then he began to play, slowly at first, with implications of unease, fear, in the key of G minor. But he quickly moved to the major, and the music began a climb to exaltation.

For a moment, Michael tried to analyze that music. Then he simply shut his eyes and let the music penetrate him. Without analysis, without the feeling that there was a score behind the sounds—there wasn't, of course—the music could do what it was meant to do. It could define and create a language of worlds, not words or thoughts, guiding Michael at the same time that it put the audience in a spell. They would learn the differences between worlds, and they would discover they had a choice . . .

For Mozart's playing was virtually a definition of sanity and peace and order. It was not lacking in conflict; it did not sugar-coat. It calmly and confidently outlined a place in which it would be wonderful to live.

From what Michael remembered of Mozart's music in Waltiri's collection of records, that was what virtually all of his music had done. In a world of people adapted to hard times and social infighting and inhospitable realities, it had gracefully outlined an alternative.

The best that we can be.

Michael looked down at his hands, folded before him.

Something glowed between the intertwined fingers. Ulath was still watching him. There was apprehension in her eyes. The Ban of Hours, listening to Mozart's music, had clasped her own hands before her breast and lowered her head as if in prayer.

"Shiafa," he said softly, raising his hands. "Will you join with me, this once?"

She was trembling. "We will die," she said. He thought of Eleuth, trying powerful magic before she was ready.

"I don't think so. If we don't try, we'll die anyway, and everybody with us."

"My father will protect me," she said. "He is the God of the Realm."

"He has left you to me," Michael reminded her. *Would Tarax interfere?*

"What do you want from me? That which I will give only in mating? I don't even know what that is."

"No mating," Michael said. "No loss. I need what you have inside you, but I cannot take it. You can only give it to me—to us—and I will not keep it."

Shiafa lifted her eyes to the sky. The music was not so much heard as lived, now. Mozart was succeeding. "I am so afraid," she said, shuddering.

"So am I." Michael unclasped his hands, and the light between them went out. He held his right hand out to her. All around, save for Ulath, the audience paid them no attention, entranced by the music. "There isn't enough time to train you and give you all the discipline. I cannot make you what your father would have you be. The old traditions are inadequate. Help me forge new ones."

Shiafa took his hand and grasped it firmly. White light escaped from between their fingers.

In the palm of his other hand, Michael felt time come apart like a squeezed clot of dust. The sky went from uncertain blackness to the nonexistence and nonquality of death. The arena skewed and bled upward, all of its coral redness fragmenting and smearing.

Now we begin, Michael told Shiafa through their joined hands. The humans in the arena had been enchanted by Mozart's music, but they had not had time to transport. It was necessary for Michael to make his first small world and wrap them in it.

Where are we? Shiafa asked.

We are dead, I think, Michael said. There was no seeing, no feeling, only their thoughts and joined energy. Around them—if "around" could be used to describe relations without space or coherent time—were the people who had been in the arena and Mozart's music, pure pattern without sound. Michael used the pattern as a model.

There was no time to lay down solid underpinnings for the world. Instead, he began a "gloss"—warmth, distance, some semblance of time. What else did a world need? Limits. He established a size.

And saw three hands. His hand and Shiafa's, joined, and his other hand. In his free hand he saw a pearl the size of a walnut. The pearl blossomed and became a coral-red rose. The edges of the rose's petals spread out as red lines, vibrating to Mozart's pattern. The red lines marked out a space, twisting to meet and close off the space. The lines then vanished. Again, in his free hand was a pearl, this time the size of a baseball. He closed his fingers around it and pushed it back— not necessary. He would save it for another time.

Space and warmth surrounded the five thousand. Michael listened for the Earth. It was, of course, quite close, singing its complex, steady, but somewhat out-of-tune melody. *Do you feel the Earth?* he asked Shiafa.

Yes.

This is what war between Sidhe and humans left behind—a garden gone to seed. Hatred and pain and deception.

Yes.

Our people are more alike than either would suspect.

Yes.

I need you to help me bring all of us to the Earth. Do you feel how it must be done? Training through necessity. . .

She replied that she could feel the necessity but not yet the method.

Just listen . . . he suggested. *Feel the addings and takings away. We must come to the Earth when it is neither adding nor taking away, and then we must synchronize.*

She was no longer afraid. He felt in her some of the confidence he had experienced earlier.

Dare, he said.

Together, they dared.

He saw the between-worlds arrayed beneath them like

nightmare relief maps, all the shadows and discarded possibilities. He veered away from them, toward the song of the true and finished Earth.

The limits of his little world were fading. His first creation would hold together only briefly.

The Earth unfolded, and around it, all the possible points of space and time. He disregarded those possible points—*how the Sidhe felt their way between the stars, back when the world had not joined with so many other worlds and was so much smaller*—and concentrated on the familiar.

Young, homesick Michael Perrin rose up and asserted himself. Shiafa did not object. Neither did the newer, more powerful Michael. Los Angeles spread its night tapestry below them.

They needed a place to let the bubble burst, a place that could accommodate everybody, an empty place . . .

Dodger Stadium, dark and deserted under the warm night skies

Accepted them, and Michael's first world died.

31

Five thousand people, some of whom had not seen the Earth for millennia, stood on the turf and soil, spread out over the diamond, infield and outfield, all the way to the fence.

Moon and sun briefly arced with shadow and fire in the sky as the dead Realm spread across and through the Earth. Everybody fell to their hands and knees as the ground shook. The noise and quaking went on for a very long time; Michael wondered if Mahler's symphony had been enough to cushion the fall. Then the noise subsided, and the ground became still.

Michael released Shiafa's hand in the silence after.

"Thank you," he said.

Shiafa sat up with her legs crossed beneath her. "This is Earth?" she asked, staring up at the dark seats arrayed in concentric rows and the few scattered security lights.

"It is," Michael said.

"It doesn't *feel* right," she said. "It feels harsh."

He did not disagree.

32

Morning light was already touching the high cirrus clouds above Los Angeles. Michael, Shiafa, Nikolai and Ulath walked through the people sitting, standing, conversing or just staring—at the sky, the walls, the tiers of seats—while Michael tried to assess the extent of their problem.

Five thousand people. Frightened, most of them unfamiliar with the Earth. Soon to be hungry. Brought abruptly into a world already upset and confused. Most of them illegal aliens.

"I need some organization," he said. "How did the Ban administer them all in the *Sklassa?*"

"They have speakers—one for every fifty—and a knotmaker for every ten speakers. The knotmakers address the assistants of the Ban," Ulath explained.

Michael pursed his lips, thinking rapidly. "Where is Biri? The other assistants?"

"I saw Biri inspecting the walls around the field," Nikolai said. Michael probed for him, found him and sent a dubious Nikolai to bring him into the center of the group, near second base.

"Nobody should leave the stadium until I've learned what

conditions are like outside. I think"—he knew, actually, but the feeling was unfamiliar—"that Biri will cooperate with us. Together, we can keep order—where is the Ban?" He could feel her presence but could not pinpoint her location.

"She has chosen to spread herself among her children," Ulath said.

"What does that mean?"

"She is diffuse now. She will attend to us all and to the Sidhe of Earth."

"How do we communicate with her?"

"I speak to her," Ulath said.

"Yes, but why did she do this now, when we need her?"

"Because Tarax is here. He has brought the Realm to its end and now begins his rule on Earth. She protects us best by spreading herself."

Michael closed his eyes briefly to feel for her. *What has happened to you now? Are you dead?*

"The Ban is not dead."

"I still have a lot to learn about the Sidhe," he said.

"Perhaps about the Ban only," Ulath suggested, smiling.

Nikolai and Biri approached, Biri trailing the Russian by several steps. "This is a foul place," Biri said. "It is dirty and painful."

"There's no place like home." Michael told him they would need a perimeter of protection to prevent people from entering the stadium and to discourage the captives from leaving.

"That is simple enough," Biri said.

"Ulath and the Ban's other assistants will help you."

"I can do that alone."

"Fine. I have to leave to make arrangements outside. Is everybody here except the Ban?"

"The Ban is here," Ulath reiterated.

"Yes. Well?"

"I think so," Nikolai said.

"Where are Mozart and Mahler?"

"I will find them," Nikolai said, running off between the crowds of people.

They're still remarkably well-behaved, Michael thought. *No clamoring, no confused milling about. And it's not because they're dazed, either.* Perhaps there would be fewer problems than he had imagined, at least among the five thousand inside the stadium.

Savarin approached Michael alone. His robes were stained green with grass and smudged with dirt. "This is truly Earth?" he asked.

"Yes," Michael said. "You aren't by any chance a speaker or knotmaker, are you?"

"Henrik is a knotmaker," Ulath said.

Savarin grinned sheepishly. "I am always the organizer," he said.

"Good. Then you'll help us—" He spotted Nikolai returning with Mahler and Mozart. "Excuse me."

Michael hugged Mozart firmly and shook Mahler's hand. "You've done it," he said to them.

"Wolferl played magnificently," Mahler said.

"Yes, well, such an audience, *nein?*"

"Would both of you be up to accompanying me?" Michael asked. "I'll need help outside. Nikolai, you too . . ."

"Gladly," Nikolai said. Mahler inhaled deeply and shook his head. "The air smells very bad here."

"There's lots to get used to. But there're some people—friends of mine—who would very much like to meet you. I have to make some phone calls—talk to them." *If phones are still working.*

"I will go," Mozart said. "This is exciting, really." He sounded more willing than he looked. Mahler rubbed his hand back across his high forehead and gray hair.

"Ja," he said. "But be careful with us. We are not young men, you know."

"Speak for yourself," Mozart said.

In a group, they made their way off the field and down a ramp. Michael was searching for a pay phone, though he didn't have any money in his ragged clothes.

"There is a frightened man ahead," Shiafa said as they passed the door of a locker room. Michael had felt him also —and he was armed.

"A security guard, probably," Michael said. "Best to be open." He cupped his hands to his mouth. "Hey! We need help."

A portly, middle-aged man in a gray uniform came out of the shadows with his gun drawn. "Who in the hell are you?"

"We need help," Michael said, holding his hands in the clear and nodding for the others to follow suit. "I need to make a call. There're a lot of people on the field—"

"I saw them. They're like those freaks coming out of everywhere."

"No, no they aren't," Michael reassured him. "They're people, most of them, and so am I. But they need help. We have to call the police, the city. They're going to need shelter, food, clothing."

"What in hell is this?" the guard asked, clearly out of his depth. He was close enough now that Michael could see his sweating face and the wicked gleam on the black barrel of his service revolver.

"I need to get to a phone," Michael said.

"They're not working. I mean, they're only working some of the time. Who are you?"

Michael approached the guard slowly, hands extended, and gave him his name and street address. The guard finally acquiesced and took them to a pay phone near the end of the corridor. He did not put away his gun, however, and he stood well back from them.

Michael smiled his thanks and dialed for the operator. He got a beeping noise and then a recording: "All phone connections are for emergency use only. An operator will be on the line soon. If this is not an emergency, please hang up. Penalties may be levied for abuse of emergency services."

Half a minute passed, then a weary male voice answered. "Emergency service only. May I help you?"

"Yes. I need to reach the office of the Mayor."

"You're whistling in the wind, buddy," the operator said. "You're on a pay phone. Unless you need the police or are reporting an accident with injuries, we don't service pay phones."

"Fine," Michael said patiently. "Connect me with LAPD Central."

"It's your head."

Several minutes passed before he was able to get a line through, and then an even more weary female voice answered.

"I'd like to speak to Lieutenant Harvey in homicide," Michael said.

"Lieutenant Harvey is no longer on homicide. He's on Invasion Task Force."

"Wherever he is, I need to talk to him."

"Is this an emergency?"

"Yes," Michael said. He glanced at the guard. "I'm talking to the police now," he said, cupping his hand over the mouthpiece.

"Invasion Task Force, Sergeant Dinato."

"My name is Michael Perrin."

There was a sharp intake of breath and then a quick, stuttered, "Hold on. I'm transferring you to Lieutenant Harvey's office now."

"Thank you," Michael said. He banked his *hyloka* carefully, realizing how tired he was. The guard held his ground, but he had lowered his pistol a few inches and was mopping his forehead with a handkerchief. He inspected them closely, his eyes darting from Mozart's blue silk jacket and white breeches and hose to Mahler's dark robe and Shiafa's ragged pants and loose blouse. "Where all did you come from, anyway?" he asked nervously.

"From Dreamland," Mozart said. "We've just awakened."

"You're all German?"

"I'm Russian," Nikolai said.

"All of you?"

Michael recognized Lieutenant Harvey's resonant "Hello" immediately. "Where the hell have you been?" Harvey asked. The lieutenant sounded exhausted.

"Not far. I'm calling from Dodger Stadium. I have something of an emergency here."

"Oh?" Harvey asked cautiously.

"I'll need food, supplies and shelter for about five thousand people. Human beings. There are a few Sidhe here, as well."

Harvey's silence was prolonged. "That will stretch us a bit," he said. "Dodger Stadium? Where?"

"On the field."

"I mean, where did they come from?"

"The Realm," Michael said.

"All at once?"

"All at once."

There was a sharp edge to Harvey's laughter. "You know," he said, "I'm almost accustomed to this crap now. You gave me the basic tools to help me accept it. I guess I owe you. Are these people dangerous?"

"No," Michael said. "Mostly, they're frightened. Some

have been away for a long time."

"All right. I'll see what I can do. Are you going to stay there?"

"I don't think so," Michael said, thinking rapidly. "I have a lot of other work to catch up on. We'll have a committee here to meet your people and work with them."

"I'll put together a team now. I feel silly asking you this, but when will I hear from you again?"

"I don't know," Michael said. There was simply no way of telling how much time his next few challenges would take. "Can you get me an open phone line? I need to call my parents."

"Sure," Harvey said. "Hold on for a sec."

"Thanks," Michael said.

33

The taxi driver—a portly Lebanese with a well-trimmed mustache and curious, darting eyes—took Michael, Shiafa, Mahler and Mozart from the stadium parking lot to the Waltiri house in record time. The streets were almost deserted. "I'm the only one out this time of day. Everybody else, they stay home," he said. "I'm not afraid of these spooks. It's fear hurts people." He glanced nervously in his mirror at Shiafa. "Don't you think that's what hurts people?"

Nobody answered. Mahler and Mozart seemed to be in dreamy shock. The modern buildings and sprawled clutter of Los Angeles was completely contrary to their experience. "Ugly," Mahler said under his breath again and again, but he did not turn away. Mozart, sitting between Shiafa and Mahler in the back seat, was frozen, his hands folded and clamped between his knees, only his eyes moving away from the cab's center line.

Michael was too tired to do more than broadcast a light circle of awareness tuned to Tarax or Clarkham. His more experienced eye—helped by the driver's occasional observations—was already picking out the city's new incongruities.

The late morning sky over the city was cut through with wildly tangled clouds on several levels. Michael had never seen their like before. The air smelled electric, and his palms tingled constantly, telling him that the song of Earth had been disturbed by the Realm's death. Some of the Realm's qualities had been passed on to the Earth, perhaps by Tarax's design. Michael wearily realized that magic would not be so difficult on Earth now.

"No people at all up and down Wilshire. On a Wednesday!" the taxi driver said, waving his free hand out the window. "And you're my first fare today. God knows why I work, but I got no wife, no kids, this cab's my life."

"We appreciate your working," Michael said.

"Take my advice. You all look fashed. You belong to some rock band, some group? I notice your dress. That's a fine wig. You look all rumpled, like you've been playing a concert all night. . . . Funny." He shook his head.

"We're musicians," Michael said. He found his head nodding as if to some inner beat and had to stop it with an effort of will. "Hard couple of days."

Mozart laughed abruptly and without explanation, then grabbed the front seat and leaned forward. "Is it all this bad?" he asked plaintively. "Is there no place the eye can rest?"

"Sorry," Michael said. "We'll be home soon." He glanced at Mahler. "Arno Waltiri's house."

Mahler's eyelids assumed that languid expression Michael had seen before. "Waltiri. Brilliant youth. He must be very old by now."

"He's dead," Michael said. Time enough to explain the details later.

John and Ruth were sitting on the front steps of the Waltiri house as the cab drove up and deposited the four of them on the sidewalk. John paid the fare, and Ruth hugged Michael as the others stood on the concrete and grass, squinting and blinking in the bright sun.

"Everyone has their own tiny estate here," Mozart said, gazing at the neighborhood.

Michael and John embraced peremptorily. "Welcome back," John said. "You've been gone during the worst of it. Ruth and I thought you'd choose this morning to come back. It just . . . seemed appropriate."

"After the earthquake," Ruth said. "After the false dawn."

Michael introduced them as they walked to the house. He reached into his pocket and produced the key, still there after all he had been through, and opened the door.

A warm wind blew out of the house, redolent with jasmine, honeysuckle and tea roses. The interior of Waltiri's house was overgrown with flowering plants and vines. They ascended the walls to the ceiling, forming an arch, and covered all the furniture, leaving only the floor and a narrow passageway clear. On every branch and twig, peering from every tiny hollow, birds blinked at him through the foliage. Pigeons and sparrows rustled and backed away on the floor as the door opened wider; others regarded the intruders with sleepy black eyes, unperturbed.

"All right," Michael said slowly, stopping in the hallway and spreading his hands.

"I feel a power," Shiafa said. Ruth regarded her with frank worry, obviously thinking of the hill wife her great-grandfather had taken.

Mozart sat on the front step and leaned his head on one hand, staring out at the street, too jaded by marvels to care much about a houseful of forest and birds. "Where do we sleep? In there?" he asked, gesturing behind him.

Michael, Shiafa and Mahler walked down the flowered passage until they came to the stairway to the second floor. The birds made way for them and did not seem unduly disturbed. "Surely this is magic," Mahler commented. "All these birds, yet the place is so *clean.*"

"Do you feel anything?" Michael asked Shiafa.

"Yes. It feels powerful. Someone important is here."

A large black crow with red breast-feathers and white-rimmed eyes hopped down the stairs, ignoring them, intent on its descent, until it reached the bottom. Then it turned its attention to Michael, beak open and thin black tongue protruding, angling its head this way and that.

.

"Arno?" Michael inquired softly.

The crow lifted its head. "Arno is dead," it squawked. "Now is the time of marvels. Boy becòme man. Death of worlds. Gods die too."

Michael kneeled to be closer to the bird's level. "Were you Arno?"

"Helped be him. Arno was man. Gone where dead men go."

"Are you . . . ?"

"Am feathered mage," the crow said, strutting. It spread its wings, revealing iridescent black plumage and, under both wings, the lettering of its bondage.

Mahler shrunk back. A sparrow landed on his shoulder and chirruped, the first actual bird noise they had heard since entering. Mahler did not attempt to brush it off, but he was clearly enchanted and unhappy at once. "What does this mean?" he asked.

"It means we'll be sleeping at my parents' house," Michael said. "Doesn't it?" he asked the crow.

"Come back. Time to confer. The bonds soon will break. We choose you. Come back."

"All right," Michael said, standing. "I'll be back."

Outside, as they walked the few blocks to his parents' house, John asked, "Pardon the cliché, Michael, but what does it all mean?"

"There's magic on Earth again, and the Sidhe are no longer its only masters," he said.

"That sounds suitably portentous, son," John commented dryly. "Bring it down to my level."

"I think I understand," Ruth said. "We're all together again. There's no other place to go. Fairyland is dead. We have to live together."

"We will share the rent," Mozart said muzzily. "Do we have to walk much farther?"

They did not.

34

John seemed dazed. He followed Mozart, Mahler and his son up the stairs to the second floor. Mozart peered into the bathroom while Michael pulled towels from the linen closet.

"There's plenty of room," John said. Mahler squared his slumped shoulders and yawned. John suddenly seemed to focus on the two men, and his eyes grew wider as he stared at them. Michael walked past him with the towels. "They can stay in the guest room; there are two beds in there," John suggested.

"One can stay in my room," Michael said. "I don't think I'll be sleeping."

"Right. Michael's room."

Mozart inquired where that was, and John opened the door for him.

"Good. Crowded and busy. I'll stay here." He thanked John and shut the door behind him. John stood in the hallway, hands in pockets, blinking owlishly.

"We are very appreciative of your hospitality," Mahler said. "I do not know why your son brought us here."

"I don't either," John said. "But we're glad . . . to have you."

Michael emerged from the bathroom. "There. All set out. Do you sleep?" he asked Mahler.

"I haven't slept in many years, but today . . . yes. I'll sleep." He entered the guest bedroom and swung the door shut, smiling at John briefly through the crack before the latch clicked.

Michael put his arm around his father's shoulder. "I'm sorry to upset everything on such short notice."

"Don't mind me," John said. "I just can't accept what's happening. Those two—they're *really* Mahler, Gustav Mahler, and Wolfgang Amadeus Mozart?"

"They are," Michael said.

"They were held by the Sidhe . . . for all this time?"

"However long that was for them," Michael said. He paused at the head of the stairs. Ruth was in the living room, busily making up the couch, apparently intending it as a bed for Shiafa, who stood near the front door watching her. "I don't think Shiafa sleeps, either," Michael said.

"Who is she?" John asked softly.

"Where are you from?" Ruth asked her in a high-pitched, nervous voice clearly audible on the stairs.

"She's the daughter of a Sidhe named Tarax," Michael told John, too low for his mother to hear.

"I was born in the Realm," Shiafa said to Ruth.

John glanced at Michael. They had stopped halfway down the stairs, eavesdropping by silent and mutual consent.

"Oh? That's what we called Faerie, until now, isn't it?"

"I do not know."

"Yes. I think it is. You know, you remind me of. . . . Well, never mind that. Have you known my son long?"

"Not long," Shiafa said.

"Is he important to you?"

"Yes."

"Oh," Ruth said breathlessly, fitting the top sheet and blanket over the couch cushions. She kept a constant watch on Shiafa from the corner of her eye. "Will you be staying with us for some time? I'm sorry. That's not polite." She stood, smoothing her hands down her legs, and tossed a strand of hair back. "This is not easy for me to accept. Are you and Michael, my son . . . lovers?"

"Jesus," Michael breathed, immediately resuming his descent.

"No," Shiafa said. "He is my teacher."

"Mother, no time for this now," Michael interrupted. "Shiafa probably won't be sleeping. She may want to clean up—"

"Good . . . GOD," Ruth said, staring at Michael with a fierce expression. "John, is any of this happening?"

"You know it is," John said.

"She looks just like my great-grandmother. She could *be* my great-grandmother!"

"No, she couldn't," Michael said.

"They're all over the world now, aren't they? Just like her?"

"And like us, Mother," Michael said. He gripped her shoulders tightly with both hands. "Listen. You're better prepared to accept what's happening than most people. Shiafa is a pure Sidhe. I'm training her, or at least going through the motions. The men upstairs—"

Her expression changed from anger to pain. "Michael," she interrupted, "what can we *say* to those men? John, what can we say to them? To Mozart!"

John shrugged.

"What can we say to people centuries old, to ghosts? Dead people? Famous dead people?"

Michael grinned despite himself. "I'm sorry," he said. "I should have called ahead."

"DAMN you," Ruth said, but she was beginning to laugh and cry at once. "God damn everything." She turned to Shiafa. "I'm sorry. We don't know how to react to all this."

Michael could feel tension radiating from Shiafa. If he didn't isolate her soon, he wasn't sure what would happen.

"We have to leave now. I'll be back in a few hours. There are people I have to call—but the phones are restricted. So I may have to talk to them in person. Mahler and Mozart are just the beginning. I came back with many others—about five thousand of them."

Ruth's face went white. "Here?"

"They're in Dodger Stadium. That's where I called you from. I have to make arrangements for them. They've been in the Realm for a long time, some of them thousands of years."

"All right," Ruth said. She pointed with a nod of her chin at Shiafa. "Will she go with you?"

"Yes," Michael said. "This is difficult for her. She can't go home."

"There is no home," Shiafa said distantly.

"So please, bear with me, with us," Michael said. "If I don't miss my guess, Mahler and Mozart are going to be asleep for hours. I hope to be back before they wake up. I don't have much time."

"We'll manage," John said, hugging his wife to him with one arm. "Won't we?"

"We'll have to," Ruth said. "What will they eat?"

"Go easy on the meat," Michael advised. "They haven't had much of that where they've been." Shiafa's skin grayed noticeably at the mention of meat.

"You look very tired," Ruth said. "Both of you. I'm sorry about reacting badly . . ."

"No time to rest. And no self-recriminations. We'll be back soon."

"Why was the Waltiri house full of birds?" Ruth asked.

"Please, Mother."

"All right. Go."

Michael reached out to feel for Edgar Moffat and found him sitting in the recording room in the studio where they had first met. His probe seemed to be surrounded by razors, the harsh reality now that the Realm had beached itself on Earth's shoals.

"Will we take the machine again?" Shiafa asked.

"It's the easiest way," Michael said. "I think my car is still full of gas."

They walked back to the Waltiri house under the gray, overcast afternoon. "You're wasting energy," he said, as they walked up the driveway.

"This place smells horrible," Shiafa said sharply. "It smells like death."

"Right here?" he asked, glancing at the sidewalk where Tommy had shot himself and turned into dust and rags.

"Everywhere. The entire city."

Michael shrugged. "I've gotten used to it. I don't notice."

"It smells like dead forests," Shiafa said. "Like one of Adonna's abortions."

He realized that what she was objecting to was not just the smell of smog—very light this day, he thought—but of technology and human habitations in general. The houses around them, including Waltiri's, had been made from unconsecrated wood. The power lines overhead could upset a Sidhe's sensibilities. If other human technologies were still working, the air would be full of beamed energy—radar and television and radio. How were the tens of thousands of other Sidhe reacting to this sudden change in environment?

Shiafa's mood was upon *him* now. He brushed it aside with a small shudder and told her to stand away from the driveway. He then went to the Saab and unlocked it. The engine caught quickly and rumbled to life, murmuring with twin-exhaust throatiness.

As he backed the car down the driveway, he glanced through the opposite window at the wall of the house and the entrance to the crawl space.

The wine bottles in the basement.

During the first few minutes of his first visit to the Realm, Michael had crossed a decaying vineyard behind the ruined Clarkham mansion, covered with the twisted, blackened and thick-boled stumps of thousands of dead vines. *What was their purpose?* Nothing Clarkham did was uncalculated.

Clarkham brought Waltiri bottles of wines as a gift. Waltiri passed some of them on to his neighbors.

He almost stopped the car. *One thing at a time. Priorities.* Reaching over to open the car door for Shiafa, Michael felt a buzz of excitement. Clarkham had failed at creating a personal Song of Power; he had always relied on the genius of others, even at the height of his sorceries. He had interfered with poets, composers, dancers. . . . He had failed at architecture. Had he cultured vines simply to please himself—and perhaps anger the more abstemious Sidhe . . . or had he an ulterior motive?

Shiafa sat reluctantly on the seat. "Close your door," Michael instructed her. She stared at him, eyes burning. He sighed and reached across. "Like this," he said, grabbing the handle to pull it shut.

"There is too much iron," she said quietly. "It kills."

"You can stand it. The Sidhe use iron for their own purposes."

"Not like this."

He drove out onto the street. The trees cast long shadows. Time was passing too quickly; the Realm's chronometry was evident on Earth now. What that ultimately meant, there was no way of knowing. Was it a temporary effect—no pun intended, he though wryly—or a permanent distortion?

He frowned as he guided the Saab through the largely empty streets of the city. Other things were changing. The leaves on the trees seemed darker and the streets and buildings less hard-edged, as if viewed through a fog.

"Your world is sick," Shiafa said as he turned onto Melrose.

"How do you mean?"

"It is suffering."

"Because of the Realm?"

She nodded, staring at him with an expression he had never before seen—a mix of barely subdued greed and deep concern. It shook him.

"How do you know?" he asked, arguing more out of pique than disagreement.

"Even beyond the dead smell, it is afflicted."

He pressed his lips together and shrugged. But now he was really worried. Who was working to set things right again— Tarax, who had plowed the Realm onto a reef and perhaps started the disintegration of the reef? Clarkham, hiding somewhere . . .

in a bottle of wine

"Jesus," he whispered. *A wine of power. Flavor that seduces, a finish that lasts forever.* It seemed quite possible that Clarkham had kept that art as a backup, almost inaccessible to the Sidhe, who—as Clarkham had stated—"love human liquor entirely too much." What they loved, obviously, was not the flavor but the numbing effect. Because of that, the best of the Sidhe—those who might be interested in Songs of Power —would fastidiously avoid alcoholic beverages.

What was the word for the art of wine-making? The study of wines? *Oenology.* Having failed at everything else, Clarkham could have hidden himself, biding his time, waiting for the proper moment. Preparing to spring a surprise.

In the Realm, Clarkham had served not wine but brandy . . . hiding his craft for decades in Waltiri's cellar, where not even the mage of the Cledar would suspect chicanery.

Michael was so excited he had to bank his *hyloka* to keep from flaming his clothes and the car seat. Shiafa regarded him with that same new hungry, greedy expression . . . and he felt himself responding. He had used her magic. That had somehow bonded them, and it could draw them together . . .

Shocked, he avoided Shiafa's gaze and focused his attention on the road.

The studio's Gower gate was open. The guard blinked passively at Michael and Shiafa as they walked through the door, leaning forward to say, "Hey. Nobody's here. Everybody's home."

Michael smiled at her and nodded. "Edgar Moffat's here."

"Yeah," the guard said. "Edgar's here. Is he expecting both of you?"

"No," Michael said.

"But he knows you."

Michael nodded again.

"I remember you, but not her. Where's Kristine Pendeers?"

"I don't know," Michael said. "I'm looking for her, and I thought Edgar might help." That was a minor fib, but he hoped it would play. It did. The guard shrugged and leaned back in her seat.

In the hallway of the music building, Michael knocked on the recording studio door. Moffat himself answered this time, wearing gray slacks and a very rumpled white business shirt. His crown of hair looked as if he had been running his hands through it all night long, pushed back stiff and dark with sweat. He hardly reacted when he saw Michael, but his expression changed to nervous anxiety as he stared at Shiafa.

"We need your help," Michael said.

"I'm the only one working here. I think Hollywood packed up its bags and went to hide in the hills. Did you feel the earthquake?"

"Yes. We need you to organize things for us. You and Crooke."

"I haven't talked to Crooke for days. I don't even know where he is."

"This is important. Did Kristine ever tell you what she knew?"

"You mean, about you and the man who disappeared in front of her?"

"Yes."

"She told me a little. Enough to make the rest of this . . . into a real nightmare. A little knowledge is worse than none at all."

"I have some men I want you to meet," Michael said. Edgar opened the door wider and motioned for them to come in.

"Who's your designer?" he asked Shiafa. "You could be the toast of the garment district."

"And when you've met these men, I'll need you to organize a rescue operation. All the artists and musicians and writers you know. We'll need houses—hundreds of houses—and we'll need them in just a few days, maybe sooner."

"Why?"

"Refugees," Michael said.

"Who am I going to meet?"

"Gustav Mahler and Wolfgang Amadeus Mozart," Michael answered.

Edgar smiled warily. "Napoleon, too? Maybe Christ?"

Michael shook his head. Edgar's smile vanished. "Jesus. Crooke said he'd dreamed about Mahler, just as if he was still alive." Edgar swallowed convulsively, and his hands fluttered. "The real McCoys?"

"And five thousand others."

"Brought back by the concerto and the symphony?"

"In a way. Are you up to it?"

Edgar glanced at the banks of electronic equipment and ran his fingers through his hair again. "I just want one question answered, if you haven't answered it for me already. Is the world coming to an end because of what we did?"

"No," Michael said.

"All right. I'm just wasting my time here anyway. Nobody's going to be making movies for some time. Who needs fantasy now? The world's full of the real thing."

35

One thing at at time. Michael had located Crooke sitting on a bench near the Griffith Park Observatory—simply sitting and staring out over the city. Griffith Park, Michael sensed, was full of hidden Sidhe, and the police and National Guard had unofficially made it off-limits. Michael and Shiafa, working their discipline together, had penetrated makeshift barricades and driven up the winding road to the observatory, where they spoke with Crooke and persuaded him to come with them.

Moffat waited in his car in front of the Perrin house. Moffat and Crooke followed Michael up the steps and through the front door, held open by his father. Michael then introduced them to Mahler and Mozart. Crooke gaped.

"You did not do a bad piece of work," Mahler said to him. Mozart hung back, frowning. His frown changed to consternation when Moffat approached with an almost worshipful look on his face.

"You *are* Mozart," Moffat said. "Jesus. Everybody said the portraits were bad, but I recognize you. I know you through your music."

"Well," Mozart said, still edging away. He shook Moffat's hand quickly. "All this. What is it for?"

"You came back with how many, again?" Crooke asked. Michael had given him a brief explanation in the car.

"Five thousand, approximately."

Crooke took Moffat aside, and they conferred for a few minutes. When they returned, Moffat said, "I think this is a job for Mrs. Pierce-Fennady."

Crooke agreed. "She raises money for the Huntington. She knows lots of people."

"We'll introduce her to Mahler and Mozart."

"Mein Gott," Mozart moaned. "Society women!"

"She's much more than that," Crooke said. "She's a real mover and shaker."

"Does she keep her rooms warm?" Mozart asked, but he did not explain what he meant.

One thing at a time.

"I'm leaving now," Michael said. "Shiafa's going with me. We may or may not be back soon."

"What are you going to do?" Ruth asked, her face pale. She kept glancing at Shiafa, with anything but approbation.

"I'm not sure," Michael said.

You are what you dare.

36

Dusk was a wall of fire above the treetops. The air was cool and sharp, faintly electric. As Michael and Shiafa approached the Clarkham house on foot, he saw little streaks of darkness shoot inches above the black grass of the nearby lawns. Roses in a well-tended garden glowed in unnaturally bright pinks and blood-reds.

The two-story Clarkham house seemed covered by a shadow darker than the evening around it. Michael edged the door open slowly. Behind him, Shiafa kept her eyes on his back, as if willing him to do something. He could feel her attention, but he could not riddle her thoughts. Still, he felt he might need her; his own magic might not be strong enough for what lay ahead.

And if he resorted to using her buried power one more time. . . . What then? What commitment would he feel, and what would she demand in return?

She was getting little formal training from him. *I must be teaching her very bad habits*.

He ignored the stairs and looked through the service porch and kitchen for the doorway he knew must exist. Shiafa seemed to know the unspoken object of his search; she summoned him to the back of a walk-in pantry and pointed to a small door sealed with an ancient brass padlock. Michael drew a small percentage of his strength from his center and melted the hasp, singing the wood behind it. A small, ghostly curl of smoke rose and spread under the low ceiling. Shiafa breathed deeply. He glanced at her and turned away quickly. Her face was the color of the moon in the dark confines of the pantry.

The door opened easily and without noise. He descended

the narrow steps after asking Shiafa to remain above. The basement was larger than he had had reason to suspect; it spread under the length and breadth of the house, broken only by dark outlines of vats and racks and large square supporting beams.

In one corner was a large Archimedean screw nestled at the bottom of a metal trough—a grape crusher. Wooden boxes in the opposite corner held the dried and dusty remains of crushed grapes and their stems—looking not unlike Tommy. Michael peered closer at the remains and saw a faint rainbow-hematite-oil sheen hovering about them.

"Vintage," he murmured. Their smell was sweeter than any grapes he remembered, as sweet as the perfume he had exuded in the Realm whenever he had come in contact with water, or the fragrance of the manuscript of opus 45.

The racks were empty of bottles. He searched the corners of the cellar meticulously and found no evidence of hidden caches. The cellar had not been used for some time—perhaps fifty years.

There was no choice but to return to the Waltiri house and disturb the birds—the Cledar—again.

Shiafa blocked him at the top of the stairs. Her face was a cool, mellow beacon, lovely in the darkness. Her lips were parted expectantly, and the teeth behind them were a beautiful shade of gray mother-of-pearl. Her red hair spread like feathers around her head, loose and fragrant. "Nothing?" she asked.

He shook his head, regarding her steadily.

"We can join to search out what you're looking for," she suggested.

"I don't think that's a good idea."

"You've taken my power from me once already," she said. "It's not as if we'll be doing anything unfamiliar. Isn't that why you brought me with you?"

He nodded. "It is. But I don't need help just now."

"Perhaps I need yours," she said.

Kristine suddenly seemed far away and not very well-suited to be the partner of a mage. How could he live with a purely human woman, who had no idea of his problems and abilities?

Michael took another step up, and Shiafa backed out of his

way reluctantly. "I know where we—I need to go," he said. She followed him out of the house.

In the darkness, the leaves of the trees around the neighborhood sparkled like crystals. The stars overhead wobbled almost imperceptibly. The cold had intensified and chilled him even with his *hyloka* in effect. Reality was becoming most inhospitable—why? Because of the weight of the Realm's demise? Or by plan . . . Tarax's plan, or Clarkham's?

Even from a distance of half a block, Waltiri's house radiated an aura of life and energy. It seemed filled with anticipation and joy. Michael's spirits took an abrupt upswing as he approached, and Shiafa seemed less enchanting and menacing. He removed the key from his pocket on the front step and opened the door.

"Life for you is opening doors," said the mage of the Cledar, who stood nestled among pigeons and sparrows in the hallway. His white-rimmed eyes flashed at Michael with an inhuman but not unwelcome (and not unfamiliar) humor. Michael could feel the connection quite clearly now. This creature had once been part of Arno Waltiri, a buried but considerable part.

Shiafa chose to remain outside, standing in the razor chill at the end of the front walk. Michael did not think about her now. He walked through the birds, who parted without complaint, to the service porch.

The birds had not occupied the basement. The armoire had not been disturbed since it had been emptied of its papers, months before. All that remained were a few odds and ends— stone paperweights, an andiron in one corner, and at the bottom of the armoire, the little rack of three wine bottles, each bearing the label, "Doppelsonnenuhr, Feinste Geistenbeerenauslese, 1921."

Drink me, Alice.

He sensed the Cledar mage's presence above him, waiting patiently for his decision, tendering neither judgment nor advice. Full of life, full of joy. *They feel something beyond the edge of harsh, sickened reality, beyond the razor cold and the night.*

They feel me.

They trust me.

If this wine did indeed take him to Clarkham's hidden ex-

perimental reality, his embryonic attempt to replace this world
with another, then it was likely Kristine would be there, or
accessible once he was there.

Then his agreement with Tarax would be unnecessary.
Michael had never been comfortable with Shiafa; now he felt
a kind of dread at the thought of her.

She could demand so much of him, and he did not know if
he could resist. Easy paths to—

What? Damnation?

Away from Kristine, at the very least.

Away from honor and self-trust. Michael could feel the tiny
Sidhe part of him struggling to go to Shiafa and unite with her.
The compulsion was barely controllable now.

The easy path, finally offered—similar to the path Clarkham might have taken. And Clarkham was filled with ever-
regenerating evil. There were so many things Michael did not
know, so many things he had to puzzle out for himself . . .

And still, he had made it this far.

He removed a bottle of wine from the rack and examined it
in the cellar's dim light. The cork had disintegrated beneath
the lead cap, and the wine inside had long since dried to black
paste. Putting the first bottle aside, he lifted the second; liquid
still shimmered within.

His father had taught him something about wines; he did
not shake it nor in any other way disturb the sediment cast off
to the side of the reclining bottle. Sediment could take years to
settle out again. Spoil the purity.

The contents were a deep, rich green-brown through the
green glass, as clear and suggestive as the depths of a gem-
stone. All summer and winter caught in a swallow, fogs and
soil, earth and sky and sun, distillations of time and reality. A
core-sample of a universe, not the cultural universe of books
and music and art, but of the world itself as shaped by
humans.

Oenology. The one art the Sidhe would almost certainly
ignore. The one art the Sidhe had not passed on to the re-
evolved humans.

His respect for Clarkham grew. *Never underestimate your
enemies.* He took his knife from his pocket and contemplated
removing the lead wrapping, but found himself paralyzed with
indecision. Drink it here, or elsewhere? Share it with Shiafa?
That idea particularly disturbed him.

Swallowing this vintage might do more than transport. It might teach, give clues. He did not want Tarax's daughter to be more powerful than he was.

He pushed the knife blade into the foil around the lip of the bottle. Pulling the lead and impressed wax away, he unfolded the corkscrew from the base of his knife and pushed the tip into the dark cork. The cork seemed brittle. The screw finally found purchase, and he twisted the knife handle. With less dexterity than he might have wished, holding the bottle between his knees and glancing up the stairs to see that nobody was watching, he pulled the cork free of the neck.

The base of the cork was stained with a dark reddish-purple glaze. He sniffed the cork and smiled—his father's ritual—and then smelled the open bottle. The odor was not strong; it reminded him more of dust than flowers or fruit. Should he let it breathe for a while for maximum effect? How fastidious should one be, uncorking a wine between worlds?

He lifted the bottle to his lips. In other circumstances, he might take days to make this decision and follow every little precaution—including his father's wine rituals.

The liquid met his lower lip, cool and slick. It spilled across his tongue in a thin dribble, and he swirled the small amount of wine across his palate and over the full surface of his tongue.

His eyes widened.

With a barely controlled gag, he spit the wine out onto the dusty floor and wiped his lips hastily. Sour and bitter. The wine had turned. He held the cork up to the light; it was brittle and crumbling. Too much oxygen had gotten into the bottle.

But even so—

For a moment, he felt his skin warm and his hair stand on end. The basement's outlines seemed to change. With a blink, the effect vanished. He might have imagined everything.

Michael recorked the bad bottle. The wine the Dopsos had served had been very good but certainly not a wine of power. Perhaps he was on the wrong track after all. Or Clarkham had reserved the finest bottles for his own use, giving the Waltiris only *vin ordinaire*.

He returned the corked bottle to the rack and removed the last. This one seemed dustier, less clear behind the glass. The sediment lay thick within, covering almost a quarter of the bottle's circumference.

He removed the foil and the cork and lifted the bottle to his nose. Eyes closed, he inhaled.

When he opened his eyes again, the light bulb sang like an insect. The walls flexed outward. He smelled the sweetness deep in his nose and all down his throat, into his stomach and down into the center of his being. His eyes felt encrusted with rainbows. Curiously, he examined the cork's bottom and saw that the varnished darkness there was absolute.

He took a swallow from the bottle.

The sweetness was that of a season—late summer.

The tickle in his nose was like a burst of sunlight in his eyes, drawing him closer to a sneeze.

The rounded, almost oily sensation was a distant lake slowly rippling under hazy sun. In the lake, the Serpent wallowed, and in the Serpent's memories, a mix of dangers and opportunities.

The smell of distant raspberries: a vine on a trellis in a garden with no guardian, no Tristesse to menace and frighten. The way is open.

Choose.

From a multitude of possible places to go.

The wine was not a passkey to a distinct world. It was
as he had barely suspected
a skeleton key

Clarkham being far more powerful than Waltiri or even the mage of the Cledar, and in his own way far more subtle, an instigator of unrest and trouble and a prompter of actions
a skeleton key to the dozens of worlds or more that Clarkham had created; an open invitation, for the wine would not have been left here had Clarkham wished otherwise; a challenge—*find me in the manifold of my creations*

Michael saw the Isomage's house as a kind of skeleton on a background the shade of the cork's varnished bottom. He also saw the pleasure dome and the house in Los Angeles. These were the shadows of Clarkham's creations, no longer accessible. The taste of the wine continued to quietly massage his tongue, revealing layer after layer of finish.

Here was the primitive, stark world in which Michael had been imprisoned. Beyond it was something more complex but difficult to distinguish; the taste seemed muddy. At another level, Michael saw a city stretching across a valley, a sprawled and sunny place . . . not unlike Los Angeles in the 1930s and 1940s, he realized. The Hollywood hills and Griffith Park seemed to stand out, as well as the large barn-like studios and great stretches of empty fields where more of the city would lie in Michael's time. A derivative creation.

He probed that world and watched his energies spread from end to end of the tiny creation, barely twenty miles wide. The creation was empty; like Michael's former prison, it contained only pale shadows, architectural mannequins indicating where people might be.

The next layer of taste unfolded across his tongue. He saw a field of yellow grass with intensely blue, almost purple sky rising above the field and the low golden hills beyond.

David Clarkham stood under the hot sun in the field. He appeared younger—in his thirties perhaps—with thick brown hair and a wide mustache. His face was narrow with a narrow hawk nose and high cheekbones, and his eyes were langorous, relaxed. His lips curved in a faintly bemused smile. Michael swallowed the wine and felt the grass part around his solidifying body. His shoes sunk into the dirt as he took on substance.

"Hello," the young Clarkham said.

Michael shaded his eyes against the glare and built up all of his *hyloka* for a defensive surge. But Clarkham's assault did not come. Michael probed quickly, and Clarkham allowed him to perceive of his reality and character before blocking.

It was indeed Clarkham, but not quite real and not quite a shadow; this Clarkham was almost as much a creation as the prairie around them. Even so, behind the image lay the merest hint of Clarkham's inescapable foulness.

"Hello," Michael replied, feeling the sweat start out on his brow. The sun was almost unbearably hot. Clarkham, dressed in a dark corduroy suit with a white linen shirt, appeared to be mimicking a Western pioneer. Through the grass, Michael could see he was wearing scuffed leather boots with his cuffs pulled down over them.

"I'm surprised," Clarkham said, hitching his thumbs in the pockets of his coat. "You're much more resourceful than I thought. More powerful, too."

"I'm looking for Kristine," Michael said.

"She's not here. I can't return her to you, especially now. I took her for just such an eventuality."

"Why? That's the only reason I'm here." Michael realized the shallowness of that particular untruth; and yet, as he said it, he believed it. Part of him would have forgiven all, just to have the Earth return to normal and Kristine back.

Clarkham's smile broadened. "You have no other ambitions, after making it this far? Surely you've faced . . . let's call them opportunities, if not temptations?"

Normality was as impossible now as a peaceful settlement of the disputes between them. Michael could not have a normal life; Clarkham had never had one. Michael threw aside that especially tenuous shadow-self's wish and faced Clarkham on his own terms. Nothing visible had changed between them, but Michael's new stance was apparent to Clarkham immediately.

"That's more like it," the ex-Isomage said. "More honest."

"I didn't want to become a mage," Michael said softly.

"I did. I've been working through my apprenticeship, or whatever it should be called, for centuries longer than you've been alive. Your interference is unsettling and unwelcome. You've caused me much grief."

"This whole dispute . . ." The magnitude of grief caused by the Sidhe-human conflicts was beyond Michael's ability to describe. All of human history. . . . He shrugged.

"Your maturity is a sometime thing, weak at best," Clarkham said. "Yet you don't seem unreasonable. And your ambition isn't nearly as strong as mine. Perhaps we can discuss things, and you can realize how hopeless your prospects really are and how much harm you might cause if you try to fight both Tarax and myself."

"All right," Michael said.

"We're in one of my test environments," Clarkham explained. "Like an artist's sketch. It's part of my larger world. It's quite accomplished, I think. It has firm roots and mimics most of the complexity of our birth universe. It is not nearly so large, of course."

"Is it complete?" Michael asked.

"No," Clarkham admitted. "Come with me. We'll find a cool place."

They walked over the fields. Michael felt the quality and density of this test-world with the palms of his hands. It was indeed fine, almost indistinguishable from Earth. He could not do something this powerful and real—not yet, perhaps not ever.

Yet he itched to try. The part of himself that aspired to be a mage—the ultimate poet, creator of worlds—was impressed but not overawed.

In a depression within the prairie lay a small town hammered together from gray planks and splintered posts. On one side of the single dirt street was a barber shop, a saloon and a hotel, on the other a gunshop and a feed and general store, all deserted. Michael stretched his mental fingers wide, searching for the facts in this world he might need to know, and he curled those fingers back empty. This world was a test case, finely wrought, but not profound.

Derivative. For the first time since he had swallowed the wine, Michael smiled. Clarkham saw the edge of that smile, and his face became thinner, nose sharper, cheeks paler.

They walked the single dirt street, and Clarkham held open the swinging doors to the saloon. Michael passed through into welcome, cool shadow. Clarkham pulled out a seat at a rickety round table, and Michael sat.

"This is all I have," Clarkham said, indicating with his arms the room and the world beyond, and not just one world, but the others Michael could still feel at the back of his palate. "You helped remove the rest from me. I cannot return to Earth now. Not in person, not physically."

Michael thought of the footprints on the dusty floor. *Whose, then? A Sidhe—perhaps Tarax himself, or Biri—clearing out Clarkham's gate to the Realm, disposing of Lamia and Tristesse—carrying them to the Tippett Hotel. . . . Leaving them there as a warning to the Ban, perhaps, that humans must not cross there . . .*

Would he ever know? Probably not.

"I could not go to the Realm, but now that's dead too, and soon the Earth with it, no? So no regrets. You've taken nothing from me I didn't deserve to lose. Complacency is a mage's worst enemy. Complacency and lack of vigilance."

"The Earth is dying?" Michael asked, feeling like a child again, asking questions of a teacher. *The role he wishes upon me. Power lies in placing others in their weakest postures.*

"Tarax didn't do a very good job of bringing his ship up on the reef, did he? Pushed out the captain and then couldn't navigate. He forgot to toss away the unnecessary, the deadly cargo—the underpinnings of the Realm. Chaos, the mist of creation. Now they pollute the Earth. Soon anything will be possible. When anything is possible, nothing is real. Might as well spread turpentine across a fresh oil painting." Clarkham sat across the table from Michael and folded his arms, looking strong and young and satisfied, his face dark in the saloon's cool gloom. "His qualifications to be the mage of the new Earth seem weaker to all of us day by day. Perhaps even to himself."

"All of us?"

"The Serpent still dreams. And who can say there aren't others? They might be less apparent in this than even you. And you have moments when you don't even want to be a mage." His smile was perfectly candid and friendly. "The contest must be decided soon. We all have loyalties to our people, and without the people, what use is a world? Like Adonna, I once considered populating my own worlds, but . . ." He sighed. "You've seen the results. By the way, how *did* you escape? Mine was a particularly nasty trap."

Michael saw no reason for lies. "Tarax released me."

"On what condition?"

"Part of a pact. I would train his daughter, and he would tell me where you've hidden Kristine."

Clarkham's smile broadened. "Interesting. The law of mages. No candidate shall harm a fellow candidate or lessen his chances. But as you see, I don't necessarily follow those rules. Tarax's daughter—a Sidhe? I seem to recall his woman was a pure Sidhe. Adonna made the same mistake." He leaned forward and put his elbows on the table. "Thirsty?"

Michael shook his head. He did not want the taste of the wine diluted or washed away. "Why is it a mistake?"

"It *can* be a great mistake for a mage. If you choose not to be a mage—if you sensibly decline this position you've half unwittingly put yourself in—then there is no threat. But I tell too much. You are still my enemy."

Michael nodded. "Yes," he said. "You killed Tommy."

"His death was easy. He killed himself. Do you know humans, Michael? You think you are one of them. You are, mostly. But you don't know them. Have you followed your history lessons, read the newspapers? We are not fighting each other in order to serve an exalted race, Michael. We strive to serve animals . . . unprincipled, cruel, blind and willful. When the Sidhe last left Earth for the Realm, humans were already on their merry path to making it unlivable even for themselves. Now they have the power to destroy everyone.

"Humans are willful and blind. They do not appreciate. They look upon those possessed by genius and chew them over and spit them out. Artists and poets are just so many . . ." His face had paled again, and he brought color back with another broad smile. "Their scientists have the upper hand. Taming a garden gone to seed."

"The Sidhe tried to take magic away from us," Michael said. "Without magic, we could only learn how to use the world. The scientists have made us strong."

"Us?" Clarkham mimicked incredulously. "You rank yourself with the scientists?"

"I would hope to," Michael said.

"A candidate mage condoning the worship of a corrupt and runaway world. Amazing how far humans have fallen."

Michael suddenly felt a surge of boredom. He pushed it aside lest it dull his apprehension and sense of peril. "You are about to try to strike a deal with me," he said.

"I am?" Clarkham feigned surprise.

"You are," Michael said, the insane self-assurance coming to the fore again. *So much to keep in balance.*

"All right. But it might not be the deal you imagine. Your talent is strong but undeveloped. We could help each other. Alone, I can create a suitable world. . . . But together, the three of us can control Tarax's ambitions *and* create a new Earth for all the races, or as many as will accept us."

"Three?"

"You have a certain attraction to Tarax's daughter. Her power can be most useful, if handled properly. And I can keep the worst from happening between the two of you, once you merge." His eyes seemed to cloud. "Euphemisms. Once she seduces you, or you her."

Michael made as if to consider this, but there were alarms in his head. What he had felt in Shiafa . . . Tonn's wife on the Blasted Plain. Connected. Horribly connected. Those who aspire to become mages . . .

"What about her loyalty to Tarax?"

"I doubt she feels any loyalty."

Michael glanced down at the worn-smooth table top. "What kind of world would you make for all the races?"

"The world-building is relatively easy," Clarkham said. "It's control of the world's inhabitants that causes trouble. Humans are especially difficult. They would likely start tinkering with the very foundations, unless they're kept tightly reined in. Sidhe might be more manageable. At least the Sidhe have a sense of their limits."

"How would you control them?"

"Rigidly," Clarkham said, eyes narrowing. "They have opposed me. They must never be that strong or willful again."

"Isn't there any other way?"

Clarkham shook his head slowly. "If you think otherwise, you're being foolish. Human history, Michael. Wars and exterminations and crimes and cruelty. Distorted minds and distorted societies. I doubt you have any idea of the depth of depravity humans are capable of."

"The Sidhe are responsible for many of our problems."

"Probably," Clarkham conceded. "But the roots are still there. The Sidhe merely tried to train the branches. And whoever caused the problems, as mage—I still have to solve them. Rigorous weeding and trimming. Could you face up to that?" Michael did not answer. He pushed his chair away from the table. The wine's finish was losing definition. "If I cooperate and bring Shiafa's power to you, will you free Kristine?"

Clarkham made a magnanimous swing of one hand. "She is of no use to me except as a means to control you. I certainly do not lust after her."

"Nobody implied that you did," Michael said, his face flushing.

Clarkham stood and leaned across the table on his extended arms, fingers splayed against the dark wood. "Do not try to join this conflict, unless you join on my side. You have certain abilities but no sophistication. You do not know the potentials. Whatever you do, you must not oppose me. I've taken your measure, Michael Perrin. I know your weaknesses."

Michael nodded agreeably.

"We cannot afford the virtues of patience and kindness and honor," Clarkham continued, his eyes contemplating the distances beyond Michael. "If we are to be mages, that is."

Michael's palms tingled. He lifted one hand as if to rub his nose and saw a pearly excrescence beginning there. "You've always wanted to be a mage, haven't you?" he asked.

"Yes."

"I didn't," Michael said. "I've never really had a choice." That much had become quite clear to him. He rubbed his tongue against the back of his palate, drawing forth saliva to further dilute the taste of the wine.

"Consider my offer seriously. The alternatives are not pleasant," Clarkham said.

The saloon darkened, and the walls of the basement returned. The bottle lay spilled on the floor, where it had slipped out of his hands. Michael bent to pick up the cork and reinsert it, but there was no liquid left.

When he straightened, he saw a spot of color on the opposite wall. The wall itself seemed intensely grainy, detailed, every speck and shadow of it clear. Michael squinted, and the spot of color resolved itself into a sleeved arm and hand. As his eyes swept up the arm, he seemed to paint with his gaze a flat figure on the wall, dressed in white garments that partook, in their transparency, of some of the wall's concrete gray. Still flat but now complete, the figure's face became animated. Michael backed away; he dimly recognized the Sidhe.

"You must think your house very full," the Sidhe whispered, his voice a mere vibration of the wall.

"Tonn," Michael breathed.

"I had hoped to bring you more, but even a mage cannot survive the forces I've faced. This is a very weak shadow to bring you, a weak bequest . . ." The figure smiled and seemed with that expression to almost lift from the concrete. Michael pressed close to the stair rail.

"You cannot best the Isomage without far greater knowledge than you currently possess. There is only one place for you to gain this knowledge . . . the Serpent. This shadow cannot convey it to you. Adonna favored you for some time; you sensed that? You hold much promise, and the others . . . well, Adonna had reasons for being less fond of them. You must take what the Serpent has; he will not give it to you without his own freight of past evil. But take it you can, if you are careful, without breaking the law of mages. You must act soon. . . . This is the last shadow the Realm can conjure. There is no forest with wood enough to contain a mage."

The shadow of Tonn faded as if bleached by the cellar's darkness rather than light, until nothing but the grainy wall remained and even the sharpness of detail blurred.

Michael swallowed. *Will I ever become as insubstantial as that?*

37

On the first floor, Michael knelt before the mage of the Cledar. The bird regarded him straight on, nictitating every few seconds. "You brought me into this," Michael said, half-accusing.

Better to be a part of change than to simply stand aside and react. The bird had abandoned spoken words, communicating with Michael by *evisa*.

"How much of Waltiri were you?"

Enough to love Golda. This war has made strange demands on us all.

"Did you know Tonn's shadow was here?"

Yes.

"Were you cooperating with him all along?"

Our goals evolved in the same direction, separately.

"And why are you waiting here?"

For the end, or for you to fulfil your promise.

Michael stood and shook his head slowly. "I'm not the boy you lured into Clarkham's house. I've lost so many selves since then, I hardly know who I am."

That is the curse of a leader.

"I've never been a leader," Michael said softly. His eyes misted over, and he looked around the living room, covered with birds of all kinds, from large white owls and red-tailed hawks to pigeons and sparrows. There were only a few of the robin-colored, crow-sized birds the Dopsos had once seen covering the house on a misty morning. "You're much younger than the Serpent," Michael said. "Are you as old as Tonn?"

Older, now.

"The writing . . . it contains the terms of your curse?"

The mage of a race must wear its shackles.

Michael nodded, lips drawn together ruefully. "How long will your curse last?"

Until we again have faces. The bird opened its beak and cocked its head to one side. *The Serpent will soon be released. Tonn's death and the end of continuity among the Sidhe mages will break his bonds. Those who were born in their present forms, however, will not be released. None of my people will be released.*

"The cockroaches won't rise up to become Urges, and the Spryggla will not drown at sea . . ." Michael mused, smiling at his vision of the apocalypse avoided.

Be warned about the Serpent.

"I'm warned."

And accept my apologies.

"I'll consider it," Michael said. "One last question. Is Shiafa a danger to me?"

Either mortal danger, fatal diversion, or ultimate boon. Her fate is in your hands.

"I've been led to believe it's the other way around."

You can change. She cannot. You determine.

"Tonn's wife . . ."

Adonna was a failure.

Michael could not decide how to say good-bye to the mage of the birds, so he simply turned and walked out the front door. Shiafa sat cross-legged on the lawn, surrounded by grass green-black and jewel-like under the bright nacreous sun. She watched him closely as he locked the door.

"How long was I in there?" he asked.

"I am not well-acquainted with time," Shiafa replied.

"You and I are going to have to talk," Michael said. "But first, we're traveling."

"Where?"

"To meet with the Serpent Mage."

For the first time, he saw an expression of deep horror on her face. But she did not protest.

With no regard for any observers in the neighborhood—

none were visible, anyway—Michael drew aside a slice of air, revealing darkness and a spot of green, and beckoned Shiafa to pass through. She did, and he followed, closing the rent behind.

Night lay like a warm, black ceramic bowl over the grass fields surrounding the loch. The water was still and silent and practically invisible; without a probe of his surroundings, he would have hardly known where the shore was. Deep in the lake, hundreds of feet below the surface and under a rocky overhang, the Serpent slumbered. Michael could not detect his Breed assistant anywhere.

"Do you feel him?" he asked Shiafa, a patch of dark gray in the obscurity.

"Yes," she said, her voice unsteady. "He stole our souls . . ."

"Tit for tat," Michael said, not entirely stifling the upwelling of crass levity again plaguing him. *You do not know the perils . . . you do not feel the true danger.* The voice in his head was his own, a part of himself having assumed the role of Clarkham, the Serpent and the mage of the Cledar all at once. "He's not going to hurt anybody now, least of all you."

"He makes *me* harm myself," Shiafa said. "What my people feel . . . anger and horror weaken us. We cannot draw from the center. We become like hunted animals in our minds."

Michael walked down to the shore and held out his hands. The pearly excrescence still covered one palm; he had been at some pains to hide it from Shiafa, even from the bird mage. He did not know precisely what it meant now, and what few clues he did have did not comfort him.

His function, he thought, was similar to that of an organ activated within a body during trauma. That would imply a connection between the worlds and their inhabitants that was completely beyond anything he had learned before, but it was not implausible. Perhaps even Clarkham knew such a "truth," if it could be called that.

At any rate, all questions of his own needs, his own decisions, might soon be swept completely away. In an emergency, his assignment might be predetermined, and if that was so, then very likely what remained of his individuality—all he had left to hold on to—would fall away like some bothersome hangnail.

He hoped to find a way to avoid that.

Kristine.

He held back the anger and impatience. *You* must *find her ...soon....* But first, he must keep hold of a world to bring her back to.

I know your plans, Michael. The Serpent's words came out of the loch as clearly as if they were side by side. *You are Tonn's final revenge for his people.*

Shiafa groaned softly, hearing the words in her own head. Her disgust was almost palpable.

"I have been told twice that I need what you have," Michael said. "You told me so yourself."

And it can be yours.

"I don't think you ever seriously intended me to have it. You would have fashioned me into a weapon. That shows how little you understand, after all."

You could have had my heritage.

"I don't think you would have given me all of it. You didn't tell me your curse is soon done with."

The Serpent began a long, undulating rise to the surface. *You make your way between worlds, and around this one, as if you were a mage. Your candidacy was only in doubt because you spurned what you most need.*

"I'm a flower," Michael said. "I've had the relationship all wrong, all along. We don't make worlds. Worlds make us. Or both. Or neither. There is no priority. I am a rose put forth by a bush grown by a world. So were you, once. But you rotted. Your whole generation ... all the Sidhe and humans of your time ... just rotted."

If you want what I have, you should come swim with me ...

Michael removed his shoes and shirt. He stepped down to the waterline in the tar-like darkness and hesitated. The water smelled of peat and age. Walking in up to his ankles, he considered the depth of the lake and how easy it would be for a body to be lost there, forever—nibbled by the salmon the Serpent fed upon, stripped until its tea-colored bones lay scattered on the silty bottom like so many pieces of broken crockery.

Come live the life I've lived. Maybe then you'll deserve to raid my memories.

The Serpent swam several hundred feet below the surface, its watery darkness no more profound than the clouded night over the loch. Michael dived into the water, pulling himself

toward the middle with the strokes he had learned in a high
school gym class. The water tasted sour. It was quite cold. He
drew more heat from his center and kept on swimming until
he dog-paddled directly above the Serpent.

*My curse comes to an end soon. Adonna's last power
fades, and the words he wrote on my belly will fade, too. Then
I'll take my place with the other candidates. No need for a
feeble boy to carry on in my place.*

Michael could feel the pressure of the Serpent's ascent beneath him. A harsh metal moon cast a weak gray light through
a gap in the clouds and revealed the water around him as so
much mercury, rippling slowly around his stroking arms.
"What in *hell* am I doing here?" Michael asked himself, spit-
ting out water. The Serpent was barely a hundred feet below
him now, insinuating its coils through the murk. Sixty feet.
Thirty. Twenty.

Michael took a deep breath and sank, letting the water
close over his head. His eyes stung, but he forced them open
and stared down. Ten feet. Five feet. With the few scattered
photons of filtered moonlight, he made out an oblong shape,
now stationary beneath him.

My world, the Serpent said. *Have you earned what you
wish to take?*

No, Michael responded. *But I'll try anyway.* And if he
succeeded, wouldn't he, too, be breaking the law of mages?
Adonna's shadow had implied he would not, but that seemed
most convenient.

He set aside the confusion. That law, doubtless, had been
devised during times of prosperity and calmness, when transi-
tions of mages could be leisurely and honorable. Such ex-
cuses, at least, came easily to his mind. He was still a thief.
And if it all turned out well in the end—would it justify what
he was about to try?

Strong motivations. Even bravery.

The Serpent's head gave off its own light now. The small,
clouded eyes and underslung scythe of a mouth, with two
curves of tiny white teeth, were all too apparent. Michael felt
as if his heart would stop. The Serpent could swallow him
whole in a couple of bites, an act of topsy-turvy, turned-
sidewise cannibalism . . . or simple survival.

Then it's a contest, the Serpent said. *You're worthy of a contest. See if you can take what you need.*

The Serpent broke the surface. Michael did likewise. At the same moment, the moon shed a rich, cold platinum light on the smooth loch. The beam drew a line down the Serpent's wake, and Michael saw its skin glittering with jewels and the fresh strong arms it was using along with its tail and thickened fins to propel itself through the water.

"You really are part of the original sin, aren't you?" Michael accused, his voice echoing from the hills and rocks of the opposite shore. He realized what he was doing. Despite everything, he had come away from his first meeting with the Serpent intensely impressed. He was shedding those last bits of regard; what he had to try now, he could not in all conscience do to something—someone—he truly respected.

Michael swam to the shore. The Serpent followed, matching his pace, its blunt eel nose never more than three yards behind.

Michael stood in the shallows. The Serpent was quiet. It was no more than a few yards from the shore, and the moonlight was fading. He did not try to probe the Serpent's thoughts; what was coiling and tensing within him could be given away by that.

My time has come around again, Michael Perrin. My face returns.

The Serpent pushed itself onto the pebbly surface, the moon glistening on its skin through sporadic breaks in the slick black clouds. Michael's palms tingled furiously now, making his arms ache. Shiafa—

He touched her mind lightly. He still had not found sufficient strength within himself to accomplish what he needed to do. Ashamed, he asked for her help—again—and felt a surge of sexual response, magical strength, intertwined. She did not know what to do with her power, but she knew what his "borrowing" meant. He could hardly avoid entanglement now.

She very nearly had him.

The sadness that welled up in Michael was as painful as the feeling in his hands. *Kristine.*

Sixty million years of mixed sanity and madness, dreaming and plotting. The Serpent, whatever he had done, deserved this coming moment of freedom from the Sidhe curse—

Michael recognized the subtle wash of the Serpent's persuasion and blocked it. His emotions were being played with on more levels than he could watch carefully. The Serpent's probes were incredibly subtle, undetected until now...

Which meant it knew the danger Michael presented.

Michael asked himself, *What in God's name are you*

The loch shore exploded, bushes and grass flaring for an instant into daylight brilliance, burning with a horrifying gasp of air that shook the waters and made them shrink back toward the center

Who did that

And the Serpent writhed on the shore, arms pulled from their grasp on the rocks, a face emerging from its carp-eyes and underslung, moon-shaped mouth, it is changing, now it has a face again, who is

The horror of my people carried in this (Shiafa)

mixing the fires, going out after such fury, the moon gone and the sky like a helmet

Uncoil. Lunge. Who is

Michael, not the Serpent, which seems stunned. Michael stands over it, the Serpent's thickness rising to above his waist, the face coming out and a handsome face, not very unlike that of a Sidhe, the first face of ur-human seen on Earth for sixty million years, brother to Sidhe one would think.

And within its mind Michael works his way rapidly, putting to work utilities he did not know he had, tossing out the Serpent's personality and thieving from those reserves of knowledge he knew he would need. Unable to avoid some aspects of becoming the Serpent, for knowledge is the man (and becoming more entwined with Shiafa with every instant of his use of her powers) and breathless above the Serpent watching

Who flamed the bushes—diversion but by whom?

How many minds have I

The sixteen-year-old boy has shrunk to nothingness, leaving only a trail of memory

Shiafa is in his place

Lord, lord of my youth, wherever you have gone, whatever you may be unless you are just another stronger of us who aspire to make worlds I cannot ask your help this is not right but I need your help

The Serpent fought back suddenly, and Michael's head seemed to explode in fire as had the brush along the shore.

The flames crisped the letters of the Serpent's curse onto Michael's soul.

You have not earned any right to do this to me.

"Then give me what I need!" Michael cried out into the night. Shiafa shouted some of the words with him, a poorly slaved extension.

You would have us live with them, after what they did to us . . .

"And no revenge! An end to the war!"

Never.

But Michael was already learning from the Serpent, taking what he needed. He saw the meaning of the excrescences on his palms and knew what he was. Once there had been many like himself, sixty million years ago; with their passing, the world's unruliness had been practically guaranteed.

They had not been mages. They had served the mages that had created this world and many others (!) like it. They had been called makers. In the absence of the intricate organization that the Serpent remembered, Michael would have to be both maker and mage, craftsman and creator.

The Serpent struggled against him, kicking up the rocks. Several large stones struck Michael and Shiafa, drawing blood from his outstretched hand and forehead and doubling her over with a gasp, but he did not flinch.

Even as the transformation continued, the symbols on the Serpent's belly did not fade. Instead, they glowed with a new malevolence and with new life. Its sounds, as it rolled and flopped on the beach, knocking free some of its jeweled scales, were agonized beyond any pain caused by Michael.

More and more, the Serpent was returning to the form of Manus—the mage's name, sixty million years ago, before humans had lost their final battle with the Sidhe, and he had been made to carry the eternal burden of defeat.

Michael consumed its—his—memories as rapidly as he could, but they were fading and contorting horribly under his anchored probe. Manus writhed on the shore, steam rising from the letters on his dark, golden-colored skin. The jeweled scales had all fallen away, littering the beach like a spilled chest of treasure.

The mage now had two arms and two legs. His tail had diminished to a black nubbin at the base of his spine. With a moan, he turned over on his back. His face was once again completely human—but it was blank.

Michael's probe thrashed around within a vast cavern.

"There's nothing," Michael said, rising to his knees. He felt a wave of nausea; his exhaustion was little short of insensibility. "Where did he go?"

Shiafa backed away from the water and the combatants on her hands and knees, crab-wise. Michael had released her from the conflict. "Where did who go? He's there." She pointed with one long finger at the body barely visible near the quivering water.

"He's empty. There's nothing in his memory."

The one-time Serpent Mage stared up at the sky, face as blank as a corpse's, chest heaving and hands clenching and relaxing. He made small mewling sounds and writhed feebly on the pebbles. The moon reflected from the mage's eyes, as flat and dull as the eyes of an old dead fish, as empty of thought as a snake's. The letters marked by the Sidhe millions of years past lay like gold-encrusted welts on his stomach.

Using the knowledge he had stolen, Michael could read them now and could see how they had changed as the Serpent's form had changed.

For as long as the Sidhe know darkness, what is within, without. That had been the curse marked by the Sidhe mage, sixty million years past. But now a new line had appeared.

What is without, within.

Michael crawled closer to the mage, reaching out to touch him. The flesh was warm. He appeared to be in healthy middle age, though the subtle differences in his features precluded accurate judgment.

Michael felt the presence of an opening gateway and saw the mage's assistant running toward them. Dawn was a blue patch to the east. The Breed woman stood in vague silhouette against that blueness, between her master and the loch's still waters, and knelt on the pebbles. She touched him, her hand just inches from Michael's.

Then she turned her eyes to Michael, squinting to see him more sharply in the half-darkness of the moon and infant day. "You are not him," she said flatly. "You've come back, but you are not him."

Michael was too sick and tired to answer. He pulled back from the naked man and lay beside Shiafa, with whom he felt an intense connectedness, not love or lust or even need, but something *a priori*. They lay pressed against each other on the rocks, waiting for the sun to warm them. The mage's assistant could have done anything to them then; they were as helpless as beached jellyfish. But she simply crouched with her hand resting on the mage's stomach, near the letters that glittered with a light of their own. Slowly, she drew back her fingers into a fist, raised the fist as if to strike something, anything, and then stood. "So long," she said. Michael wondered vaguely if she were leaving.

"I've been with him, off and on, for a thousand years," she continued. "He waited for this day, when Tonn's death and the confusion would free him."

"What's wrong with him?" Michael croaked. "I did nothing that would have . . . left him like this."

" 'What is without, within,' " she quoted. "For sixty million years, he had a man's mind confined in the body of a serpent. *Blessed* Adonna," she croaked, her words thick with sarcasm. "Blessed, forgiving mage of the Sidhe. One curse was not enough. Now that the first has ended, he's made a second by twisting the words. The mage has a man's body—"

Manus rolled over and stared blankly at Michael and then at his assistant, eyes as shallow as road scum after a light rain. He opened his mouth and made a noise like air escaping a balloon.

"—and now, the mind of a serpent," she finished, nudging him lightly with a toe. Manus recoiled. "Adonna has finished with him. What do you have?"

"I'm sorry," Michael said, feeling a wash of distant horror, as if an inner crowd were screaming through a thick stone wall. "I don't know what you mean."

"Did he lose it all, then?" the Breed asked. "All his knowledge, all his thoughts?"

Michael closed his eyes and followed a trail of light through the darkness behind his eyes. Once, he had been a boy and had lived in a boy's body, with a boy's mind, like a very small but well-made cottage.

Now the boy was gone, and the man who replaced him lived in a palace, crumbling and crooked, but magnificent beyond description and filled with mysteries. It would take him years to explore that palace and learn all its passageways and perils.

"No," the Breed said, standing over him. "You did the

mage a favor. He didn't even know. You've taken from him and preserved. Now what will you do with what you've stolen?" She turned to Shiafa. "So it starts again. The whole sad chronicle starts again." She shook her head vigorously, hair flying out against the gray sky, and marched back to the rent in the air, lifting her leg and hopping through, drawing the ripped edges together after her.

Manus rotated his head to stare at the gray, stone-like sky above them, his human jaw opening and closing rhythmically, his human legs twitching.

Michael managed to pull some strength from his *hyloka* and got to his feet, helping Shiafa to stand beside him.

"You have his knowledge?" she asked, watching him with eyes feverishly bright.

Michael nodded. "Some of it." He felt a sob coming and could not stop it; the sound shook him once, violently, and he hiccoughed it back, covering his lower face with one hand. Some seconds later, in control again, he removed his hand from his mouth and said, "I don't even know how I took it."

His head was full of voices, all unfamiliar. He stumbled over an image of the mage's youth, when the child Manus had wandered through a grove on old Earth, surrounded by huge trees beside which sequoias were puny—trees of no shape Michael had ever seen, with trunks like rubbed ivory and leaves as translucent as glass.

Tumbling after this came memories of the meeting with the last serious human candidate. Manus had used all his remaining powers to cast a shadow, appearing to the Nazarene on a rocky hill in Judea, almost two thousand years before.

Michael saw the face of Christ, strong and fine-boned, eyes black but hair brown almost to red, his eyes drawing almost all attention away from the body, which was broad-shouldered and of medium height.

Michael held his hand over his face, squeezing his temples and nose, and saw Elme and Aske and the garden where their children had played—and the infant Crane Women, grandchildren of Adonna, dancing around the bejeweled Serpent, while Adonna himself played the larger game of godhood among the mountains of Ararat and across the river plains of the Tigris and Euphrates.

And then Michael saw the position above all worlds, where those who would seriously make worlds must stand. The place called Null.

The tears returned to Michael's eyes. Now that he had part of the mage within him, he could assess the truth of Manus's long, tortured life . . .

And he could feel the emotions that had stayed alive within the mage for sixty million years—the horror and rage at what had happened to his people, the dismay at how what had once been paradise had decayed into factional fighting and self-destruction.

None had deserved what had been visited upon them.

Even the giants of those past ages had been as powerless as children against circumstance.

The depth of Michael's pretension was beyond assessment. But it was far too late to take another course. Adonna had removed a potential rival from the contest; Michael had not broken the law of mages, for Manus had never truly been a candidate; the curse would obviously have prevented that.

Now there was only Tarax, Clarkham and Michael. And at last Michael had most of the expertise he needed to begin applying his talents with some small hope of success.

"I know where we should go next," he said. Already, he thought of Shiafa as a part of him, practically inseparable.

"To battle my father," Shiafa said.

The vacant Manus tried to rock back and forth. Michael pressed his hand to the mage's forehead. Applying Manus's own knowledge, he brought to an end the life of the world's oldest living creature, the last of the first race of humans. The mage's eyes became flatter, and finally the last faint gleam of awareness went out of them. Michael lowered the corpse's eyelids with two fingers.

"No," Michael said, "not to fight Tarax."

Shiafa seemed almost disappointed. "To find Kristine?" she asked hesitantly.

Kristine.

He shook his head. A far voice said, *One step at a time,* and he hardly recognized it.

Michael held out his hand to her, and she grasped it. Something not entirely pleasant passed between them. Manus's memories now told him specifically what would happen if he stayed with Shiafa much longer, but for the moment, he could not stop himself. He still needed her power.

38

There was no need to return to Los Angeles. To Michael, all places on Earth were pretty much alike now; all places offered equal opportunities for entry to Null, and that was the next step he must take.

A mage or maker could not create mature worlds within worlds already established. He wondered that this had not been obvious to him sooner; young worlds contradicted old in fundamental ways and could not thrive when bound by the *a priori* rules. The pearlescent globes that had extruded from his hands had been suppressed by his location, not stillborn because of his inexperience. He wondered, then, that Clarkham had made as much progress as he had—for he was certain the Isomage had never been to Null.

Had the possibility been made clear to him, Michael realized through Manus's knowledge, at age two or three he could have functioned as a maker and spun tiny infant worlds, toy worlds as it were. What potentials lay buried in humankind; what potentials might be released now that the altered Earth suggested so much?

They buried the mage Manus in the hills beyond the lake, under a crisp copper-green sky shot with ribbons of cloud. Shiafa helped him move the body without a sign of her previous fear and disgust.

When that was done, Michael stood on a hill overlooking the loch. Shiafa stood beside him, glancing at him now and then uncertainly, hopefully.

"You are no longer Tarax's," Michael said finally.

"No," she admitted.

"You cannot serve him now."

She shook her head.

"Do you know why he sent you to me?"

"To be a trap," she replied, eyes narrowing as if in anticipation of a blow to the face.

"How many curses were exchanged during the War!" Michael mused. "Overt curses, hidden curses, curses doubling back on each other. How clever in their cruelties our ancestors were. But this curse. . . . That Sidhe men and women can be the destruction of each other. Did you know this?"

"No."

"If I become a mage after taking a Sidhe mate," Michael said, "the Sidhe part of me, however small, will assert itself. I will become obsessed with my mate, bury myself in her, adore her until all my powers are drained. We will eat each other alive. And yet to have the power necessary to make the highest sorceries, I need to draw power from a woman. Sidhe women carry the magic. And because I have Sidhe in me, I cannot become a mage of humans alone . . .

"I must love, and steal, and then . . . I must escape. And I will not escape unless my mate is transformed, otherwise I will continue to be held by her. The second part of the initiation. First, you kill your favorite horse . . . and then, you kill or transform your mate." Michael shuddered. "Females do not know this?"

"I did not."

"The Ban of Hours knew. This is what it takes to be a mage among the Sidhe. Since I have Sidhe blood, I could be trapped. Tarax took his chances. Your father."

Shiafa was shivering. "You do not have all my power," she said.

"I haven't tried to take it all at once, only to borrow it. The more I borrow, the more I need. But I cannot take any more without mating."

"Use the Serpent's power. Leave me here."

"I took no power from the mage. What little he had left, I've already exceeded. His other powers were blunted at the end of the War, when he was cursed."

"But you have to leave me—"

"I can't," Michael said. "If I face Tarax in Null, just as I am, I will lose, and all my people will suffer. I can probably defeat Clarkham, who acquired his magic in other ways. But not Tarax."

Shiafa sat down on the grass. Her shivering had progressed almost to the point of convulsions. Michael touched the top of her head. "What are you feeling?" he asked.

"Lost," Shiafa said. "Full of hatred."

"Do you hate me?"

She shook her head, a motion barely distinguishable from her shivering.

"Draw from the center," Michael suggested.

"There's *nothing* at my center," she countered. "I'm as empty as a gourd. I've never been anything. Not to myself."

"What would you be?" he asked.

The question seemed to calm her. "A fine lady of the Sidhe. I don't want powers or importance. I reject the courts and councils. I reject my father's goals. I would take all of that and give it away . . . to you, if you need it. . . . But it won't be given away. It sticks with me. I can't give, and it is useless within me, and if you take it, it destroys both of us."

Michael sat beside her. He had lost all sense of urgency. He knew precisely how much time the world had left—three days and some hours before time itself became completely unreliable. Plenty of time to accomplish whatever he would accomplish. "What does a fine lady of the Sidhe do?" he asked.

"I imagine my mother was a fine lady. She worked hand in hand with her mate and—she was gone. I never knew what happened to her. Ideally, a Sidhe woman should aspire to the simple joys of living within a well-tended world, among Sidhe—"

"And humans?"

Shiafa seemed unable to absorb the suggestion. Michael sighed. "Still your father's daughter."

"Then reject me!" she spat, edging away from where he sat. "Find what you need somewhere else!"

"If only I could," he said. *How close to Tarax's trap have I come? The easy way, the obvious way—borrow what you need, rather than face the uncertainty.* He tried to find a solution in all of Manus's memories, but there was none. Just as Manus had not understood souls, only stripped them from the Sidhe, so had he taken away love from Sidhe mages.

Nobody's solutions worked perfectly for Michael.

If you would do everything you can to avoid losing and waste all your energies before the battle truly begins—seek-

ing ultimate assurances and security—then you only destroy yourself.

And where did that wisdom come from? Not from Manus. Not from Adonna. Not even from the Crane Women or the mage of the Cledar.

It came from young, unpolished, uncertain Michael Perrin.

"All right. I won't use your powers any more," Michael said.

"Who will, then?" Shiafa asked, not believing him.

"I don't know. Perhaps you."

"To do what? Work for my father's cause?"

"I don't know." He was still attracted to her. He would have to fight that; right now, compared to Shiafa, Kristine seemed a pale and feeble object of passion.

What could Kristine offer a mage? She was mortal, human, not even especially beautiful compared to some of the beauties he had seen—the Ban of Hours, for example. What good would she do a young mage, what could she teach him or give to him?

Nothing. She was a totally impractical love. He didn't even know that what they had was truly love. It might be evanescent. He might rescue her and find her drifting away from him within weeks or months, leaving him alone. If he bonded with Shiafa, they would never be able to leave each other . . .

He might—he *would* find some way to hold back the mutual destruction. *You are what you dare . . .*

But that was not something he would dare. He would not defy the warning image of Adonna's wife, nameless, turned into a monster and condemned to slide across the Blasted Plain.

No wonder the Sidhe mage had hidden his final revenge.

No wonder all of history was cruel, revenge stacked upon revenge, punishment upon punishment.

Break the cycle.

"I'm returning you to Tarax," Michael said.

"I don't even know where he is," Shiafa said.

"I think I do. He's where I should be now. So we'll go to him together."

39

Stolen memories:

Of a time when the Earth occupied the center of all space-time, and the sky was full not of stars but of jeweled lights, other worlds not far away to which one could travel on *epon* in a few days' time . . .

And when *days* were determined not by the orbit of a sun but by the duration of a haze of light that suffused all creation.

Manus, initiate and candidate for the position of mage of humans—one among tens of thousands of candidates—undergoing his discipline in the forests and mountains, among immortal trees and clean, sweet snow-smelling peaks that never rebelled to kill but sometimes managed a little defiance simply to *challenge* . . .

Consorts and wives Manus shared with other candidates . . . some of the consorts themselves candidates to be the supreme creator, maintainer, master of the craftsmen makers, tenders and designers bearing the honorific of *Gardener* or *Weaver of Lace*, keepers of the paradise where a thousand different varieties of beings lived, dominant (in numbers only) being Sidhe, humans, Spyrggla, Cledar—and Urges, from whom most but not all of the makers were chosen, hence the legend of the demiurges, workmen of the gods.

Memories of a sky as pure and entrancing as sapphire or lapis, filled with the airborne Sidhe Amorphals and the Cledar, master singers and the inventors of nonvocal music; and of oceans so pellucid that swimmers and sailors could see a thousand feet below the surface and witness the deep sports of the Pelagal Sidhe.

Manus was young in those times. By his maturity, the

golden age had tarnished and the sweetness between races soured. By his accession to magehood, his inherited realm was a welter of skirmishes and infighting, threatening to erupt into outright warfare.

Accustomed to the purity of sweet reason and orderly debate, very few in his time were prepared to face the upwellings of hatred and suspicion. Almost none were immune to the sickness that passed among all the races. Sides were chosen, and those who supported the humans—virtually all races but the Sidhe—quartered creation and gave the Sidhe the least desired section.

That was when the war truly began . . .

And Manus had been powerless to prevent it. He had, in fact, been swept up in the sickness, as had the then-mage of the Sidhe and the mages of the other races.

The outcome Michael had known already, but Manus's memories added horrifying detail. The true Fall . . .

What many thought of as humanity's fall, distorted in the myth of Adam and Eve and the serpent, had been in fact the beginning of a climb to a new maturity in a creation left to go completely out of control.

Space had spread almost without limit. The creation had merged with wild and discarded continua, and in the necessary coming together of laws for existence, the fine-tuning of the mages and makers had been abrogated. Unfamiliar and alien intelligences had appeared at these distant borders. The triumphant Sidhe, alarmed that in their victory they were declining into easeful ways, had set out across the Great Distance, as these newly accessible regions were called. Followed the war called Quandary, lasting millions of years, of which Manus knew very little, imprisoned as he was on Earth.

Then the Sidhe had returned, neither victorious nor defeated, but somehow lessened by their journeys. . . . And only one of them had aspired to be maker and mage: Tonn. Tonn had been the last to go to Null, where creations were arranged, and to work true magic to shape the Realm.

For the ten thousand years since, Null had gone unoccupied.

Michael knew the combinations of discipline necessary to open a mage's gate. From the hill overlooking the loch, he used Manus's memories and spread wide a black gash in the rock and dirt, unlike the gates in the air he had made before.

This gash led into a near-total lack of qualities, with the most minimal of enforced patterns.

Michael and Shiafa stepped into Null.

"Beneath" Null was the mist Michael had seen beneath the Realm, but even more unstructured and painful to witness. "Above" Null was a negative plane of dissolution, where badly contrived creations could be recycled, falling back to the mist. Null could be used as an eraser, should a maker or mage decide a new creation must be eliminated.

These two, mist and negative plane, spread across all manner of distances and dimensions; and "between" them, where no untrained human eye could track or decipher, lay Null itself, a simple structure of black cubes resembling an enormous mineral specimen. But Null was not made of rock or of anything else.

It was a place marker, a beginning point.

It had never been "made" by anybody. Existing before all creations, or all peoples, Null had a timeless and *a priori* reality that Michael found difficult to comprehend, even with Manus's memories.

Tarax already stood on the uppermost cube, lost in concentration. In his hands he held a pair of calipers, the two points of the calipers spanning a featureless ivory-colored sphere floating before him.

Michael entered Null on the next cube down. Shiafa closed her eyes and moaned as she appeared on the surface of a third cube a short distance away, if distance meant much here— which it did not.

Tarax glanced away from his measurements and smiled at Michael as an equal. *Welcome, candidate,* he said. There was no sound in Null and hence no voices but those conveyed by mind. Even those communications seemed tinny and weak. It was obvious to Michael that nobody could remain in Null for long without losing all material form, and perhaps all mental order as well. It was not meant for habitation; it was meant for the highest kinds of creation.

Thank you. The chivalric politeness did not seem out of place here. The sheer, oppressive lack of order had to be compensated for.

My daughter should not be here. She is not equipped for these reaches.

I have given part of myself to her that she might come and witness.

Witness what, our struggle?

Perhaps.

Tarax indicated the sphere between the calipers. *This is almost finished. It can support all those now alive on Earth. Would you condemn both our peoples to destruction to assume your own petty prominence?*

Michael was fascinated by the difference between Tarax's nascent creation and the tiny pearls he had grown. *You would abandon the old world completely?*

What use is it? It is harsh and uncontrolled. My people live there with difficulty. As flawed as the Realm was, it supported us in comfort.

Do you have room for all the races?

Tarax spread his arms wide. *All are welcome.*

I don't think my people would know how to live in a creation so isolated from Earth.

They would learn.

Michael now knew the full extent of the law of mages. Candidates could not simply "have it out" in Null; they were here by sufferance. What that meant precisely—who was suffering their presence?—Michael could not find in Manus's memories. But at any rate, while they were here, they could not settle the issue by any form of combat—

Except one.

Michael felt the pearly excrescences spread across both of his palms. He had an advantage over Tarax . . .

His creation would not begin from scratch. The example of an unruly, unpredictable garden gone to seed, hothouse growths subsumed, wild and self-sustaining growths dominant—the example of Earth and all space-time around it lay buried within Michael, innate, felt if not understood. And the maker part of him could use that as a beginning.

Tarax would try for a pure creation, outside and beyond the despised Earth. He would attempt what Adonna had ultimately failed at—creation *ex nihilo*. That was a very Sidhe thing, style and bravado. Michael admired that.

But even with Manus's memories, he could not compete on that level. (If you merge with Shiafa . . .)

He tossed that murmur aside and glanced at Tarax's daughter. She stood bravely on the black surface. *I've brought your daughter to you.*

Is her training finished?

It is. She knows as much as I knew when you brought her to me. I trained her as the Crane Women might have.

Tarax's creation increased in apparent diameter. He expanded his calipers and measured it again, nodding. *Then you will learn where your human woman is.*

Did you send Shiafa to me as a trap? Michael inquired.

Is that relevant? You have evaded the trap, if I did.

There are people on Earth who would consider such a trap villainous, the tactic of a desperate coward.

Tarax seemed unperturbed. *I wonder that you would believe I care for the opinions of humans.*

Where is Kristine?

I can tell you where she is, but not how to get there. Clarkham has her in one of his endless sketches for a creation.

I already know that much. I've fulfilled my bargain. Tell me what you promised you would tell me.

In number, it is Clarkham's fortieth creation, and you may find it among one of the bottles of wine he made in the Realm . . . or in the wine he stole from Adonna, the celebrational nectar of the Sidhe mages.

Wine for the Sidhe? *Where does he keep these wines?*

You've tasted some of them already. He hid them in various places.

Michael subdued the anger he felt. *This is not our bargain,* he said, the nacre spreading between his hands as he brought them together. Shiafa looked on, squinting against the unaccustomed nonquality of Null's space-time extension.

Never trust a Sidhe. You've heard that adage, no doubt.

Michael grinned and turned to Shiafa. *You are free to choose. I do not need your power now.* His confidence had taken a perverse leap with Tarax's statement. Whatever etiquette existed in Null, whatever rules were implied by the law of mages, simply masked a jungle law—

Survival of the fittest. Or more succinctly, the *finest.*

And Michael had grown up in a jungle creation, not in the hothouse Realm Tarax carried in his deepest instincts.

Michael withdrew all his balancing judgments and restraints. He pulled back all the controls, those he had known and those he had never even been aware of.

A maker has no conscience, he said to Tarax. *Where is your maker, Priest?*

I am my own maker.

Michael's grin became positively feral. *Did you discover this talent within you, or learn it?*

Tarax did not reply. His ivory globe was now nearly as broad as he was. The calipers vanished from his hands. *We cannot compete here, Man-child.*

But this is the only competition that matters, Michael responded.

He spun the nacre between his palms into a pearl the size of a baseball. Rose-colored lines washed around the little sphere. Manus's memories approved—this was a vigorous creation. It carried its own inner light and confidence. Tarax's large bone-colored globe was a patchwork, virtually stillborn effort. It would grow, perhaps even become a coherent creation, but it would be no better than Adonna's Realm, and probably worse. Tarax was aware of this, Michael suspected.

Within his own pearl, Michael felt all the contradictions and difficulties of the unruly Earth. Spice in the mixture. Give the creation a little autonomy; allow it to surprise the maker. Leave the sting in the bee, the thorn on the rose, and the spider in the garden. These incongruities will remind the inhabitants of the thorns within themselves, the evils that spring not from worlds but from individuals, and perhaps they will not soon forget, and not soon succumb to the disaster that befell all races sixty million years before.

Michael's little pearl-creation fairly pulsed with its own confidence and eagerness. *This world already lives,* he thought. *I simply have to give it freedom. It requires very little power from me, merely encouragement.*

This world is like a child.

Michael felt a burst of joy within him that transcended any emotion he had ever known before. He was once again a child rolling mud into a ball. The greatest art of all time—creation of a world—was really no more profound and exalted than a child's play.

And into the pearl went this aspect of innocent enthusiasm, to counter the wisdom of the bee's sting and the rose's thorns. The pearl threatened to burst into light.

Tarax kept his bloated bone-sphere close to him, apparently worried lest it be released too early.

Michael lay his fingers on the surface of his pearl and, lifting it above the black surface of Null, pushed it away from him across the "distance" to the mist. Shiafa's thoughts as she watched were like a song.

You do not need me, she said. *I am free.*

Michael turned with tears in his eyes, his face glowing red. *I don't know what it is I've done. You helped me come here. But you are right. I do not need you.*

With his thoughts, there poured forth a residue of the energy he had put into the pearl. Shiafa added part of her own self, her own thoughts. And in those thoughts lived a small, self-contained world that impressed itself on both of them for the merest instant.

And in this tiny world—

Michael and Shiafa lay down under the spreading boughs of an ivory-trunked tree in the lost creation of their ancestors. They removed their simple hand-spun and hand-sewn clothes and reveled in their beauties and flaws, taking as much pleasure in the flaws as the beauties. They cataloged their differences, Sidhe and mostly-human. They replaced the tensions that had once plagued them and savored such flavors like bitter herbs in a rich stew.

They held each other in the suffused light of the old world, moving against each other, their friction bringing on a delicious passion cut free of all guilt and necessity.

They *loved*. Michael was no longer a teacher and Shiafa no longer a student. For a dangerous instant, they were totally connected; but that instant existed only in a shared fantasy, and the connection was robbed of all its dire consequences.

They parted.

The little world dissolved.

Shiafa wavered in the uncertain reality of Null, her face as bright as the moon, eyes closed, still savoring the dreamworld they had made for each other. Then she did something she had never done for Michael or for anybody else in her life; she opened her eyes and smiled at him, directly and without reservations.

Michael nodded to her—respect, relief, all his best wishes.

Shiafa pulled aside a curtain, revealing sunlight and rugged desert hills—perhaps Israel—and departed from Null. She had been released from both Michael and her father.

Michael's pearl had orbited Null several times, then dropped abruptly to the mist, where it waited like seed in a womb for the proper moment to lay itself over the desperately ill Earth. Tarax still held on to his bone-egg, now nearly as broad as Null itself, if Null had any breadth.

There is no battle between us, Michael said. *I wish you luck.*

The desperation in Tarax's face then was beyond what Michael had expected or desired. The Sidhe was failing as a maker, but no others were available.

The Maln had destroyed the last of the Urges long ages ago.

Michael moved forward to help. The bone-egg bubbled, wildly overextending, developing far too many qualities for a single creation. To Michael, it was obvious Tarax had been overdeliberate, overcautious.

It's dangerous, he told the Chief of the Maln. *Send it out to dissolve. Start again.*

No, Tarax said. *It is the best I can do . . .*

It's flawed.

Leave!

Michael watched the bone-egg swell between the mist and the hideous solvent "sky," Tarax laboring beside it like an ant with a boulder. For a moment, he wondered if Tarax's world-sized abortion would harm the Earth and his own nascent creation.

But Manus's memories told him, this is what Null is for. Nothing that goes wrong here can affect the worlds beyond. Only if Tarax tried to apply his abortion beyond Null—something he did not have the strength to do, in Michael's judgment—was there danger. At any rate, there was nothing Michael could do to stop him.

Before he departed from Null, he allowed himself one last comment to Adonna's self-proclaimed successor.

There's no substitute for talent, he said.

Tarax did not respond. White hair sticking out from his head with the effort of controlling the bone-egg, he looked after Michael with a pitiful yearning totally uncharacteristic of the Sidhe priest.

The past makes victims of us all, Michael realized even more sharply. The last of his animosity simply evaporated.

He pulled the gap shut after him and stood on the sidewalk

before his parents' house, in the glow of a sizzling streetlight, the night a frightening dark sheet of warm metal laid over the city and half the Earth.

The pearl's convergence with Earth had not begun yet. Whatever would happen, would happen in its own due time.

He opened the door. In the living room, his father was presiding over a meeting of neighbors. The electricity was out, and candles had been placed around the room, on the fireplace mantle and on top of the entertainment center and hall credenza. As Michael entered, a plump middle-aged man wearing a golfing sweater and baggy slacks interrupted a vehement diatribe on the lack of city services. Michael glanced around the room. He recognized most of the people there: Mr. Boggin, the plump speaker, and his wife Muriel; the Wilberforce family, six- and seven-year-old daughters sitting before the blank television; grandmotherly Mrs. Miller, widowed before Michael's return from the Realm; the Dopsos; and Warren Verde, a bookseller friend of John's.

"Any news?" John asked quietly.

"Your son is involved in all this, that's what Ruth and Mrs. Dopso have been saying, isn't it?" Mr. Boggin asked. John didn't answer. "Well?" Boggin persisted, facing Michael. "What do you know? What can we expect?"

Michael frowned. He could feel the man's mental state all too acutely; his thoughts smelled of sweat and the fear of his own inadequacy. Mr. Boggin knew he was not the sort of man to survive a major crisis on stamina or wits. Clarkham's words on whom the candidates would be creating worlds for returned to Michael, and he mentally brushed them away.

"There's been a kind of battle," he said.

"These invaders," Warren Verde interjected. "Have you been talking with them?"

Michael nodded. "More than that."

Mrs. Miller moaned and twisted her hands in her lap.

"I've been working to see what can be done to put things right again." That, he knew, was about as much as they could take right now. "Where are the guests?" he asked his father.

"Moffat and Crooke and several other people took them away. They've arranged for rooms at some downtown hotels."

One thing at a time. And the time had come.

"Dad, did Mr. Waltiri ever give you bottles of wine?"

John smiled. "Two bottles," he said. "We never drank them. Waiting for a special occasion."

"Are they in the wine closet?" John kept a fair collection of wines in a cool first-floor hall closet.

"I think so. Ruth?"

"I haven't touched them," Ruth said. Her eyes had not left Michael since his entry.

"Then they should still be there. Do you need them?"

"Who's Waltiri?" Mr. Boggin asked.

"The composer," Verde said. "John used to know him, didn't you?"

John had told the guests very little, perhaps for the same reasons Michael had chosen to cut his explanation short. People who rigorously lived their normal lives could not stretch their imaginations to encompass what he now knew.

"I'll get them for you," John said.

"I'll come with you." Michael followed his father into the hall. John took out his keychain and unlocked the closet door, then shook his head. "Can't see anything in there. I'll get a flashlight or a candle." He came back with a candle, but Michael had already located the two bottles on the bottom of the right-hand rack, using his sense of smell more than anything else. One bottle carried the double sundial of Clarkham's winery. The second carried no label whatsoever; this dark, almost black container was oddly shaped, slightly pinched in the middle. The glass had a glazed, metallic sheen.

"Arno had no idea what was in that one," John said. "He said I might save it for a *very* special occasion. I take it this is that occasion?"

"Perhaps not yet," Michael answered. "May I take them?"

"They're yours. Arno . . . wasn't exactly human, was he?"

"Part of him was human," Michael said.

"The part that died."

"Yes."

"You sound distant," John commented. "Something big happened, didn't it?"

"Yes."

"Your mother is worried sick, more about you than the way the world's going, I think. Can you reassure us?"

Michael hugged his father tightly. "I'm still my father's son and my mother's son," he said. "It'll take me some time to tell you what's been happening. Right now, I have one more thing I have to do."

"Involving the Sidhe?" John asked. Ruth came into the hallway and leaned against a wall, her arms crossed. Michael went to her and hugged her, as well.

"Not involving the Sidhe," Michael said.

"Where's Shiafa?" Ruth asked.

Michael laughed and shook his head. "She's not with me. I'm not sure where she is. But she's fine."

"It's not that I'm prejudiced," Ruth said.

"I'm going to look for Kristine," Michael explained.

"In a bottle of wine?" John asked.

Michael lifted the unlabeled bottle. "It's probably just as well you didn't try this," he said. "It's very old."

"How old?"

"Maybe sixty million years."

"That's impossible," John said, and then laughed dryly. "But then, I suppose it isn't. Let me know what it tastes like?"

Michael nodded. "What did the people with Moffat and Crooke say about Mahler and Mozart?"

"I don't think they were convinced at first," John said. "Everybody's out of whack these days. Nobody knows what to do or where to turn. But Moffat seemed to have things in hand."

"I'm going out the back way," Michael said. "Try to keep the people calm. I think everything's going to work out."

"But you're not sure?" Ruth asked.

"No. I'm not sure."

She gave him a sad and intense look, her face pale and tight in the vibrating light of the candle. "I can't believe you're still my son," she said. "Have you met your great-great-grandmother yet?" Her eyes narrowed to slits.

"No," Michael said, smiling now, knowing what she was getting at. "Great-great-Grandpa's Hill wife hasn't come my way."

"If she does," Ruth said, "be sure to tell her something for me."

"What's that?"

"Tell her, 'Boo!'" Ruth said. John took her outstretched hand, and she extended her other hand to Michael. He grasped it firmly.

40

Michael was certain that there was more to Clarkham than had met his eye. Clarkham's concealment of his creations' gateways in bottles of wine was a master stroke. That all of Clarkham's worlds were derivative might or might not be relevant; he certainly did not wish to underestimate the Isomage.

Clarkham had, after all, escaped the combined plots of the Sidhe Councils—with Michael as the barb on the end of a spear-shaft centuries long. And Clarkham was much older than Michael.

That was balanced now by the millions of years of memories from Manus. But Michael had hardly had time to catalog the broad features of those memories, much less take full advantage of them. (What would he become when he had absorbed the entire treasure?)

He carried the bottles down the dark street, vaguely making his way by the candlelighted windows of the houses. He avoided the few people he saw—some drunk, some young and rowdy, some furtive and frightened. They carried Coleman lanterns and flashlights and made a great deal of noise. Their world was crumbling. He did not want to think about them now, or about the responsibilities of a maker and mage—

He was concentrating on Kristine. How long had it been since her kidnapping? Weeks? Months? What had happened to her in that time?

What did she remember? Had Clarkham locked her in some dismal dream-world, as he had Michael? Did she think Michael was dead?

He was going back to where his first journey had begun,

Clarkham's always-empty, always-full house. Once inside, he would drink a toast.

But from which bottle?

The stolen bottle of mage's nectar, however old it was, did not seem the most promising. Clarkham had not considered it important enough to take along with him. Or perhaps Waltiri had hidden it from him. And Clarkham had simply given away or abandoned the other wines, perhaps thinking it next to impossible that anyone would divine (no pun intended, Michael thought wryly) the secret of his worlds' gateways.

But Clarkham knew the secret was out. Michael had intruded once already. No doubt the Isomage, or whatever was left of him, would be on the alert.

Michael stood on the front porch of Clarkham's house. Despite all that had happened, the house still seemed nothing more than a slightly run-down dwelling in a moderately ritzy neighborhood.

In the upstairs dusty-floored guest bedroom, Michael took his Swiss army knife from his pocket and cut the lead foil on Clarkham's bottle. With a pop, the cork came out cleanly and in one piece. Michael smelled the varnish-like stain on the cork's end and then smelled the bottle.

It had not soured.

The gate was clearly inviting him.

He took a sip and sprayed it across the back of his tongue, as his father had taught him. He closed his eyes.

The flavors paraded, and he tasted again the distinct divisions. He counted carefully, using all of his heightened senses to mark the borders on each range of tastes.

Thirty-five, thirty-six different flavors—one dusty and grassy, the world where Clarkham had last conversed with him—and then thirty-seven, richer by far, thirty-eight, thirty-nine—

Like counting the iron gates in the alley between worlds.

And forty. He bore down with all his discipline on that flavor. It was harsh, metallic and stony, and yet behind it lurked the most complex subtleties of all the succession. He thought for a moment, as he crossed, that this fortieth flavor might have once been the finest but had somehow begun to turn, separately from all the others.

Michael was nearly hit by a car as his feet touched hot asphalt pavement. The car screeched to a halt, and the driver cursed at him, then swerved into another lane.

Stunned, Michael left the intersection and stood on the sidewalk. There, he looked up at the street sign. The placards for streets in both directions were blank.

A hot, mellow sun shined down on the pastel stucco-walled buildings with awnings stretched out halfway across the sidewalks. Old streamlined cars—Buicks, Fords, Chevrolets and a single white Packard—with bright paint jobs and glittering chrome drove down the streets, wide white sidewalls on their tires. Men and women in summer attire passed by—Bermuda shorts, sunglasses, Hawaiian shirts, spaghetti-strap print dresses with short-sleeved jackets.

Michael stood off to one side under a black and white striped awning. *So many people.* . . . Where had they come from? For that matter, where was he? He had never suspected Clarkham was capable of creating a world this complex, with such a distinct feel of reality.

Michael entered a men's clothing store to gather his wits. The sunlight through the windows was dazzling. Legless and headless mannequins modeled wide-lapel sports coats and Arrow shirts in the window, surrounded by a small mock-up split-rail fence. A smiling cast-iron black jockey in red and white livery offered a silver ring beside a chair. Michael sat and rubbed his eyes. The taste on his tongue was fading, yet the world was still here, detailed and undeniable. It felt real.

All but the blank street signs.

"May I *help* you, sir?" asked an unctuous salesman in a pinstriped suit. Michael looked up. The salesman's face was round, black hair greased slick, a thin pencil mustache beneath his sharp nose. The salesman smiled, revealing brilliant white teeth.

Michael quickly probed his aura. He had no aura. He was as alive as the mannequins in the window, and as thoughtful.

Michael got up from the chair without replying. The salesman looked over his shoulder at two other salesmen toward the rear of the store. "Sir?"

"I'm fine," Michael said.

"I should hope so, sir. May I help you find suitable apparel?"

"No, thank you."

"Very well."

"What's the date?" Michael asked abruptly.

"September 19th, sir. We're having a summer's end sale. You know that summer apparel is never really out of date in Los Angeles. Some fine buys."

"The year, I mean."

The salesman smiled quite broadly. "The gentleman has been reading too much John Collier, perhaps?"

"I'm serious."

"Nineteen and thirty-seven, give or take a few minutes."

"Thank you."

"Think nothing of it."

Michael left the shop and strolled down the street, delicately probing the people he passed. None were more than animated figures—brilliantly animated, but no more real for all that.

He passed the alcove entrance to a stone-walled office building. A shoeshine stand squatted in one corner, attended by an elderly white-haired black (*Negro*, he almost wanted to say) in a powder-blue wraparound apron. The black smiled at several men as they passed. "Shine? Finest shine." He focused on Michael, starting from Michael's shoes and glancing upward. Michael's suede Hush Puppies did not invite an inquiry.

The shoeshine man was empty, also.

Clarkham had populated his world with vacuous ghosts. In a way, these inhabitants were worse than the dark figures Michael had avoided in Clarkham's dream-prison. Without the discipline, one would probably accept these as people.

He turned back abruptly and entered the alcove, passing through the revolving glass door. In the lobby, he glanced at the magazine stand replete with issues of *Life* magazine and stacks of newspapers and pulps. The vendor, a young, skinny woman with her hair netted in a tight bun, smoked a Camel cigarette, lost in some blank reverie. *Truly blank,* Michael thought. *Emptiness mimicking emptiness.*

His respect for Clarkham grew, tinged with horror. Why did Clarkham wish to populate worlds with simulacra? That seemed a perversion of what being a maker or a mage was all about—providing a habitat for real people.

But perhaps he was missing the big picture, Michael thought. Perhaps these were simply test subjects, architect's toy figurines. He stepped into a wood-paneled elevator with three other simulacra, one of whom—a gray-haired woman in a black silk suit—smiled at him with matronly good-humor.

He returned the smile. The operator, a Latino with deep-set black eyes, asked what floor he wished. Michael said, "Fourth, please."

Anyplace where he could get off and be quiet, away from the simulacra. Where he could spread a large-scale probe across this world and measure its extent. . . . Feel for Kristine.

The door opened at the fourth floor, and Michael stepped out into a cool, shadowy hallway. Near the end of the deserted hall, adjacent to an etched glass-front door marked "Pellegrini and Shaefer, Novelties and Party Favors" in gold letters, he paused by a white ceramic water fountain. Michael spread his probe.

And screamed, withdrawing it immediately.

Head crawling with fire, he slumped to the floor. His mouth seemed to instantly fill with the taste of decayed meat. *Trap,* he thought, pulling in all his senses and calling up a rejuvenating pulse of *hyloka.*

But after a few minutes of silent recuperation, he realized this world was not a trap. What he had felt had not been intended for him. The boundaries of this world—no more than five or six miles on a side—were truly corrupted.

He pulled in the range of his probe and braced himself, taking a deep breath. *Kristine.*

Point by point, he swept the streets and buildings, touching briefly on the hundreds of empty caricatures populating the mock-up city. *It's a film set,* he thought. It wasn't as hollow as the sets he had seen in the Western lot at Moffat's studio, but it was nearly so.

It was a sham.

It couldn't be intended as a serious rival for the worlds the other candidates had constructed. And it obviously wasn't the last of Clarkham's tests. How many mock-worlds had Clarkham created? And how accomplished had he finally been?

Kristine.

As he probed, he felt the foundation of the little world, riddling its secrets, automatically comparing its rules and qualities with the overlay he had recently set loose on Earth. The underpinnings here were smoothly textured, almost slick, difficult to analyze, even more difficult to get a grip on. *The words of Tonn's wife.*

For a moment, he felt a trace of Clarkham, but that passed,

and he could not recover it. And almost immediately after, he forgot about that brief touch, for he found *her*.

Michael's release of breath was clearly audible up and down the length of the still hallway. She was alive, she was reasonably well—and she did not remember who she was.

Kristine was wrapped up in Clarkham's world and thought herself a part of it—just as Michael had.

He punched the button for the elevator and anxiously watched the brass arrow point to the raised floor numbers. The arrow passed the 4, and the doors did not open. At the end of the hall, he heard heavy footsteps shuffling. But he could feel nothing.

The chair. The turning chair.

In the house next door to Clarkham's, on his first passage through to the Realm, Michael had paused to look into the living room and had seen an overstuffed swivel rocking chair with its back turned toward him. The chair had been rocking, and as Michael had watched, it had started turning . . .

With a chill, he had passed by the living room, the chair and its unseen occupant.

The guardians of Clarkham's gateway could have numbered more than two. Tristesse had been stationed by the Sidhe; Lamia had acted as a watcher for both Clarkham and the Sidhe. But the third—

Whatever had been in the rocking chair—

Might have been controlled solely by Clarkham.

Michael had little doubt that the shuffling footsteps he heard at the end of the hall and the occupant of the chair were one and the same.

He swore under his breath and tried to open a gate. But he could find no purchase; the seamless glass-smooth creation allowed for no exits. He swallowed, hoping to wipe the taste of the wine from his tongue, but it lingered. Thinking of the water fountain, he walked quickly to the ceramic basin and turned the handle. The cool water did not erase the taste.

For a moment, Michael felt very foolish. He had just spun loose a thing of incredible complexity and power, an improving overlay for the sick and injured Earth; he had absorbed the knowledge of the world's oldest living being—

And yet he still was afraid. He damped the fear quickly and stood in the middle of the hall, wrapped in a grim calm. Being merely human could get him killed. He explored Manus's knowledge of guardians and other artificial and altered beings. The brief tastes of memory—changelings, conjured devils, witch-waifs, abortions like Ishmael and transformed monsters like the vampiric Tristesse—did not match what he heard approaching.

A door opened and closed around the corner at the end of the hall. Something sniffed delicately. "Hello," a muffled voice said. "I see you've gotten this far."

The voice was barely recognizable.

"Clarkham?" Michael asked.

Again the delicate sniff. "Yes. Have you found her yet?"

"I've found Kristine."

"That's good. You'll pardon me if I don't show myself. I still have some pride. We've never met, you know."

Michael raised his eyebrows. "I beg your pardon?"

"No, we never have. Puzzle it out. Reports from distant shores. Corruption and bad decisions. Vicarious thrills."

"I don't understand."

"I won't get in your way. My ambitions, at least, are few now. And don't confuse the other with me, though we are both failures. The other brought your woman here. You'll contend with him, not me. I regret many things, not least of all . . . him. You can go now."

"Who are you?" Michael asked, confused.

"I've identified myself. Let that suffice. To tell all would be most painful. Find out for yourself. Earn the facts."

Michael thought of the rocking chair. "You were in the house next door to Clarkham's."

"Yes."

"Who were you waiting for?"

"Arno. To apologize. I told him I'd be waiting when I left him the key."

"Did you expect me?"

The sniff was less delicate this time, and much less pleasant. "You can go."

The elevator door opened with a chime. Michael hesitated, then entered. The simulacrum operator smiled toothily at him. "Lobby?" he asked.

Michael nodded.

"Nothing on the fourth floor," the operator said, smirking.

The door closed with a squeak, but behind that squeak, Michael thought he heard a distant groaning wail of anguish. Even through his controlling discipline, his neck and scalp prickled.

The brightness of the sunlight had diminished slightly. He passed the shoeshine stand and turned left down the street in Kristine's direction. When he had first located Kristine, he had seen a distinctively narrow three-story white wood-frame building wedged between two other brick and stone structures. Considering the limited size of Clarkham's creation, Michael didn't think it would take him long to find the site.

The street changed character within a few hundred yards. The buildings became darker and older; brick and stone replaced stucco, and styles seemed to revert to the teens and twenties. The air was cooler, grittier.

The people were different, too. Much less care was being spent on the details of the simulacra. Their faces were blander, more standardized; the worst of them were mere blank-eyed mannequins.

Michael became aware, after walking a mile and a half, that he was much closer to the edge of corruption. He took care to limit the extent of his probe in that direction.

Despite his discipline, he couldn't help becoming more excited—and anxious—the closer he came to Kristine. The undercurrent of his anxiety was excruciating. So much had happened since they last met; even if he could bring her out of this creation and back to Earth—even if Earth was recovering through the influence of his overlay—would they still feel for each other with as much intensity and depth?

So little time together, and the time so strange . . .

Memories of Manus's ancient loves came to him unbidden, colored by rich emotions and contexts he couldn't begin to interpret. There were hardly words in English to describe what the memories conveyed.

Now the figures around him were little more than place markers walking around in barely-sketched clothes. Michael could see and feel the shifting qualities of their presence, holding them together only marginally here on the edge of a corruption that burned.

He saw the narrow white building, sandwiched between two five-story brick apartment complexes. A fire escape crisscrossed its front and ended a few feet above arm's reach over the sidewalk. Beneath the folded ladder, a simple square wooden overhang shadowed the building's double glass and wood doors.

Michael felt for Clarkham's presence, gingerly skirting the painful borders of the creation. There was nothing definite; his probe kept being drawn back to the office building where the unseen figure had addressed him, and Michael kept pulling away from that sensation of lostness and resignation.

He pressed down the latch on the brass handle of the right-hand door and opened it slowly, stepping inside. A wall of tarnished mailboxes waited with timeless patience on the left, beside a janitorial door shut and padlocked. To his right, an ancient map of Los Angeles hung behind dusty and cracked glass.

So much detail . . .

Stairs covered with frayed oriental-style carpet rose beyond the wall of mailboxes. He began climbing, not needing to refer to the building's directory, knowing which floor. *She is here.*

Kristine, Michael knew, sat at this very moment in a cracked leather armchair behind a glass-topped desk in a small office on the top floor, the third.

He climbed the next flight of stairs, past the second floor landing and doorway, the door hand-lettered in black: "Pascal Novelties amd Party Supplies." Not and—amd. The detail was repeating, and inaccurately.

Clarkham had made much of his creation out of rubber-stamped combinations, prefab units, as it were. Michael thought of the large teeth on both the salesman and the elevator operator. Identical.

On the third floor doorway, in gold letters on the clear glass, he read

TOPFLIGHT DETECTIVES
Ernest Brawley Rachel Taylor
Divorces Investigations Confidential

Behind the door, at the end of the very narrow hallway that ran the length of the building against the right-hand wall, Michael heard Kristine speaking to someone in an undertone.

He walked at a measured pace down the hallway, restraining an urge to run and find her immediately, simply to see her and know by the evidence of his eyes that she was alive and well.

The corruption was so close, barely a few hundred yards away, practically singing against the fabric of the streets and buildings, vibrating in the wood like a threatened quake or tremor. How had she stood it for so long?

The door to the last office was half-open. Michael pushed it all the way. Kristine sat facing the door, black Bakelite desk phone sitting on the glass-topped wood desk in front of her. She held the receiver pressed against her ear and slightly lowered from her heavily lipsticked mouth.

Kristine's hair been arranged in an upswept, split bun above her forehead and pulled tightly back behind into a more full bun. The style was not particularly attractive. She looked hard, weary. Her eyes barely reacted when she saw him.

"Yeah," she said into the phone. "Bring me the timecards, and I'll believe Jimmy was there, like you say. Look, I've got company, I gotta go." She hung up the receiver decisively. "There's a buzzer downstairs. We come down to meet you. What can I do for you?" She appraised him coldly.

He smiled. "It's time to leave," he said.

She stiffened and dropped one hand below desk level. "Where are you going, then?" she asked.

What came next was pure inspiration. He remembered Bogart and Stanwyck going through their timeless motions on the television screen the night his father had first introduced him to Waltiri.

"You mean, where are *we* going," Michael said casually.

"The persuasive type, eh?" Kristine asked, eyes sweeping him again with faint amusement. "You aren't dressed for the part. Ernie has a good tailor—"

"It's not what I'm wearing that counts," Michael said. "It's what I'm thinking."

"Is a penny payment enough?" She still had her hand below desk level, and Michael sensed that it was just an inch or two away from a gun. She knew how to use it, too.

"More than enough. For you, it's free." Michael began to feel gloriously giddy. "I'm thinking you don't belong here. You look and act tough, but I know you better."

"We never met before, Mister."

"Think back. Think back to before you came here. Remember a kiss?"

She smiled wryly. "So sing me the tune the radio was playing. Maybe that'll refresh my memory."

Just the words Stanwyck had used.

Michael wet his lips and walked slowly into the office, sitting on the corner of her desk, watching her hidden arm closely. He began to whistle, hoping he could reproduce at least the basics.

She stopped appraising him. Her large green eyes opened wide with wonder. The face behind the makeup softened noticeably.

"I know that . . ." she said.

"You should. It's our song."

"What's it called?" she asked, both hands on the desk, empty. She seemed about ready to stand, perhaps run.

"Opus 45," Michael said. "Concerto for piano and orchestra, Infinity."

Kristine pushed the chair back. "There's no music like that here," she said.

"It's a simple case of kidnapping."

"Who?"

"You," Michael said, pointing. "Now we have to go."

Her confusion put an end to the enjoyment. Michael held out his hand, and she reached for it, hesitated, then grasped it firmly. The warm touch of her skin was ecstasy.

"Your name is Kristine," he said.

"Yes, of course I know that—Kristine Taylor. I mean . . . Kristine Pendeers."

"And who am I?"

She smiled, and a tear traveled down one cheek, bringing a streak of mascara with it. "You're *Michael*," she said, taking a deep, tremulous breath. "Oh, God. Michael! Where in hell are we?"

"Not far from hell at all," he said. "Come with me."

But first, she ran from behind the desk and wrapped her arms around him. Not so much had happened after all, he decided—not enough to matter. He was crying, too.

41

The difficult part now began: getting home. Michael led Kristine out onto the street. "Something hurts my head here," she said. "I haven't really been able to think about it until now, but it's been hurting for a long time."

"The whole place is rotting away at the edges," Michael said.

Kristine made a face. "That's what it feels like. Can we leave?"

"I'm trying."

"What's happened to you? How long has it been?"

Michael shook his head and held his finger to his lips. "I have to think." He pulled her close to him and nuzzled her cheek, then let her go and drew his palms together to feel for a way out.

"God, all this *gunk*," she said, touching her lips with her finger.

Michael tried again to locate a seam in the apparently seamless matrix of Clarkham's world. The substratum beneath the detail and solidity was masterfully smooth, smoother than it needed to be—as if Michael's father were to spend weeks polishing the underside of a table. Again, there was more craftsmanship than practicality or actual achievement in this world.

"It's going to be hard," Michael said finally, letting his hands drop.

"We can't leave?"

"There has to be a way." He was calling up facts from the Serpent Mage's memories, but in all that Manus knew about makers and creating worlds, there was little about one-way entries. *Detail*, he thought. *How do I use Clarkham's crafts-manship to get out?*

"We're going to walk toward the center. That's where the reality is most complete," he said.

"I'm ready. I have some questions. I think I have some questions, anyway. How long have I been there—months, years?"

"Months, maybe. No more."

"Am I older? I feel older."

"You don't look any older."

"Is this place like the Realm you talked about?"

"Somewhat," Michael said. "It's much smaller, and it's . . . not made the same." They looked at each other intently. "I love you," Michael said. "It's been awful, not being able to find you."

Kristine's face was almost comically serious. "I haven't felt the time, however long it's been. He made me into some-body else. And the funny part is—nothing happened, and *I didn't really notice*. I wasn't bored, but most of the time I just sat behind that desk or walked around the city, thinking I was on a case. . . . Taking phone calls. God, I don't remember what people said to me. It's all jumbled now, but it didn't feel like it when . . . I was in it. Like a bad dream. Not a night-mare, I mean, but badly thought out, artistically bad."

They brushed past figures that became more and more con-vincing and detailed as they approached the center of Clark-ham's creation. "I have a thought," Michael said. "It's crazy, but no crazier than anything else. . . . Do you know a liquor store or a good restaurant around here?"

"Of course," Kristine said. "There's a fancy French place called La Bretonne. Lots of mobsters go there."

"Take me there," Michael said.

"Why?"

"We need to order a good bottle of wine."

La Bretonne was on the ground floor of a stately stone building at the very heart of Clarkham's creation. At four or five in the afternoon—the apparent time of day—it was just beginning to open for its supper "crowd." Neither Michael nor Kristine was dressed for the occasion, and a haughty maitre d' with slicked-down black hair and prominent teeth adamantly refused them service.

This did not stop Michael. Leaving Kristine at the front, he walked to the prominent oak rack of wine bottles on one wall and paced before it, finger to his lips. The maitre d' followed and berated him for his crudeness and bad manners.

"I will call the police, *m'sieur*," he threatened with a terrible French accent.

Michael chose a sauterne—Chateau d'Yquem 1929—and skirted around the man, uncorking the bottle as he rejoined Kristine.

The maitre d', red-faced and huffing like a pigeon in heat, stalked off with loud threats to call the police. Other employees—penguin-like waiters and busboys—stood well clear of the scene, watching with mixed empty amusement and empty irritation.

Michael offered the bottle to Kristine, more out of politeness than any expectation she would be able to use the taste as he intended to. She took a swallow and nodded. "Good wine," she said, returning the bottle.

"Clarkham's a connoisseur of wine. I'd expect him to stock his world with a good cellar." He brought the bottle to his own lips and took a hearty swig. It was indeed a good sauterne, bloody gold in color, and it carried a distinct message—a sweet message of warm sunny fields and evening mists, of a definite *place* on Earth. Michael gripped Kristine's hand as the maitre d' returned, still livid and voluble.

A shadow fell over the restaurant's interior. Kristine paled and held Michael's hand with painful pressure. "I know who that . . ." she began, not needing to finish. Michael recognized it, also.

Out in front of La Bretonne, hidden behind a stone pillar, was the presence he had met on the fourth floor. The simulacra in the restaurant froze and lost definition.

Michael tried to place himself in the middle of the wine's flavors and to take Kristine with him, but the wine was souring on his tongue. The livid gold liquid in the bottle foamed black, and he hastily set it on a table top.

"It came around the agency sometimes," Kristine said quietly, her face drawn with fascination and fear. "I didn't know what it was—it didn't fit in. I never saw it, but I always knew when it was there."

"Mr. Perrin," a voice called behind them. They turned. Standing between the dark, gritty black outlines of the maitre d' and a simulacrum waiter was David Clarkham. He appeared much older than when Michael had last seen him, pallid of face and long of arm, as gaunt as a scarecrow. "You're disrupting everything. That's not unusual for you, is it?"

Michael smiled confidently, though he did not feel very confident. He had once thought himself a match for Clarkham. . . . That the Isomage did not present much of a danger to him.

Now, he was not so sure. The presence outside the restaurant was stranger and more frightening than Tristesse or Lamia, for all its seeming coherence and lack of aggression.

"How clever that you head for my wine collection. I never would have thought of that. It's brilliant, but it won't work. You think the battle—the competition—is over, don't you? I trust you believe you've won, too."

"I don't know that," Michael said. Kristine stared at Clarkham with rising color, her face grim.

"I know you, too," she said. "You're the one who threatened me on the phone and brought me to this foul place."

Clarkham sighed deeply. "I would be quite proud of this world, but for some major difficulties, not entirely my fault," he said. "One of the difficulties is that creatures of genuine, original flesh and blood cannot escape. As you've no doubt discovered, this world has a smooth and flawless foundation. For any would-be mage, it's the equivalent of a pit with sheer ice walls. That was not my original intention, believe me. You cannot leave."

"And you?" Michael asked.

"Whatever advantage it is, I can come and go as I please. How did your entry in the competition fare?"

Michael shook his head. "I haven't been back yet to see."

"Eager to rescue your woman. Laudable enough—if your ambitions are purely human. A mage has to be more deliberate and disciplined. What will you do if things are going wrong on Earth? You're not there to protect your people."

That was true enough. Michael felt a surge of guilt—and anger that Clarkham, of all people, could chide him. He probed Clarkham quickly, shielding his reactions against the expected suffusion of evil. But the Isomage was almost free of corruption.

"I've shed my latest accumulation of dross," Clarkham said. Outside, the unseen presence made a deep, unpleasant noise like coughing. Clarkham appeared momentarily irritated. "This world accepts my difficulties . . . sanitation facilities are abundant, you might say." He put his arm around one of the low-resolution simulacra. "Better than finding humans to dump my disease upon, no?"

Kristine looked as if she might be sick. Her hand tightened on Michael's, and his anger compounded. He brought it under control immediately. *Null*, Manus's memories recommended. *A world ill-conceived can be aborted . . . in Null.*

And if the world envelops the maker?

No creation is absolutely seamless. That came to Michael almost as a truism, compounded of Manus's knowledge and his own experiences in Null.

The presence approached the door of the restaurant slowly. Michael caught a glimpse of it through the front window before it passed behind a wall again; it was large, dark and of no definite color.

"If you can leave here," Michael said, drawing conclusions rapidly, "then you must not be flesh and blood."

"That should have been obvious to you long before now," Clarkham said. He walked to a table and pulled out four chairs. "Let's have a light supper and talk. The food here is exceptional. You can even have that magnificent sauterne served in a glass, which would be more appropriate, don't you think?"

Michael gently urged Kristine forward. She glanced at him resentfully, and he read her combined weariness, fear and hatred of Clarkham without a probe. She was on the edge. She did not know what Michael had become; all she knew was that he had been delayed for quite some time before rescuing her, which implied he was not necessarily more adept or powerful than Clarkham.

"We have another guest," Clarkham said. "Michael has met him already. My dear," he addressed Kristine softly, "do not be frightened of him. He is in some ways my better half, though sorely afflicted. He made this world. He made me."

Clarkham gestured toward the doorway. Silhouetted against the late afternoon light, a small, corpulent man entered La Bretonne, darkness sloughing off him like dust. His skin was pocked and riddled with lesions, giving it a quality of distressed and decaying wood. He wore a wool suit as well-tailored as could be expected, considering his shape and condition.

"Excuse me," he said.

His voice was the same as Clarkham's.

"My original," Clarkham said. "More than a father to me."

"And you are something less than a son," the presence said, waddling slowly toward the table.

Judging from Kristine's expression, there was no question of sitting at table with the two. She was not in the least interested in their relationship; all she saw was a walking horror and a spectral, smiling captor. Michael, though suddenly and almost coldly curious, deferred to her.

"We won't eat with you," he said.

The corpulent presence stopped a few yards from the table, shuffled its feet in indecision, and then said, "I understand."

"How disappointing," said the other.

"Michael," Kristine moaned.

"It's all right," Michael said.

She obviously didn't believe him. "It can't be. This is horrible. I'd rather be back in the office, talking on the phone, not knowing. . . . What are you going to do?"

He took her hand and felt for how much strength she had left. Very little. Facing her, he put his hands on her shoulders and stared at her. "I'll never do this to you again," he said.

"Do what?"

He held the palm of his hand before her eyes and spun a brief, soothing dream of UCLA's grassy quadrangles and mock-Renaissance buildings. Then he pulled out a chair at a nearby table and sat her there. Face blank, she relaxed.

"Gentlemen," Michael said, indicating the table where the more presentable Clarkham stood, hands still resting on the back of a chair, "let's talk."

"I thought you'd be interested."

"I apologize to her," the presence said. A small, sooty layer pooled around his feet.

"You're both David Clarkham," Michael said cheerfully, sitting in the chair indicated. The others sat, the presentable one next to Michael, laying his napkin in his lap, and the dark, corrupted one opposite.

"Yes," said the dark one. The presentable figure smiled and raised a hand in deferment.

"And you are the only Clarkham I've met until now," Michael addressed the presentable one.

"He is the only one," said the other.

"You made him."

A nod.

"He's a shadow? Or a simulacrum?"

"He *is* me. Like you, I had some of the talents of a maker. Curious that two such rarities as you and I should occur within a millennia, both springing from Sidhe and humans—you more human than I, and more rare for that."

"Makers spin worlds, not people."

"Worlds are extensions of one's self. They are solid dreams. Since I ..." The dark Clarkham made a half-swallowing, half-choking sound and called for water. A poorly resolved waiter, white smudging into black, brought a glass goblet to him, and he drained it quickly. "You know the mistakes I made, long ago."

Michael raised an eyebrow. "Not in detail."

"The details are not important. Suffice it to say I chose a less tortuous path to express my talents, to gather discipline about me. I did not have the boon of the Crane Women's teaching. ... That is reserved for those favored by the Councils, and I have never been their favorite. The "down side" of this path, as one of your businessmen might currently express it, was a wasting spiritual disease. I found I had not prepared myself properly. I gained power enough but could not avoid the corruption. It is a cruel malady, for I could only shed myself of its effects by passing it off to others. For a time, I managed to control the worst effects ..."

"Shahpur, for example."

"Yes. Shahpur. The Sidhe compounded the effects of my malady when I was defeated in the Realm and the Blasted Plain was scorched around the Pact Lands. I could not remain on Earth or in the Realm. My disease was so hideous then that I would have quickly polluted thousands, perhaps millions. I could not kill myself; I would have, had there been a way. I would have done that simply to atone for what happened to my ... women. Lovers. But death is not an option and never will be."

"Had you created this world then?"

"I was working on it even as they defeated me. You are

aware that in its latter days, time in the Realm, compared with time on the Earth, was most unreliable? Occasionally it would speed up, occasionally slow down. But that's of little relevance here. I had a luxuriously long and peaceful time to 'spin' this world, as you say. I put everything I was capable of into it. And after . . . I retreated here."

"We always end up in civilized discussions, don't we?" the presentable Clarkham commented. Michael ignored him.

"I had to come here. I was corrupting everything around me. At least here, I could shed my evil on the periphery."

"A serious problem," the other said. "When one's production of nastiness exceeds the capacity of whole populations of sacrificial victims. When only a world can hold it all."

"Yes," his original agreed. "I had had enough of making worlds. I became convinced I was not good at it, and my handicaps were hideously distracting. So I spun something other than a world. I remade myself. Something of a shadow, something of me. . . . Finely tuned, finely wrought. This is what the Sidhe Councils set you against." He indicated the dapper Clarkham, who nodded and smiled.

"This has been my adversary . . . and you control him?"

"Not at all. He is too like my younger self, centuries ago. Willful. He made plans on his own. He discovered he also had some ability to spin worlds. He tried a few—of little quality, quite derivative, worse than my own. You have encountered at least one, I believe.

"In the Realm, when you confronted him, you removed most of the reality I had given him. You almost destroyed him."

The facsimile's smile went away. "You made a ghost of me. That's why I lured you here. What little I can do outside, I will not have you there to interfere with. And what little I can do is more than what Tarax can do, now that *he* has failed."

"Like you, I had real talent," the original declared to Michael. "This much must be obvious." A soot-dripping arm waved at the surroundings. "Not even Adonna could spin a creation so solidly detailed and appointed."

"I still don't think you have a real grasp of the problems involved in being a mage," the facsimile said, leaning forward and putting one elbow on the table. "Especially a mage of humans. I cannot imagine a more fractious and divided audience. Split by religions and philosophies so distorted by the Sidhe that some are beyond redemption. . . . And we cannot blame the Sidhe for all our sins. Have you considered what sort of policing a mage would have to do? What sort of punishments he would have to mete out? A mage is more than a creator; he must also control, and guide."

Michael said nothing, concentrating instead on finding a seam in the foundations around them. *Let them talk.*

"My life has been full of bitterness," the original said. "It is only fair that my other self should be given an opportunity, free of interference."

"He hasn't escaped your malady," Michael said.

There—something too small to squeeze travelers through, but large enough for a ribbon of chaos—

"No," the facsimile said. "I haven't. It eats at me, too. And I have to divest myself of the results now and then. But I cannot do otherwise. Like my original, I do not have the option of suicide."

"What sort of mage would you be, dropping your corruption on innocents?" Michael asked. "You've done enough damage already."

"What about the damage done to *us?*" the original wailed, standing abruptly. The chair legs caught in the plush carpet, and the chair went over backward, knocking into a hazy simulacrum as it delivered a fresh bottle of wine. The wine spilled to the floor, part of it landing on the dark Clarkham. The liquid hissed and blackened. "I can't even enjoy wine now! It sours before it ever touches my lips."

"I enjoy it for him," the other said, face blank. He looked at Michael intently. "What are you doing?"

Michael did not answer.

"He's doing something."

"What are you up to?" the original asked, backing around the fallen chair, away from the table and Michael.

"There's really nothing you can do," the facsimile said doubtfully. "Still . . ."

"Hold his woman," the original commanded.

Michael pushed back his chair casually and stood between the facsimile and Kristine.

"There's something wrong," the original said, raising his dark, woody palms and feeling the space around them.

"You cannot escape," said the other, brushing a hand through his hair. He had aged visibly in the past few minutes and was now roughly as old in appearance as he'd been when Michael first confronted him in the Realm.

"You must flee!" the original instructed his second.

"You're staying," Michael said. With remarkable ease, he bound the facsimile to the floor with a clinging, tenuous skein of shadow-cords, the arms of a dozen ghosts of himself.

"You *are* a monster," the facsimile said, struggling only for a moment. "A sport. You're still a weapon of the Sidhe. Still aimed and fired by Tarax!"

Michael ignored him; his charges weren't worthy of comment. There was nothing in particular he had to say to either of them. He pitied both, a little—but his thoughts were on Shahpur, bound in white sheets and filled with Clarkham's corruption; on Tommy, disintegrating on the sidewalk before the Waltiri house; on Emma Livry, lying burned, in agony, until rescued by the Ban of Hours; on Coleridge and Mozart and all the dozens of human geniuses ultimately tormented by Clarkham's struggle to find someone capable of expressing his desires strongly enough to make them real.

Himself included.

Michael circled the original Clarkham and picked up the bottle, gently nudging away the leg of the simulacrum waiter. The bottle had landed on its side and still contained some fluid. Michael had thought he recognized the label—*Doppelsonnenuhr,* the double sundial. It had seemed only reasonable that Clarkham would have brought some of this vintage with him. It would probably not give them a way out; it had been grown in the Realm, after all, and its flavor led either into Clarkham's worlds or back into the Realm, which was no more. Besides, it seemed likely that both Clarkhams were telling the truth—once in this world, there was no way out . . .

But the wine provided the seam in the smooth foundation. It was neither flesh and blood nor of this world; its reality was subtly *other,* and through it, Michael could feel the qualities of the chaos "above" Null, eager to come in and erase, devour.

Michael partly corked the bottle with his thumb and began sprinkling its contents around the tables. A large spot of wine was already seething at the original's feet. Orange light seemed to glow beneath the dark stain.

"I don't know what you're doing," the original Clarkham said quietly, dabbing at himself. Larger flakes of soot fell away beneath the glistening wine. "Are you going to destroy us, after all?"

Michael didn't respond. Grimly, he shook the bottle and continued sprinkling.

"You were wrong, then," the original said to the facsimile.

"He's making a bloody mess, I'll give him that."

Michael was aware that the second Clarkham, without moving, was working against the bonds. Soon he would be free.

"I think he knows what he's doing. He's more capable than even you imagined."

The shadow-bonds broke and disappeared. The facsimile shrugged his coat back up on his shoulders. Michael gave him a sharp glance: *stay away from her.* The facsimile did not challenge him.

"It's best," said the original, folding his hands over his ample belly. "I can almost feel relief."

The second Clarkham was fading. Michael glanced at the bottle; there was still a half-inch or so of the wine, the dregs. Turning quickly, he splashed the dregs over him.

The surprise on both their faces was at once comical and horrifying. Where the wine stained his suit and dripped from his face, the second Clarkham began to glow orange. He tried to wipe away the wine, but couldn't. He was held by the advancing chaos.

"You do things even I would not have guessed possible," the original said, with an air of peculiar enthusiasm. "Incomprehensible things. My wine. You use me against myself." His eyes were full of wonder.

The wine stain expanded and shot fingers out under the wall, into the street. The daylight outside was suddenly clouded over.

I've done this before—something like it—to Lin Piao Tai.

"You're going to destroy my world, aren't you?" the original said.

"Yes," Michael answered.

"You know, if I had known a way, I might have helped you and the woman escape. It was really his idea to bring you here. I have nothing against you. Truly. I've grown tired—"

The waiters, maitre d' and all the other simulacra vanished. The original's sloughing, sooty evil fell more rapidly. He was surrounded by a thick blanket of black, formless dust.

Michael stood before Kristine and passed his hand over her eyes again. She looked around quickly. Before she could speak, Michael lifted her to her feet and wrapped his arms around her. "Just a little world," he said. "For us. For now."

Between his palms spread the purest and whitest nacreous sheet. "Are we leaving?" she asked.

"We're going home," Michael said. "But first, there're going to be some special effects." He gripped her tightly as the nacre spread around them both. "Take a deep breath," he said.

"I hold you no ill will," the original Clarkham said. "This is truly best. I can see that."

Michael turned to look at him. In the middle of a prodigious fall of soot from his head, in the span of his now-featureless face where his eyes would have been, two molten drops of silver flowed.

"My regrets," Clarkham said, and the silver fell to the carpet. The La Bretonne shook, and the walls bloated and spun outward like released balloons. "Dear God above us all, I wish I had it to do over again—"

The nacre closed, and that was as Michael preferred it.

42

As Michael held Kristine tightly within the whiteness, eyes half-closed, weary and resigned to whatever might come, he knew he had done his best. No one could have asked more of him, not even the Crane Women.

"Where are we?" Kristine asked.

"I've made a little world to protect us," Michael said.

"Oh." Then, "What does that mean?"

"It means I'm holding you," he said. "And I'm happy."

"Don't talk down to me," she said, not at all in anger. "Where are we, and where are *they?*"

"We are somewhere near Earth. They are dying or dead by now, and their world with them. Erased."

She considered this for a moment, conflicting emotions crossing her face in rapid succession. "You're positive?"

"As positive as I'll ever be about David Clarkham." He nuzzled her. "I'm very tired, and I'm very happy to have you. Let's wait until later for explanations."

She stroked his cheek. "What in hell are you?" she asked tenderly.

"Later. Please."

Kristine suddenly relaxed. "All right," she said. "I don't know what it is about you. I feel very safe. I don't know what's going on, and I still feel safe."

The thought of what he had just done to the two Clarkhams and of all he had been through—and all he had lost, most of it never to be regained—and the long path he had taken to come here, wherever *here* was, and that Kristine should tell him this, putting her seal of approval on him . . .

"You're crying again," she said. His back began to knot up and his shoulders to curl inward. "No," she crooned. "Relax."

But it had to come. He felt the Serpent Mage's memories within him, filled with tales of all his ancestors culled from a million years of "listening," and he thought of Manus in defeat.

He thought of Eleuth.

"Shh," Kristine said, holding him as tightly as she could, as if he might fly away.

And of Shiafa, sad Shiafa finally free—she at least was not lost—and even sadder Tarax, power and desire without, finally, the necessary talent.

Within the tiny lifeboat world, settling slowly down to Earth, Michael wept and shivered and came to terms with what he was and what he would have to be.

"I'm not going away," Kristine said. "Whatever you are. You make me safe."

The whiteness took on color and dissolved around them.

They stood in Clarkham's house, on the second floor, with the ancient bottle of wine sitting upright and undisturbed a few feet away.

The Earth still existed and accepted them.

43

Fall gave way to winter, and winter to a dry, clear spring.

44

A different dawn.

To the eyes of most, the pale rose horizon and dusty gray zenith would not have seemed any different. But to Michael, who did not even look with his eyes, the changes were obvious.

For one thing, there had been less violence around the Earth during the night. Strife between humans and Sidhe had decreased markedly in the past few months; now, he could see a decline in strife between humans and humans. He was pleased; there was good reason to believe he was responsible.

For weeks he had worked to lift a mental haze that had lain over the Earth for thousands of centuries. The accumulation of discarded dreams, lost memories, cast-off fragments of personalities from the migrating human dead—the general miasma of a mental environment gone ages without cleansing —had created a mind-muffling "smog." The smog was now largely gone.

His people could think more clearly. Their passions did not magnify and distort, and they were less quick to destructive anger.

If he did nothing for the rest of his life—however long that was—then his creation of the overlay and cleansing of the mental environment would be sufficient, he thought.

But he did not intend to stop. He had other responsibilities.

Kristine slept beside him, a large, very pregnant pale shape in the bedroom's dawn-lit obscurity. They had moved into the Waltiri house just after their return; John had made new furniture for them to replace what had been ruined by the birds.

Michael seldom slept. Night was the time he voyaged out on a spreading wave of perception and kept track of his Earth. On such nights, there seemed to be ineffable rustlings in the world. When Kristine had become round-bellied and big-breasted, she had told him, "I don't know who's more pregnant, you or I. At least on you, it doesn't show."

The Earth turned beneath him, a truly remarkable pearl covered with rock and soil and oceans and people and clouds and sky. Much had changed since the Sidhe migrations and the death of the Realm, and much had remained the same. Sidhe, for the most part, avoided human cities and human machines and usually chose desolate parts of the land and sea to rebuild their own communities. So it was that Sidhe now lived among the hills and cinder cones of Death Valley, and in the sandy wastes of the Sahara and the Gobi and scattered across the outback of Australia, where they could work their magic and adjust their ways in relative peace.

There were exceptions. A large Sidhe community now existed in Ireland, mostly Faer and Amorphals; a thousand Sidhe had settled in the heart of London, a thousand more in Jerusalem and several hundred in Peking.

Life went on. In Los Angeles, cars still crowded the freeways and power still pulsed through the wire networks across the country. The Sidhe would have to adapt to these things.

Pelagals prevented all killing of cetaceans and other marine mammals and regulated the fishing of certain ocean regions. Humans would have to adapt to this.

Riverines frequently harried rafters on the Colorado River. Apparently, both humans and Sidhe took this as a kind of sport, and firm friendships had been made.

Airline pilots frequently found their craft inhabited by Amorphals. There had been no air disasters since such occupations began.

Sidhe horses and riders, under tough restrictions, had begun to be grudgingly accepted in equine competitions.

And on the negative side—

Sidhe tribal sorcerers in the Middle East had been called upon by Moslems to raise the dead of past wars, that they might fight the Jews again. Human dead could not be literally resurrected, but the sorcerers had obliged by raising shadows and dreams of ancestors, breathing a kind of life back into the ghostly residues of the past. These "dead" had promptly occupied Arab villages, driving out the living and refusing to fight or do much of anything else. The Moslems had sworn vengeance against the Sidhe. There was little Michael could do about such travesties.

The five thousand human captives of the Sidhe had been repatriated. Their presence so far had not made much difference in the arts, but less than a year had passed, after all . . .

The mage of the Cledar and his retinue had moved to jungles in Mexico for the time being, to establish an enclave where they would wait until a way could be found to return them to their ancestral forms. Michael spoke with him frequently, traveling sometimes to Mexico or sometimes just conversing by thought.

Michael spent much of his time consulting with Sidhe and with the deep cetacean minds of the Spryggla and the scattered, tragically fractured cockroach minds of the Urges.

Their time was coming again. Much had been lost, but there was a grudging cooperation between the races now. The sundering was done with. Years, perhaps centuries, would pass before most things could be set right, but that was a short time indeed.

Michael pressed his thigh against Kristine's and she sighed, adjusting her bulky abdomen without waking. He smiled and felt a love for her beyond expression, and with that love came not fear but apprehension.

What stability the Earth had now, as always, was very fragile. At any moment, his magehood could topple into singing shards. There was no final security, no certainty. He could not see the future. Yet he was not afraid. Fear would only paralyze him.

Michael lay his head gently on her stomach and listened, smiling. She stirred again but did not awaken.

Michael and Kristine arrived at the front door of the trendy little Nicaraguan restaurant on Pico, just before opening time. Bert Cantor came down the street with Olive's arm in the crook of his own and saw the pair. Olive responded to his elbow-nudge, focused on them and smiled broadly.

"I know you," Bert said brusquely, shaking Michael's hand. "Didn't you used to work here or something? But who's this?" Bert eyed Kristine's obvious condition.

"This is my wife, Kristine Pendeers. Kristine, Bert and Olive Cantor."

"Very pleased to meet you," Olive said, smiling at her delightedly. "Oh, when are you due?"

"Three weeks, roughly," Kristine replied, resting her arms on her abdomen and smiling with anticipation of relief.

"Men, they just don't know, do they?" Olive sympathized, clucking and urging Bert to open the door.

Kristine agreed with Olive, to be polite, but her glance at Michael was sufficient. He knew what her pregnancy felt like. Sometimes he even read the child's burgeoning, liquid-dreaming thoughts and conveyed them to her.

"You know, you have a lot of explaining to do," Bert said, slipping his key into the lock. "About what's happened. I read things in the newspaper that are nothing like what we used to read in the newspaper." He sighed and held the door open for them. "Not *good* newspapers."

"Not everything's perfect," Michael conceded.

Jesus shouted "¡Hola!" from the kitchen, and Michael waved back with a big grin.

"The beautiful lady, she's your girlfriend?" Jesus asked, twirling a plastic bag full of dried black beans.

"She's my wife," Michael said proudly.

"Eh! Wait until Juanita hears. Juanita, the *brujo* has a *bruja*."

"Such talk," Olive said, waving both hands at the kitchen. "Your folks, how are they? And why didn't you invite us to the wedding?"

"They're fine," Michael said.

"It was a small ceremony," Kristine explained.

"You've told her all about...?" Bert asked, raising his brows and corrugating his forehead.

"I have," Michael says.

"And she marries you anyway!" Bert marveled.

"I would, too," Olive said, casting a defiant look at her bemused husband. "Bert and I, we think... we think you had something to do with what's been happening."

"Yeah, a *hypothesis*, call it," Bert said. "How things got so much worse, then better, though all confused. You were the only one who knew anything... I admit, though, you sounded quite..." He twirled one finger around his ear. Then he glanced at the front windows and door and said, "Business hasn't been worth much lately. Oh, what the hell, let's close today and celebrate. And talk. You have to fill us in."

And Michael did, Kristine helping him with certain parts he left out. Jesus fixed black bean tortillas, and Juanita served, and everybody ate as Michael spoke in a quiet voice of what had happened. He told very few people these things; there was no pride in him now, only practicality, and he knew there were few who would believe, and most of those he did not want to deal with.

Juanita crossed herself several times.

"No more meat? Not beef or chicken?" Bert asked at one point.

Michael shook his head. "Plants are growing that will replace meat," he said. He had modified a number of existing plants just a few weeks before. The changeover, like everything else, would take time, but at least the groundwork was laid.

"And what about the people?" Olive asked. "How will we get along with all these others here now—the faeries and others?"

"Not eating meat's part of the way we'll get along better," Kristine said. "They can't stand it."

"Oh, don't we know!" Bert said, shaking his head vigorously. "Had a few of them walking up the street a month ago, out of place, dressed like they dress, acting like tourists, and they came in here.... Such looks! Made me feel ashamed, somehow, and mad, too. No worse than going around in black coats and wide-brim hats, I suppose, and frowning at the gentiles—but still . . ."

"It's partly guilt, Michael thinks," Kristine said. "They feel like they'd be eating their enemies . . ."

"So many peoples were transformed into animals," Michael reminded them.

Bert's face paled. "I think we're going to have to come up with new definitions for *traef*."

"And what about us?" Olive persisted. "What's going to happen to us, all the people here? Can we just accept them, accept all the changes?"

"This is the way things are," Michael said, and there was a finality in his tone that made Olive draw her head back and purse her lips, on the edge of disapproval.

"And you're responsible for all this?" Bert asked, preparing to be astonished again.

"Oh, no," Michael said. "Not at all." He laughed, and Kristine laughed with him, thinking it very likely that some of Michael's advisors were even now hiding out in the garbage behind the restaurant. "Not at all!"

"I knew there would be something different tonight," Kristine said, weary of attendant marvels. She sat awkwardly on the Morris chair John had dragged onto the patio behind the Perrin house.

"What's that?" Michael asked.

"The mage hasn't guessed?" She mocked surprise. She was getting testier as her time narrowed to days. "Your mother. She's keeping mum, but she's a nervous wreck, and John looks absolutely terrified."

"So what is it?" Michael asked.

"Somebody's joining us for dinner. Somebody *not* human, I'd say. You're usually the one responsible for nonhuman guests, but not this time, I take it?"

Michael shook his head, all innocence.

"Who does your mother know that isn't human?"

Michael's eyes widened. "She's never met her in person,

but—my great-great-grandmother," he said.

Salafrance Underhill arrived at seven in the evening, her long red hair tied back in a prim bun, dressed in a cloak the color of autumn leaves. Ruth answered the door herself, turning down Michael's offer flatly. "She's my problem, really," Ruth said. "When she called, I invited her here. I'll greet her at my own front door."

For a moment, the two women faced each other over the threshold, and Michael saw his great-great-grandmother for the first time. Side by side, Ruth and Salafrance Underhill looked remarkably alike, but there was no denying Salafrance was a pure Sidhe and Ruth was largely human.

"Great-granddaughter," Salafrance said, her voice even more beautiful than Ulath's, almost as entrancing as the voice of the Ban of Hours. "You have dreamed of me. I've felt your dreams, even across the world and beyond."

"Hello," Ruth said, struggling with remarkable success to control her shivering.

"Is it customary that I should wait out here?"

"No," Ruth said smoothly. "Come in."

Salafrance drifted through the door, seeming as tall and slender as a tree, her long face and cold eyes difficult to read as she looked from person to person, lingering on Kristine and her improbably wide belly and then turning her full attention to Michael, who stood by the couch in the living room, feeling awkward and young all over again.

"I did not know my love for men would lead to this," she said. "I followed the way of Elme for five hundred years, but out of an inner perversity, not by plan. Granddaughter, this is your husband?" She indicated John with a nod of her long chin.

"His name is—" Ruth began.

"Yes. I have been watching you all for some time. I hope that does not upset you."

Ruth swallowed hard but shook her head.

"I have much to apologize for. I did not prepare my children adequately. I am afraid they issued foolish edicts and did not understand who or what they were, and how they must choose mates wisely. You suffered for this, Great-granddaughter."

Michael could read his mother's emotions, barely held in check—half an urge to order Salafrance from her house, and

half simply to weep. She did neither. Salafrance sat in the
living room at Ruth's invitation and gestured for Kristine to sit
beside her.

"Does he read your child for you?" she asked.

"Michael?" Kristine asked, embarrassed. "Yes. He does."

"And is it a maker, as well?"

"We don't know," Michael said.

"Male or female?"

"Female," Kristine said. "The doctors confirmed it."

Salafrance smiled ironically. Her almond eyes could have
been regarding anybody in the room at any given moment,
without the slightest impression of darting about. "Power is
carried by the female. . . . Great granddaughter," she said, fo-
cusing her full attention now on Ruth.

"Yes?"

"I am proud of you, most proud."

Ruth smiled. Michael knew then that his mother would
never come to love or even be comfortable around Salafrance
Underhill, but she could now be comfortable within herself.

She had not failed her heritage.

At dinner, as Salafrance picked at rice and vegetables, she
asked, "Where is the nectar of mages?"

"I gave it back to my father," Michael said.

"It's in my wine-cellar. Closet, actually," John said.

"It has waited long enough, don't you think?"

"Sidhe don't drink, Grandmother," Michael said quietly.

"Do you know the rule—always forbidden, on occasion
mandatory?"

Michael nodded.

"This is such an occasion," Salafrance decreed.

"I'll bring it," John said, pushing his chair back from the
table.

"I am told, and I have felt, that you are in control of this
world now, of its making and its song," she said to Michael.
"This is so?"

"It is so," Michael said.

"And what sort of mage are you?"

Michael smiled. "That's a broad question."

"Are you an obvious one, dancing with the song at all
times, watching the steps of all who dance with you?"

"He doesn't meddle," Kristine said defensively. "Hardly

anybody knows what he does or who he is." Michael patted her hand.

"I . . . don't want to control everybody or act as a policeman," he said. "I don't think I should have any real authority over how people behave or make moral judgments. I won't impose my will on others. I'm a poet, not a master. I may tune the instruments, but I don't lay down every note of the song."

"And if it comes about that the races try to destroy the balance again?"

"I'll write that bridge when I come to it," he said, irritated that she should see so quickly what worried him most about the future.

"You are a very young mage," Salafrance said. John returned with the opaque, time-darkened bottle of wine.

"What is its provenance?" Salafrance asked.

John was puzzled, uncertain how to answer. "Arno Waltiri gave it to us."

"The human who shared his body with the Cledar mage . . . ?"

"The same," Michael said. "He had it from David Clarkham. I've heard Clarkham stole it from Adonna."

"We should all drink . . ." Salafrance said. "Except for Kristine, who bears perhaps another maker, one who will drink this wine in her own due course."

"I don't think I could stomach it anyway," Kristine said.

The bottle was sealed with a thick slug of wax impressed with a tiny sharp design, two triangles nested like a Star of David. When John cleared out the wax plug from the bottle's neck, working carefully to avoid breaking the ancient glass, an almost palpable aroma filled the room, richer by far than Clarkham's wines, beyond a bouquet and into the realm of a summer-heated fruit garden.

"Who took this bottle, and when, I do not know, but I know whence it comes," Salafrance said. "The sigil tells me. It was once in the collection of Aske and Elme themselves. It may be the last bottle of its kind, and it carries special virtue. It is fitting that the first human maker and mage in untold ages should drink of it and be confirmed by the experience. That is what Elme would have wished, and Aske would have been proud beyond his time."

"You knew them?" Ruth asked, awe-struck.

"I am not *that* old, Great-granddaughter," Salafrance said, and Michael sensed the depths of her humor. "I have met those who knew them. So has Michael." Her look was potent with meaning. Michael almost shivered.

"Now that both Councils have dissolved, and new orders are found, and new songs to which we dance, let us toast the new mage in humble surroundings, toast a humble creator who vows not to enslave for order's sake but to do what he must, and that alone: tend a garden fit for all God's creatures and weave a lace pleasing to all."

Not once, in all his time with Sidhe, had Michael ever heard them refer to a god beyond Adonna or Adonna's Yahweh.

"Which god is this, Grandmother?" Michael asked.

"You feel this God in your blood, do you not?" she asked. She held up her glass, and the others followed suit. "The God that requires only our remembrance in extremis. The gentle, the mature, the ever-young, that demands nothing but our participation and growth. The composer of the Song of Earth and all worlds. Invoke this God, Michael, and be a maker and mage."

Michael examined the color of the wine in his glass: both golden and brown, all wines become one wine, and said, "To all of us, of all races, and the matter we are made of, and the ground beneath our feet, and the worlds over our head. To strife and passage and death and life." He held his glass higher. "To horror, and awe, and all strong emotions, and most of all, to love."

Salafrance drank, and the others drank as well.

When they were finished, John put down his glass and said, "I think it must be an acquired taste."

"It's wonderful," Ruth said.

Michael frowned, drawing the flavors back and forth. He honestly did not have an opinion. In a few decades, perhaps he would appreciate what he was tasting now.

"What's it like?" Kristine asked.

He shook his head. "I don't know," he said.

"All that suspense, and you don't know?" she chided.

The rest of the evening went well, with Salafrance telling her own story and Ruth listening closely. There was much about life in the hills and alleged witchcraft and conflict between the early farmers and the clannish Sidhe. Salafrance told of a lonely and rebellious young Sidhe female—herself —coming down out of the hills into the communities of humans, enchanting and being enchanted in turn by a strong young human male and being taken to his cabin to bear children. In time, Salafrance could not stay apart from her kind; the love was strained by forces neither could control, and they parted, Salafrance leaving their children with the man, who found his house filled with witches and warlocks: his own offspring.

Kristine slept in the crook of Michael's arm as the hour passed midnight. Salafrance said near dawn that she must leave, and Ruth escorted her to the door, where they had a few words alone.

Then Salafrance extended her arms and took her great-granddaughter into them, hugging her close. "Humans have always taught us how to love," she said.

She departed into the dawn, and Ruth returned to the kitchen, her face wet with tears. John sealed the bottle again and placed it in the wine closet. Michael took Kristine home in the Waltiris' old Saab.

The birth was late. Three days later, on a bright spring morning after a long-awaited night's rain, the sidewalks dappled with moisture and the grass still beaded, Michael opened the front door to retrieve the newspaper. Something feather-touched his aura, and he paused, listening.

"Man-child," came a voice above his head. He looked up and saw Coom staring down at him from the roof, her long fingers tightly gripping the tile.

"You still have much to learn."

He turned. Nare stood on one leg on the lawn to the left, wriggling her long fingers before her flat chest.

"Even a Lace-Maker and Gardener needs a few tens of years to mature and reach his potential," said Spart, sitting cross-legged on the lawn to his right, smiling at him with her head cocked to one side. "May we teach?"

Michael's chest swelled with gladness, and he laughed. "Only if you'll teach our child, too."

"Man-childs," Coom said. "Our specialty!"

So it was that Michael Perrin came into his time, and the Earth found its youth once more.